Nick Drake was born in 1961. He is the author of one previous novel featuring Rahotep, *Nefertiti: The Book of the Dead*, which was short-listed for the Crime Writers' Association Best Historical Crime Novel Award. He is also a screenwriter and an award-winning poet. He wrote the screenplay for *Romulus, My Father,* starring Eric Bana, which won Best Film at the Australian Film Awards 2007.

D1395350

www.**rbooks**.co.uk

Tutankhamun

The Book of Shadows

Nick Drake

BANTAM PRESS

LONDON • TORONTO • SYDNEY • AUCKLAND • JOHANNESBURG

TRANSWORLD PUBLISHERS
61–63 Uxbridge Road, London W5 5SA
A Random House Group Company
www.rbooks.co.uk

First published in Great Britain
in 2009 by Bantam Press
an imprint of Transworld Publishers

A CIP catalogue record for this book
is available from the British Library.

ISBNs 9780593054024 (cased)
9780593054062 (tpb)

Addresses for Random House Group Ltd companies outside the UK
can be found at: www.randomhouse.co.uk
The Random House Group Ltd Reg. No. 954009

The Random House Group Limited supports The Forest Stewardship
Council (FSC), the leading international forest-certification organization. All our
titles that are printed on Greenpeace-approved FSC-certified paper carry the FSC logo.
Our paper procurement policy can be found at www.rbooks.co.uk/environment

Typeset in 11.5/15.5pt Electra by
Falcon Oast Graphic Art Ltd.
Printed and bound in Great Britain by
CPI Mackays, Chatham, ME5 8TD

2 4 6 8 10 9 7 5 3 1

Mixed Sources
Product group from well-managed
forests and other controlled sources
www.fsc.org   Cert no. TT-COC-2139
FSC   © 1996 Forest Stewardship Council

Cast List

Rahotep – Seeker of Mysteries, Chief Detective in the Thebes Medjay (police force)

His family and friends
Tanefert – his wife
Sekhmet, Thuyu, Nedjmet – his daughters
Amenmose – his baby son
Thoth – his baboon
Khety – Medjay associate
Nakht – noble
Minmose – Nakht's servant

The royal family
Tutankhamun – Lord of the Two Lands, the 'Living Image of Amun'
Ankhesenamun – Queen, daughter of Akhenaten and Nefertiti
Mutnodjmet – aunt of Ankhesenamun, wife of Horemheb

The palace officials
Ay – Regent, and 'God's Father'
Horemheb – General of the Armies of the Two Lands
Khay – Chief Scribe
Simut – Commander of the Palace Guard
Nebamun – Head of the Thebes Medjay
Maia – wet nurse to Tutankhamun
Pentu – Chief Physician to Tutankhamun

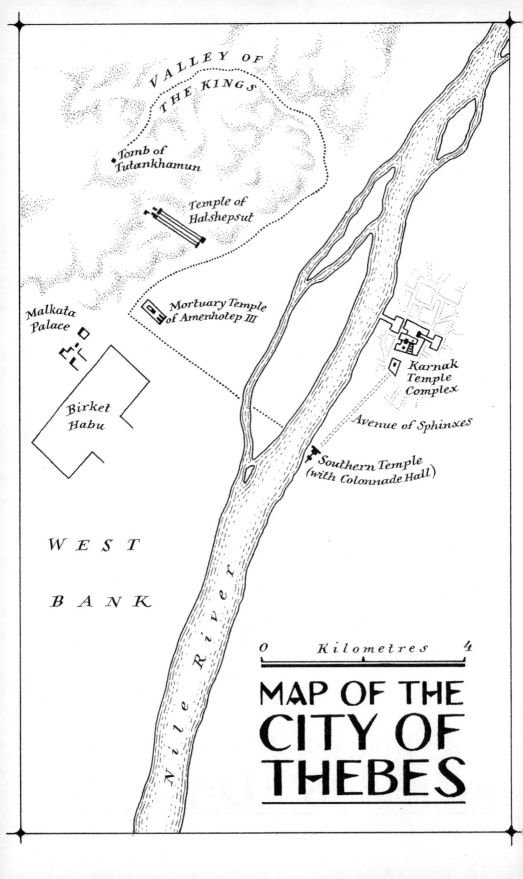

VALLEY OF
THE KINGS

• Tomb of
Tutankhamun

Temple of
Halshepsut

Malkata
Palace

Mortuary Temple
of Amenhotep III

Birket
Habu

Karnak
Temple
Complex

Avenue of Sphinxes

Southern Temple
(with Colonnade Hall)

WEST

BANK

Nile River

0   Kilometres   4

MAP OF THE
CITY OF
THEBES

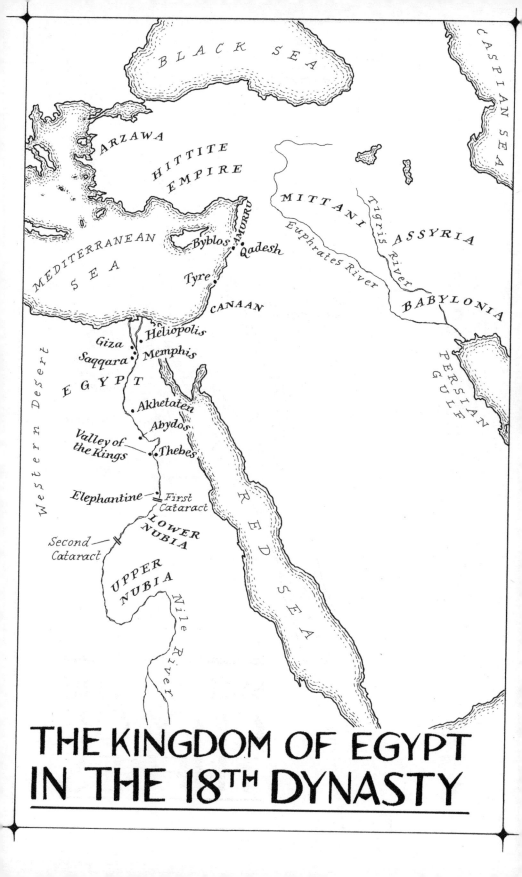

THE KINGDOM OF EGYPT
IN THE 18ᵀᴴ DYNASTY

DYNASTIC FAMILY TREE

Amenhotep III ══════ Tiy

Kiya ══════ Amenhotep IV/ ══════ Nefertiti
              Akhenaten

Meritaten   Meketaten   Neferneferuaten   Neferneferure   Setepenre   Mutnodjmet

Tutankhamun ══════ Ankhesenpaaten/
                   Ankhesenamun

?

Now when His Majesty was crowned King, the temples and the estates of the gods and the goddesses from Elephantine as far as the marshes of lower Egypt had fallen into decay. Their shrines were fallen into ruin, become mere mounds overgrown with grass. Their sanctuaries were as if they had not yet come into being, and their buildings were footpaths. The land was in chaos. The gods had turned their backs upon it. When an army was sent to northern Syria to extend the boundaries of Egypt, it had no success. If one prayed to a god to ask something from him, he did not come at all. If one beseeched any goddess in the same way she did not come at all. The gods' hearts were faint in their divine statues. What had been made had been destroyed.

From the Restoration Stela, set up in the temple complex at Karnak in the early years of Tutankhamun's reign

Part One

I know you, I know your names

Coffin Texts
Spell 407

1

Year 10 of the reign of King Tutankhamun, Living Image of Amun

Thebes, Egypt

Three short knocks. I listened to the silence that followed, my heart thudding in reply. Then, to my relief, came the familiar last short knock of the signal. I let my breath out slowly. Perhaps I was getting old. It was still dark, but I was already awake, for sleep had betrayed me once again, as it often does in the melancholy small hours before dawn. I rose from the couch and dressed quickly, glancing at Tanefert. My wife's head was resting elegantly on its sleeping stand, but her beautiful, disturbed eyes were open, observing me.

'Go back to sleep. I promise I will be home in time.'

I kissed her lightly. She curled into herself like a cat, and watched me leave.

I drew back the curtain and looked for a moment at my three sleeping girls, Sekhmet, Thuyu and Nedjmet, on their beds, in their shared yellow room crammed with clothes, old toys, papyri, slates, drawings from their childhood, and other objects whose significance eludes me. Our house is too small now for such grown girls. I listened for a moment to the rattle of my father's strained breathing in his room at the back. It ceased for a long moment, but then another breath worked its way laboriously through his old body. Lastly, as always before I leave the house, I stood beside my young son, Amenmose, sleeping entirely peacefully, his limbs thrown every which way like a dog before a fire. I kissed him on his head, damp with warmth. He did not stir.

Taking my night passes with me, for the curfews were in force, I closed the door soundlessly. Thoth, my clever baboon, loped over to me from his sleeping place in the yard, his short, tufted tail curved upwards, and he rose on his hind legs to greet me. I let him smell my palm, then ran my hand through his thick, brown mane. I made a brief gesture of libation to the little household God in the niche, who knows I do not believe in him. Then I opened the gate and stepped into the shadows of the lane, where Khety, my assistant, was waiting for me.

'Well?'

'A body has been found,' he said quietly.

'And you woke me for that? Could it not wait for dawn?'

Khety knows how bad my mood can be when I am disturbed too early.

'Wait until you see it,' he replied.

We set off in silence. Thoth strained on his leash, excited to be out in the dark, and eager to explore whatever lay ahead. It was a beautiful clear night: the hot harvest season of *shemu* had ended, and with the appearance of the sign of Sirius, the Dog Star, the inundation had arrived to overflow the banks of the Great River, and flood the fields with rich, life-giving silt. And so once again the time of festival had returned. In recent years the waters often did not rise far enough, or else they rose too much, causing vast devastation. But this year they had been ideal, bringing relief and joy to a population subdued, even depressed, by these dark times of the reign of Tutankhamun, King of Upper and Lower Egypt.

The bright face of the moon cast enough light for us to walk as if she were our lamp. She was almost full, with the great drift of stars about her like a fine mantle: the Goddess Nut who the priests say our dead eyes will gaze upon as we lie back in the little boats of death that carry us across the ocean of the Otherworld. I had been brooding about this as I lay sleeplessly on the couch, for I am one who sees the shadow of death in everything: in the bright faces of my children, in the over-crowded ways of the city, in the golden vanity of its palaces and offices, and always, somehow, in the corner of my eye.

'What do you think we see after death?' I asked.

Khety knows he must humour my occasional philosophical musings, as he must humour so much else. He is younger than me, and despite the grim things he has seen in his life of service in the Medjay, his face has somehow preserved its openness and freshness; and his hair, unlike mine, remains naturally as black as midnight. He is still as fit as a thoroughbred hunting dog, with the same passion for the hunt – so different from my own pessimistic and often weary nature. For as I grow older, life seems to me simply an endless succession of problems to be solved, rather than hours to be enjoyed. 'What fun I am these days,' I reproached myself.

'I think we see green fields, where all the pompous aristocrats are slaves and all the slaves pompous aristocrats, and all I have to do all day is hunt ducks in the reed marshes and drink beer to celebrate my glorious success.'

I let his jest pass unacknowledged.

'If we are supposed to see anything at all, why do the embalmers push onions into our eye sockets? *Onions!* The bulb of tears . . .'

'Perhaps the truth is we see the Otherworld only in our mind's eye . . .' he replied.

'Now you are sounding like a wise man,' I said.

'And yet those who have been born into wealth laze about all day

15

enjoying their luxuries and their love-affairs, while I still work like a dog, and earn nothing . . .'

'Well, that is a much greater mystery.'

We passed through the maze of old, narrow passageways zigzagging between precarious houses built to no plan. By day this quarter would be noisy and crowded, but by night it was silent under the curfew: the expensive shops and their luxury offerings were protected behind shutters like the grave goods of a tomb; the carts and stalls of the Alley of Fruit had gone for the night; and the workshops of wood, leather and glass were deserted and shadowy; even the birds in their cages hanging in the moonlight were soundless. For in these dark days fear keeps everyone in obedience. The disastrous reign of Akhenaten, when the royal court and temples were moved from Thebes to the new desert temple city of Akhetaten, collapsed ten years ago. The powerful priests of Amun, who were displaced and dispossessed under Akhenaten, had their authorities, vast landholdings and incalculable worldly riches reinstated. But this did not restore stability; for harvests were poor, and plague killed countless thousands, and most believed these disasters were punishment for the grave errors of Akhenaten's reign. And then as if to prove the point, one by one the royal family died: Akhenaten himself, five of his six daughters, and finally Nefertiti, his Queen of great beauty, whose last days remain a cause of much private speculation.

Tutankhamun inherited the Kingship of the Two Lands at the age of nine; and he was then immediately married to Ankhesenamun, the last surviving daughter of Akhenaten and Nefertiti. This was a strange but necessary alliance, for they were both children of Akhenaten, by different mothers; and as the last survivors of their great dynasty, who else could be crowned? But they were merely children; and it was Ay, the Regent, 'God's Father' as he was officially entitled, who since then ruled implacably, establishing his rule of fear, through officials who seemed to me loyal to fear alone. Unreal men. For a world with so much sun we live in a dark place, in a dark time.

We arrived at a house that was no different from most of the others in this quarter: a high crumbling mud-brick wall to defend it from the narrow lane, a doorway with one old, warped wooden door ajar, and beyond it the simple mud-brick house, several floors of new accommodation stacked precariously on top of each other – for there is no space to spare in the over-crowded city of Thebes. I tied Thoth to a post in the courtyard, and we went inside.

It was hard to guess the victim's true age; his face, almond-shaped, almost elegantly delicate, was both young and old, and his body was that of a child but also that of a crone. He might have been twelve or twenty years old. Normally his poor bones would have been twisted and bent into each other from the life-long errors of his crippled body. But I could see, in the dim light cast by the oil lamp in the wall niche, that they had been broken in many places, and re-arranged, like the fragments of a mosaic. I carefully raised his arm. It was as light as a snapped reed pen; the fractured bones made it both jagged and floppy. He was like a strange doll made of fine linen and broken sticks.

He had been laid out in funereal fashion, his crooked legs straightened, his thin, uneven arms crossed, his clawed hands like a falcon's talons prised open, and laid over each other. His eyes were covered with leaves of gold, and the Eye of Ra, in black and green, had been drawn around them. I carefully lifted the leaves away. Both his eyes had been removed. I stared at the mystery of the empty sockets, and then replaced the gold leaves. His face was the only thing that had not been successfully re-arranged, perhaps because its contortions – think how many muscles it takes to make a smile – could not be persuaded from their habitual lopsided grin by the hammers and tongs and other instruments that must have been used to reshape the imperfect material of this body. That grin remained like a little victory in the face of so much cruelty. But of course, it was no such thing. His pale skin – a sign that he had rarely been allowed into the sun - was cold as meat. His fingers were long and fine, the carefully clipped nails undamaged.

His twisted hands seemed to have been little use to him in life, and not to have struggled against his grotesque fate. Strangely there were no marks of binding on his wrists or ankles or neck.

What had been done to him was vicious and cruel, and would have required considerable physical strength, as well as knowledge and skill in anatomy; but it wouldn't necessarily have killed him. I had once been called to a victim of the gang wars in the poor suburbs. The young man had been rolled in a reed mat, with his head exposed, the better to observe his own punishment, which was to be beaten with heavy clubs. I still remember the look of terror on his face as the mat, dripping with his own blood, was slowly unrolled, and his body fell apart, and he died.

Most murder victims reveal the story of their end in their postures and in the marks and wounds inflicted upon their bodies. Even their expression still sometimes speaks, in the clay-like emptiness of death: panic, shock, terror – all these register, and remain in traces for a while after the little bird of the soul, the *ba*, has departed. But this young man seemed unusually calm. How so? A thought occurred: perhaps the murderer had placated him with some kind of narcotic. In which case he must have knowledge of, or access to, pharmacopoeia. Cannabis leaf, perhaps; or else the lotus flower in an infusion of wine? But neither would have had more than a mild soporific effect. The root of the mandrake plant, when extracted, is a more powerful sedative.

But this level of violence, and the sophistication of its concept, suggested something even more potent. Possibly the juice of the poppy, which could be obtained if you knew where to go. Stored in vases shaped like inverted poppy-seed pods, it was imported only by the most secret routes into the country, and most of the crop was known to be cultivated in the lands of our northern enemies, the Hittites, with whom we are engaged in a long war of attrition for control of the strategically vital lands that lie between our empires. It was a forbidden, but highly popular, luxury commodity.

*

The victim's room, which was located on the ground floor, giving directly on to the yard, was as characterless as a store chamber. There were few mementos of the boy's short, private life, other than some rolled papyri and a rattle. A simple wooden stool was set in the shadows from where he could have watched the passing life of the street through the frame of the doorway – and through which his murderer could have easily entered in the darkness of the night. His crutches leaned against the wall by the bed. The mud floor was swept clean; there were no traces of the murderer's sandals.

Judging from the house and its location, his parents were of the lower bureaucratic class, and they had probably kept their son hidden from the critical and superstitious eyes of the world. For some people believed such infirmities signalled abandonment and rejection by the Gods, while others believed they were a mark of divine grace. Khety would interrogate the servants and take statements from the family members. But I already knew he would turn up nothing; for this killer would never allow himself to commit any mundane errors. He had too much imagination, and too much *flair*.

I sat in silence, considering the strange puzzle set out before me on the couch, intrigued and confounded by the deliberate strangeness of the act. What the killer had done to the boy must be a sign of something else: an intention or a commentary, written on the body. Was the cruelty of the act an expression of power? Or was it, perhaps, the expression of a contempt for the imperfections of flesh and blood, signalling some deep need for a greater perfection? Or, more interestingly, did the boy's possible similarity to the King, with his own infirmities – although I had to remember these were but rumours – have a specific implication? Why had his face been painted as Osiris, God of the Shadows? Why had his eyes been removed? And why, strangely, did all this remind me of an old ritual of execration, in which our ancestors used to damn their enemies, first by smashing clay tablets on which were written their names and titles, and then by executing and burying them, decapitated, upside down? Here was sophistication, and intelligence, and meaningfulness. It was almost as clear as a message. Except it was in a language I could not yet decipher.

And then I saw something. Around his neck, hidden under his robe, was a strip of exceptionally fine linen on which hieroglyphs had been written in beautiful ink. I held the lamp up. It was a protection spell, specifically for the deceased during the night passage through the Otherworld in the Ship of the Sun. It concluded: '*Your body, Oh Ra, is everlasting by reason of the spell.*'

I sat very still, considering this rare object, until Khety coughed discreetly at the entrance to the boy's chamber. I put the linen away in my robe. I would show it to my old friend Nakht, noble in wealth and character, expert in matters of wisdom and spells, and in so much else besides.

'The family are ready to meet you,' he said.

They were waiting in a side room lit by a few candles. The mother was rocking and keening quietly in her grief; her husband was sitting in uncomprehending silence beside her. I approached them, and offered my futile condolences. I nodded discreetly to the father, and he accompanied me out to the little courtyard. We sat down on the bench.

'My name is Rahotep. I am Chief Detective in the Thebes Medjay division. My assistant Khety will need to talk to you in greater detail. I'm afraid it is necessary, even at a time like this. But tell me, did you hear or notice anything unusual last night?'

He shook his head.

'Nothing. We keep no night guard, for everyone here knows us, and our house is not rich. We are ordinary people. We sleep upstairs, for the cool air, but our son slept here, on the ground floor. It was much easier for him if he wished to move about. And he liked to watch what was going on in the street – it was all he saw of the life of the city. If he needed us in the night, he would call.'

He paused, as if listening to the silence in the hope of hearing his dead son's voice calling. 'What sort of man would do this to a boy of such simple love and soul?'

He looked at me, desperate for an answer. I found I did not have one that would help at all, at this moment.

The vivid grief in his eyes had changed suddenly into the desperate purity of revenge.

'When you catch him, give him to me. I will kill him, slowly and mercilessly. He will learn the true meaning of pain.'

But I could not promise him that. He looked away, and his body began to shudder. I left him to the privacy of his grief.

We stood in the street. The eastern horizon was swiftly turning from indigo to turquoise. Khety yawned widely.

'You look like a necropolis cat,' I said.

'I'm as hungry as a cat,' he replied, once he had finished his yawn.

'Before we think of breakfast, let's think about that young man.'

He nodded. 'Vicious . . .'

'But strangely purposeful.'

He nodded again, considering the almost visibly changing darkness at his feet, as if it might provide him with a clue.

'Everything's upside down and back to front these days. But when it comes to mutilating and re-arranging lame, helpless boys . . .' He shook his head in amazement.

'And on this day, the biggest day of the festival . . .' I said, quietly.

We let the thought settle between us for a moment.

'Take statements from the family and servants. Check the room for anything we might have missed in the dark . . . do it while it is all still fresh. Find out if the neighbours saw anyone unusual hanging around. The killer selected this boy carefully. Somebody may have seen him. And then get off to the festival and enjoy yourself. Meet me back at headquarters later.'

He nodded, and turned back into the house.

Taking Thoth by his leash, I walked away down the lane and

F/2156197

turned into the street at the end. The God Ra had just appeared above the horizon now, reborn from the great mystery of the Otherworld of night into a new day, silver-white, spreading his sudden, vast brilliance of light. As the first rays touched my face it was instantly hot. I had promised to be at home with the children by sunrise, and I was already late.

2

The streets were suddenly crowded. People were emerging from different quarters, from the upper-class villas behind their high walls and reinforced gates, as well as from the poor back streets and rubbish-strewn alleys. Today, for once, the city's mules and their burdens of mud-bricks and rubble, vegetables and fruits, were not on the streets, and the immigrant labourers who would normally be hurrying to their harsh work were enjoying a rare day of rest. Elite men of the bureaucracies in their pleated white clothing clung on to the back of their little horse-drawn chariots as they bumped and rattled along the ways of the city, some accompanied by running bodyguards. Men of the lower hierarchies walked with their servants and sunshades, along with rich children and their guardians, and expensively groomed women setting forth on early visits accompanied by their excited maids; everyone making their way, as if in time to some unheard drumbeat, towards the Southern Temple at the end of the city's territory in order to attend the ceremonies of the festival. Everyone wanted to watch the arrival of the sacred boats bearing the shrines of the Gods, and even more importantly to get a glimpse of the King receiving them in public – before he entered the most secret and sacred of the temple shrines to commune with the Gods and receive their divinity into himself.

But whereas, once upon a time, everyone's concern would have been about making sure the whole family was as finely dressed, as neatly styled, as well-fed, and as impressive as possible – in these days of strained obedience, the wonder and the awe had been replaced by uncertainty and anxiety. The festivals were not as I remembered them from my own childhood, when the world had seemed like a boundless fable: the processions and the visitations, station by station, of the divine figures in their gold shrines, carried on gold barges, all unfolding and passing in pageant, revealed to the over-heated crowds like great images on a living scroll.

I entered my courtyard, and untied Thoth from his leash. He immediately loped over to his bed, and settled down to watch from the corner of his eye one of the cats working at her exquisite toilet, an elegant front paw thrust out in the air as she licked it clean. She looked like the coy mistress of an older gentleman, playing up to her audience.

Inside, the house was in chaos. Amenmose was sitting cross-legged at the low table like a little king, beating his clenched fist in time to some tune in his cheerful head, as the milk in his bowl slopped out on to the floor for another of the cats to lick up. The girls were running to and fro, getting themselves ready. They barely registered my presence. 'Good morning!' I shouted, and they chorused back some semblance of a greeting. Tanefert kissed me briefly as she passed. So I settled down at the table with my son, who regarded me with mild curiosity for a moment, as if he had never met me before. Then, suddenly, he honoured me with one of his vast smiles of recognition, and continued to bash at his dish to show me how well he could do it. He is the golden child we did not expect, the surprise and delight of my middle years. At his age, he still believes everything I tell him, so I tell him the best of everything. Of course, he doesn't understand a word. I tried to amuse him by feeding him his milk, and as if it were a special occasion, he solemnly drank.

As I watched him, I thought about the dead boy in his shattered condition; his grotesque image suddenly like a shadow at the table of life. That he had been killed in this fashion on the very day of the festival might not be a coincidence. It might not also be any kind of coincidence that the victim's imperfections recalled those of our young King. Although of course no one publicly dares make any mention of his infirmities – his *alleged* infirmities – it is rumoured that Tutankhamun is less than perfect in his earthly body. But since he is rarely seen in public – and even then he always rides in a chariot, or sits on a throne – no one can say for sure what truth lies in the matter. But it is common knowledge he has never exercised power on his own account, even though he must now have come of age.

I had met his father several times, years ago, in the city of Akhetaten. And on one of those occasions I had also glimpsed the boy who had now become the King, if in name only; I remembered the *tap, tap, tap* of his cane down the echoey corridor of that vain, tragic and now surely derelict palace. I remembered his face, charismatic, angled, with a small, shy chin. He had looked like an old soul in a young body. And I remembered what my friend Nakht had said to me about the boy, who in those days was called Tutankhaten: '*When the time of the Aten is over, the Amun will be restored. He may yet be called by a new name. Tutankhamun.*' And so it had proved to be. For the maddened Akhenaten had been confined to his palace in the dusty Otherworld of his crumbling dream city. And after his death, all its vast open temples and multitudes of great statues of the King and Nefertiti had begun their inevitable return to rubble; the very bricks of the city's hasty construction were now said to be turning back into the dust of their making.

After Akhenaten's death, throughout the Two Lands of Egypt and its dominions, his cult of the Aten had been abandoned. The image of the sun disc, and its many hands reaching down with the Ankh, sign of life, to bless the world, was no longer carved upon the walls of the temples in any of our cities. Life in Thebes had continued as if everyone had agreed to pretend that none of these things had ever

25

happened. But of course people's private memories are not so easily wiped clean of history; the new religion had had many committed supporters, and many more who, in the hope of worldly preferment, had placed the fate of their livelihoods and futures upon its triumph. And many remained privately opposed to the Amun priests' astounding earthly powers, and to the absolute authority of one man in particular: Ay, a man not truly of the natural world, his blood cool, his heart as deliberate and indifferent as the *drip, drip, drip* of a water clock. Egypt in our times is the richest, most powerful kingdom the world has ever known, and yet no one feels safe. Fear, that unknowable and all-powerful enemy, has invaded us all, like a secret army of shadows.

We set out together in a hurry, for we were, as usual, late. The intense light of dawn had given way to the broad, powerful heat of morning. Amenmose sat on my shoulders clapping his hands and yelling with excitement. I pushed ahead, shouting at people to make way. The official insignia of my Medjay office seemed to have less effect than Thoth's bark; he helped to clear a path through the excited mass of sweaty bodies jostling for space and air, congesting the crooked, narrow lanes and passageways leading to the Great River. Music from strings and trumpets warred with shouts and songs and jeers as men called out to each other in cheerful recognition or fantastic abuse. Tied monkeys jabbered and caged birds shrieked. Street-sellers bellowed their wares and their snacks, and insisted on the perfection of their offerings. A lunatic, with a bony face and wild eyes searching the heavens, proclaimed the coming of the Gods and the end of the world. I loved it all as much as my son.

The girls followed, dressed in their finest linens, their hair shining and scented with moringa and lotus oil. Behind them Tanefert made sure no one got lost, and no one tried to approach. My girls are becoming women. How will I feel when the three great glories of my life leave me for their adulthood? I have loved each one from before the moment they entered the world yelling in answer to their names. As the thought of their leaving began to hurt me, I glanced back. Sekhmet, the oldest, smiled quietly; the scholar of the family, she claims she can hear me thinking, which is an alarming thought, given the nonsense that makes up most of my musings.

'Father, we should hurry.'

She was right, as usual. The time of the arrival of the Gods was approaching.

We found seats on the official stands under the shade of the riverside trees. All along the east bank, offering booths and shrines had been set up, and large crowds had gathered, full of expectation, waiting for the ship to appear. I nodded to various people I recognized. Below us, young Medjay officers were failing to impose much order on the crowd, but it has always been this way during the festival. I glanced around; the numbers of troops seemed surprisingly high, but security has become a national obsession in our times.

Then Thuyu shouted and pointed at the first of the towing boats as it came into view from the north; and at the same time we glimpsed the boat gangs on the riverbank struggling to pull the *Userhet*, the Great Ship of the God Amun. At this distance the famous and ancient floating temple of gold was just a glow on the glittering waters. But as it drew closer and made a turn towards the shoreline, the rams' heads at the prow and stern became clear, and the sun's full glory hit the polished solar discs above their heads, sending blinding light scintillating across the vast green and brown waters, glancing and flashing among the crowds. The girls gasped and stood up, waving and shouting. From the flagpole of the ship, and from the oar at the rear, brightly coloured streamers fluttered. And there at the centre was the golden shrine, veiling the hidden God himself, which would be carried ceremonially through the crowds for the short distance from the dock to the temple entrance.

The rowers at the rear of the ship, and the gangs on the shore, efficiently brought the vessel alongside the great stone dock. Now we could see the protecting frieze of cobras above the shrine, the crowns above the rams' heads, and the gold falcons on their poles. Amenmose was utterly silenced, his little mouth wide open, amazed by this vision of another world. Then, to a vast and deafening roar, which made my son nestle into my chest anxiously, the God's carrying shrine was raised upon the shoulders of the priests. They struggled to balance the burden of so much solid gold as they processed slowly and carefully down the gangplank on to the dock. The crowds surged forward against the linked arms of the guards. Dignitaries, priests and foreign potentates knelt down and made their offerings.

The temple was only a short distance from the riverbank. There was a ritual way station where the shrine would pause briefly for the hidden God to accept offerings, before being carried across the open ground towards the temple gateway.

It was time to move, if we were to get a good view of the carrying shrine's arrival.

3

We pushed our way through the crowds to Nakht's grand city house that stands close to the Avenue of Sphinxes, to the north of the temple entrance. Here are the residences of only the richest and most powerful families of the city, and my old friend Nakht belongs to that select group, although in person he could not be less like the haughty, arrogant grotesques that make up the vast majority of our so-called elite class. I noticed again my own stiff contempt for these people, and tried to prepare myself for the inevitable condescensions this party would involve.

He was waiting to greet his many rich and famous guests inside the large main door, wearing his finest linens. His face has sharp, delicate features that have become more pronounced with the passing of time, and unusual, flecked topaz eyes that seem to observe life and people as a fascinating but slightly remote pageant. He is the most intelligent man I have ever met, and for him the life of the mind, and of rational enquiry into the mysteries of the world, is everything. He has no partner, and seems to need none, for his life is full of interest and fine company. There has always been something of the hawk about him, as if he is merely perching here on earth, ready to fly into the empyrean with a brief shrug of his powerful mind. Why we are friends I am not sure, but he seems always to relish my company. And he truly loves my family. When he saw the children, his face filled with delight; for they adore him. He embraced them, and kissed Tanefert – who I think adores him a little too much – and then hurried us all through into the sudden tranquillity of the beautiful courtyard, full of unusual plants and birds.

'Come up to the terrace,' he said, handing special festival sweets to each of the children, like a benign sorcerer. 'You are almost late, I don't want you to miss anything on this special day.' Sweeping the delighted Nedjmet into his arms, and followed attentively by the two older girls, he bounded up the wide stairs, until we reached his unusually spacious roof terrace. Unlike most people who use their tiny city roof space for sun-drying vegetables and fruits, and hanging out the washing, Nakht uses his larger quarters for more glamorous pursuits: for example, to observe the transit of the stars in the night sky, for this mystery is his deepest passion. And he uses it for his famous parties to which he invites people from all walks of life; and today a large crowd was milling about, drinking his excellent wine, eating the exquisite morsels of food from many trays set on stands every-where, and chattering away under the protection of the beautifully embroidered awning, or under the sunshades held by patient, sweating servants.

The view was one of the best in the city. The rooftops of Thebes spread away in every direction, an umber and terracotta labyrinth crammed with the reds and yellows of drying crops, unused and derelict furniture and crates, caged birds and other groups of people who had gathered on these lookout platforms above the chaos of the streets. As I gazed at the panorama, I realized how much the city had expanded in this last decade.

Tutankhamun wished to be seen to demonstrate the royal family's renewed loyalty and largesse to Amun, the God of the city, and the priests who owned and administered his temples, in the construction of new monuments and ever more ambitious and glorious temple buildings. For these, great numbers of engineers, artisans and especially labourers were required, whose shanties and settlements had sprung up around the temples, pushing the city's boundary further into the cultivation. I looked north, and saw the ancient dark lanes of markets, pigpens, workshops and tiny houses of the ungovernable heart of the city bisected by the unnatural straight line of the Avenue of Sphinxes, built before I was born. To the west ran the glittering silver serpent of the Great River, and on either side the fields shone blindingly bright, like a carefully shattered mirror, where they had been flooded by the inundation.

Much further away, on the west bank, beyond the strips of cultivation, lay the vast stone mortuary temples in the desert, and beyond them the secret underground tombs of the Kings in their hidden Valley. To the south of the temples lay the Royal Palace of Malkata with its suburb of administrators' offices and homes, and in front of it the vast stagnant expanse of the Birket Habu lake. Beyond the city and its territories was the definitive border between the Black Land and the Red Land; there it is possible to stand with one foot in the world of living things, and the other in the world of dust and sand, where the sun vanishes each night, and where we send our spirits after death and our criminals to perish, and where the monsters of our nightmares roam and haunt us in that great, barren darkness.

In front of us, running north to south between the great temple cities of Karnak and the Southern Temple, the Avenue was as empty as a dry riverbed, apart from the sweepers who were working fast to clear the last specks of dust and debris so that everything would be perfect. Before the vast painted mud-brick wall of the Southern Temple, phalanxes of Theban army units and crowds of priests in white robes were massed silently in their orders. After the lively chaos of the dock, here all was regimented order and conformity. Medjay officers held back the crowds that pressed together on all sides of the open ground and on either side of the Avenue, until they faded into the shimmering blur of distance; so many people, drawn together by the dream of a propitious glimpse of the God on this Day of Days.

Nakht appeared at my side. For a moment we were alone.

'Am I imagining it, or is the atmosphere strange?' I said.

He nodded. 'It never used to be so tense.'

The swallows, alone in their delight, zoomed about our heads. I discreetly produced the linen amulet, and showed it to him.

'What can you tell me about this?'

He looked at it in surprise, and read it quickly.

'It is a Spell for the Dead, as even you must know. But it is a very particular one. It is said to have been written by Thoth, God of Writing and Wisdom, for the great God Osiris. In order for the spell to be ritually effective, the ink must be made from myrrh. Such a thing is usually reserved only for the funerals of the very highest of the high.'

'Such as?' I asked, puzzled.

'High priests. Kings. Where did you find it?'

'On the dead body of a lame boy. He was certainly no king.'

Now it was Nakht who looked surprised.

'When?'

'First thing this morning,' I replied.

He pondered these strange facts for a moment, and shook his head.

'I cannot yet make sense of that,' he decided.

'Neither can I. Except that I do not believe in coincidence.'

'Coincidence is merely a way of saying we recognize a connection between two events, but cannot discover the meaning of that connection,' he replied, concisely.

'Everything you say always sounds exactly right, my friend. You have the gift of turning confusion into an epigram.'

He smiled. 'Yes, but it is a kind of tyranny with me, for I am far too neat for my own good. And life, as we know, is mostly chaos.'

I observed him as he continued to ponder the linen and its strange spell. He was thinking something he would not tell me aloud.

'Well, it is a mystery. But come now,' he said in his peremptory manner, 'this is a party, and there are many people here I wish you to meet.'

He took me by the elbow and led me into the great, chattering crowd.

'You know I can't abide the great and the good,' I murmured.

'Oh don't be such an inverted snob. There are many people here today who have remarkable interests and passions – architects, librarians, engineers, writers, musicians, and a few businessmen and financiers for good measure – for art and science also depend upon healthy investment. How is our culture to improve and grow unless we share our knowledge? And where else would a Medjay officer like you get to consort with them?'

'You are like one of your bees, going from flower to flower, sampling the nectar of this and that . . .'

'That is quite a good analogy, except that it makes me sound like a dilettante.'

'My friend, I would never accuse you of being a dilettante, nor a dabbler, nor an amateur. You are a kind of philosopher mixed with an inward-seeking adventurer.'

He smiled, satisfied.

'I like the sound of that. This world and the Otherworld are full of curiosities and mysteries. It would take many lifetimes to understand them all. And disappointingly, it seems to me we only have one . . .'

Before I could escape with grace, he introduced me to a group of middle-aged men who were conversing together under the awning. They were all affluently dressed, in linens and jewellery of finest quality. Each of them examined me curiously, like an object of strange interest that perhaps they might purchase, at a bargain price.

'This is Rahotep, one of my oldest friends. He is a chief detective here in Thebes – he specializes in murders and mysteries! Some of us think he should have been made Head of the city Medjay at the last opportunity.'

I tried to deal with this public flattery as best I could, although I loathed it, as Nakht knew very well.

'As I'm sure you are all aware, my dear friend's rhetoric is famous. He can turn mud into gold.'

They nodded all at the same time, apparently delighted by this.

'Rhetoric is a dangerous art. It is the manipulation of the difference, one might say the *distance*, between truth and image,' said a small, fat man with a face like a sat-upon cushion, the startled blue eyes of a baby, and an already-empty cup in his fist.

'And in our times, that distance has become the means by which power is exercised,' said Nakht.

There followed a little awkward silence.

'Gentlemen, this gathering is sounding almost subversive,' I said, to lighten the moment.

'Surely it was ever thus? Rhetoric has been a force for persuasion since man began to speak, and to convince his enemy that he was indeed his friend . . .' said another of the men.

They tittered.

'True. But how much more sophisticated it has all become now! Ay and his cronies sell us words as if they were truth. But words are treacherous and untrustworthy. I should know!' said the blue-eyed man, ostentatiously.

Several of them laughed, raised their hands and wagged their dainty fingers at that.

'Hor is a poet,' explained Nakht.

'Then you are a craftsman in the ambiguity of words. You master their hidden meanings. That is a very useful gift in these times,' I said.

He clapped his hands in delight, and hooted. I realized he was slightly drunk.

'True, for these are times when no one may say what he really means. Nakht, my friend, where did you find this remarkable creature? A Medjay officer who understands poetry! Whatever next, dancing soldiers?'

The company laughed harder, determined to keep the mood light and easy.

'I'm sure Rahotep will not mind if I reveal he too wrote verse when he was younger,' said Nakht, as if to smooth over the hairline cracks that were beginning to appear in the conversation.

'It was very bad indeed,' I replied. 'And no evidence exists of it any more.'

'But what happened, why did you give it up?' asked the poet solicitously.

'I don't remember. I suppose the world took over.'

The poet turned to the company, wide-eyed with amusement.

' "The world took over",' that is a good phrase, I may have to borrow that.'

The company nodded back, indulgently.

'Be careful, Rahotep, I know these writers, they say "borrow" when they mean "steal". You will soon read your words coming back to you on some privately circulated scroll of new verse,' said one of them.

'And it will be a vicious little satire and not a love poem, if I know Hor,' said another.

'Very little of what I do belongs in a poem,' I said.

'And that, my friend, is why it is interesting, for otherwise all is artifice, and how easily one tires of artifice,' replied the poet, thrusting out his empty cup at a passing servant. 'Give me the taste of truth any day,' he continued. The girl approached, refilled our cups, and departed, taking her quiet smile and the attention of several, although not all, of the men with her. I thought how little of reality this man would know. Then the conversation resumed.

'The world has certainly changed greatly in these last years,' said another of the men.

'And despite the advances in our international power, and the achievements of our great new constructions, and the standards of affluence which many of us now enjoy—'

'Blah blah blah,' mocked the poet.

'. . . not all the changes have been for the better,' agreed another.

'I am against change. It is overrated. It improves nothing,' said Hor.

'Come now, that is an absurd opinion, and goes against all sense. It is merely a sign of age, for as we get older, so we believe the world gets worse, manners decline, standards of ethics and knowledge are eroded—' said Nakht.

'And political life becomes more and more of a dismal farce . . .' interrupted the poet, draining his cup again.

'My father is always complaining about such things, and I try to argue with him, and find I cannot,' I offered.

'So let us be honest at least with each other. The great mystery is that we find ourselves ruled by men whose names we hardly know, in offices that remain inscrutable, under the governance of an old man, a megalomaniac without even a royal name, who seems to have cast his gruesome shadow over the world for as long as I can remember. Under the ambitions of the great General Horemheb, we have been engaged in a long and so-far fruitless war with our ancient enemies, when surely diplomacy might have done far more, and saved us the endless drain upon our finances. And as for the two royal children, it seems they are never to be allowed to grow up and take their rightful places at the centre of the life of the Two Lands. How has this come to pass, and how long can it continue?'

Hor had spoken the unspeakable truth; it seemed no one had the courage to answer.

'From our point of view we are very comfortably off, and we thrive within the circumstances of our lives. There is affluence and work, and we keep our fine houses and our servants. Perhaps for us it is a fair compromise. But I imagine you witness a very different side of life?' said a tall, elegant gentleman, bowing and introducing himself to me as Nebi, an architect.

'Or perhaps you really do see the awful reality of things as they are, from which we, living within the charmed circle of our comfortable lives, remain defended,' added the poet with a touch of the supercilious in his tone.

'Why don't you accompany me one night, and find out?' I said. 'I could show you the back streets and the shanties where honest but unlucky people survive on the rubbish we all throw out without thinking. And I could introduce you to some very successful career criminals, experts in viciousness and cruelty, who trade in humans as a commodity. Many of them have fine offices in the city, and beautiful wives and children set up in lovely homes in the comfort of the new suburbs. They throw lavish dinners. They invest in property. But their riches are made in blood. I can show you the reality of this city, if that is what you are looking for.'

The poet put his stubby hands to his forehead theatrically.

'You are right. I leave reality to you. I cannot bear too much of it – who can? I admit I am a coward. Blood makes me faint, I hate the look of poor people and their awful clothes, and if someone even knocks into me accidentally in the street I shriek in fear I am about to be robbed and beaten. No, I prefer to stay within the safe, well-behaved company of words and scrolls in my comfortable library.'

'Even words are not perhaps safe in these times,' said another man, standing at the back, in the best part of the awning's shade. 'Remember we are in the presence of a Medjay officer. The Medjay itself is part of the reality of this city. It is not immune from the corruption and decadence of which we speak.' And he looked at me coolly.

'Ah. Sobek. I wondered whether you would join us,' said Nakht.

The man he addressed was of late middle age, with short grey hair untouched by dye. He had striking grey-blue eyes, and a touch of anger at the world written into his features. We bowed to each other.

'I do not think speech is a crime,' I said carefully. 'Although others might disagree.'

'Indeed. So crime depends on its enactment, not its intention or articulation?' he asked.

The others glanced at each other.

'Yes, it does. Otherwise we would all be criminals, and all behind bars.'

Sobek nodded thoughtfully.

'Perhaps it is the human imagination that is the monster,' he said. 'I believe no animal suffers from the torments of the imagination. Only man . . .'

'The imagination is capable of enacting the very best in us, and the very worst,' agreed Hor, 'and I know what mine would like to do to some people.'

'Your verse is torment enough,' quipped the architect.

'And that is why civilized life, morality, ethics and so on, matter. We are half-enlightened, and half-monstrous,' said Nakht assertively. 'We must build our civility upon reason and mutual benefit.'

Sobek raised his cup.

'I salute your reason. I wish it every success.'

He was interrupted by a roar from below in the streets. Nakht clapped his hands, and shouted:

'The moment has come!'

There was a general rush towards the parapet of the terrace, and the men dispersed to compete for the best vantage points.

Sekhmet appeared at my side.

'Father, father, come or you will miss everything!'

And she dragged me away. Another vast cheer rolled like thunder all along the Way below us, and on and on through the crowds packed into the heart of the city. We had a perfect view of the open area before the temple walls.

'What's happening?' asked Thuyu.

'Inside the temple the King and Queen are waiting for the right moment to appear and to welcome the Gods,' said Nakht.

'And what's inside the temple?'

'A mystery within a mystery within a mystery,' he said.

She squinted at him, annoyed.

'That doesn't mean anything at all,' she commented, correctly enough.

He smiled.

'Inside there is an extraordinary new construction, the Colonnade Hall. It has just been completed after many years of labour. There is nothing else like it upon the earth. Its columns reach to the sky, and they are all carved and painted with wonderful images of the King making offerings; and the roof is painted with uncountable gold stars around the Goddess Nut. Beyond is the vast Sun Court, surrounded by many tall, slender columns. And beyond that you must pass through portal after portal, as the floors get higher, and the ceilings lower, and the shadows darker and darker – and these all lead to the heart of everything: the closed shrine of the God, where he is woken at dawn, and fed with the finest of foods, and clothed in the best of linens, and put back to sleep at night. But only a very few priests, and the King himself, are allowed to enter there, and no one who does can ever speak of what he has witnessed. And *you* must never speak of what I have just told you. For this is a great secret. And great secrets bring with them great responsibilities.' He stared at her sternly.

'I want to see it.' She grinned her clever grin.

'You never will,' said Sekhmet suddenly. 'You're just a girl.'

Nakht was just thinking about how to respond to that when trumpets blasted out a deafening fanfare; at this signal the ranks of priests knelt down as one in the perfect dust, and the soldiers stood tightly to attention, their spearheads and arrowheads glittering in the unforgiving sun. Then, from out of the shadows of the vast enclosure wall, two small figures appeared, seated upon thrones carried by officials, and surrounded by men of the offices and their assistants. The moment they moved from the shadows to the sun, their robes and high crowns caught the powerful light, and they shone dazzlingly bright. An absolute hush descended upon the city. Even the birds were silenced. The most important moment of the festival's ritual had commenced.

But nothing happened for a few moments, as if they were too early for a party, and no one had quite thought what to do to keep them entertained. The royal sunshade holders produced sunshades and protected the royal figures within circles of shade. Then a roar up ahead announced the God in his gold shrine, borne on the shoulders of his bearers, as the procession slowly and laboriously turned the corner, and appeared in a flash of light. The royal figures waited, seated like dolls, costumed, stiff and small.

Preceded by high-ranking priests chanting prayers and spells, surrounded by acrobats and musicians, and followed by a white sacrificial bull, the God approached. Finally the King and Queen stood up: Tutankhamun, the Living Image of Amun, and next to him Ankhesenamun.

'She looks frightened.'

I looked down at Sekhmet, then back at the Queen. My daughter was right. Under the paraphernalia of power, the crown and the robes, the Queen looked nervous.

From the corner of my eye I saw, from out of the dense crowd standing under their sunshades against the intense light of the sun, several figures raised up by other figures as if on the joined hands of acrobats, and then a series of swift movements, arms casting something – small, dark balls that arced high in the air, over the heads of the crowd, on an inexorable trajectory towards the standing figures of the King and Queen. Time seemed to stretch and slow, as it does in the last moments before an accident.

A series of bright splashes of red exploded suddenly across the immaculate dust, and over the King and Queen's robes. The King staggered backwards and slumped into the throne. The silence of profound shock suspended everything for a long moment. And then the world exploded into a thousand fragments of noise, action and screaming.

I feared Tutankhamun was dead; but he slowly raised his hands in horror or disgust, reluctant to touch the red stuff that ran down his royal robes into a puddle in the dust. Blood? Yes, but not the King's, for there was too much of it too quickly. The God's shrine now wavered, as the carrying priests, uncertain how to respond, waited for instructions, which did not come. Ankhesenamun was looking about in confusion; then as if waking from a slow dream, the orders of the priests and the army suddenly broke ranks.

I became aware of the girls screaming and crying, of Thuyu huddling into me, of Tanefert holding the other girls to herself, and of Nakht's quick glance communicating his shock and astonishment at this sacrilegious act. On the roof terrace, men and women were turning to each other, their hands raised to their mouths, or appealing to the heavens for comfort in this moment of disaster. A tumult rose beneath us as the crowd began to panic, turning in confusion, pushing against the ranks of Medjay guards, trying to spill out on to the Avenue of Sphinxes, where they stampeded away from the scene of the crime. The Medjay guards responded by piling into the crowd, hitting anyone they could reach with their batons, dragging innocent bystanders by the hair, tackling men and women to the ground – where some were trampled by others – and herding as many people as they could capture together.

I looked back down to the place the balls had been thrown from, and noticed a young woman's face, tense with trepidation; I was sure she had been one of the people who had thrown the balls; I watched as she looked around, assessing whether she had been seen, before turning purposefully away in the middle of a group of young men who seemed to gather about her as if in protection. Something occurred to her, and she looked up and saw me watching her. She held my gaze for a moment and then hid herself under a sunshade, hoping to disappear into the pandemonium of the streets. But I saw a group of Medjay guards rounding up everyone they could catch, like fishermen, and she was trapped, along with many others.

The King and the Queen were already being carted with indecent haste back into the safety of the temple walls, followed by the hidden God in his gold shrine and the crowds of dignitaries who ducked and scurried, alert to their own anxieties. Then they all vanished through the temple gates, leaving behind an unprecedented pandemonium at the heart of the city. A few bladders of blood – weapons suddenly as powerful as the most sophisticated bow and the finest, truest arrow – had changed everything.

I looked at the solid ground far below me, crowded with people, swirling in eddies of panic, and then for an instant what seemed solid changed to an abyss of dark shadows, and within it I saw the serpent of chaos and destruction, that lies coiled in secret beneath our feet, open its golden eyes.

4

I left the family with instructions to wait in Nakht's house until it was safe for them to return home under the care of his household guards. Then I took Thoth with me, and stepped carefully out of the doorway into the street. Medjay officers swept up the last of the crowds, taking prisoner and binding any they suspected of wrongdoing. Shouts and cries came distantly through the thick, smoky air. The Avenue seemed like a vast papyrus scroll on which the true history of what had just happened was now recorded on the trampled sand, scribbled with the scuffed signs of footprints as people had fled, abandoning thousands of sandals. Litter drifted pointlessly. Gusts of hot air went around in angry circles, and then died out in a flutter of dust. Little groups gathered around the dead and injured, weeping and crying out to the Gods. The detritus of all the festival flowers, smeared and crushed, made an inadequate propitiatory offering to the god of this havoc.

I examined the patches of spattered blood, now sticky and congealed in the sun to black puddles. Thoth sniffed delicately at the blood, his eyes flickering up at me. Flies fought furiously over these new riches. I carefully picked up one of the bladders, and turned it in my hand. There was nothing sophisticated about it, or about this act. But it was radical in its originality, and the crude effectiveness of its abomination; for the perpetrators had humiliated the King as well as if they had just hung him upside down and smeared him in dog shit.

I walked beneath the carved stone image of our standard, the Wolf, Opener of the Ways, and entered the Medjay headquarters. I was instantly assailed by chaos. Men of all ranks hurried about, yelling orders and counter-orders, and generally demonstrating their status and appearance of purpose. Through the crowd, I saw Nebamun, Head of the Thebes Medjay. He stared at me, obviously annoyed to find me here, and gestured bluntly in the direction of his office. I sighed, and nodded.

He kicked the door shut in its shoddy frame, and Thoth and I sat patiently on our side of his not very neat low table, covered with papyrus rolls, half-finished snacks and dirty oil lamps. His big face, always shadowed with bristles, looked darker than ever. He glanced disdainfully at Thoth, who gazed back at him undaunted, as he pushed the various documents about with his stubby fists – he had the wrong hands for a bureaucrat. He was a man of the street, not a papyrus man.

He and I had avoided speaking directly to each other, but I had tried to show I bore him no resentment at his promotion over me. His was not the job I desired, despite my father's disappointment, and Tanefert's wish. She would prefer me to inhabit the safety of an office; but she knows I hate being trapped in a stuffy room mired in the tedium and nonsense of internal politics. He was welcome to it all. But now he had power over me, and we both knew it. In spite of myself, something rankled in my guts.

'How's the family?' he asked, without much interest.

'They are well. Yours?'

He gestured vaguely like a bored priest waving away a troublesome fly.

'What a mess,' he said, shaking his head. I decided to keep quiet about what I had seen.

'Who do you think is behind it?' I asked innocently.

'I don't know, but when we find them, and we will, I am personally going to rip their skin from their bodies in long, slow strips. And then I will stake them out in the desert under the midday sun as lunch for the bull ants and the scorpions. And I will watch.'

I knew he did not have enough resources available to investigate any of this properly. In these last years, the Medjay budget has been cut again and again, in favour of the army, and too many ex-Medjay were now unemployed or else working – for better remuneration than they had ever received within the force – in private security operations for rich clients and their families, at their homes or their treasure-filled tombs. It created an uncomfortable circumstance in which to run the city force. So he would do what he usually did when faced with a real problem; he would arrest some likely suspects, invent a case against them, and execute them for show. Such is the process of justice in our time.

He lolled backwards, and I saw how his belly had expanded since he had been appointed to his new role. Fat, with its implication of wealth and ease, seemed to be part of his new self.

'It's been a while since you had one of your big projects, eh? I expect you're sniffing around for a place in the investigation . . .'

The way he eyed me made me want to walk out.

'Not me. I'm enjoying the quiet life,' I replied. He looked offended.

'So why the hell are you here? Sightseeing?'

'I examined a dead body this morning. A boy, a young man, under interesting circumstances—'

But he didn't let me finish.

'Nobody gives a fuck about a dead kid. Write a report, file it . . . then do me a favour and go away. There's nothing for you here today. Next week I might be able to find you a few bits and pieces to mop up, when the others have finished. It's time to let the younger officers have their chance.'

I forced myself to smile, but it felt more like the teeth-baring of an angry dog. He saw this. He grinned, stood up, walked around the table and with mock officiousness opened the door. I walked out. It slammed shut behind me.

Outside, hundreds of unfortunate men and women of all ages were crowded into the courtyard, crying out their innocence and their petitions, or yelling abuse at each other. Many thrust out offerings of anything they possessed at this moment – jewellery, rings, clothing, even an occasional message scratched on to a shard of stone – to try to secure freedom from the guards. No one took any notice. They would be held arbitrarily, for as long as required. Medjay officers methodically and mercilessly bound the wrists and ankles of any not yet trussed-up.

I passed through the low dark entrance to the prison block, and immediately smelt the hot, stable stench of fear. In small cells, shackled prisoners were being tortured, their feet and hands twisted, or struck with hard blows, while their confessors quietly repeated the same questions, over and over, as a father might address a lying child. The prisoners' pitiful laments and pleas went unacknowledged. No one could endure such pain, and fear of pain; and so of course long before the cutting knives were produced, and their sharp blades shown to the victims, they would say anything they were told to say.

I saw her in the third holding cell. She was crouched on the fetid ground in a dark corner.

I entered the cage. The prisoners made way for me, fearfully, as if I would kick them. She kept her face hidden under her black hair. I stood before her.

'Look at me.'

There was something about her face, when she raised it – perhaps its pride, perhaps its anger, perhaps its striking youth – that touched me. I wanted to know her story. I had a feeling that the kind of injustice that deforms a whole life had been visited upon her.

'What is your name?'

She maintained her silence.

'Your family will be missing you.'

She sagged a little. I knelt down closer to her.

'Why did you do it?'

Still nothing.

'You know there are men here who can make you say anything they want?'

She was shivering now. I knew I should report her. But I realized in that moment I could not do it. I could not deliver this girl alive into the hands of the torturers. I could not have lived with myself.

She turned her face away, waiting for her fate to be decided. I stared at her. What should I do?

I pulled her up roughly, and took her out of the cell. I was well known enough not to need to show any of my identity papers to the guards. I simply nodded at them, as if to say – 'she's mine'. Then I pushed her before me along the stinking passage.

We turned a corner, into my office, and fearing the worst, she began to struggle violently.

'Be quiet, and be still,' I whispered urgently. I quickly cut the ropes that tied her hands and feet. A look of grateful astonishment dawned on her face. She was about to speak but I gestured to her to remain absolutely silent. I cleaned her face as best I could, with a rag dipped into the water pot, and as I did so I questioned her.

'Speak quietly. Who ordered this action?'

'No one ordered it. We acted ourselves. Someone has to protest against the injustice and corruption of this state.'

I shook my head at her naivety.

'Do you think throwing blood at the King will make a difference?'

She looked at me with contempt.

'Of course it will make a difference. Who has ever had the courage

47

to take a stand before? No one will forget this gesture. It is only the beginning.'

'And for this you were prepared to die?'

She nodded, convinced of her ideals. I shook my head.

'Believe me, the real target you need is not this boy in gold robes. There are others, far more powerful, who deserve your attentions.'

'I know what is done in the name of justice in this land, by men with power and treasure. And you? You are a Medjay officer. You are part of the problem.'

'Thank you. Why are you doing this?'

'Why should I tell you anything?'

'Because if you don't tell me, I will not do what I intend to do, and let you go free.'

She stared at me in amazement.

'My father . . .'

'Go on.'

'My father was a scribe in the offices of the former King. In Akhetaten. When I was young, he moved us all to the new city. He said the new regime offered him the chance of preferment, and stability. And so it seemed. We lived well. We had the nice things he had dreamed of giving us. We had some land. But when everything collapsed, we had to move back to Thebes with nothing. He was stripped of his work, and his land, and everything he owned. And it broke him. And then one night, there was a knock on the door. And when he opened it, soldiers were waiting for him. They put him in fetters. They wouldn't even let us kiss him goodbye. And they took him away. And we never saw him again.'

She couldn't continue for a moment, but I saw it was rage not grief that gripped her.

'My mother still sets a plate of food for him every night. She says the day she stops doing that is the day she knows he is dead. The men of this King did this to us. And you wonder why I hate?'

It was not a new story. Many men of the old regime had suffered:

enforced labour and dispossession and, in some cases, disappearance. Husbands, fathers and sons were arrested and removed in fetters, in silence, and never seen again. I have also heard stories of body parts washing up further to the north along the Great River. Of eyeless, rotten corpses fished up in the nets, missing fingernails, and fingers, and teeth, and tongues.

'I'm sorry.'

'Don't be.'

At least now she looked reasonably presentable. I led her out into the courtyard. The great risk was that we would be noticed, but taking advantage of the general chaos, we hurried through the crowds, under the entrance with its carved wolf, and then out into the busy street.

'I understand how you feel. Injustice is a terrible thing. But think carefully. Your life is worth more than a gesture. Life is short enough. Your mother has lost enough already. Go home to her now, and stay there,' I whispered. I insisted she gave me her name and address, in case I needed them for the future. And then, as if she were a wild animal, I let her go. She disappeared into the city without once looking back.

5

It was late when I returned to the house. Thoth and I passed through the gate. But instead of loping to his bed in the yard he stood poised, his tail up, listening intently. The house seemed unusually quiet. Perhaps Tanefert and the children had not yet returned from Nakht's house. But the oil lamp was lit within the front room, where we never sit.

I moved across to the kitchen door, soundlessly pushed it open, and stepped across the threshold. Another lamp was lit in the wall niche, but there was no sign of the children. I moved towards the door into the front room. Tanefert was sitting on a stool by the wall paintings that still, after all these years, we have not found the funds to complete. She had not yet seen me. She looked tense. I moved further and saw another shadow lying across the floor. Then the shadow's arm moved, and I slipped quickly into the room and grasped the man's arm behind his back.

A goblet clattered to the floor. Wine spread in a small puddle. I was staring into the condescending face of an elite gentleman, of late middle age, expensively dressed, surprised but still composed. Tanefert stood up, as if to attention. It seemed my nerves had betrayed me.

'Good evening,' said the man, in a smoothly ironic tone.

I let him go. He readjusted his impressive gold Collar of Praise –

an exceptionally fine one – and then noticed he had spilt wine on his robe. He looked down at the red stain with disappointment. It was probably the worst thing that had happened to him in years.

'This gentleman has been waiting to see you . . . *for quite a long time.*' My wife looked less than pleased with me. I imagined there would not have been much conversation. She disappeared into the kitchen to fetch a cloth and water, giving me the eye as she passed.

'I should apologize for appearing in this way. Unannounced. Unexpected . . .' he said, in his grand, hushed voice.

'And unexplained . . .' I added.

He looked around the room. He was not impressed by what he saw. Eventually his gaze returned to me.

'How shall we continue this discussion? I find myself in a quandary. A dilemma . . .'

'A predicament.'

'If you like. A predicament. And the predicament is this: I cannot tell you why I am here. I can only ask whether you will come with me to meet someone.'

'And you cannot tell me who.'

'You see my predicament.'

'It's a mystery.'

'But then one hears you are something of an expert at mysteries. A "Seeker of Mysteries". I never thought to meet such a person, and yet here I am.'

And he graced me with his most withering stare.

'At least you could tell me your name and titles,' I said.

'I am Khay. Chief Scribe, Keeper of the Royal Household. Well, that is all I can tell you at this moment.'

What was a very high official, at the heart of the palace hierarchy, doing in my front room, on this strange day of omens and blood? I was annoyed with myself for being so intrigued. I poured us each a fresh goblet of wine. He glanced at his, clearly unimpressed by its quality; but nevertheless he drank it as if it were water.

'You are asking me to come now?'

He nodded, almost casually, but I saw he needed me badly.

'It is late. Why should I leave my family with no certain knowledge of where I am going, or when I will be back?'

'I can guarantee your safety, of course. Well, I can guarantee my commitment to your safety, which I suppose is not quite the same thing. And I can certainly guarantee you will return home before dawn, if you wish.'

'And if I refuse?'

'Oh . . . It would be rather difficult . . .' he trailed off.

Then he reached into his robes and from a leather pouch brought out an object.

'I was asked by my *client* to show you this.'

It was a toy. A wooden man and a big dog with wide red eyes, worked by strings and pulleys. There was a peg. I knew if you turned the peg the man's arms went up to defend him as the wooden dog rose to attack him. I knew this because I had seen it before, many years ago, in the nursery of the royal family. When the young Queen, who today had been spattered in blood, was a child.

I explained everything to Tanefert in the kitchen. The girls crept out of their room now, and gathered in the safe circle of the lamplight.

'Who is that man?' demanded Thuyu.

'He's a high official.'

'A high official of what?' whispered Sekhmet, thrilled by the arrival of a real, live elite bureaucrat in our home.

Tanefert shushed all their questions, and persuaded them to return to their bedrooms. Nedjmet, the Sweet One, stood there, hardly even looking at me. I picked her up, kissed her, and promised I would return in time for breakfast.

'Where are you going? It's dark.'

'Out to see someone.'

'Is it work?'

'Yes. It's work.'

She nodded gravely, and I passed her to Tanefert, who gave me one of her looks.

'I'll leave Thoth on guard.'

She kissed me carefully, and retired to our chamber.

We arrived at the docks, at the place where the ferries cross. By day it is crowded with boats and ships of all sizes, from little reed boats and passenger ferries through to the large commercial ships of the kingdom, and the transporters of stone. The economy that keeps the city thriving and affluent, and supplied with luxuries, construction materials and food, is based here; deals are sealed or betrayed, and goods imported or smuggled. But by night it is quiet. No trade happens in the night hours because it is so dangerous to sail the Great River after dark; crocodiles cruise invisibly, disguising their predatory manoeuvres in the currents and swirls of the black water.

But the sophisticated and beautiful vessel we boarded would need a herd of crocodiles to capsize it; we settled ourselves within the curtained privacy of the cabin and passed the brief crossing in silence. Khay offered me more wine, which I refused. He shrugged and poured some for himself and sat down to drink. I played with the toy, turning the wheel so that the dog, with its crudely sawn ridge of raised wooden hackles and its red fangs, rose repeatedly up to the man. And I thought about the child who had said to me many years ago: *Look! It's you . . . !* But I was not going to open the sealed box of those memories. Not yet. I gazed at the low rooftops and white walls of Thebes lit by the moon as we sailed towards the west bank. Most of the city's multitudes would be asleep now, to prepare for tomorrow's return to their perpetual labours; only those with wealth and liberty would still be up, at their private festivals of wine and pleasure, gossiping about the events of the day, and the politics, and the consequences.

We did not dock directly on the western bank, but instead sailed past the guard stations, then up a long, dark channel between the trees and fields, now stirring with nightlife. The channel, built in the straight lines beloved of engineers, opened suddenly into the great T-shaped basin of the Birket Habu lake. Flocks of night birds squabbled on its flat, still surface. Ramps of hewn rock, which protected the surrounding complex of buildings from the inundation, hid the landscape from view. But I knew what lay beyond those ramparts: the Malkata Palace, a vast assemblage of buildings, where the royal family maintained their closely guarded royal quarters and those of the thousands of officials, officers and servants who work to make their strange life possible. It was known as the 'Palace of Rejoicing', but there seemed little about the dark construction that now began to come into view to earn it such an optimistic title. It was famous for the elaboration and expense of its construction under Tutankhamun's grandfather, and for its remarkable water system that, it was rumoured, supplied bathrooms, pools and gardens even in the heart of the palace. It was said the beds were inlaid with ebony, gold and silver. It was said the doorframes were solid gold. Such are the things people say about the dream palaces they will never visit.

We docked at the vast palace jetty that spread all along the lake's frontage. Copper bowls of oil on wrought stands burned, giving off a thick, sinister yellow and orange light. The palace guards bowed low as Khay and I stepped off the boat. The depth of their obeisance gave a clear indication of this man's status here. In any case, he utterly ignored their existence, as these high-ranking men always do.

We set off down a long processional way, lit by lamps, and the welcome, familiar moon, towards the long, low silhouette of the palace complex, and then – my heart compelled by the mystery ahead, and my feet by necessity – we entered a great gloom.

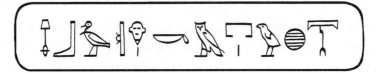

6

The Keeper of the Royal Household took a lit oil lamp from a niche. Everything seemed hushed, lavishly decorated and sealed from the outside world. All along the corridor, down which we marched at speed, were beautiful statues and carvings set upon plinths. I wondered what went on in these side chambers; what meetings, what discussions, what resolutions with what great consequences reaching down through the hierarchies, and out into the unsuspecting and powerless world? We moved on, taking turns to the right or to the left, passing through high, echoing halls where occasional groups of officials conferred and guards were stationed, making our way deeper and deeper into the complex. It was a labyrinth of shadows. Sometimes a servant or a guard passed, their heads bowed low, pretending not to exist as they tended the lights of the oil lamps.

Chamber after chamber of walls painted with glorious scenes of elite pleasure and leisure – birds in the reed marshes, fish in the clear waters – appeared and disappeared in the light of the lamp. It would be difficult to find my way back. My footsteps sounded all wrong – a disturbance in the vast hush. Khay moved ahead on his costly, quiet sandals. I decided to make more noise, just to annoy him. He refused to dignify my behaviour with even a backwards glance. But it is strange and true that we can read a man's face by the back of his head.

We passed swiftly through a checkpoint, as Khay waved away the elite guards of the royal quarters, and then he led me into the inner sanctum, along another high passageway, until finally we paused before great double doors of dark wood inlaid with silver and gold, beneath a carved, winged scarab. He knocked precisely, and after a pause the doors opened, and we were admitted into a large chamber.

Opulent surfaces and furniture were illuminated by large hammered bowls, set all around the walls, whose flames burned very still and clear. The furnishings and decor were immaculately restrained. Here, the room seemed to say, life could be lived calmly, with elevated feelings. But it also had the air of a stage spectacle: as if behind these glamorous facades one might discover masons' rubble, painters' brushes, and unfinished business.

A young woman entered quietly from the courtyard beyond the open doors, and paused at the threshold, between the firelight from the great bowls and the dark shadows that surrounded everything. She seemed to carry something of both with her. Then Ankhesenamun stepped into the light, closer now. Her face, for all its youthful beauty, was engagingly confident. She wore a fashionable, braided, lustrous wig that framed her features, a pleated linen gown tied beneath her right breast, whose flowing cut seemed to sculpt her elegant, neat form, and a broad gold collar, fashioned from row upon row of amulets and beads. Bangles and bracelets shifted and tinkled elegantly around her wrists and ankles as she moved. Rings of gold and electrum flashed on her delicate fingers. Gold disc earrings glittered in the lamplight. She had carefully painted around her eyes with kohl, and drawn out the black lines in a style that was slightly old-fashioned – I realized, as she gazed at me, the ghost of a smile on her lips, that she had deliberately made herself look very much like her mother.

Khay quickly bowed his head, and I copied him, and waited, as protocol demanded, for her to begin the conversation.

'I am not sure if I remember you, or if what I remember is from stories I have been told.'

Her voice was full of self-possession, and curiosity.

'Life, prosperity and health. You were very young, majesty.'

'In another life. Another world, perhaps.'

'Things have changed,' I said.

'Look up,' she said, quietly; and with an enigmatic flash of her dark eyes, she turned away, expecting me to follow her.

We moved into the courtyard. Khay did not withdraw but followed discreetly, at a distance where he could still hear us, but pretend not to. A fountain trickled somewhere in the shadows. The dark air was cool and scented. She moved along an ornamental pathway, lit by more flickering lamps, further into the moony dark.

I remembered the little girl I had met years before: full of petulance and frustration. And here was an elegant and accomplished young woman. Time itself seemed to be mocking me. Where had the years gone? Perhaps she had grown up very suddenly, too quickly, in the way people do when devastating change falls upon them in youth. I thought of my own girls, their ease with their changing lives and themselves. They had no need, thanks to the gods of fortune, for such strategy and appearance. But they too were growing up, growing away, into their own futures.

'So you remember me,' she murmured, as we walked.

'You had a different name in those days,' I replied, carefully.

She glanced away.

'I have had little choice in the matter of myself. I was an awkward unhappy girl, never much of a princess, unlike my sisters; and now they are all dead, it turns out I must be so much more. I have been reinvented, but perhaps I have not yet felt worthy of the role for which I have been – appointed. Is that the word? Or destined?'

She sounded as if she were talking about a stranger, not about herself.

We arrived at a long pool of black water at the centre of the courtyard, with oil lamps placed at each corner. The moon was reflected there, lilting slowly in the water's dream. The place felt romantic, and secret. We strolled along the pool's edge. In some way I felt we were moving towards the heart of the matter.

'My mother told me that if I was ever in real danger, I should call for you. She promised me you would come.'

'And here I am,' I replied quietly. I had sealed her mother's memory in a box in the back of my mind. It was too potent, and too hopeless, to do anything else. And the fact that she was dead now made no difference, for she lived on where I had no power to control her, in my dreams.

'And since you have called for me, and I am here, you must be in real danger.'

A fish broke the immaculate surface of the water, and concentric rings spread out, lapping silently at the pool's walls. The moon's reflection broke apart, and then slowly unified again.

'I am concerned by signs. Portents . . .'

'I am not a great believer in signs and portents.'

'So I have heard, and that is important. We are too easily alarmed, my husband and me. We need someone with less superstition and less fear. I think of myself as modern, as a person not easily frightened by things that are not there. But I find it is not so. Perhaps this palace does not help. It is so vast and empty of life that the imagination populates it with everything it fears. A wind blows from the wrong direction, down from the Red Land, and already I sense malicious spirits stirring at the curtains. These rooms are too big to sleep in without fear. I keep the lamps lit all night, I rely upon magic, I clutch amulets like a child . . . It is ridiculous, for I am no longer a child. I cannot afford to indulge the fears of a child.'

She looked away.

'Fear is a powerful enemy, but a useful friend.'

'That sounds like something only a man could say,' she replied, amused.

'Perhaps you should tell me why you are afraid,' I said.

'I hear you listen well.'

'That is not what my daughters tell me.'

'Oh yes, you have daughters. A happy family . . .'

'It is not always as simple as that.'

She nodded. 'No family is simple.'

She paused, thinking.

'I was married to my husband when we were both very young. I was older by a few years. But we were children, united by the state for the purposes of alliances of power. No one asked us if we wished it. Now we are brought out like statues for state occasions. We perform the rites. We make the gestures. We repeat the prayers. And then we are put back inside this palace. In return for this obedience, we are given luxuries and indulgences and privileges. I do not complain. It is all I know. This beautiful shrine is as much of a home as I have known for many years. It is a prison, and yet it has felt like home. Is it strange that I should think of it that way?'

I shook my head.

Again she paused, thinking ahead.

'But lately – I do not feel safe, even here.'

'Why?'

'For many reasons! Partly, perhaps, because I sense something changing in the atmosphere. This palace is a very restrained, highly disciplined world. So when things change, I notice at once: objects that are not where they ought to be, or that appear out of nowhere. Things that could mean nothing, and yet seen another way might imply something mysterious, something . . . And then, today . . .'

She ran out of words. Shrugged. I waited for more.

'You mean the events at the festival? The blood . . . ?'

She shook her head. 'No. Something different.'

'Can you show me?'

'Yes. But first, there is something more I must tell you.'

She drew me down on to a long bench in the shadows, and spoke in a more cautiously hushed voice, like a conspirator.

'What I am about to tell you is a secret known only to myself and a very few trusted men. You must give me your word you will keep silence. Words are powers, and silence too has its great power. Those powers are mine, to be respected and obeyed. If you do not, I will know it, and I will not spare your punishment.'

She looked at me gravely.

'You have my word.'

She nodded, satisfied, and took a deep breath.

'Tutankhamun will announce his coronation and his ascendancy to the kingship shortly. It would have happened today, after he had communed with the Gods. But that could not happen. Obviously. We were thwarted, on this occasion. But we will not be stopped. The future of the kingdom is at stake.'

She watched for my reaction.

'He is already King,' I commented, carefully.

'But in name only, for Ay is Regent, and he holds all power, in reality. His government is the ruling authority of the kingdom. It remains invisible, and under that cloak he does as he wishes, while we are merely his puppets. So we must grasp power now. While there is still time.'

'That will be very difficult. And very dangerous.'

'Obviously. So now you understand better why I have called for you.'

I felt the shadows of the palace darkening around me with every word she spoke.

'May I ask a question?'

She nodded.

'Can you be sure Ay would not support him in this?'

Ankhesenamun suddenly looked as lonely as any woman I had ever seen. It was as if the door into her heart had been blown open by a gust of wind. In that moment, I knew there was no way back from this strange night, or escape from the dismal labyrinth of this palace.

'He would destroy us both if he knew.'

There was both determination and fear in her eyes.

'And can you be certain he does not know?'

'I cannot be certain of it,' she said. 'But he has shown no sign. He treats the King with contempt, and maintains him in a dependent childhood he should have outgrown. His authority depends upon our subservience. But he has made the most dangerous assumption: he underestimates us. He underestimates *me*. But I will not endure it any longer. We are the children of our father. I am my mother's daughter. I have her inside me, calling to me, encouraging me, persuading me against my fear. The time has come for us to reassert ourselves, and our dynasty. And I believe I am not alone in not wishing to live in a world ruled by a man of such cold heart.'

I needed to think carefully.

'Ay is very powerful. He is also very clever and very ruthless. You will need a powerful and remarkable strategy to outwit him,' I replied.

'I have had a great deal of time to study him, and the stratagems of his mind. I have watched him, and yet I think he has not seen me. I am a woman, and therefore I am beneath his notice. I am almost invisible. And – I have had an idea.'

She dared to look proud of herself for a moment.

'I am sure you realize what is at stake,' I said, cautiously. 'Even if you manage to proclaim the King's accession to power, Ay will almost certainly still hold the reins of its management. He controls many powerful factions and forces.'

'Ay's ruthlessness is notorious. But we are not without allies, and he is not without great enemies. And then there is his obsessive love of order. He would rather cut himself in half than risk a renewal of disorder in the world.'

'I think he would always choose to cut a thousand others in half before himself.'

She smiled, for the first time.

'Ay is more concerned with others who threaten his supremacy. Horemheb, the general, is waiting for his chance. Everyone is aware of this. And remember, we have one other great advantage over Ay. Perhaps the greatest advantage of all . . .'

'And what is that?'

'Time itself. Ay is old. His bones hurt. His teeth hurt. Time the destroyer has discovered him, and is taking his revenge. But we are young. Time is our ally.'

She sat there in all the simple beauty of her youth, dressed in the gold of the God of the Sun, smiling at the thought.

'But time is also famously a betrayer. It has us all at its mercy.'

She nodded.

'You are wise to say so. But our time is now. We must seize this moment, for our sakes, and for the sake of the Two Lands. If we do not, then I foresee an age of darkness ahead of us all.'

'May I ask one last question?'

She smiled.

'I heard you like questions. I see it is true.'

'When will Tutankhamun announce his coronation?'

'It will happen in the next few days. The ceremonial opening of the new Colonnade Hall has been re-arranged. At that time the King will enter the innermost shrine. It is the most propitious moment for change.'

How clever and quick she was. The King would visit the Gods. An announcement after such an event would be perfect timing. It would carry the authority of the divine sanction. I felt a stirring of excitement, of the possibility of change – something I had not felt for a very long time. Perhaps this could work. But I knew my optimism was danger-ous, and could betray me into carelessness; for now, we remained in the world of shadows.

'You said you had something to show me.'

7

It was a small carving of Akhenaten and Nefertiti, together with their older daughters, worshipping the Aten, the sun disc, which had been the great symbol of their revolution. Many rays of light extended down from the disc itself, ending in divine hands which offered ankhs, the sacred symbol of life itself, to the strange little human figures whose arms were raised to receive the divine blessings. Despite the fluid, strange elongations of their limbs, done in the style of the period, it was recognizably a family portrait. The stone was not very old, for it had not been roughened or eroded around its edges by wind and time. It could only be from the city of Akhetaten.

There were several other striking things about it. First, the signs of the name of the Aten had been chiselled out. This was significant, for names are powers, and this desecration was intended as a threat to the soul of Ra himself. Second, the disc of the Sun, the great circle, the sign of life, had also been obliterated. But neither of these things was unexpected, for since the abolishment of the religion, such iconoclasm was common. What mattered more was that the eyes and the noses of all the royal family had been gouged out, so that they would have neither sight nor smell in the Otherworld. And I saw too that Ankhesenamun's own royal names had been excised. This was a very personal desecration.

The carving had been discovered in a box earlier that day, within the royal quarters, during the hours of the performance of the festival. It bore a label offering the contents as a gift to the King and Queen. No one recalled its arrival, and there was no record of its presentation at the gate to the royal offices. It just seemed to have appeared from nowhere. The presentation box itself was unremarkable – a carved chest, probably made of acacia wood, of Theban design and craftsmanship. I rummaged through the straw in which it had been packed. No note. No message. The desecrated carving *was* the message. It would have taken some effort to acquire it, for Akhetaten, the City of the Horizon, although not entirely deserted, was slowly returning to the dust of its making, and almost no one went there any more. It had the reputation of a cursed and abandoned place now. Together with Khay, we stood pondering this enigmatic object.

'And you think this stone is connected to what happened today at the temple, and that between them they constitute a threat against your lives?' I asked.

'Each event by itself would be considered alarming. But both in one day . . .' she replied.

'What happened today, and the appearance of this stone, are not necessarily connected,' I said.

'How can you be sure?' said Ankhesenamun quickly.

'The public event was a consciously political act of dissent. But this is more personal, and private.'

'That sounds a bit vague,' said Khay, airily.

'The first was a crude gesture made by a group who had no other means by which to express their opposition and anger. They had no other way to approach the powers that be than to throw something at the King during a ceremony. For all the drama of its effect, that is hardly the action of powerful people. They are outsiders, without real influence, on the margins of society. This is different: it is more potent, more meaningful, and more sophisticated. It implies knowledge of writing, and of the power of names, and of the effect of iconoclasm. It has needed considerable preparation, as well as inside knowledge of the security of the royal quarters. Therefore we can assume this act has been committed by a member of the elite, and probably by someone within the hierarchies.'

'What are you implying?' said Khay, stiffly.

'That it was delivered from within the palace.'

'That is quite impossible. The royal quarters are carefully guarded at all times.'

'And yet here it is,' I said.

His narrow chin was raised now. He bristled with righteous indignation, like an angry bird. But before he could interrupt, I continued: 'Also the perpetrator is very sure of what he is doing, for this has the intention of creating fear where it does the most damage. In the mind of the King, and those close to him.'

They both stared at me, disconcerted. I had probably said too much, by imputing to the King any kind of human weakness. But it was too late now for protocol and correctness.

'. . . Or so the culprit would seem to hope. Can I assume no one knows anything of this?'

Khay looked as if he had eaten a sour fruit.

'Ay has been informed. He requires to be informed of everything that happens within the royal quarters.'

No one spoke for a moment.

'You will know what I am going to ask you,' Ankhesenamun said, quietly.

I nodded.

'You wish me to find out who is responsible for sending this object, and for its hostile desecration.'

'Someone malicious has access to the royal quarters. They must be discovered. But me need more than that: I want you also to attend my husband and me as our – private protector. Our guardian. Someone to watch over us. Someone unseen by others . . .'

'You have the Palace Guard,' I said.

'I cannot trust the Palace Guard.'

Each sentence of this conversation felt as if it was leading me deeper and deeper into a trap.

'I am one man.'

'You are the only man. And that is why I have called for you.'

Now the last of the doors that might still have led away from here and back to my own chosen life closed silently.

'And what is your answer?'

Many answers jostled in my mind.

'It will be an honour for me to fulfil the promise I made to your mother,' I replied eventually. My heart was knotted tight at the consequence of these few words.

She smiled with relief.

'But at the same time, I can't abandon my family . . .'

'Perhaps that is all to the good. This must remain a secret between us. So you should carry on normally, and then—'

'But Ay knows me. Others will know of me. I cannot be here in secret. It would make my task impossible. You should simply say you are employing me, in addition to the Palace Guard, because of the threats you have received. Say I am independently assessing the internal security arrangements.'

She glanced at Khay, who considered the options, and then nodded once.

'We accept this,' she said.

The thought of the double life ahead made me anxious. And, I had to confess, excited. I had promised Tanefert I would not forsake the family. But I reasoned I would not be breaking that vow, for I would not need to leave the city to pursue this mystery. And there was little enough work for me at the Medjay headquarters, under Nebamun's thumb. I wondered why I was persuading myself.

Khay was making the kind of noises that indicated it was time for us to depart. We offered our formal farewells. Ankhesenamun held my hands between her own, as if she wished to seal there the secret things that we had spoken about.

'Thank you,' she said, her eyes brimming with accomplished sincerity. And then she smiled, more openly and warmly this time, and instantly I glimpsed her mother's face; not the beautiful public mask, but the warm, living woman.

And then the great double doors were silently opened behind us, and we retreated, backwards, bowing, until the doors closed again and we found ourselves in that endless, hushed corridor, with its many identical doors, like a scene from a nightmare.

I needed to piss, and I wanted to see whether the rumour about the water supply was true. Khay took me down a side corridor. 'Third doorway on the left.' He sniffed. 'I will await you before the Queen's chamber doors.' He turned away.

I entered. The space was long and narrow with a stone floor on which were painted pools of water, with gold fishes swimming. A lattice drew in the cool scents of the night. A few tapers swayed in the breeze of my appearance. I did what was necessary. It sounded too loud, in the awful, almost religious, hush. I felt as if I were pissing in a temple. Then I washed my hands in the basin, pouring water from the jug. No miracles of plumbing here. I was drying my hands, when I sensed something – a prickle of the hairs on my neck, a blur of something across the polished surface of the copper mirror – and in an instant I turned.

The woman watched me knowingly, her clever eyes shining in the dim light, her black hair tied severely behind her head, her face angled and strangely gaunt, her robes like a dress of shadows.

'Do you know me?' she said, low and quiet.

'Should I?'

She shook her head, disappointed.

'I came to tell you my name.'

'In the *toilet*?'

'I am Maia.'

'Your name means nothing to me.'

She clicked her tongue in annoyance.

I finished drying my hands.

'I was the wet nurse to the King. He fed from me from the day he was born. Now I care for him as no one else can.'

She must have lived in the city of Akhetaten. She must have witnessed the life of Akhenaten, and the royal family, from close quarters. It was known the King's mother was Kiya, who had been a rival royal wife to Nefertiti. But Kiya had disappeared. And then, later, Tutankhamun, son of Kiya, had been married to Ankhesenamun, the child of Nefertiti. The children of enemies, both fathered by Akhenaten, last survivors of their lines, married to each other. From a political point of view it was a great alliance. From theirs it must have been hell, for stepchildren rarely love each other, even less so when great power and treasure are at stake.

She nodded as if she watched me work this out.

'What do you wish to say to me?'

She glanced around, cautious even here.

'Do not trust that girl. She has the blood of her mother.'

'She is the Queen. As was her mother. Why should I not trust her?'

'For all your power, you know nothing. You cannot see what is there. You are dazzled like a fool before gold.'

I felt the grip of anger at my throat.

'Man of pride. Man of vanity. Think! Her mother disposed of her rival, Kiya, the mother of my King. That must not be forgotten. It must never be forgiven. It should be avenged. And yet you come like a dog to wait at her door.'

'You sound like a marketplace storyteller. And you have no proof of anything you say. And even if you are right, it was all a long time ago.'

'I have the proof of my eyes. I see her for what she really is. She is

68

the child of her dynasty. Nothing changes. So I come to warn you. Her care is not for her husband. Her care is all for herself.'

I moved closer to her. She drew herself deeper into her robes.

'I could have you arrested for this.'

'Arrest Maia? The King will not allow it. He is my child, and I speak out from love for him. For no one else loves him. Without me he is alone in this palace. And besides, I know their names. I know the names of the shadows.'

'What do you mean?'

'Shadows have powers,' she replied, and with those enigmatic words she slid away along the dark wall, and vanished.

8

At the jetty, Khay gave me a papyrus of authority that would allow me to enter the Malkata Palace again, and to request an audience with him at any time. He told me he lived within the royal quarters. I should make use of him whenever I needed. Everything he said made it clear he was the pass to all gates, the man whose word was law, whose every whisper was heard in the ear of power. As I turned away, he offered me a leather bag.

'What's this?'

'Consider it a small advance.'

I looked inside. It contained a good-quality gold ring.

'Why is it a small one?'

'I trust it will be adequate.'

His voice ground the words like grit under a millstone. He turned and left without waiting for any response I might have cared to offer.

I stood at the stern of the boat, looking backwards as it was rowed away, until the palace containing its lonely Queen and its strange, clandestine young King disappeared behind the ramparts of the great lake's defences.

The boat left me discreetly in a far corner of the docks, and I walked back past the hundreds of moored boats, each with their painted eyes, shifting and knocking against each other on the surface of the river's dark currents, their sails folded and stowed, and their crews and some of the dock workers sleeping on the decks and in the shadow of the heaps of goods, curled into their dreams like ropes into a coil. At the far end of the dock, in the dark, I noticed, to my surprise, two boats being unloaded of their cargo. No torches were lit to illuminate the work – but the moon's light was almost adequate. The men worked silently, efficiently transferring a number of clay containers from the ships to a convoy of carts. I saw a tall, thin man walking among them, directing affairs. Smugglers, probably, for no one else dared to navigate the dangerous river in the dark. Well, it was none of my business. I had other concerns.

Walking is my cure for confusion; it is the only thing that makes me feel sane sometimes. I made my way back through the deserted streets, and now the night city felt like a vacant theatre, a construction of papyrus, shadows and dreams. I set myself to a proper consideration of everything this extraordinary day had set before me. The festival ceremonials with their strangely repressed atmosphere; the astonishing act of sacrilege; the girl in the cells, and her rage, which had matured like a wine into something dark and powerful; this night meeting with the Queen of the kingdom – anxious with fear; the encounter with the King's wet nurse. And perhaps most shocking of all, the dead boy, his cruelly shattered limbs, his appalling posture of perfection, arranged for death, and the linen spell. What did these things, the events of this day, have to do with each other? If, indeed, they had anything to do with each other – for I am given to finding patterns where, perhaps, none exist. Still, I sensed something – an intuition, elusive, just out of the reach of thought, like the glinting edge of a shard flashing for a moment among ruins – but then it was gone again. At this moment nothing added up. I know I love to consider the ways disparate things may be surprisingly related – more as in a dream or a poem than in reality. My colleagues ridicule me, and perhaps they are right, and yet somehow I do not find the mystery at the heart of human beings is ever as logically fathomable as they say it is. But then again, what use was that to me now?

Next, I considered the carving. Superficially, it expressed animosity towards the previous regime of the Aten, of which the King was the inheritor, survivor and (as had been made clear by his public pronouncements, acts and new buildings) now the destroyer. The iconoclasm, however, was not exceptional, and the interesting question was: why had it been delivered in such a deliberate, even intimate, manner to the King? More subtly, it expressed a severe threat: for the annihilation of the sign represented the annihilation of the reality. The King was also the Sun. And the Sun destroyed, and still worse the royal names destroyed, represented the destruction of the King and Queen in the afterlife. And there was something else: the sheer fury of those chisel-marks spoke of deep, almost mad, anger. It was as if each stab of the chisel was a stab into the King's eternal spirit. But why, and who was responsible?

I looked up at the moon, now sunk low over the rooftops and the temple pylons, like the sickle of light in the left eye of Horus; and I remembered the old fable we tell our children about how this was the last missing fragment of the God's destroyed eye, which was finally restored by Thoth, God of Writing and Secrets. Now we know better – we know the actions and movements of the celestial forms from observation; our star calendars record their perpetual motions and great returns over the year, and over infinities of time. And then – suddenly it occurred to me: what if the stone represented a more obvious meaning? What if it said: *eclipse?* Perhaps it meant a true eclipse? Perhaps the eclipse of the Living Sun was just a metaphor. But what if it wasn't? It seemed a possible link, and somehow I liked the thought. I would talk to Nakht, who knew all about such things.

I walked up my street, pushed open the gate, and entered the courtyard. Thoth was waiting for me, alert on his haunches, as if he knew I was about to arrive and had prepared to present himself smartly. Tanefert had insisted I acquire him a few years ago, for the city's streets had become more and more dangerous for a Medjay man like me. She claimed she wanted him as a household guard, but her real intention was for me to have more protection at work. To please her I had acquiesced. And now I could almost admit I loved the animal for his intelligence, loyalty and dignity. He sniffed the air around me, as if to divine all that had happened, and then looked me in the eye with his old, gentle challenge. I passed my hand over his mane, and he walked around me, ready to receive more attention.

'I'm tired, old man. You've been dozing here while I've been out working . . .'

He moved back to his place and settled down, his topaz eyes on guard, seeing everything in the dark.

I closed the outer door, and moved silently into the kitchen. I washed my feet, then drew a cup of water from the clay pot, and ate a handful of dates. Then I moved along the passage, and as quietly as I was able I drew back the curtain to our room. Tanefert was turned on her side, the form of her hips and shoulders like an elegant cursive upon a dark scroll, described by the light from the lamp. I took off my robe, and lay beside her, placing the leather bag by the couch. I knew she was awake. I drew close to her, put my arms around her warm body, fitted my form around hers, and kissed her smooth shoulder. She turned to me, half-smiling, half-annoyed, in the dark, kissed me, and moved into my embrace, soft and comfortable. More than anywhere in the world, this felt like home. I kissed her sleek black hair. What should I tell her of the evening's events? She knew I rarely spoke about work, and understood my reticence. She never resented it, because she knew I needed to keep it apart, separate. But then again, she can always read me: she sees something wrong or troubling in my face, or in the way I enter a room. There could be no secrets. So I told her.

She stroked my arm as she listened, as if calming her own anxiety. I could feel her heart beating – the bird of her soul in the green tree of her life. I finished my story, and she stayed like that for a while, quietly considering everything; looking at, but also somehow beyond me, the way someone looks into a fire.

'You could refuse her.'

'Do you think I should?'

Her silence was eloquent, as always.

'Then I will return this tomorrow.'

I held up the bag, and shook out the gold ring into her palm.

She looked at it, then handed it back.

'Don't ask me to tell you what to do. You know I hate that. It's not fair.'

'But what, then?'

She shrugged.

'What is it?'

'I don't know. I have a bad feeling . . .'

'Where?' I reached out for her.

'Don't be a fool. I know each day is full of dangers, but what good can come of this? Palace intrigues, and attempts on the life of the King? These are dark matters. They frighten me. But look at you: your eyes are sparkling again . . .'

'That's because I'm worn out . . .' I yawned extravagantly for effect.

Neither of us said anything for a little while. I knew what she was thinking. And she knew what I was thinking.

Then my wife spoke.

'We need this gold,' she said. 'And you can't help yourself. You love a mystery.'

And she smiled sadly, in the dark, at the implication of her words.

'I love my wife and my children.'

'But are we mystery enough for the Seeker of Mysteries?'

'Our girls will be leaving us soon. Sekhmet is nearly sixteen. How did that happen? It's a great mystery to me how time has passed so swiftly since they were crawling and throwing up and grinning their proud, toothless smiles. And now look . . .'

Tanefert slipped her hand into mine.

74

'And look at us. A middle-aged couple that need their sleep.'

And so she settled her head on its stand and closed her elegant eyes.

I wondered if sleep would honour me on this night. I doubted it. I had to think about how I might approach this new mystery when the sun rose, as it very soon would. I lay back and stared at the ceiling.

9

I arrived soon after first light at the office of the treasury. A cleaner, with a brush and pot, worked backwards across the great floor, scattering fresh water with deft gestures then wiping it away until the stone shone brightly before his feet. He worked methodically, impassively, his head down, as the first of the bureaucrats and officials arrived for work; men in white robes who glanced at me and Thoth with brief curiosity, but passed the cleaner as if he did not exist, leaving the dirty prints of their dusty sandals upon his immaculate floor. He wiped these away, over and over, with endless patience. He was a man who would never walk on shining, clean stone. At no point did he look up at the stranger sitting on the bench, his baboon patiently beside him, waiting for someone.

Finally a senior official, the Deputy of the Treasury, invited me into his office, slightly anxious under his affable competence. I knew his kind: loyal, quietly proud of his merits, relishing the just rewards of his profession – the comforts of a good villa, productive land and faithful servants. I left Thoth tied up outside. We sat on stools opposite each other. He adjusted the few objects – statuettes, trays, the tube of his reed pen, his mixing palette, two little bags for the red and the black ink – on his low table, and recited his long list of titles, from the beginning of his professional life until this very moment. Only then did he ask how he could be of assistance. I told him I wished to be granted an audience with Ay.

He feigned surprise.

I pushed Khay's papyrus of authorization at him. He unrolled the document, and glanced along the characters swiftly. Then he looked up at me with a different expression.

'I see. Could you wait here for a few moments?'

I nodded. He disappeared.

I listened to the irrelevant sounds of the corridor and the distant chorus of the river birds for a while. I imagined him knocking on doors, one after the other, like a box within a box, until he arrived at the threshold of the innermost shrine.

When he reappeared, he looked as if he had gone on a long march. He was out of breath. 'If you would follow me . . .'

We passed through the deep shadows and the long angles of sunlight laid out along the corridors. The guards at the doors lifted their weapons respectfully. The official left me at the last threshold. He would go no further. A supercilious, brittle assistant – one of three who sat in tense attendance outside the office – knocked on the door like a nervous schoolboy, and listened to the following silence. He must have heard something, for he opened the door, and I passed through.

The chamber was empty. It contained the bare minimum of furniture: two couches, both exquisitely wrought, were set perfectly opposite each other. A low table, beautiful in a purely functional way, was placed just so, equidistant between the couches. Walls undecorated, but clad in stone so fine that the very grain matched up all the way along. Even the light that entered was somehow minimal, perfect and composed. I loathed the immaculate order. For pure pleasure, I nudged the table out of its perfect alignment.

There were two doors in opposite walls, set like choices in a game. Without my noticing, one of them had opened silently. Ay was standing on the threshold of the dark, in his white robe, which glowed in the light from a high window. He looked like a priest. His face was hard to make out.

I bowed my head. 'Life, prosperity and health,' I said, according to the formula. But when I looked up I was surprised to see that for all Ay's great powers, as Ankhesenamun had said, in the years since we had last met time the destroyer had begun his work on him. He moved cautiously, stiffly, as if he did not trust his own bones. He was obviously suffering from ague, although he made every effort to disguise it. But his sharp reptilian eyes had tremendous focus and concentration. He observed me intently, like a connoisseur assessing an object of dubious value. His thin mouth expressed inevitable disappointment and disapproval. I gazed back. There were lines on his forehead, and wrinkles around his chilly eyes, and the skin was stretched tautly across the planes of his face; those eyes were sunken, almost as in death. There were red spots where his blackheads had been erased. I could smell the scent of the lozenge he held under his tongue: cloves and cinnamon, the remedy for toothache, the curse of age.

'Sit,' he said, very quietly.

I obliged, observing the difficulty with which he lowered himself on to one of the exquisite couches.

'Speak.'

'You will be aware that I have —'

'Stop.'

He raised his right hand. I waited.

'If the Queen had ventured to ask my opinion, I would have forbidden her to send for you.'

He looked me up and down.

'I do not like the city Medjay interfering in the administration and the business of the palace.'

'She called for me in a private, personal capacity,' I replied.

'I am perfectly aware of the nature and history of your involvement with the royal family,' he said quietly. 'And if this does not remain an entirely private, personal affair, you may be sure I will show you and your family no mercy.'

I nodded, but said nothing.

'In any case, I have decided that carving is irrelevant. It must simply be destroyed and forgotten.'

His hand, mottled and bony, quivered as it gripped the head of his walking stick. I looked around the pure order of his chamber. The room seemed to lack life, and its natural state of disorder, entirely.

'And yet it seems to have alarmed the King and Queen.'

'They are children. Children fear the insubstantial. The ghost in the tomb. The bad spirit beneath the couch. It is superstition. There is no place for superstition in the Two Lands.'

'Perhaps it is not superstition but imagination.'

'There is no difference.'

Not to you, you slice of emptiness, I thought.

He continued: 'Nevertheless, this represents a failure of order. The officers of the palace should have detected it. That it came to enter the precincts of the palace at all is gross negligence. This will not be tolerated.'

'No doubt there will be an investigation, and the flaws will be remedied.'

He ignored the contempt that inflected my tone.

'Order is the priority of power. After the arrogant catastrophes of the past, the glorious reign of Tutankhamun represents the triumph of the divine universal order of *maat* by the will of the Gods. We have set these lands aright. Nothing will be allowed to threaten that. Nothing.'

'You called him a child just now.'

He gazed at me, and for a moment I thought he would throw me out. He didn't, so I continued.

'Forgive me for labouring a point, but when the crowd start to splatter the King with the blood of slaughtered pigs, in public, at the height of the Opet Festival—'

'An isolated incident. These elements of dissent are unimportant and they will be crushed out of existence.'

He noticed the table was out of alignment, frowned, and returned it to its perfect position.

'And then the carving. Discovered on the very same day? Someone within the palace hierarchy is conspiring against the King. And bearing in mind the rumours of the failure of the Hittite wars, and the long absence of General Horemheb—'

I had hit the spot. His walking stick slammed down on the low table between us. A glass figurine tipped over and shattered. He barked: 'Your job is to apply the law. Not to question the ethics or the practice of its application.'

He tried to calm himself.

'You have no authority to speak of any of these issues. What are you doing here, wasting my time? I know what the Queen has asked of you. Why should I care if she wishes to indulge her little fantasies of fear and protection? And as for you – you imagine yourself as the hero in a romance of truth and justice. And yet who are you? Others have been promoted before you. You languish in a middle-ranking position, alienated from your colleagues, lacking accomplishments. You think of yourself as complex and subtle, with your interest in poetry, and yet you are uncertainly engaged in a profession that exalts the violent business of the execution of the law. That is the sum of you.'

Silence. I stood up. He remained seated.

'As you say, I'm a figure from a romance: absurd, old-fashioned and out of date. The Queen prevailed upon me. I can't help myself. I have a weakness for ladies in distress. Someone shouts the word "justice", and I appear like a dog.'

'*Justice* . . . what has that to do with all of this? Nothing . . .'

The mocking way this old and rotting man spoke the word at me made me think of everything that was not just.

I moved towards the door.

'I'll assume I now have your approval to continue with the investigation of this mystery, regardless of where it takes me.'

'The Queen is sufficient authority. I support her wishes in all things.' And he meant: 'You will have no authority from me.'

I smiled, opened the door, and left him and his aching bones in his perfect chamber. At least I had now asserted my role in the situation. And I knew one other important thing: he had no idea of Ankhesenamun's plan.

10

I returned to my own shabby office at the wrong end of the last passage-way, where the light gives up in disappointment, and the cleaners never bother. No signs of power here. Ay was right, of course. I was going nowhere, slowly, like a fallen leaf in a stagnant pool. Indeed, the glamour of last night's encounter was now giving way to the harsh light of day, and I realized I hardly knew where to begin. On days like this I felt, as the saying goes, worse than the dung of vultures. Thoth rambled ahead of me, knowing the way, as he knows everything that matters.

Khety was waiting for me. He has a way of brimming with information which I find tolerable only on good days.

'Sit.'

He faltered for a moment, disconcerted.

'Speak.'

'Last night—'

'Stop.'

He paused, his mouth open, looking from me to Thoth, as if the animal might explain to him the reasons for my temper. We sat like a trio of fools.

'Do you believe in justice, Khety?'

He looked a bit dazed by the question.

'What do you mean, *believe* . . . ?'

'It is a matter of faith over experience, is it?'

'I *believe* in it, but I don't think I've ever seen it with my own eyes.'

I nodded at this good answer, and changed the subject.

'You have some information.'

He nodded.

'Something you have seen with your own eyes,' I continued.

He nodded again.

'Another body has been found.'

'That's disappointing,' I said, quietly. 'When was it discovered?'

'Early this morning. I tried to find you at home, but you had already left. This one is different.'

She would have been beautiful. Last night she would still have been a young woman, eighteen or nineteen, just arriving at the perfect possession of her beauty. Except that where her face and hair should have been there was now a mask of gold foil. With my knife-blade I carefully peeled back a sticky corner, and saw that under the gold there was no face; nothing but skull and bloody tissue and gristle. For someone had, with an exquisite and appalling skill, scalped her, front and back, and removed her face and her eyes. There still remained a vivid trace of her features in the contours of the mask, where the foil had been pressed into shape. This had been done before someone had butchered her beauty. It might help us to identify her.

Around her neck, tucked under her white linen robe, was an ankh amulet on a delicate gold chain; an exceptionally beautiful piece of jewellery bestowing protection, for this was the symbol that writes the word for Life. I carefully removed it and held the cold gold in my palm.

'That never belonged to this girl,' said Khety.

I looked around the plain room in which she had been discovered. He was right. It was far too valuable an item. It seemed a treasure, an heirloom perhaps, of a very wealthy family. I had an idea about who might have owned it. But if I was right, the mystery of its appearance made things very much worse.

'She has a tattoo. Look—' said Khety, showing me a snake, curling around her upper arm. The workmanship was crude, and cheap.

'Her name was Neferet. She lived here alone. The landlord says she worked nights. So I think it's safe to assume she worked in the clubs. Or the brothels.'

I gazed at the lovely body. Why, once again, were there no signs of violence or struggle? No one could endure such agony without struggling, biting and gnawing at their own tongue and lips, as they strained for life against the bonds that must have tied wrists and ankles. But there was nothing. It was as if all this had been accomplished in a dream. I moved around the room, looking for clues, but could see nothing. As I walked back to the bare couch, sunlight filtered in through the narrow window, and across the girl's body. And it was only then that I noticed, on the shelf next to the sleeping couch, caught in the angle of the strong, elongated morning light, the faintest trace of a circle in the dust; the mark of a cup that had been placed there, and was now gone.

A ghost cup; a cup of dreams. I thought back to my first instinct, that the killer of the lame boy had administered the juice of the poppy, or some other potent narcotic, to his victim to placate him while he undertook his gruesome labour. The secret behind the Two Lands in our time – behind its great new buildings and temples, its powerful conquests, and its glittering promises of wealth and success to the luckiest of those who come here to labour and serve and somehow survive – is that the grinding miseries, daily sufferings and endless banalities of life are mitigated, for more and more people, by the delusions of narcotics. Once wine was the means to artificial happiness; now things are much more sophisticated, and what was one of the great secrets of medicine has become the only bliss many find in this life. That this euphoria is an illusion is irrelevant, at least until its effects wear off, leaving the user abandoned to the same miseries that motivated the flight from reality. The children of elite families now regularly relieve the tensions and so-called pressures of their affluent, meaningless lives in this way. And others, who have for one reason or another fallen through the support network of their families, find themselves soon descending the staircase of shadows to the under-world, where people sell the last things they possess – their bodies and their souls – for an instant of bliss.

In these days, trade of all kinds has extended its routes and tracks into the furthest and strangest parts of the world. So along with the essentials of the kingdom's economic power – timber, stone, ores, gold, labour – the new luxury commodities make their way here, by land and sea and river: rare animal skins, live clever monkeys, giraffes, gold trinkets, textiles, subtle new perfumes . . . the endless parade of fashionable and desirable objects. And also, of course, the secret things; the merchandise of dreams.

Physicians and priests have always used the potent parts of certain plants; some, like the poppy, are so powerful that just a few distilled drops in a beaker of water are sufficient to lull the senses of the patient before an exceptionally painful procedure is enacted, such as amputation. I remember one indication of this is that the pupils dilate. I know this because the prostitutes of the night city magnify their allure by taking the same thing to brighten their jaded, weary eyes. But the dosage is a delicate matter – too much and the eyes bloom in the strange, unreal light of the drug, only to close for ever in death.

I explained my idea to Khety.

'But why doesn't the killer just kill his victim with the drug, and then do his rearranging of the furniture?' he asked.

It was a good question.

'It seems to matter to the killer that the "work" is conducted on a living body,' I replied. 'It's at the heart of his obsession. His fetish . . .'

'I hate that word,' said Khety, unnecessarily. 'It makes my skin crawl . . .'

'We need to identify where this girl worked,' I said.

'The kids that end up in the city, doing what she did, have come from everywhere and nowhere. They change their names. They have no families. And they can't ever leave.'

'Go to the clubs and the brothels. See if you can trace her. Someone will have missed her.'

I offered him the gold face.

He nodded. 'And what about you?'

'I need you to do that while I follow up something else.'

He looked at me, half-amused.

'Anyone would think you didn't like me any more.'

'I've never liked you.'

He grinned.

'There's something you're not telling me . . .'

'That's an accurate deduction. Our long years together have not been wasted.'

'So why don't you trust me?'

I touched my ear to confirm my silence, and gestured towards Thoth.

'Ask him. He knows everything.'

The baboon stared back at both of us with his very straight face.

We went to a quiet inn, away from the busy part of the city. It was the middle of the morning, and everyone was at work, so the place was deserted. We sat down on benches at the back to drink our beer and eat the dish of almonds I had ordered from the silent but vigilant owner, leaning close to each other so that we might not be overheard. I told him everything that had happened the night and the day before. About the mysterious Khay, and Ankhesenamun, and the carving.

He listened carefully, but said nothing, beyond asking for more information about what the palace was like. This was unusual. Normally, Khety has a rational opinion on everything. We have known each other for many years. I made sure he was appointed a Medjay officer in Thebes, to get him and his wife out of Akhetaten. Ever since then, he has been my assistant.

'Why haven't you spoken?'

'I'm thinking.'

He drank deeply from his beer, as if thinking was thirsty work.

'That family is nothing but trouble,' he decided, eventually.

'And I should feel grateful for this jewel of wisdom?'

He grinned.

'What I mean is: you shouldn't get involved. It's bad news.'

'That's what my wife said. But what do you propose I do? Leave the girl to her fate?'

'You don't know what her fate is. And she's not a girl, she's the Queen. You can't be responsible for everyone. You've got your own family to think about.'

I felt obscurely annoyed.

He watched me.

'But you do feel responsible, don't you?'

I shrugged, drained my beer cup, and rose to leave. Thoth was already straining at his leash.

We walked out into the heat and light, Khety trotting to keep up with me.

'Where are you going now?' he said, as we dodged the crowds.

'I'm going to see my friend Nakht. And you are going to find out everything you can about the disappearance of that girl. You know where to start looking. Make sure you come and find me later.'

11

To visit my old friend Nakht at his country house is to pass from the hot, dusty chaos of the city into a different, calmer and more rational world. He has used his great wealth to make his life as luxurious and pleasant as possible, by creating his own little kingdom of art and knowledge in his walled estate outside the city. His fame as a cultivator of flowers and bees there has earned him an unusual new title: 'Overseer of the Gardeners of Amun'. All the thousands of bouquets that decorate the temples at festivals, and those presented to the Gods themselves – to remind them of the afterlife – are grown under Nakht's supervision.

I walked out of the suburbs, through the southern gateway, and continued along the path towards his house. The sun crowned the sky, and the land shimmered in the heat of midday. I had not brought a sunshade, but the palms that lined the way provided enough protection. As I walked I observed the bountiful crops in their carefully tilled rows, which spread out in every direction. Here and there the glimmer of the water canals, overflowing from the inundation, reflected in lines the clear blue-white of the sky. I passed few people, for all the labourers were taking their midday meal and beer, or sleeping in neat rows in any shade they could find, under carts, palm trees, or at the side of houses and grain barns, with their headscarves over their faces. High above us all, falcons spread their wide dark-bronze wings in the thermals, drifting and wheeling as they gazed down at the world. I have often wondered what the world looks like from their high vantage that no man, condemned to walk the earth on his two legs, can ever share. I imagine the glittering serpent of the Great River, continuing from one end of the world to the other; and fanned out on either side the green and yellow patterns of the cultivation. Beyond that, the infinity of the Red Land, where the royal families build their tombs of eternal stone, and their attendant temples, on the margins of the wilderness, the desert, the place of great solitude. Perhaps they could see what we could not: what happens to the Sun when it sets beyond the unreachable horizon of the visible world. Is there truly a vast and perilous dark ocean, populated with gods and monsters, in that great beyond, where the Sun sails its nightly course on its barque, through the perils of the night? Is that what those birds of prey were telling us, with their sharp, high shrieks that sounded like cries of warning?

I entered the first courtyard of Nakht's long, low villa. His servant Minmose came running out to greet me, and hurried me inside, holding a sunshade solicitously over my head.

'Your brain will bake in your skull like a duck's egg, master, in the heat of this hour of the day. I would have sent a servant with a sunshade to accompany you, if I had known you were going to grace us with a visit.'

'This is an impromptu call,' I said.

He bowed.

'My master is working with his hives at the far end of the garden,' he said.

He offered to escort me – keen, I knew, to hear any news of the city; for even at this short distance, the country feels as remote as another world. But I know this place well, for I have come here alone, or with the girls, for many years. He slipped away, quietly as always, to the kitchen to prepare refreshments, and I walked out through the second courtyard, and paused for a moment to enjoy the glorious vista before me. In the city, we are crammed together like animals. Here, with the luxury of space, and between the high walls that secure the property, all is peaceful; it is like finding oneself walking through a living papyrus scroll depicting the good life of the afterlife.

I walked along the tree-shaded length of a long, stone-lined pool; full of white and blue lotus flowers, it provides water for the flowerbeds and vegetable plots, as well as containing Nakht's collection of ornamental fish. Cheerful gardeners, old and young, devotedly and calmly attended to the plants and trees, watering and weeding, trimming and pruning; obviously happy in their dedicated work. Creeping vines extended their curling shade along the pergolas. Unusual and exotic plants flourished exuberantly. Birds felt free to take advantage of everything, and they sang with pleasure. Waterfowl dipped and thrived in the cool shade of the papyrus plants that grew in the long pool. It was almost ridiculously beautiful, so distant did it seem from the city's grandeur and grime and poverty.

I found Nakht among his hives, smoking out the bees from their clay cylinders. I kept my distance, being no devotee of bees or their stings, and sat on a stool in the shade of a tree to amuse myself at his expense; for he looked like the crazed priest of a desert cult as he moved about, dancing and wafting the smoke at the fuzzy cloud of demented insects. He carefully decanted the combs into storage pots, and soon he had many of them, laid out on a tray.

Then he stepped away, lifted his protective hood, and saw me watching him. He waved and came over, offering a pot of the honey.

'For the children.'

We embraced.

A servant brought him a bowl and cloth, and then Minmose arrived with wine and snacks, which he set out on a low table. Nakht washed his sweaty but always elegant face. Then we sat together on stools in the shade, and he poured me some wine. I knew it would be excellent.

'What brings you here on a working day?' he asked.

'I'm working.'

He eyed me carefully, then saluted the Gods and took a long draught of his wine.

'On what? Not that incident at the festival?'

'Partly.'

He looked intrigued.

'I imagine the palace must be going crazier than my bees . . .'

'Someone is certainly poking a stick into the royal hive . . .'

He nodded.

'So what did you make of it? A court conspiracy, perhaps?' he asked, enthusiastically.

'Probably not. I think it's an aberration. At worst, someone within the hierarchies has encouraged a bunch of foolish young people into an act of naively irresponsible violence.'

He looked almost disappointed.

'Maybe so, but still it's had a surprisingly powerful effect. Everyone is talking about it. It seems to have catalysed the dissent that's been bubbling under the surface of everything for years now. People are even whispering about a possible coup . . .'

'And who would command such a thing?' I countered.

'There is only one man. General Horemheb,' he said with some satisfaction.

I sighed.

'That would be no improvement on the present regime,' I said.

'It would definitely be much worse, for Horemheb's vision of the world is governed by his life in the army. He has no humanity at all,' he replied. 'But in any case, we are in trouble, for this has made the King look vulnerable. And what king can afford to look vulnerable? He has never been one of the warrior kings. It's as if the dynasty has grown weaker and stranger with every generation. And now he is powerless . . .'

'And more and more vulnerable to other influences,' I said.

Nakht nodded. 'He's never really been able to assert any of his own authority, partly because after Akhenaten no one would countenance it, and partly because he's grown up under the dire shadow of Ay. And what a tyrant he turned out to be. No wonder the boy can't exercise his own power.'

We enjoyed sharing our private, but profound loathing of the Regent.

'I went to see Ay this morning,' I said, watching Nakht's face.

He looked amazed.

'Why on earth would you do such a thing?'

'Not because he asked for me, but because I had to.'

'How curious,' said my friend, leaning forward and pouring me more of the excellent wine.

'I met Ankhesenamun last night,' I said, after a suitably dramatic pause.

'Ah . . .'

He nodded slowly, beginning to piece together the evidence I was carefully feeding him.

'She sent one of her people to fetch me.'

'Who was that?'

'Khay. Chief Scribe,' I said.

'Yes, I know him; walks around as if he has a gold cane up his arse. And what did she say to you?'

'She had something to show me. A stone. From Akhetaten. A carving of the Aten.'

'Interesting. But not remarkable.'

'Not until you saw someone had completely chipped out the Aten disc, the hands holding the ankhs, both the royal and holy names, and the eyes and the noses of the royal figures,' I said.

Nakht looked off into his garden's idyllic picture of colour and shade.

'A little bit of iconoclasm goes a long way, I imagine, especially in that palace.'

'Exactly. They are all terrified because they don't know what it means.'

'And what do you think?' he enquired.

'Well, it could mean nothing more than someone with an old gripe has wasted their time working out how to send the royal family a nasty insult.'

'But the coincidence . . .' he pressed me.

'I know. We don't believe in coincidences, do we? We believe in connections. The dead boy with the broken bones; the elite amulet; and now also a dead girl with a gold mask hiding her missing face.'

Nakht looked aghast.

'How awful! Such barbarity. The times are definitely getting worse.'

I nodded.

'There's something about the sophistication of all of these things, and the consistency of the style, that makes me think the object left in the palace could be connected; I was wondering if the obliteration of the sun disc could also mean something specific . . .'

'Such as?' he asked, doubtfully.

'An eclipse,' I ventured.

'Well now, that is a very interesting idea,' he said, absorbed by the ramifications. 'The Sun in battle destroyed by the force of darkness, and then restored and reborn again . . . the symbolism is potent. And very much to the point at the moment . . .'

'Something like that,' I replied. 'So I thought I would consult the man who knows more about the stars than anyone else I know.'

'Well, it's an allegory,' he smiled, quickly warming to his subject.

I had no idea what he meant.

'Tell me more.'

'Let's walk.'

So we strolled up one of the paths, between the flowerbeds, and he began to explain. As always, with Nakht, I listened without under-standing everything, for I know that to interrupt him with questions will only lead to another, equally wonderful, but endlessly perplexing digression.

'Think about how we understand the mysteries of the world around us. Ra, the God of the Sun, sails across the blue ocean of the day in the Golden Ship of Day. But at sunset the God crosses to the Ship of Night and disappears into the Otherworld. The black ocean of the night is revealed, with its bright stars – the Sharp One, the brightest, and the five stars of Horus and the stars of Osiris, the Pathway of the Further Stars in the height of the sky, and the travelling star of the dawn – all sailing the dark waters, following the Sun whose night journey, with its perils and tests, we can never see but only *imagine*. We liken this in the Book of the Dead to the journey of the soul after death. Are you following me so far?'

I nodded.

'Just about . . .'

'Now, it gets subtler. Listen and concentrate. The most significant, and indeed mysterious, of those perils is the union of the Sun with the body of Osiris at the darkest point of the night. *"The Sun at rest in Osiris, Osiris at rest in the Sun"* as the saying goes. This is the most secret moment when the Sun descends back into the original waters and their powers of chaos. But it is precisely at this dark moment when he receives new powers of life, and Osiris is reborn. Again we the living can never witness such an event, for it is hidden from human sight in the remotest part of the Unknown. But once again we can *imagine* it, although with great mental effort. Then, at dawn, the Sun returns, apparent and reborn, for Ra is the self-creator and the creator of every-thing that exists. And we call that returning form of the God the Scarab, *khepri*, the evolving one, pushing himself into being from non-being. And so begins the new day! And so all things follow ever onwards, day by day, year by year, life by life, death by death, rebirth by rebirth, perpetually and eternally.'

I knew he loved talking like this. My problem was it sounded too much like a good story. And like all the stories that we tell ourselves, and our children, about how things happen, and why things are as they are, it could never be proved.

'But what has all that to do with my question?' I asked.

'Because there is one time when we the living *can* witness this divine union.'

'During an eclipse?'

'Precisely. Of course, there are different explanations of such an event, depending upon which authority you consult or accept. One is that the Goddess Hathor of the West covers the God with her body. A divine union of light and dark, as it were. Another, opposite one is that some dark power whose name we do not know, and therefore cannot speak, conquers – but light recovers and triumphs in the sky's divine battle.'

'Luckily for us.'

'Indeed. For without light, there can be no life. The Kingdom of Darkness is the land of shadows and death. But there are things, even now, we do not understand. However, I truly believe our knowledge will some day be able to explain all things that exist.'

He stopped at a pomegranate bush, and fiddled with its pink flowers – the latest fashion – and plucked a few fading blooms as if to demonstrate his own god-like powers over his creation.

'Like a Book of Everything . . .' I suggested.

'Exactly. But words are imperfect, and our system of writing, for all its great glories, has its limitations in terms of its ability to describe creation in all its manifest and hidden glories . . . So we would have to invent another way of describing things.'

'Such as?'

'Ah well, that is the question, but perhaps the answer lies not in words, but in signs; in fact, in numbers . . .'

At this point my thoughts began to collapse, as they often do when I talk with Nakht. He has an appetite for speculation that sometimes makes me want to do something meaninglessly practical, like sweep the yard.

He smiled as he saw the baffled expression on my face.

I steered the conversation back to my subject.

'Speaking of which, using the star calendars, I know you can predict the arrival of the inundation, and the beginning of the festivals. But do eclipses appear in the charts?'

He considered the question before replying.

'I believe not. I have been compiling my own calendars from observation, but I have not yet been lucky enough to witness an eclipse of the Sun, for they are rare events indeed. However, from my roof terrace I have observed an eclipse of the moon. I am intrigued and puzzled by the consistent element of circularity, both in the returning nature of the cosmic events, and also in the implication of the curves of the shadows as they are cast against the face of the moon, for they imply a whole circle – such as we see of the moon and the sun, and such as we might witness in a total eclipse. It suggests the circle is the perfect shape of the heavens, both as idea – for the circle implies infinite return – and in actual fact.'

Grateful for a pause in this torrent of rapid speculation, I asked quickly:

'But how could we find out more? Could you take me to the astronomical archives?'

'In the Karnak Temple precinct? To which I have access?' he smiled.

'How fortunate I am to count as a close friend a man of such elevated status.'

'Your sarcasm is so . . . middle class,' he replied, cheerfully.

12

Thoth and I followed Nakht as he passed imperiously, and at his usual elegant speed, through the security-guard posts at the main pylon of the Karnak Temple. I looked up at the great mud-brick walls that soared high above us. And then we were plunged into the shadows of the 'Most Select of Places'; a forbidden, secret world within the world, for no one who is not of the elite priest class may enter this vast and ancient stone puzzle of columned halls and gloomy temples, covered in an infinity of inscrutable carvings, surrounding a labyrinth of sunless sanctuaries where, at the very heart of the dark silence, the statues of the Gods are cared for, woken, worshipped, clothed, fed, returned to sleep and guarded through the night.

We came out into an open area. All around me, men of the aristocracy, dressed in purest white linen, went about their esoteric business in a leisurely fashion. This priestly work did not seem very onerous. At set times of the year, and in return for a share of the vast income of the temple, they enter the precincts for periods of service, respecting the ancient rules of ritual purity – bathing in the sacred lake at dawn, shaving their bodies, wearing white linen robes – and observing precisely and without variation the functions and rites of worship according to the Instructions.

But all temples, from the smallest shrine in a parched trading-post town on the southern borders, to the most ancient and divine places in the Two Lands, are vulnerable to the usual range of human activities: corruption, bribery, theft, embezzlement, and everything else, from scandals of shortened services and stolen sacred food and relics, to outright violence and murder. The bigger the temple, the more wealth it controls. Wealth is power. And Karnak is the greatest of the temples. Its wealth and power have long rivalled, and have now succeeded, that of the royal family.

The great space inside the enclosure walls contained what seemed, to my eye, a chaos of ancient and modern: pylons, obelisks, avenues, statues, chapels, and inaccessible temple structures with vast papyrus columns and shadowy halls. Some of it was newly built, some of it under construction, some of it dismantled, and some even in ruins. There were also magazines, offices and housing for the officers and the priests. It was in effect a small city, grand and yet jumbled up. Priests teemed in and out of the portals and pylons, attended by even greater numbers of servants and assistants. Ahead of us was another pylon leading to further pylons, leading ultimately to the ancient sanctuaries at the heart of the temple.

'Beyond those courtyards lies the sacred lake,' said Nakht, pointing to the right. 'Twice a day and twice a night, the priests have to sprinkle themselves with water, and wash their mouths out with a little natron.'

'It's a hard life,' I said.

'It's all very well being sarcastic, but sexual intercourse is absolutely forbidden for the period when the priests are performing the offices within the temple territory, and I'm quite sure you, for instance, would find that an impossible imposition,' he replied with his usual candour on such matters. 'But of course, the priests are the more transient population here. There are the singers, the officiates at the shrine, the lector priests, the scribes, the hour priests who are responsible for keeping the correct time of the rites . . . but it's the management, and the servants, and the weavers, cooks and cleaners, who really sustain the necessities for the correct performance of the rituals. You could say the God Amun employs more people than the King himself.'

'So it's a vast government department, in essence . . .' I said.

'Exactly. There are overseers for every aspect of the running of the temple; of the domain, of the accounts, of the military, of personnel, of the fields, of the cloth, and the granaries, and the treasury . . .'

He stopped in front of the entrance to a collection of impressive buildings.

'And this is the House of Life, which contains the scriptorium, the libraries and archives, and the offices of the lector priests.'

We entered. Directly ahead of us through double doors was a large, silent room.

'That's the scriptorium,' whispered Nakht, as if to a child, for I could see men of various ages at work, meticulously copying or collating texts from old papyrus scrolls on to new ones. The atmosphere in the library was sleepy, for this was the middle of the afternoon and some of the archives' more aged users were in fact not working attentively at all, but dozing before the scrolls set out before them. Along the walls, wooden cubicles held an infinite number of papyri, scroll after scroll, as if all knowledge was here, in writing. Sunlight slanted into the chamber from clerestory windows, catching the countless motes that glittered and darkened as they drifted up or down, like tiny fragments of ideas or signs that had crumbled from the scrolls, and were now meaningless without the greater text from which they came.

Nakht continued to whisper. 'These are the oldest archives in the world. Many of the texts preserved here come from the dawn of our world. Papyrus is remarkably robust, but some are so ancient that they remain in their leather cases, unreadable. And others can be un-scrolled, but one fears even the lightest ray of sunlight might erase the last of the ink, so they may only be consulted by candlelight. In fact some consult them by moonlight, but I think that is just so much superstition. Many are in signs that are now incomprehensible, and so they are nothing but a meaningless jumble of childish marks. It is a terrible thought: whole worlds lost to nonsense. It is a great palace of knowledge, but, alas, much of it is unknowable. Lost knowledge . . . Lost books . . .'

He sighed. We moved away down a corridor lined with doors.

'Here are kept mythical and theological treatises, as well as recitations and the master originals of inscriptions from which all the carvings on the temple walls and obelisks are precisely copied. There are also studios here where Books of the Dead are copied, according to commission. And then there are the rooms for instruction and learning. And the various storage areas for texts upon many subjects, such as writing, engineering, poetry, law, theology, magical studies, medicine . . .'

'And astronomy,' I said.

'Indeed. And here we are.'

We faced an old man in the white linen dress and sash of a lector priest, standing in front of double doors that were tied with cord and sealed. He gazed at us balefully from under his magnificent white eyebrows.

'I am Nakht,' said Nakht.

'Welcome,' said the priest, in a tone that implied the opposite.

'I would like to examine some scrolls within the astronomical section,' said Nakht.

The priest stared at him, narrowing his eyes as he considered this request.

'And who is your companion?' he said suspiciously.

'This is Rahotep. He is a chief detective within the Thebes Medjay.'

'Why does a policeman need to examine astronomical charts?'

'He has an enquiring mind, and I am endeavouring to satisfy it,' replied Nakht. The priest could not seem to find another reason to forbid entry, so he moved with a heavy sigh, like a hippopotamus from the mud, grumblingly broke the seal and untied the cords. He opened the doors, and with a brief gesture of his hands proposed we enter.

It was a much larger, higher chamber than I had anticipated. Each wall was lined with shelves to the ceiling, and high storage cases also ran in an arrangement like fish-bones down the middle of the space. On each shelf were stored many papyrus rolls. I would not have known where to start, but Nakht browsed swiftly among the dockets, searching for something.

'Astronomy is merely a function of religion, as far as the world is concerned. As long as we know when the significant stars appear, so that the days and feasts and festivals coincide with the lunar charts, everyone is happy. But no one seems to have noticed that the regularity, the returning pattern of the imperishable stars themselves, implies an immense ordered universe beyond our understanding.'

'Rather than the old stories we've been told since time began about Gods and Goddesses and everything coming from the papyrus swamp of creation, and the night world being the place of eternal life . . .'

'Indeed,' whispered Nakht. 'The stars are eternal life, but perhaps not in the way we have always understood it. Heresy, of course,' he said, and grinned happily.

He unrolled several scrolls on the low tables set out between the cases, and then showed me the star charts' columns of signs and figures, written in red and black ink.

'See: thirty-six columns listing the groups of stars into which the night world is divided. We call these the *decans*.'

I let my eye run down the symbols in their columns, opening the old scroll further and further. The signs seemed to go on endlessly. Nakht tutted.

'Be careful. These have to be handled delicately. With respect.'

'And why is the information noted like this?'

'Each column shows the stars that rise before dawn above the horizon for every ten-day period of the year. See, here is the Dog Star, which rises exactly at the time of the inundation, at the start of the solar year. And here is Sah, Glorious Soul of Osiris, the bright star which rises at the start of *peret*, the time of spring . . . you know the saying, of course: "*I am the star who treads the Two Lands, who navigates in front of the stars of the sky on the belly of my Mother Nut*"?'

I shook my head.

'I sometimes think you know absolutely nothing,' he said.

'This is not exactly my usual territory. But what about the eclipse?' I reminded him.

For the next few minutes he assessed many more charts, unrolling and rolling as he went, each chart seeming more ancient and fragile than the last.

Finally, he shook his head in resignation.

'There is nothing recorded. I thought not.'

'A dead end.'

'It was an interesting thought, and at least now you know something of the subject,' he said, in his most scholarly manner.

We left the archive room, and the priest bent down stiffly to retie and reseal the cords. As we walked away, I wondered aloud: 'Where are the secret books kept?'

Nakht failed to disguise his alarm at the question.

'What are you talking about? Which secret books?'

'The Books of Thoth, for example.'

'Come now, they're a legend rather than a reality. Like many *supposed* secret books.'

'But it's true, isn't it, that there are a number of sacred texts which are only ever revealed to initiates?' I asked.

' "Initiates" of what? And texts about which secret subjects?'

'Oh, such matters as divine geometry,' I replied casually.

'I have never heard of such a thing,' he said stiffly, glancing around to make sure no one could hear us.

'Of course you have, my friend,' I said quietly.

He stared at me angrily.

'What do you mean?'

'You knew there would be nothing in those scrolls of interest to me. And I appreciate you taking the time to demonstrate that there was nothing. But I know you very well, and you are definitely not telling me something.'

He had the grace to flush.

'Sometimes important matters are not to be discussed casually.'

'What matters?'

'I really despise you when you turn your interrogation techniques on to me. I am just trying to help,' he said, not even half-joking.

'Then I will tell you what I think. I think there are secret books, on astronomy, among other things, and I think you have been initiated, and you have seen some of them, and you know where they are.'

He stared right at me, with as cold a look as I have ever seen on his face.

'What a vivid imagination you have . . .'

And then he walked away.

I followed him back out into the light and heat of the late afternoon, and we walked on together in silence. Then suddenly he stopped and drew me into an area of shade beside an old temple.

'I cannot lie to you, my friend. But I cannot reveal the contents of the books. I have taken a solemn vow.'

'But all I asked was whether they existed or not.'

'Even that is too much knowledge. Their existence or otherwise is a necessary concealment. The secret books are banned in these dark times. Secret knowledge has become dangerous again. As you well know, anyone found possessing them, or even copies of sections of them, could be punished by death.'

'But they exist, they are shared within an inner circle, and therefore they must be kept somewhere clandestine. So where are they?' I asked directly.

'I cannot say.'

I gazed around at the buildings that filled the temple enclosures. Suddenly I realized there might be another city within this secret city, too. For every secret contains another secret at its heart.

He glared at me, frankly angry now.

'You presume too much upon our friendship.'

We stood facing each other in this strange moment. To release the tension, I bowed.

'I apologize. Professional matters should never come between old friends.'

He nodded, almost satisfied. I knew I would learn little more from him in this moment of emotional heat.

'It is Sekhmet's birthday, or have you forgotten that fact, amongst these ideas of eclipses and secret books? I am dining with you and the family tonight,' he reminded me. I struck my forehead with my palm. I had not failed to remember, for Tanefert had reminded me before I left, but I still had a sacred family duty to perform.

'And I am responsible for the feast, so I had better go and buy the secret ingredients – which I must never reveal, on pain of death – before the holy and esoteric merchants of the market shut their stalls.'

He managed to smile at last, and we walked together under the great gateway that returned us to the life of the city; then we parted, he to his house, and I to the market to buy meat, spices and wine.

13

We each have our habitual places to sit on the stools around the low table: my father at the far end, Sekhmet and Thuyu down one side, with Khety and his wife, and Tanefert and Amenmose on the other, together with Nakht and Nedjmet, the Sweet One, who likes to sit next to him, hanging her arms around his neck. She watches her audience as she enacts her loving gestures. Where did she learn such flattery? I had cooked our favourite dish – gazelle in red wine – reserved for celebrations.

Sekhmet looked serene and confident in a new pleated robe, displaying the earrings we had given her for her birthday. The self-consciousness of her teenage years is giving way now to a new self-possession. She has read far more than I have, and she remembers everything. She can still recite the nonsense poems we made up when she was a child. Knowledge to her is everything. She once said to me, earnestly: 'I can't be an athlete *and* a scholar.' And so she made her choice.

As I sit with my family and friends on evenings like this, with the food before us on the table, and the oil lamps lit in the wall niches, I wonder what I have done to deserve such happiness. And in darker moments I worry my work may yet put all this in danger – for if anything were to happen to me, how would they live? I also have to ask myself: why is this life not enough? And how will I manage, when my father has passed on, and the girls have married, and are living in other houses, and Amenmose is studying elsewhere, in Memphis perhaps, and Tanefert and I face each other, in the strange new quiet of our late years?

'Father, I have been wondering why it is that girls have no opportunities for education and advancement in our society.'

Sekhmet took a mouthful of gazelle while she observed the effect of her statement.

'And this is delicious, by the way,' she mumbled.

Nakht, Khety and my father glanced at me, amused.

'But you have had many opportunities.'

'Only because Nakht has taught me about things no one else would . . .'

'And she is a spectacular student,' he added proudly.

'But it seems to me because I'm a girl, I've had fewer opportunities than boys, because everything in our society is about the priority of the man over the woman. And that's ridiculous. This is the modern world. Just because I've got breasts now doesn't mean I've lost my mind.'

My father coughed suddenly, as if something had gone down the wrong way. Nakht patted him on his back, but he coughed and coughed, tears in his eyes. I knew they were tears of mirth; but he did not want to embarrass Sekhmet. I winked at him.

'You are quite right,' I said. 'If you decide you are going to achieve something, you have to be determined.'

'I have decided. I don't want to marry yet. I want to study more. I want to be a physician.'

She glanced across at her mother. I knew at once they had discussed this. I looked at Tanefert, and she gazed back at me with a silent plea to please be considerate.

'But my dearly beloved daughter . . .' I said, wishing Nakht would say something to support me in my tenuous position.

'Yes, my dearly beloved father?'

I struggled to find the best words.

'Women don't become physicians.'

'They do, actually,' said Nakht, unhelpfully.

'What difference does it make whether they haven't in the past? It's what I want to do. There's so much suffering in this world, and I want to change that. And there's too much ignorance as well. Knowledge can alleviate suffering and ignorance. And anyway, why did you call me Sekhmet if you didn't want me to become a physician?'

'Why did you call her Sekhmet?' enquired Nedjmet, sensing her opportunity to get in on the conversation.

'Because it means *she who is powerful*,' said Tanefert.

'Sekhmet the Lion Goddess can send illnesses, but she can also recall them,' said Sekhmet herself.

'I see you have learned much from your clever godfather,' I said.

'I've been *discussing* things with him.'

For some reason, I felt like the only piece on the game board that has not moved beyond the first square.

Suddenly my father spoke from the other end of the table.

'She'll make a wonderful physician. She's calm and methodical and beautiful to look at. Unlike those smelly and cantankerous old men who shake a few burning herbs in the air and make you drink your own urine. I'd certainly trust her to look after me when I get old and sick.'

Sekhmet looked at me, and smiled victoriously.

'So you are guaranteed your first patient,' I said. 'But do you realize what this means?'

She nodded sagely.

'It means years of study, and I'll have to do twice as well as everyone else because I'll be the only girl among all the boys. And I'll have to endure the opposition of the establishment and the small-minded insults of the old-fashioned teachers. But I'll survive.'

I could not think of how to oppose her wish, and in truth I was proud of her determination. All that stopped me from supporting her wholeheartedly was the knowledge of the struggle to come – that, and the likelihood of failure – not from any weakness in herself, but from the refusal of the hierarchies to accept her.

I was about to say something when Thoth suddenly barked in the yard. An abrupt knocking on the door silenced us all. I rose and went to the door. A tall, thickset, unfriendly man in the formal dress of the Palace Guard was waiting there. Behind him were guards with swords shining in the light of the oil lamp in its niche beside the doorway.

'I know why you're here,' I said quietly, before he could speak. 'Give me a few moments, please.'

I turned back into the room. My family were staring at me.

Tanefert says there is always a choice. But sometimes she is wrong. I asked Khety to accompany me, and Nakht to stay and continue the celebrations. Sekhmet came through to the kitchen with me. She peered at the guards waiting outside, and nodded.

'Don't worry, Father. Work is important. What you do is important. I understand. And we'll all be here when you return.'

And she grinned, and kissed me on the cheek.

14

As we crossed the Great River once again – Khety sitting opposite me, and Thoth crouched down at my feet, for he mistrusts the treachery of boats and water – I gazed up at the black ocean of the night that glittered vastly with mysterious stars. I thought of an old saying my grandfather had told me: that what was important was not the uncountable stars, but the glorious darkness between them. The faded old papyrus scrolls Nakht had shown me that afternoon, with their columns and signs, seemed only the crudest human rendering of this greatest of mysteries.

The oarsmen expertly guided us to the palace jetty, and the black water slapped gently against the moon-silvered stones. Khay was waiting. In the shimmering firelight of the hammered copper bowls his bony face was transformed by an anxiety it struggled to restrain. I introduced Khety as my assistant. He remained at a respectful distance, his head bowed. Khay considered him, and nodded.

'His conduct and security are your responsibility,' he said.

I have heard of people who return in dreams to the same situations and dilemmas. The tormenting images of their fears and horrors are repeated night after night: nightmare chases down endless tunnels; or the swift rippling of crocodiles unseen but sensed in deep, black water; or glimpsing the beloved dead, unreachable in a vast grey crowd. And then the haunted dreamer wakes sweating and weeping uncontrollably for something or someone lost over and over again to that Otherworld of visions. This palace, with its long corridors, and many shut doors, and hushed antechambers, reminded me now of something like that. I imagined each closed chamber might contain a different dream, a different nightmare. And yet I did not feel fear; excitement had me once again in its monstrous and glorious grasp. *Something unexpected had happened. And so I was as happy as I could ever be.*

We passed through the guard station, and entered the royal quarters. Somewhere, a door slammed in the dark, and a young man's light voice called out a tremulous command. Lowered voices, insistent and persuasive, tried to calm him. Another slam of a door, and all returned to the tomb-like silence. Khay, alert to the meaning of these signs and wonders, hurried forward on his costly and immaculate sandals, until we arrived once more at the great double doors into Ankhesenamun's chamber. Khety glanced at me, his eyebrows raised, amused at the situation in which we found ourselves. Then the doors suddenly opened to admit us.

Inside, nothing had changed. The lights burned in the same places. The doors remained opened to the courtyard and its garden. Ankhesenamun, guarded by a soldier, was sitting very still, staring at a small, closed wooden box that was set on a low tray on the far side of the room, as if she was mesmerized. When we entered, she turned slowly to look at us; her hands gripped each other tightly, her eyes glittered.

The box was no bigger than that which might contain a wig. It was tied with a cord knotted to a complex, interwoven design. Interestingly, it seemed more like a magical knot than a practical one. The conundrum of it – the maker's fascination with frustrating, perhaps demented puzzles – seemed alarmingly all of a piece with the strange mysteries of the last days. Instead of unknotting the cord – for it was evidence, and the meaning of its design might be recognized by Nakht – I cut it. I lowered my head to the lid of the box, and caught the faintest of sounds; within, something was moving, toiling almost, on the very edge of the audible, even in the hush of the chamber. I glanced at Khety and Khay, and then very carefully lifted off the lid. The sweet stench of rotting meat billowed into the room. Everyone backed quickly away, holding their linens over their noses.

I forced myself to look into the box. White maggots moved through the eye-sockets, nose, ears and jawbones of a human head. I saw a pair of collarbones, some vertebrae knotted together on another length of cord, and some much smaller skulls, belonging to birds or rodents. Bones of all sorts – clearly animal bones as well as human ones – had been jumbled together to create this vile death mask. Death masks are usually made from precious gold to represent the dead to the Gods; but this one had been deliberately composed as a kind of anti-mask, made of the butcher's leftovers. But there was one piece of gold here: a necklace on which a name had been inscribed in a royal cartouche. I plucked it out with some tongs that stood nearby. The hieroglyphs read: *Tutankhamun*.

I examined the box itself; around the lid, inside and out, strange symbols, curves, sickles, dots and sharp lines, like a kind of nonsense writing, had been carved and then painted in black and red. I did not recognize the language at all. It looked like the language of a curse. I thought I would not want to hear such words spoken aloud. I would not want to meet the man whose speech these signs represented. I imagined a monster. And there at the centre of the inside surface of the lid was carved an image I recognized at once: a dark circle. The Sun destroyed.

Khay, holding a linen cloth fastidiously over his nose and mouth, approached reluctantly, glanced at the contents of the box, and then slipped away as if the ground was suddenly uneven. The soldier walked determinedly over and gazed at it with military self-discipline. He moved aside for Ankhesenamun. Khay tried to dissuade her from looking inside, but she insisted. Standing close to me, she struggled with her reaction to the smell, and then bravely her eyes plunged into the shambles in the box. She could take no more than a few moments.

But suddenly the great doors were thrown open, with a cry of frustration, and a young man, with a beautiful, almond-shaped face and small, delicate features, burst into the chamber. He hobbled slightly, leaning for light support on an elegant walking cane. A dazzling gold pectoral hung over his slim shoulders. Fine linens clothed his body, which was slim, but wide around the waist. A small, chattering monkey on a golden chain scamperd at his feet.

'I will not be treated like a child!' shouted Tutankhamun, Lord of the Two Lands, Image of the Living God, at the silent chamber.

Khay and the soldier moved in front of the box, and tried to persuade him not to approach it, without actually daring to touch his royal body physically. But despite his slight infirmity, he was too quick for them; he moved as deviously and quickly as a scorpion. He gazed at the carvings, and then down at the rotting image. At first he seemed mesmerized by what he saw – by the corruption of it. Then as he began to interpret it his expression changed. Ankhesenamun took his hands in hers and, speaking softly and carefully to him, more as an older sister, perhaps, than a wife, persuaded him to move away. He glanced up at me, and I saw he had his father's eyes, almost feminine, but with an expression that was both openly innocent and potentially, vicariously, vicious. He saw the necklace with the royal name, and snatched it from my hand. I lowered my gaze quickly, remembering the protocols of respect.

As I waited, my eyes trained on the floor, I thought how much more interesting Tutankhamun looked from close quarters. From a distance he had seemed as insubstantial as a reed. But at close quarters, he was charismatic. His gleaming skin evoked the life of someone who rarely appeared in the open air, in harsh sunlight. He seemed more a creature of the moon. His hands were exquisite and immaculate. And something about the long proportions of his limbs seemed to be all of a piece with the burnished elegance of his gold collar, his gold jewellery and his gold sandals. In his presence I felt earth-bound; he seemed like a rare species that could only survive in a carefully protected environment of shade, secrecy and utter luxury. I would not have been surprised to see beautiful feathered wings folded beneath his shoulder blades, or tiny jewels among his perfect teeth. I would not have been surprised to hear he only sipped water from a divine source. But I would also not have been surprised to hear he lived in a child's nursery, with the doors shut firmly against an outside world whose demands he refused to acknowledge. I could see at once how terrified he was; and I understood then that the man behind both 'gifts' knew this very well. Tutankhamun threw the necklace aside.

'This abomination must be removed from our sight and destroyed by fire.'

His voice, although quivering, was airily modulated, with a delicate timbre. Like many who speak quietly, he did it for effect, knowing he created the circumstances in which others strained to hear his every word.

'With respect, majesty, I would advise against its destruction. It is evidence,' I said.

Khay, the ultimate guide to etiquette, gasped at my breach of protocol. And I wondered if the King was going to scream at me. But he seemed to change his mind. Instead he nodded, lowered himself on to a couch, and sat hunched over. Now he looked like a haunted child. In my mind's eye I saw the world from his point of view: he was alone in a palace full of shadows and terrors, of threats and secrets and conflicting strategies. The temptation was to pity him. But that would not do.

He motioned for me to approach. I stood before him, my eyes lowered.

'So you are the Seeker of Mysteries. Look at me.'

I did so. His face was unusual; delicate planes and structures, with wide cheekbones that seemed to frame the soft but persuasive power of his large, dark eyes. Lips full and sensuous, above a small, slightly receding chin.

'You served my father.'

'Life, prosperity and health, lord. I had that honour.'

He observed me carefully, as if making sure I was not being ironic. Then he motioned to Ankhesenamun to join him. They glanced briefly at each other, with a look of tacit understanding.

'This is not the first threat against my life. But, with the stone, and with the blood, and now this . . .'

He looked at the others in the room, untrustingly, and then leaned closer to me. I felt his warm breath, sweet as a child's, fluttering across my face, as he whispered: 'I fear I am being haunted and hunted by shadows . . .'

But at that very moment the double doors opened once more, and Ay entered the chamber. The air itself seemed to turn cold with his presence. I had seen how everyone treated the King like a marvellous child; but Ay merely glanced at him with a contempt that would wither a stone. Then he examined the contents of the box.

'Come here,' he said quietly to the King.

The King moved reluctantly towards Ay.

'This is nothing. Do not grant it an authority it does not possess.'

Tutankhamun nodded, uncertainly.

Then, swift as a hawk, Ay picked up the death's head, crawling with maggots, dripping with worms, and proffered it to the King, who jumped backwards in revulsion and fright. Ankhesenamun approached as if to protect her husband, but Ay held up a peremptory hand.

'Don't,' she said quietly.

The old man ignored her, keeping his gaze focused on the King, the death's head held out on his palm. Slowly, reluctantly, the young King reached out and, steeling himself, took the vile thing in his hands.

The chamber was held in a tension of silence, as the King gazed upon the empty sockets and festering flesh of the head.

'Is death no more than these hollow bones and this absurd ugly grin?' he whispered. 'Then we have nothing to fear. What will survive of us is far greater.'

Then suddenly he threw the skull back to Ay, who struggled to catch the slippery thing like the solitary boy who is not good at ball games.

The King laughed out loud, and I suddenly liked him for his audacity. He motioned for a servant to bring him a bowl and linen towel to wash his hands. He dropped the linen deliberately in front of Ay, and then left the chamber, followed by his nervous monkey.

Ay, wheezing with fury, gazed after him without speaking, then dropped the skull into the box, and washed his hands. Ankhesenamun stepped forward.

'Why do you behave with such disrepect to the King, in the presence of others?'

Ay turned on her.

'He must learn courage. What kind of a king cannot bear the sight of decay and death? He must learn to endure and accept these things, without fear.'

'There are many ways to learn courage, and fear is surely not the best tutor. Perhaps it is the worst.'

Ay smiled, his bad teeth showing between his thin lips.

'Fear is a large and curious subject.'

'In these years I have learned a great deal about it,' she replied. 'I have had a most accomplished teacher.'

They stared at each other for a long moment, like adversarial cats.

'This nonsense must be denounced with the contempt it deserves, not given prominence in the minds of the weak and vulnerable.'

'I could not agree more, which is why I have assigned Rahotep to investigate. I will go now to the King, and leave you all to discuss a plan of action to prevent any further such events.'

She left the chamber. I bowed to Ay and followed her. Outside, in the dark corridor, I showed her the ankh amulet I had found on the dead girl's body.

'Forgive me for showing you this. But, let me ask: do you recognize it?'

'Recognize it? It is mine. My mother gave it to me. For my name and for my protection.'

The ankh – *Ankhesenamun* . . . My hunch about the connection had been right. And now, as I was actually delivering the object back to its owner, the act itself suddenly seemed part of the murderer's plan.

'Where did you get it?' She was angry now, and snatched the amulet away from me.

I fumbled for an explanation that would not alarm her.

'It was found. In the city.'

She turned to face me.

'Do not disguise the truth from me. I want to know the truth. I am not a child.'

'It was found on a body. A young woman, murdered.'

'How was she murdered?'

I paused, reluctant.

'She had been scalped. Her face was cut off. Her eyes were removed. In their place was a gold mask. And she was wearing this.'

She was suddenly breathless. She silently considered the jewel in her hand.

'Who was she?' she said, quietly.

'Her name was Neferet. I think she worked in a brothel. She was your age. For what it's worth, I don't think she suffered. And I will find out why your amulet was found on her body.'

'But somebody must have stolen it from my private chamber. Who could have done that? And why?'

She paced the corridor, anxiously. 'I was right. Nowhere is safe. Look at this place. It is all shadows. Now do you believe me?'

She held up the amulet, which twisted, shining in the dark of the corridor. I saw tears gathering in her eyes.

'I will never be able to wear this again,' she said, and walked silently away.

As soon as I re-entered the chamber, Ay turned on me.

'Don't think this supports your presence here. This is nothing. It is mere nonsense.'

'It may be nonsense, but it has worked in the way its creator intended.'

He snorted.

'And that is?'

'It has capitalized on the climate of fear.'

The climate of fear. How poetic.'

I wished I could swat him out of existence like a fly.

'And once again, this "gift offering" has managed to reach the King himself. How did that happen?' he continued.

All eyes now turned to the soldier.

'It was discovered in the Queen's apartments,' he admitted, reluctantly.

Even Ay was taken aback.

'How is that possible?' he said intently. 'What has happened to the security in the royal quarters?'

'I am unable to offer an explanation,' said the soldier, in shame.

Ay was about to shout back at him, but suddenly he scowled, and gripped his jaw, as a sudden spasm of toothache afflicted him.

'And who discovered it?' he continued, as the attack subsided.

'Ankhesenamun herself,' offered Khay.

Ay pondered the box for a moment.

'This will not happen again. You understand the penalty of failure?'

The soldier saluted.

'And I suggest you and the great Seeker of Mysteries acquaint yourselves. Perhaps two idiots are better than one, although experience suggests otherwise.'

He paused.

'There can be no more disturbances in the security of the palace. You will both report to me before the Colonnade Hall opening ceremony with your proposals for the King's security.'

And so he departed. A little of the tension in the room abated. The soldier introduced himself as Simut, Commander of the Palace Guard. We made dutiful gestures of respect, and said the right formulas, but he looked at me like a man who would relish my ruination. I was intruding on his territory.

'Who has access to this chamber?' I asked.

'The Queen's ladies . . . the King, those who serve him, those who serve here, and no others . . .' said Khay.

'There are guards stationed at every entrance to the royal quarters,' said Simut. 'Everyone must possess permissions to pass.'

'Therefore it must have been delivered by someone with high-priority access who moves with ease within the royal quarters,' I replied. 'I imagine that, once past the security points, in order to allow the family some privacy, there are no guards and no searches within the royal quarters themselves?'

Khay nodded, uncomfortably.

'The competence of the royal guards is absolutely not in question, but there is clearly a serious flaw somewhere that has allowed this object, and the carving, to appear here. I'm sure you'll agree it is imperative we put in place more stringent security arrangements for the King and Queen, both within the quarters and in public. When is the Colonnade Hall to be commemorated?' I asked.

'In two days' time,' said Khay. 'But tomorrow there is a gathering of the Council of Karnak which the King must attend.'

'Tomorrow?' I frowned. 'That is unfortunate.'

Khay nodded.

'What is "unfortunate" is that these "disturbances" could not have happened at a worse time,' he replied.

'It is no coincidence,' intoned Simut in his humourless, military fashion. 'If this were a conventional situation, such as a battle, I could see the enemy facing me. But this is different. This enemy is invisible. He could be one of us. He may be inside this palace now. He certainly seems to know everything about its layout, its protocols and hierarchies.'

'So we have a problem, for I imagine you cannot simply question elite men high in the order of power, without the strongest evidence,' I said.

'Alas, that is true,' Khay replied wearily, as if all his energy had suddenly departed.

'Nevertheless, every one of them is now a suspect. A list of names would be a start. And some simple questions about their whereabouts and so on would help to clarify the situation. We need to know who was here in the quarters tonight, and who has no alibi,' I offered.

'But at the same time we must not reveal anything of these objects. It is imperative we maintain strict silence on this matter,' said Khay nervously.

'My assistant will gladly help you assemble the information, and make the preliminary enquiries,' I replied.

Khay glanced at Khety, and was about to accept when Simut intervened.

'The security of the royal quarters is my responsibility. I will have the information prepared immediately.'

'Very well,' I replied. 'And I assume you will also include your own guards in the list of those with access to the area?'

He was about to confront me, but I interrupted.

'Believe me, I have no cause and no wish to doubt the integrity of your guards. But I'm sure you must agree we cannot afford to overlook any possibility, however unlikely or unacceptable.'

Eventually he nodded in unhappy acquiescence.

And so we parted.

15

'What a spectacle!' said Khety, blowing out his cheeks. 'That place reminds me of a particularly brutal school. There are always the big boys and the small boys. There are the ones who use their fists, and the ones who use their brains. There are the despots and the warriors and the diplomats and the servants. And there's also always one strange child somewhere, off to the side, tormenting another poor creature slowly to death. That's Ay,' he said.

The moonlit land drifted past as we sailed up the channel towards the Great River. I watched the dark water disappear under the keel for a little while before I spoke.

'Did you notice on the underside of the lid, the markings? In particular the black circle? It's some kind of language . . .'

Khety shook his head.

'What I noticed was the maker's nasty imagination, and his appetite for blood and guts,' he said.

'But he is educated, highly skilled, and almost certainly a member of the elite. His fascination with blood and guts, as you put it, is because they represent something to him. They are symbols, rather than things in themselves.'

'Try telling that to the girl with no face, or the boy with the shattered bones, or the new mystery man missing his own head,' he replied, accurately enough.

'It's not the same thing. And are we right to assume we're dealing with the same man in all cases?' I asked him.

'Well, just consider the connections, and the timing, and the style,' he replied.

'I have done. Similar imagery is deployed. The same obsessions with decay and destruction appear. And somewhere in all of this, I sense a love of beauty and perfection. There's almost a sorrow to these actions. A kind of grotesque pity for the victims . . .'

Khety looked at me as if I had lost my mind.

'When you talk like this, I'm glad no one can overhear us. How can there be sorrow in slicing off a girl's beautiful face? All I can see is the horrible, vicious cruelty. And anyway, how does that help us?'

We sat in silence for a while. Thoth at my feet gazed up at the moon. Khety was right, of course. What faced us was possibly just madness. Was I imagining patterns where perhaps none existed? And yet still I sensed something. Underneath the killings and the brutality, under the threats of iconoclasm and destruction, was something deeper, and darker: some kind of search, or vision. But if we were right, and the same man was responsible for all of these events, then there was a bigger question to answer: why? Why was he doing this?

'I also think whoever is responsible wants us to know he is an insider, in order to enhance the power of his threat. In fact, part of the game is to make us feel he is watching us all,' continued Khety. And as he said this, I suddenly realized the gifts and deaths had another element in common: *Rahotep, Seeker of Mysteries.*

We had just reached the jetty, and so rather than share it with him, I decided to let this odd thought sit at the back of my mind for a little while. It seemed too foolish and vain a thing to articulate.

I bade farewell to Khety, and with Thoth padding ahead of me walked home through the curfew streets. I released the baboon to his bed, and entered the dark house. Its silence upbraided me for my absence. Sometimes I feel I do not belong in this house of young women and old men and babies. I remained in the kitchen for a while before retiring to sleep. By the light of the oil lamp in its niche, which Tanefert had left for my return, I poured myself a large cup of decent red wine from the Kharga oasis, and set a few dried figs and almonds on a dish.

I sat down on the bench in my usual place beneath the statuette of the household God who knows I do not believe in him, and thought about families. It often seems to me that all troubles and all crimes begin with families. Even in our ancient stories, it is jealous brothers who kill each other, enraged wives who castrate their husbands, and furious children who avenge themselves on their culpable or innocent parents. I remembered how the girls still sweep from tender affection to murderous rage, from stroking each other's hair to dragging it out with their bare hands, in an instant, over some cause so minor even they blush for shame when it is confessed.

And so it is in marriage. We have a good marriage. If I have disappointed Tanefert by my lack of worldly success then she has disguised it well. She says she did not marry me for my fortune. And then she gives me one of her knowing smiles. But I know there are half-understood things between us that we keep in silence, as if words would somehow make them too painfully real. Perhaps it is so between all couples whose relations have survived for many years; the unnoticed influences of habit, and the perils of domestic tedium. Even the familiarity with each other's bodies, once so obsessively desired, leads to an undeniable hunger for the surprise of a stranger's beauty. The beauty and the contempt of familiarity . . . perhaps that is what I need to escape, when I relish the excitement of my work? The thought does not make me proud. I am now a man in the middle of the way of my life, and I am afraid of the middle way of it all . . . Why can I not be satisfied with everything the household God above me has granted?

If it is so for ordinary people like us, then how much stranger it must be to be born into a family whose purpose is public, and whose privacy has to be defended and policed continuously like a terrible secret? For all their wealth and power, the children of the royal family and of most elite families are raised in an air devoid of human warmth. What do they talk about at dinnertime? Matters of state? Manners at a banquet? Do they have to hear, over and over, the heroic stories of their grandfather, Amenhotep the Great, who they know they will always fail to emulate? And if my girls argue over the possession of a comb, then how must it have been when siblings struggled for possession of treasure, power, and the Two Crowns?

But I had seen two siblings who did not seem to be struggling for power. They seemed to be close, and supportive, perhaps bonded by their miseries under Ay's control. The affection between them had seemed entirely genuine. But Ankhesenamun's plan had one flaw. Tutankhamun was no warrior King. His virtues might be in his mind, but they clearly did not lie in physical prowess. Unfortunately the world requires its kings to demonstrate their vitality and virility in parades and protestations and adventures of power. Yes, heroic statues could be carved from stone, and impressive carvings could be set up in temples announcing Tutankhamun's feats and campaigns and restorations of the old traditions and authorities. And Ankhesenamun's own ancestry would help, for although she was still young she carried strong echoes of her mother – her beauty, her popularity, her independence of mind. And she had shown remarkable resilience this evening in confronting Ay. But the fact remained that at the heart of the great drama of state power was a flaw: the Image of the Living God was a clever, but frightened and physically not very heroic young man. That made both him and the Queen vulnerable. And whoever was tormenting the King with fear understood this.

Tanefert was standing in the dark doorway, watching me. I moved to make room for her. She sat next to me, and nibbled on an almond.

'Will there ever be a night when I know for sure no one will knock on the door, to ask you to come away with them?'

I put my arm around her and hugged her close, but this was not what she wanted.

'Never,' she said. 'Never.'

No words came to my aid to make this better.

'I think I am used to it. I accept it. I know it is your work. But sometimes, like tonight, when we are celebrating, I want you here, and I want to know you will not leave. And that's impossible. Because crime and cruelty and bloodshed are part of what people do to each other; and so you will always have more work. There will always be more knocks on the door in the night.'

She looked away.

'I always, always want to be here with you,' I stammered.

She turned to look me in the eye.

'I'm afraid. I'm afraid one day you will not come back to me. And I could not endure that.'

She kissed me sadly, rose, and walked away into the passage's darkness.

16

The royal entourage entered the great Karnak council chamber, and all the noise and the shouting ceased, as at the start of a drama. From the clerestory windows the burning light of late morning blazed down into the stone chamber. A long whisper from those gathered together echoed among the great pillars, and died away.

Tutankhamun and Ankhesenamun stepped together on to the dais, their small royal feet trampling the figures of the kingdom's enemies that were painted on to the steps. They turned and sat on the thrones, in an intense circle of light. They looked like little Gods, and yet they also looked so young. Their immaculate hands closed over the carved lions' claws of the thrones' arms, as if they commanded wild nature itself. I noticed Ankhesenamun briefly touching her husband's hand, as if for courage. In their white linen robes, and each wearing a magnificent collar emblazoned with a vulture's head and spread wings, they glittered with glory.

What a gallery of grotesques these men of the council were: ancient fellows, stooping, supported by servants, who had seen better days too many years ago, their faces thick with the curdled luxury and venality of their class, the sneer of superiority built into their expressions, whether into the wrinkles of the old or into the bland certainties of the young. Soft hands and sagging bellies. Fat cheeks trembling beneath almost effeminate mouths full, no doubt, of the stumps of rotten teeth. Committee men with quick, clever glances, assessing the constant shifts of politics, and the possible moves of the many-dimensioned game they played amongst themselves. And the tyrants: those stocky, angry bullies, always on the hunt for a victim, for someone to attack, and then to blame. I realized one of these last was staring at me. It was Nebamun, Head of the city Medjay. He looked wonderfully furious that I should be present at this elite gathering. I gave him a friendly nod, as if full of respect. I hoped he would appreciate the full depth of the irony in which it was given. Then I turned to look at the King. Finally, when there was absolute silence, Tutankhamun spoke. His voice was high and light, but it carried clearly in the stillness of the great chamber.

'The construction of the Colonnade Hall in honour of Amun-Ra, King of the Gods, has been financed equally by this temple and by our own royal treasury. It is a sign of our unity of purpose. This glorious monument was begun by order of my grandfather, Amenhotep III. He would be proud to see what he conceived many years ago being finally brought to magnificent completion by his grandson.'

He paused, and listened to the hush of expectation in the chamber.

'The Two Lands are themselves a great building, a great construction, everlasting. And together we are building a new kingdom; and this new hall, the tallest and most awe-inspiring that stands, or has ever stood, upon the face of the earth, is testament to our triumphs and ambitions, and to our closeness to the Gods. I invite all of you, great men of the council of this great city, and of the Kingdom of the Two Lands, to join us in its commemoration, for you have participated in its making, and we wish to embrace you all within its glory.'

His quiet speech was amplified in the hushed resonance of the chamber. Many nodded in agreement, approving of the way he had included them all within his vision.

'I now invite Ay, our Regent, God's Father, who has served us so well, to address you on further matters of state on our behalf.'

Perhaps I was not alone in detecting an interesting new hint of tension in his subtle use of the past tense. Ay would surely have heard it, with his ear for the finest of nuances, but he gave no sign. He came forward slowly from the shadows, disguising the pain gnawing like a dog at his old bones, and took his rightful place on the step below the King and Queen. He masterfully surveyed the faces before him. His face was gaunt, his gaze pitiless and unflinching. Then, in his almost toneless voice, he began an extensive, stony, formal response to the King and to the council. I looked around; his audience leaned forward to catch every word, as if mesmerized not by the content but by his compelling quietness, which was so much more effective than demonstrative, empty noise. And then he turned to the real agenda of the day.

'Following the ignominious and intolerable events at the festival, there has been a full investigation conducted with alacrity and efficiency by our city police.'

He gazed out at the crowd of men until he discovered Nebamun, and nodded at him. The men surrounding him also nodded with respect. Nebamun instantly swelled with pride.

'The ringleaders have confessed and have been impaled, together with their wives and children, and all the members of their extended families. Their bodies have been set out in public view on the walls of the city. Although no punishment is sufficient for the crime in question, an example has been made, and the problem has been *eradicated*.'

He paused, and surveyed the councillors as if daring them to question this account of justice, and its punishments.

'The Head of the city Medjay has persuaded me there will be no further public disturbances of this kind. I have taken his word on trust. His efficiency in the investigation of the unrest, and his discipline and commitment to arresting and executing those found guilty, have been exemplary. I only wish others laboured with the same alacrity. We hereby grant, in recognition of his achievement, a Gold Collar of Honour, as well as a doubling, with effect from this day, of the city Medjay budget under his command.'

Nebamun made his way through the admiring crowd, accepting the approbation and acclaim, the nods and the pats, until he stood before the gaunt old man, and bowed his head. As Ay lowered the collar on to my superior's fat neck, I experienced a wish to march over and relieve him of it. For who here knew of the injustices and the cruelties he had perpetrated upon innocent people for the sake of this moment, and this gold? Disgust swirled in my stomach. He looked up, made the gestures of gratitude to Ay, the King and the Queen, and then made his way back to his cronies. As he did so, he sent me a cold nod of victory. I knew he would use this honour to make my life even more difficult.

Ay continued: 'Order is everything. We have restored *maat* to the Two Lands. I will allow no rogue elements, no contending forces, to disturb the stability and security of our kingdom.'

He spoke as if, by the authority of his saying so, it would be so; and as if he alone was the arbiter of that order.

'Therefore, let us turn now to the matter of the Hittite wars. We have received reports of successes in battle, with new territory won, and existing towns and commercial routes sustained and their security improved. We expect to receive Hittite terms of negotiation. The old enemy of the Two Lands is in retreat!'

There was a smattering of obsequious applause in response to this hollow claim. For everyone knew that the wars were far from won, and the battles with the Hittites, which were only the latest skirmishes in the endless friction in the borderlands and states that lay between the two kingdoms, could not be resolved so easily.

Ay continued: 'If there are no further matters to be discussed with my esteemed friends and colleagues, we may retire to the banquet.'

He stared balefully at his audience. Silence reigned, and I saw that no one dared to contradict him.

Everyone prostrated themselves slowly and unconvincingly, like a bunch of elderly performing monkeys, as he, followed by Ankhesenamun and Tutankhamun, descended from the dais.

In the outer chamber, many trays had been set out on stands. Each one was piled with food: bread, rolls and cakes, all fresh from the bakery; roasted cuts of meat; roasted birds in thick glazes; roasted gourds and shallots; honeycomb; olives glistening in oil; fat bunches of dark grapes; figs, dates and almonds in astonishing abundance. All the good things of the land, heaped up in piles.

What followed was an instructive spectacle. For these men, who had never worked the soil under the midday sun or butchered an animal with their own hands, rushed to the stands as if they were the desperate victims of a famine. Showing no shame or manners, they elbowed each other aside, pushing and shoving to reach the fragrant mountains of good things of the banquet. Delicacies that must have taken a very long time to prepare fell from their heaped dishes, and were squashed underfoot. They were so greedy they helped themselves, rather than waiting to be served. Despite the somehow appalling quantities of food, of which most of the population could only dream, they behaved as if they were utterly terrified that there would not be enough. Or as if no matter how much was placed before them, somehow they were afraid it would *never be enough.*

Perhaps it was naive of me to compare the disgraceful luxury of this scene with the poverty, and the lack of water and meat and bread, that haunt the lives of those outside these privileged walls. But it was unavoidable. The noise reminded me of pigs at the trough. Meanwhile, as this feeding continued, the King and Queen, now seated on another dais, attended to a long queue of high officials and their retinues, each waiting to offer obsequious respects and to make their latest, no doubt self-serving, petitions.

Nakht joined me.

'What a repulsive sight,' I said. 'The rich as they really are: it is like a moral fable of greed.'

'It certainly does spoil one's appetite,' he agreed politely, although he seemed less revolted than I.

'What did you make of Ay's speech?' I asked.

Nakht shook his head.

'I thought it was quite appalling. It's another travesty of justice. What a world we live in! But if nothing else it shows that even tyrants struggle to maintain their power, beyond a certain point. The truth is, a handful of executions won't solve the overwhelming problems of this state. And although no one here would be caught dead saying so, everyone knows it. He's bluffing, and that's interesting because it means he's in deep trouble.'

I caught a brief glimpse of Ay surrounded by courtiers; I saw the little drama of his arrogance and condescension, and their sycophantic, stuck, desperate smiles. Nebamun was with him, like a stupid dog gazing with adoration at its master. Ay saw us looking at him; he recorded the moment of information, and the expressions on our faces, in the cold tomb of his brain. He nodded at something Nebamun said, and the Medjay man then looked as if he was about to summon me over for the patronizing questioning I had been dreading.

But then, as the noise of the feasting and shouting and arguing reached its zenith, a sudden fanfare from a single long silver military trumpet silenced everyone; full mouths gaped open in surprise, quail and goose legs were stuck half-way from plate to mouth, and all turned to watch a lone young soldier march into the centre of the chamber. Ay seemed caught unawares. Something other than certainty glittered in his reptilian eyes. He had not been forewarned of this man's arrival. A herald of the temple stepped forward and announced him as the messenger of Horemheb, General of the Armies of the Two Lands. The silence thickened.

The soldier made the correct prostrations and formulas of praise to

Tutankhamun and Ankhesenamun. He did not acknowledge the presence of Ay, as if he did not even know who he was. He surveyed the now-silent chamber and its population of gourmands with the moral arrogance of youth, clearly disappointed by their venality. A touch of shame appeared in the faces of many of those still gorging themselves. Exquisite glazed pottery and carved stone dishes clattered lightly as they were quickly set down on the trays. The honoured councillors swallowed, wiped their fat lips, and cleaned their greasy fingers.

'I have the honour to bear and to speak a message to the Great Council of Karnak, from Horemheb, General of the Armies of the Two Lands,' he shouted, proudly.

'We will hear this message in private,' said Ay, moving quickly forward.

'My orders are to address the general's message to the entire gathering of the Council of Karnak,' the messenger replied assertively, so that all could hear him. The old man snarled.

'I am Ay. I am your superior, and the superior of your general. My authority is not to be questioned.'

Now the soldier looked uncertain. But Tutankhamun spoke, in his quiet, clear voice.

'We wish to hear what our great general has to say.'

Ankhesenamun nodded in innocent agreement, but I saw the pleasure in her eyes at Ay's dilemma. For he had no choice but to concede, in public, to the King. He hesitated, but then bowed ostentatiously.

'Then speak at once,' said Ay, turning away, the threat still in his voice.

The soldier saluted, unrolled a papyrus scroll and began to read the written words of his general.

To Tutankhamun, Living Image of Amun, Lord of the Two Lands, and to his Queen Ankhesenamun, and to the lords of the Council of

Karnak. When rumour speaks, from out of its million mouths come the whispers of fear, the murmurs of speculation and the mutterings of suspicion. But truth speaks of things as they are. Nothing is changed in its mouth. And so when I, conducting campaigns in the plains of Kadesh, hear of public attacks upon the King, in the great city of Thebes, what am I to believe? Surely this is the work of rumour? Or is it, unthinkably, true?

The messenger paused, uncomfortably. He was nervous. I did not blame him.

The Two Lands are under the supreme command of Ay, in the name of our lord, Tutankhamun. So what need have I for alarm? But then is it rumour or truth that speaks to me of other conspiracies upon the King's person within the security of the palace itself?

Shocked at this new open accusation, everyone looked at Ay and the royal couple. Ay began to respond, but Tutankhamun, with un-expected authority, raised his hand and silenced his Regent. The audience was now entirely attentive to these astonishing new develop-ments. Then the King nodded at the soldier, who, conscious of the hazardous and ominous nature of what he was committed to read, con-tinued implacably, quickening the rhythm of his delivery.

So we have enemies without, and enemies within. The Hittites have lately renewed their assault upon the rich ports and cities of the confederacy of Amurru, including Kadesh, Sumur and Byblos, and we are struggling to defend them. Why? Because we lack resources. We lack troops. We lack sufficient weaponry. We find ourselves in the invidious position of being unable to support and encourage our crucial alliances in the region. I am ashamed to confess this, and yet truth demands it of me. It is said that in our time the business of our king-dom's foreign affairs has been neglected in favour of the building of great structures in the name of the Gods. Nevertheless, I extend to the King and to the council the offer of my presence and my services in the city of Thebes in this time of crisis. If it is imperative for me to return, I shall do so. We face the enemy on our borders. But those enemies within are an even greater threat. For perhaps they have insinuated themselves in the very heart of our government. For what else are these threats against the King, our great symbol of unity? How is it possible that we are so weak that these unprecedented attacks can be made? My messenger, whose safe passage I confer into your hands, will deliver to me your reply.

All eyes turned upon Ay. His patrician face showed no reaction. He flicked his hand commandingly at one of the scribes, who hurried forward with his ivory palette and reed pens, and as Ay began to speak, he began to write.

We welcome the communication of the honourable general. Hear our reply, in the name of Tutankhamun, Lord of the Two Lands. One. All the troops and weapons requested were assigned to this campaign. Why was this not sufficient? Why have you still not returned in a victory parade, with bound prisoners, and chariots stacked high with the cut-off hands of the enemy dead, and with vanquished leaders hung up in cages from the prows of our ships to offer to the King? Two. The general makes unfounded allegations against the competence of the city and the palace to manage their own affairs. He has listened to rumour and believed its lies. Even so, on spurious reasons he has offered to abandon his first responsibility to his position in the battle for Kadesh. It is a foolish, irresponsible and unnecessary offer. It might be understood, although I hesitate to call it so, as an act of abdication of responsibility and, indeed, of disloyalty. The imperative is victory, and in that you are clearly failing. Perhaps that is why your offer has come to us at this very moment. Your instructions, from Tutankhamun, Lord of the Two Lands, are to remain at your battle stations, and fight, and win. Do not fail.

The only sound in the chamber was that of the scribe's reed pen brushing across the surface of the papyrus scroll as he recorded Ay's reply. He passed it to Ay for his seal. Ay scanned it, rolled it up, tied it and then added his seal to the cord, before passing it to the soldier, who bowed his head as he accepted it, exchanging it for the one he had carried so far.

And then Ay leaned forward and spoke quietly into the soldier's ear. No one could hear what he said, but the effect of it was very clear on the man's face. He looked as if he had heard the curse of his own death laid upon him. I had by now conceived a considerable sympathy for him. He saluted and left the chamber. I wondered whether he would live to deliver the reply.

But Ay's words, no matter how forceful, could not put back together what was now broken. For the message of the general had had the effect of shattering the illusion of political certainty. And the low roar of excited and dismayed discussion that began as soon as the soldier left the chamber was the sound of its building blocks collapsing into rubble. I saw Ankhesenamun discreetly touch her husband's hand, and Tutankhamun unexpectedly rose to his feet. He looked for a moment to be uncertain why he had done so. But then he grasped the moment, commanded the trumpeters, whose fanfare silenced the hall again, and spoke.

'We have heard all that the great general has confided in us. He is wrong. The Great Estate is sure and strong. A kingdom as pre-eminent, as sublime and as eternal as the Two Lands draws envy and enmity. But any attacks will be dealt with swiftly and surely. No dissent will be tolerated. As for the "conspiracy" to which the general alluded, it is nothing but a distraction. Those responsible are being investigated, and they will be eliminated. We have placed our trust in this man.'

Suddenly every man turned to look at me, the stranger in their midst.

'This is Rahotep. He is Chief Detective within the city Medjay. We appoint him to investigate the accusations of the great general regarding our personal security. He has his orders. He has the powers we invest in him to follow his investigation, regardless of where it may lead him.'

There was absolute silence in the chamber. Then he smiled, and continued: 'There is much business of state to be accomplished. The work of the day has just begun. I look forward to seeing you all at the dedication of the Colonnade Hall.'

For the second time on that day, Ay was caught out. Ankhesenamun gave him a brief look. Something in her spirit seemed to have taken courage from these moments, and her eyes revealed it. A spark of determination was now kindled there, which had been dormant for too long. As she processed out of the chamber, she glanced at me with a tiny smile on her lips. Then she was gone, gathered up by the procession of guards and taken away, back to the palace of shadows.

Nebamun wasted no time in loping over to me. He was perspiring. His linens were damp, and the little red veins beneath his bleary eyes flickered almost imperceptibly. His breath came short as he held up one fat little finger in my face.

'Whatever you're up to, Rahotep, remember one thing. Keep me informed. I want to know everything that's happening. No matter what powers the King gives you, do this, or else, believe me, when this is all over, and your little private assignment is concluded – assuming you get anywhere at all, which I doubt – you'll have to come and see me. Come and see what's left for you at the city Medjay.'

I smiled and bowed.

'All glory is brief, and it's a long way back down to the bottom of the heap. I'm going to be busy. I'll write you a report.'

Then I turned and walked quickly away, knowing with these words I was risking my future for the sake of my contempt, but hating him too much to care.

17

As I left the temple gate, Khety appeared suddenly out of the crowds assembled behind the security lines.

'Come quickly,' he said, breathlessly.

'Another victim?'

He nodded.

'But this time the killer was disturbed at his work. Hurry.'

I hesitated. I was supposed to attend the interviews of all those who had access to the royal quarters, with Simut. But I knew I had no choice.

We ran through the crowds to reach the house, which was in a distant quarter of the city. Everything and everyone moved too slowly; people turned or stopped right in our tracks, mules loaded with mud-bricks or rubbish or vegetables blocked narrow passages; all the old people of the city seemed to be taking for ever to cross the ways – so we dodged and darted, shouting for precedence, pushing and throwing fools, workmen, officials and children aside, leaving a wake of aggravation and disturbance behind us.

The young man lay on his couch. He was about the same age as the first boy, and with a similar infirmity. The bones of his body had been shattered as well. His skin was horribly bruised from the attack. But this time, over his head, the killer had fitted the scalp, the long, black, dull hair, and the now-distorted face, like a leather mask that had melted in great heat, which must have belonged to the young girl. The cut edges of the skin of her face had been sewn around the top of the boy's own face with an exemplary precision – but he had not had time to finish his gruesome work. The dead girl's lips, dried out and curling up, opened around the small, dark hole which would once have been her mouth. I put my ear carefully to it. And then I heard it: the faintest respiration, slight as a feather brushing my face.

Very carefully, very gently, and as quickly as possible, I used my knife to snip away at the stitches and eventually, carefully removed the hideous mask. Sticky fluids and traces of blood had helped the girl's face adhere to the boy's, and I had to tease it off; the two faces peeled apart reluctantly. His own face was very pale, as if bloodless, and embroidered now with spots of blood that sprang from the killer's needlework. More terribly, where his eyes should have been were empty, bleeding sockets. I passed Khety the girl's face, for even in this lamentable state it was still an identity – something to go on.

Then suddenly the boy drew a tiny inward breath, more like a small cry. He tried to move, but the shattered bones made no sense; and then a flash of pain arched through him.

'Try to stay still. I am a friend. Who did this to you?'

But he could not speak, for the bones of his jaw were broken.

'Was it a man?'

He struggled to comprehend me.

'A young man or an old man?'

He was trembling now.

'Did he give you a powder or a juice to ingest?'

Khety touched my shoulder.

'He cannot understand you.'

Now the boy began to moan, a low, mournful sound like an

animal in appalling distress. He was suffering the memory of what had happened to him. Drawing breath seemed suddenly impossibly painful. Instinctively I touched his hand with mine, but the moan became a terrible wail of pain. Desperate for him not to die, I moistened his lips and brow with a little water. This seemed to revive him. He opened his mouth a fraction, as if pleading for more water, which I gave him. But then he slipped from consciousness. Horrified, I leant down to listen again at his mouth and heard – thanks be to the Gods – the lightest of breath. He was still alive.

'Khety – we need a doctor. Now!'

'But I don't know any doctors,' he stammered.

I racked my brains. And then suddenly it came to me.

'Quickly, we have to carry him to Nakht's house. We don't have much time.'

'But how . . . ?' he began, his palms waving uselessly in the air.

'On his bed, you idiot, how else?' I shouted back at him. 'I want him kept alive, and Nakht can do it.'

And so, to the amazement of the boy's family, I covered the boy's body with a linen cloth as if he was already dead, and the two of us took up the bed – which was light enough, and his frail weight added very little to our burden – and made our way through the streets. I went first, shouting at everyone to make way, and trying to ignore the curious faces of the people, all pushing to get a glimpse of what we were carrying, and what was causing such a stir. But when they saw the linen over the body they assumed we carried a corpse, and backed away, losing interest quickly. Their reaction was very different to Nakht's, when I revealed the damaged body beneath the cloth to him. Khety and I were drenched in sweat, and desperate for a long draught of cool water; but my priority was the boy. I had not dared to check on his state in the street, only praying that the inevitable rocking and jostling of the bed in our hands would not cause him too much agony. I hoped he was only unconscious, but not, please the Gods, already in the Otherworld.

Nakht ordered the servants to carry the boy into one of his chambers, and then he examined him carefully. Khety and I watched him nervously. Once he had concluded, he washed his hands in a bowl, and nodded sternly to us to join him outside.

'I have to confess, my friend, this is the strangest gift you have ever brought me. What have I done to deserve it? A boy's lame body, the bones shattered, the face so curiously scored by needle-holes, and the eyes removed? I am at a loss, a complete loss, to understand whatever persuaded you to bring him to me, like a cat bringing home the remains of her kill . . .'

He was angry. And so, I realized, was I.

'And to whom else should I bring him? Without expert attention he will die. But I have to keep him safely, until he is well. He is my only lead. Only he can tell me who did this to him. He might be able to help us identify his attacker. He will recover?'

'He has a dislocated jaw. His arms and legs are both broken in several places. I fear infection in the cuts around his face and in the eye-sockets. And among all the great mysteries of the cruelties that have been so precisely inflicted upon this boy's body, why does he have the marks of needles upon his face?'

I pulled the girl's face from my bag and showed it to him. He turned away in revulsion.

'We found this sewn on to his face. It belongs to a body we also found. The face belongs to a girl. Her name was Neferet.'

'Please, put that thing away. I simply can't talk to you while you are thrusting the remains of a human face at me,' he cried.

I saw his point. I passed the face to Khety, who took possession of it reluctantly, fastidiously placing it back in the bag.

'Now can we talk?'

He nodded.

'I am not accustomed, as you are, to the more brutal acts of our kind. I have never been in battle. Never been robbed or attacked. Never even been in a fight. I abhor violence, as you very well know.

The thought of it makes me sick. So forgive me if what, for you, is all in a day's work, is for me something more of a profound shock.'

'I forgive you. But tell me now: can you save him?'

He sighed.

'It is possible, provided there is no infection. Bones we can set. Blood we cannot heal.'

'And when might I be able to speak to him?'

'My friend, this boy has been literally shattered. It will take weeks, months, for these injuries to heal. His jaw is a mess. If he lives, he will need time to recover from his blindness. It will be some time, a month at the very least, before he can speak. This is assuming his mind remains undamaged by the experience, and that he is capable of articulation and comprehension.'

I gazed down at the boy. He was my only hope. I wondered what he could say to me, and whether, in a month, it would all be far, far too late.

'So what do we do now?' asked Khety quietly, as we stood outside Nakht's house. He looked shocked.

'Have you got a lead on Neferet's place of work?'

'I've narrowed it down to a couple of places. We should visit them,' he replied.

He showed me a list of establishments.

'Fine. When?'

'After sunset would be best. When they get busy.'

I nodded.

'Meet me at the first one. Bring that with you,' I said, meaning the face which he had replaced in its leather bag.

'What are you going to do now?' he asked.

'I feel like going home and drinking a bottle of decent red wine, and feeding my son his dinner. But I have to return to the palace. The interviews of all those who have priority access to the royal quarters took place this afternoon. I should have been there.'

I glanced up at the afternoon sun, which was now descending to the west. I might already have missed everything.

'Do you want me to come, too?'

I shook my head.

'I want you to go back to the boy's family and explain we're taking care of him. Tell them he's alive, and we have good hopes. And above all make arrangements for the boy to be guarded. Set a pair of guards inside the entrance to Nakht's house at all hours. We don't want anyone to hurt the boy any more. We can't risk losing him.'

'What happens if he dies?' asked Khety quietly.

'I don't know,' I replied. 'Pray to the Gods he lives.'

'You don't believe in Gods,' he replied.

'This is an emergency. Suddenly I am reconsidering my point of view.'

18

I tried to stop myself breaking into a run as I made my way, by memory now, towards the royal quarters. By day, I noticed more people: groups of officials, foreign ministers, delegates and potentates being entertained in various chambers. I showed my permissions to the guards, who scrutinized them carefully before allowing me to pass. At least the security had improved.

'Take me to Simut. At once,' I commanded.

He and Khay were waiting in Khay's office. As I entered, they both looked at me sourly.

'I am sorry. I had another emergency.'

'What emergency could possibly be greater than this one?' wondered Khay, airily.

Simut silently handed me a papyrus scroll. I glanced down the list of no more than ten names: the chiefs of the royal domain; viziers of the north and south; Huy, Chancellor; the Chief Steward; the Chamberlain; the Fan Bearer of the King's Right Hand . . .

'All of those who have entered the royal quarters in the last three days, I have called together and interviewed. It is a pity you could not be there. They didn't like being kept waiting, and they didn't like being questioned. It is contributing to the feeling of uncertainty within the palace. I'm afraid I could find no evidence against any of them,' he said.

'You mean they all claim to have alibis?' I asked, irritated by him and by my own anxiety at the lack of progress. He was right. I should have been there. He nodded.

'Of course, we are now in the process of checking these, and I will have another report for you in the morning.'

'But where are they now?'

'I asked them to remain here until you could speak to them. What else would you have me do? It is now dark, and they are angry not to be able to return to their homes and their families. Already they claim they are imprisoned in the royal quarters.' He snorted.

'Well, given what is at stake, that is the least of our concerns. Who are these men? I mean, where do their loyalties lie?'

Khay pounced on me at once.

'Their loyalties lie with the King, and with the Two Lands. And how dare you suggest otherwise?'

'Yes, that's the official version, I know. But which of these are Ay's men?'

They exchanged an uncertain glance. But it was Simut who replied:

'All of them.'

As I entered, the great men of the royal domain all turned as one from their discussion to gaze at me with frank hostility, but remained seated in a gesture of contempt. I saw abundant wine and food had been laid on for them. Khay as usual made a fussy introduction, and I interrupted him as soon as I could.

'It is no longer a secret that, somehow, someone is leaving objects within the royal quarters whose aim is to alarm and threaten the King and the Queen. We have come to the conclusion that the only way these objects could be left inside the palace, despite the excellence of the palace security, is if someone with a high level of clearance is delivering them. And I'm afraid, lords, that means one of you.'

There was a moment of icy silence, and then suddenly they were all up on their feet, bellowing in indignation at me, at Khay and at Simut. Khay patted at the turbulent air with his diplomatic hands, as if calming children.

'Lords, please. Remember that this man has the public acclaim of the King himself. He is merely pursuing his duties in the name of the King. And as you may recall, he has permission to follow his investigation, and I quote the royal words: "regardless of where it may lead him".'

This was effective.

'I am sorry to inconvenience you in this way. I realize you all have busy lives, and very important roles to fulfil, and no doubt anxious families at home . . .' I continued.

'Been spared that at least,' huffed one of them.

'And I would like to be able to say the time has come for me to thank you and open the door for you to leave. Alas, that is not the case. Regrettably, I will now need to speak to each one of you individually, and I will also need to interview all the officers and staff who are in any way connected to your work here at the palace . . .'

Another roar of indignation greeted that, during which I gradually became aware of a loud knocking on the door to the chamber. This had the effect of gradually silencing everyone again. I strode over to the door, furious at being interrupted, and saw, to my shock, Ankhesenamun standing there, holding a small object in the palm of her hand.

The magical figurine, no bigger than the span of my hand, had been wrapped in a linen cloth and dropped outside the King's chamber. It might almost have been possible to mistake it for a toy, except for the vile air of malevolence that emanated from it. Fashioned from dark wax into a shape that represented a human figure, it lacked all character or detail, like a half-formed foetus from the Otherworld. Copper needles had been driven through the head from ear to ear, and back to front through the eyes, as well as through the mouth, and directly downward into the centre of the skull. None pierced the body itself, as if the curse was intended only for the head, the seat of thought, imagination and fear. A few strands of black human hair had been inserted into the navel to transfer the essence of the intended victim into the inert matter of the figurine. I wondered if it was the King's own hair, because otherwise it would not be magically effective. On the back, the names and titles of the King had been precisely inscribed in the wax. The ritual of execration would call down the curse of death upon the person and his names, so that the destruction of the spirit extended to the afterlife. Such figurines were powerful, ancient magic to those who believed in their authority. It was another attempt to terrify; but it was a much more intimate threat than any of the others, even the death mask; for this was a great curse on the immortality of the King's spirit.

At the back of the figurine a slip of papyrus had been worked into the wax. I prised it out and unrolled it carefully; tiny signs had been written there in red ink, like those that had been carved into the rim of the box that contained the death mask. Of course, they might just be nonsense, for curses are often expressed in such a way, but then again they might well be an authentic magical language.

Ankhesenamun, Khay and Simut waited impatiently while I finished my examination of the object.

'This cannot continue,' said Khay, as if saying it would make it so. 'It is an absolute catastrophe . . .'

I said nothing.

'Three times the King's privacy has been invaded. Three times he has been alarmed—' he continued, bleating like a goat.

'Where is he now?' I interrupted him.

'He has retired to another chamber,' replied Ankhesenamun. 'His physician attends him.'

'And what effect has this had upon him?'

'He is – troubled.' She glanced at me, sighed, and continued:

'When he found the death figure, his breath seized in his chest, and his heart tightened like a knot in a rope. I feared he might die of the terror. And tomorrow is the dedication of the Colonnade Hall. He must appear. This could not have come at a worse moment.'

'The timing is deliberate,' I said.

I looked again at the figurine.

'Whoever did this seems to have been able to attach the King's own hair.'

I showed Khay. He looked with revulsion at the figurine.

'But in any case,' said Simut, in his slow, stentorian voice, 'no one seems to have noticed that all the suspects, so-called, have been gathered together in one room, at exactly the time this was found. It is not possible for any of them to have delivered this.'

He was right, of course.

'Please return to the chamber and, with my apologies, release them all. Thank them for their time.'

'But what am I going to tell them, exactly?' moaned Khay.

'Tell them we have a new lead. A promising new lead.'

'If only that were true,' he replied bitterly. 'We are powerless, it seems, against this peril. Time is running out, Rahotep.'

He shook his head and left, accompanied by Simut for protection.

I wrapped the death figure in a length of linen cloth, and placed it in my bag, as I wanted Nakht to see the signs, in case he recognized the language. Ankhesenamun and I remained standing in the corridor. I did not know what to say. I suddenly felt like a creature in a trap, acquiescent to its fate. Then I noticed the doors to the King's bed-chamber were still ajar.

'May I?' I asked. She nodded.

The chamber reminded me of a child's fantasy of a room in which to play and dream. There were hundreds of toys, in wooden boxes, on shelves, or stored in woven baskets. Some were very old and frail, as if they had belonged to generations of children, but most were fairly new, especially commissioned no doubt: inlaid spinning tops; collections of marbles; a game box with an elegant *senet* board on the top, and a drawer for the ebony and ivory playing pieces, the whole object resting upon elegant ebony legs and runners. There were also many wooden and pottery animals, with moving jaws and limbs, including a cat with a string through its jaw, a collection of carved locusts with wings that worked intricately in exact imitation of the real thing, a horse on wheels, and a painted pecking bird with a wide tail, beautifully balanced on its rounded breast, the perfect colours muted with long handling. Here were chubby ivory dwarfs set on a wide base with strings that could make them dance from side to side. And by the sleeping couch, with its blue glass headrest, gilded and inscribed with a spell of protection, was a single carved monkey with a round, grinning, almost human face, and long moving limbs for swinging from imaginary tree to tree. Also paint palettes with indentations crammed with pigments. In amongst the toy animals were hunting sticks, and bows and arrows, and a silver trumpet with a golden mouthpiece. And in gilded cages along the far wall of the room, many bright, tiny birds rustled and fluttered delicately against the thin bars of their elaborate wooden palaces, complete with tiny chambers, towers and pools.

'Where is the King's monkey?' I asked.

'It is with the King. That creature gives him great comfort,' Ankhesenamun replied. And then, as if to explain the King's childishness, she continued: 'It has taken me years to encourage the King in our plan, and tomorrow is its fulfilment. Somehow he must find his courage, despite this. Somehow I must help him to do so.'

We both gazed around the chamber and its bizarre contents.

'He cares about these toys more than he cares about all the riches in the world,' she offered quietly, and without much hope in her voice.

'Perhaps there's a good reason for that,' I replied.

'There is a reason, and I understand it. These are the treasures of his lost childhood. But it is time to put away such things. There is too much at stake.'

'Perhaps our childhoods are buried inside all of us. Perhaps they set the pattern for our futures,' I suggested.

'In that case I am doomed by mine,' she said without self-pity.

'Perhaps not, for you are aware of it,' I said.

She glanced at me warily.

'You never talk like a Medjay.'

'I talk too much. I am famous for it.'

She almost smiled.

'And you love your wife and your children,' she replied, oddly.

'Yes I do. I can say that, for certain,' I replied, in truth.

'But that is your vulnerability.'

I was taken aback by the observation.

'How so?'

'It means you can be destroyed through others. I have been taught one thing: to have care for no one, for if I care for someone I know they will be condemned by my love.'

'That is survival, not life. And also, it disallows the love of the other. Perhaps you have no right to do that. Or no right to make that decision for them,' I said.

'Perhaps,' she said. 'But in my world it is a necessity. The fact that I wish it were not so cannot alter the fact.'

She was now moving about the chamber, anxiously.

'Now it is I who talk nonsense. Why do I say such things when I am with you?' she continued.

'I am honoured by your honesty,' I replied, carefully.

She gave me a long, long look, as if assessing the polite equivocation of my reply, but said nothing more.

'May I ask you a question?' I said.

'Of course you may. I hope I am not a suspect,' she said, half-smiling.

'Whoever is leaving these objects can move about within the royal quarters with relative ease. How else could these things be left? So I need to know who could have access to this chamber.

148

Obviously his chamber-men and women, and his wet nurse . . .'

'Maia? Yes. She performs all the most intimate tasks for the King. She despises me, of course. She blames my mother for everything, and she thinks because I might have benefited from crimes committed before I was born, I should pay for them now.'

'She is only a servant,' I observed.

'She whispers her hatred into the ear of the King. She is closer than a mother to him.'

'But her love for the King is unquestioned . . .' I said.

'She is famous for her loyalty and her love. It is all she has,' she replied, almost casually, as she wandered about the room.

'So who else could come in here?'

She picked up the monkey figure, and regarded it coolly.

'Well, me, of course . . . But I rarely enter this chamber. I would have no reason to come in here. I do not wish to play with toys. I have encouraged him in other directions.'

She put the monkey back down.

'And in any case, I can hardly be a suspect, since I asked you to investigate in the first place. Or does it sometimes happen that the very person who initiated the investigation, also turns out to be the guilty party?'

'Sometimes. I imagine in your position, others will make of your situation what they will. After all, they might say, for example, that you wanted your husband crippled with fear, in order to assume power for yourself.'

Her eyes turned suddenly lightless, like a pool when the sun departs.

'People speculate, they love it. I can do nothing about that. But my husband and I are bound to each other by much more than mutual necessity. We have a deep bond of history. He is all I have left of that history. And I would never harm him, for, apart from anything, that would hardly enhance my own security. We are necessary to each other. To each other's survival and future. But we also share a deep care and affection . . .' She ran her carefully manicured fingernails across the fretwork of one of the birdcages, tapping gently, so that the bird within regarded her with one eye, then flitted away as far as it could.

Then she turned back to me. Her eyes glistened.

'I feel danger in everything, in the walls, in the shadows; the fear is like millions of ants in my mind, in my hair. See how my hands tremble, all the time?'

She held them out, and gazed at them as if they were disloyal. Then she summoned back her confidence.

'Tomorrow will be a life-changing day for all of us. I wish you to attend us at the ceremony.'

'Only priests are allowed within the temple itself,' I reminded her.

'Priests are only men in the right clothing. If you shave your head and dress in white linen, you will pass for a priest. Who would know you were not?' she said, cheering up at the thought. 'Sometimes you have the face of a priest. You look like a man who has seen mysteries.'

I was about to reply, when Khay reappeared. He bowed ostentatiously.

'The lords of the royal domain have left. Full of threats and indignation, I might add.'

'That is their way, and it will pass,' replied Ankhesenamun.

Khay bowed again.

'Rahotep will accompany us to the inauguration tomorrow,' she continued. 'He will need to be dressed appropriately, so that his presence causes no disturbance to protocol.'

'Very well,' he said, in the dry tone of someone who is only obeying orders.

'I wish to meet the King's physician,' I said, suddenly.

'Pentu attends the King,' replied Khay.

'I am sure he will spare Rahotep a few moments of his time. Ask him as a favour from me,' said Ankhesenamun.

150

Khay bowed once more.

'I must go to the King now. There is so much to be accomplished, and so little time,' she replied.

Then she added quietly: 'Can you remain here, in the royal quarters, tonight? The thought of your presence would be a comfort to me.'

I remembered the appointment with Khety.

'Alas, I must return to the city. I have another line of inquiry that I must pursue tonight. It is imperative, I'm afraid.'

She gazed at me.

'Poor Rahotep. You are trying to live two lives at once. You will attend us in the morning.'

I bowed, and when I looked up again, she had disappeared.

19

Pentu was pacing backwards and forwards, his hands clenched behind his back, his angular, haughty face desiccated with tension. As soon as I entered, and the curtain was drawn behind us, he efficiently assessed me, as if I were an annoying patient.

'Why do you need to see me?'

'I appreciate you are busy. How is the King?'

He glanced at Khay, who nodded, indicating he should reply.

'He has suffered an attack of anxiety. It is not the first time. His mind is sensitive, and easily affected. This will pass.'

'And how do you treat him?'

'I contended with the affliction by reciting the effective prayer of protection by Horus against the night demons.'

'And was it effective?'

His brow furrowed and his tone implied this was none of my business.

'Of course. I also persuaded the King to drink a curative water. He is much calmer now.'

'What kind of curative water?' I asked. He huffed.

'To be magically efficacious, the water must be passed over a sacred stele and, once it has absorbed the effectiveness of the carving, collected.'

He gazed at me, daring me to question him further.

We paused.

'Thank you. The world of medicine is unknown to me.'

'Clearly. Now, if that is all . . .' he said, exasperated, making as if to leave, but Khay made soothing gestures, and he stayed.

It was time to make my mark.

'Let me be plain and to the point. There have now been three successful attempts to infiltrate the very heart of the royal quarters. On each occasion, an object has been left which has threatened the King in ways both physical and, at least in intention, metaphysical. I also have reason to believe whoever is doing this has knowledge of pharmacopoeia—'

'What are you implying?' Pentu shouted. 'Is this man implying that I or my staff are under suspicion?' He glared at Khay.

'Forgive me if I spoke carelessly. My reasons are drawn from other things, events outside the palace. But I would say this state of affairs, and the consequences for the King's state of mind, should be our absolute priority. For if the instigator of all this can do the things he has done so easily, then what else might he not do?'

He and I looked at each other in silence.

'Why don't we all sit down?' suggested Khay, diplomatically, taking advantage of the moment.

So we sat on low benches placed against the wall of the chamber.

'Firstly, since I have reason to believe this man may indeed be a physician himself, it would be helpful to understand how the palace physicians are organized, and who has direct access to the King,' I said.

Pentu cleared his throat stiffly.

'As the Chief Physician of the North and the South, only I have access directly to the King. No other physician may be in his presence unless I am there also. All treatments are authorized and prescribed by me. Of course, we are also charged with the care of the Queen and the other members of the royal family, and with that of all members of the royal quarters, including the servants.'

'You said other members of the royal family. Who else is there, apart from the Queen?'

He glanced at Khay.

'I meant by that members of the extended families who serve the King and Queen,' he replied, with a curious indifference.

'How many physicians are affiliated to the palace?'

'All physicians in the Two Lands are under my ultimate authority. There are only a few of us who are fully competent in all aspects of the mysteries, but there are specialists of the eye, either the left or the right, the belly, the teeth, the anus, and the hidden organs, who can be called upon instantly as required.'

'And as I understand it, there are distinctions between the different professional hierarchies?'

'*Obviously* there are distinctions. Don't you think it is important to discriminate between marketplace bone-setters, and those of us with academic training and knowledge of the books, which qualify us to administer proper healing through plants and magic?' he hissed.

'I am intrigued about these books,' I said.

'You may be intrigued, but they are secret books, that is the whole point.'

I smiled, pleasantly.

'I apologize. Is the King receiving any treatment at the moment? Apart from the curative water?'

'He is strong, physically, and his health is perfect; but I have also prescribed a sleeping potion. He has suffered a severe shock. He must rest before tomorrow. He must not be disturbed. I will sit with him throughout this night.'

Simut had made sure this time the security of the royal quarters made it into a sealed sanctum. At every turn of the corridors, pairs of guards were stationed. And when we arrived at the chamber itself, there were two guards on either side of the door, and two others stationed opposite them. The doors were closed, but Pentu quietly opened them, and gestured for me to look briefly within.

The King's temporary bedchamber was lit with oil lamps; they were set in the wall niches, and on the floor, and in even greater numbers around his bed, so that he appeared like a young god in a constellation of lights. The candles were lit to banish the darkness of the world around him, but they looked weak against such threatening, dangerous forces. Ankhesenamun was holding her husband's hand, and talking quietly to him. I saw the intimacy between them, how she made him feel safe, and secure, and how she was the braver and the more powerful one of the pair. But I still could not imagine how such a delicate couple could, tomorrow, assume authority from demagogues and dictators of ambition such as Ay and Horemheb. However, I knew I would prefer Ankhesenamun's rule to either of theirs. And I knew she was clever. They had underestimated her. She had watched and learned from their example, and perhaps too she had now learned some of the absolute ruthlessness she would need in order to survive in this labyrinth of monsters. They both looked up for a moment, and saw me framed in the doorway. I bowed my head. Tutankhamun, Lord of the Two Lands, stared at me coldly, then flicked his hand with a gesture of dismissal.

Pentu closed the door in my face.

20

I hurried to meet Khety in the quarter of the town where men go after their hard day's work in the offices of the bureaucracies. It was long past our arranged meeting time; the only light in the ways and lanes came from the small windows of the houses where oil lamps had been lit. The narrow passageways were full of drunken men, bureaucrats and labourers, some hurrying silently, furtively; others in vociferous groups, calling and shouting to each other as they lurched from place to place. Girls with their breasts displayed, and slim, sly boys, and some who could have been either, threaded through, brushing against the men, and glancing back over their shoulders as they passed into shady doorways that led to the tiny curtained cubicles where they worked their trade. One of them accosted me.

'I can teach you such pleasures as you cannot imagine,' she offered, in a worn-out voice.

I found the low, anonymous doorway in a long mud-brick wall that ran off the main thoroughfare. Past the thick doorkeeper and his thick door, I went down the passageway. Usually these places are a warren of airless, low rooms, their ceilings besmirched with many nights of black tallow smoke, but this one was very different. I found myself in a series of rooms and courtyards. The quality of everything was luxurious: high-quality wall paintings, very good art, and the best tapestries hung on the walls. The place had the rich sheen of success; and it was thronged with fashionable, successful men, their acolytes and female attendants, drinking and talking – roaring with opinion, laughter and contempt over jugs of beer and goblets of wine, and plates piled with excellent food. Faces swam in and out of my vision: a painted woman in expensive robes braying like a mule, her eyes thrilled; an older, red-faced man with his mouth wide open like a baby screaming; and a young man's tough, greasy, thin profile, hidden in a corner, not talking to anyone, but watching everything, waiting for his opportunity, a hyena at the feast.

On the walls were paintings of copulation: men and women, men and men, men and boys, women and women. Each figure wore a cartoon grin of ecstasy, sketched in a few lines of red and black. Inconceivably massive cocks jutted. Various penetrations occurred. I had seen such things circulated on confiscated satirical papyri, but not reproduced on a larger scale.

Khety was waiting for me. I ordered a jug of wine from the middle-aged servant whose blotched, pallid skin looked as if it had not seen sunlight for many years.

'I've been drinking very, very slowly,' he said, to remind me how late I was.

'Top marks for self-discipline, Khety.'

We found a corner, and both turned our backs on the crowds, not wanting our presence to register more than it must – for no Medjay officer walks carelessly into a place like this. There were plenty of rich men, whose businesses were less than orthodox, who would frequent such a place, and perhaps take great pleasure in confronting law-keepers such as Khety and me, in a place where we could count on few friends.

The wine arrived. As I expected it was over-priced and under-whelming. I tried to adjust to the strange adjacency of the two worlds:

the Malkata Palace with its silent stone corridors, and its elite characters in their hushed drama of power and betrayal, and this playground of noisy nightlife. I suppose the same things were going on in both places – the nightly demand of male desire, and the supply of satisfactions.

'Any more leads?' I said.

'I've been asking around. It's tough because these kids come from all over the kingdom now. Some of them are slaves or prisoners, while others are just desperate to escape and make their way to the golden streets of the city from whatever fly-infested nowhere they call home. Most come on the promises of a recruiter in their local area, but many are even sold by their own families. Babylonians, Assyrians, Nubians . . . if they're lucky they end up in Thebes or Memphis.'

'Or, if they're unlucky, somewhere less romantic, a garrison town like Bubastis or Elephantine,' I said. 'They don't last long anywhere. All they've got to offer is their beauty and their freshness. But once that's passed . . . they're only fit for the human junk-heap.'

I looked around, and saw in the young faces the damage caused by servicing all these demanding clients, night after night. Desperate, sunny faces smiling too widely, too deliberately, trying too hard to please; pretty girls and pretty boys like living dolls on the knees of the repulsive-looking men who could afford new flesh every week, or once a year. Everyone looked exaggerated and wild. A young woman with ruined eyes walked past us; her nose had been cut off. She looked as if she moved on invisible strings worked by an invisible puppet-master. She drifted away through the crowds.

'But interestingly, many of them also carry illicit drugs across the borders or downriver as part of the deal. It's a cheap delivery method. Everyone knows it happens, and individually the amounts are too small to bother with; and the border guards are bribed, or they'll take a quick fuck as a backhander, and even when the odd few are caught for show, the profit far outweighs the loss.'

'What a beautiful world this is,' I said.

Khety chuckled.

'It could do with some improvement.'

'It's getting worse,' I said gloomily.

'You always say that. You wouldn't know what to say if something good actually happened,' he replied, with his usual aggravating optimism. 'You're more miserable than Thoth, and he's a dumb animal,' he replied.

'Thoth is not miserable. Nor is he remotely as dumb as most of the two-legged creatures around here. He is thoughtful.'

I drank my wine.

'Who owns this place?'

He shrugged.

'Whoever owns most of this quarter of the city. Probably one of the big families, connected with the temples, who no doubt take a big percentage of the profits.'

I nodded. It was well known that the temples' enormous wealth depended upon varied and very profitable business investments throughout the city and the nomes of the kingdom.

'And who are we meeting?'

'The manager. She's a smart woman.'

'I'm sure she has a heart of gold.'

We made our way through the braying crowds, past the blind musicians plucking at their instruments, despite the fact that no one was listening, and then slipped down a silent passageway lit by a few oil lamps.

Off this ran other passageways, with elegant curtains concealing spaces big enough for a comfortable mattress. Fat old men retreated into the cubicles to avoid us, and small girls and giggling boys slipped past like silly, ornamental fish. Despite the incense burning everywhere, the air was stale, tinged with human odours: sweat, tainted breath, stale feet and rank armpits. Somewhere someone was panting and groaning, in another cubicle a girl was sweet-talking and giggling, and from another a woman performed, low-pitched and ardent as a court singer. Further off I heard the splash of water, and laughter.

At the end was a door, and outside the door stood two thugs as big and expressionless and ugly as unfinished statues. They searched us wordlessly.

'Can anyone smell onions?' I said, catching a whiff of rank breath.

The thug who was patting me down paused for a moment. His face reminded me of a battered cooking-pot. The other thug put a thick, calming hand on his colleague's broad shoulder, advising him with a wordless shake of the head to ignore my sarcasm. The thug snorted like a bull, then pointed a stubby finger right between my eyes. I smiled and pushed it away. The other guy knocked on the door.

We entered. The room was low and small, but mitigated by a vase of fresh lotus flowers on the table. The manager greeted us politely and distantly. She wore a long auburn wig in the latest style, but her fine, sculpted face was still, almost frozen, as if she had long forgotten the uses of a smile. She offered us stools and cushions. She elegantly arranged herself opposite us, her chin in her hand, and waited for what would come.

'Please tell me your name.'

'Takherit,' she replied, clearly.

So she was Syrian.

'I am Rahotep.'

She nodded and waited.

'This is an inquiry, that's all. You have no personal cause for concern.'

'I feel none,' she replied, coolly.

'We are investigating a series of murders.'

She raised her eyebrows in a little mocking gesture of anticipation. 'How thrilling.'

'These slayings have been unusually brutal. No one deserves to die in the way these young people have done. I want to try to stop any more perishing in the same manner,' I replied.

'In these dark times people prefer to look away from everything they would rather not see,' she said, evasively. Her tone was so flat I could not tell whether she spoke with a rich irony, or with none.

'I want you to understand how serious this is.'

I threw the dead face, with its tarnished crown of black hair, on to the table in front of her.

Her face remained frozen, but something altered in her gaze; a reaction, at last, to the blunt facts before us. She shook her red hair.

'Only a monster could do this to a woman.'

'What he has done is cruel, but it is almost certainly not meaningless. This is not some unpremeditated act of violence or passion. This man kills for reasons and in ways that are meaningful to him, if to no one else. It is a question of discovering the meaning,' I said.

'In that case, there are no monsters.'

'No, only people.'

'I don't know if that makes me feel better, or worse,' she replied.

'I sympathize,' I replied. 'We need to discover who this girl was. We thought she might have worked here.'

'Perhaps she did. We have many girls who work here.'

'But have you missed anyone in particular?'

'Sometimes these kids just vanish. It happens all the time. No one cares what happens to them. There are always more.'

I leaned forward.

'This girl died a horrible death. The least we can do is call her by her name. She had a snake tattoo on her upper arm. Her landlord told us her name was Neferet.'

She glanced at the face, considered me, and nodded.

'Then yes, I knew her. She worked here. I didn't know much about her. You can never believe the stories they tell. But she struck me as one of the more innocent and trusting of the girls. She had a strange, sad smile. It made her even more attractive to some of our clients. She seemed like she belonged to a better world than this one. She claimed she was stolen from her family, who loved her, and one day she was sure they would come for her . . .'

'She did not say where she was from?'

'A farming village north of Memphis, I think. I can't remember the name.'

'We can assume she met the killer here. That means he is a client. He is an older man, from the elite class. Educated. Possibly a physician.'

She gazed at me.

'Do you know how many men like that pay their discreet visits to places like this? And in any case, my workers are instructed never to ask questions about the clients' personal lives.'

I tried another line of inquiry.

'Are there any clients or workers who use drugs on these premises?'

'What kind of drugs?' she asked, innocently.

'Soporific drugs. The opium poppy . . .'

She pretended to think about it.

'We would accept no one who was notorious for it. I do all in my power to prevent such things. I run a clean business.'

'But these drugs are everywhere . . .'

'I cannot be held responsible for the private behaviour and the inclinations of my clients,' she replied, firmly.

'But they must acquire the drug somehow,' I said.

She shrugged, avoiding my eyes.

'There are always merchants, and middlemen, and suppliers. As with any business, especially where there is gold to be made.'

I glanced at Khety.

'I have long been puzzled by how it is possible for such popular demand to be satisfied. I mean, the number of young people who are apprehended as they make the journey across the borders is small, therefore many must make it successfully to places just like this in each city. It is a route of supply, direct and convenient, and low risk.

We know that the kids who come here to work are carriers. And yet even if there were thousands of them, they could still not transport a sufficient quantity of such a highly desirable luxury to satisfy the demand. It is a mystery to me.'

She dropped her gaze.

'As I said, I do not involve myself in such things.'

I watched her carefully. I realized her pupils were dilated. She saw me looking.

'It would be no trouble for me to bring a team of Medjay officers down here to search the place. I doubt many of your clients would appreciate the exposure,' I said.

'And I doubt you realize how few would appreciate your doing such a stupid thing. Who do you think comes here? Our clients are from the highest levels of society. They would never allow a low-level officer, such as you, to cause any trouble.'

She shook her head and stood up, ringing a tiny bell. The door opened and the two thugs stood there, not smiling.

'These gentlemen are leaving now,' she said.

We had left quietly enough, but once we were outside, the thugs looked at each other, nodded, then the one I had teased punched me once, very hard. I confess it was accurate, and it hurt. The other one punched Khety less viciously, just to be equitable.

'Don't be so sensitive,' I said, rubbing my jaw, as they slammed the door. We stood in the dismal and suddenly silent street.

'Don't you dare to tell me I deserved that,' I said to Khety.

'Fine, I won't,' he replied.

We set off into the darkness.

'So,' said Khety, 'how does all that stuff enter the Two Lands? It can't possibly be managed just through these kids.'

I shook my head.

'I think these kids, these couriers, are a distraction. They're irrelevant. The transportation and shipping must happen in much greater quantities. But if it comes in on ships, then harbour officials are bribed, and if it comes by land routes the border guards would be getting a backhander.'

'Someone, somewhere is making a fortune,' he said. 'But whoever it is must be very powerful and very well-connected.'

I sighed.

'Some days this work we do feels like holding back the waters of the Great River with nothing but our bare hands.'

'I wonder about that almost every morning,' replied Khety. 'But then I get up and go to work. And of course, I get to spend my time with you, which is some compensation.'

'You are a very lucky man, Khety,' I said. 'But think: at least the connections are becoming clearer. Each murder has involved stupefying the victims, most likely with the drug. The girl worked here. Most likely the carriers deliver the drugs here. Probably they are distributed from places like this throughout the city. That is something.'

'And remember also that the killer is keeping you dancing between two worlds,' he said, and smiled wryly.

If we were right, and the same man was responsible for both crimes, then all I was doing was leaping from clue to clue, like a dog following a trail of food, eyes focused on the ground, not seeing anything else.

I bade Khety goodnight, and turned wearily away towards my own home for once.

21

The white sun of late morning exonerated nothing and no one from its terrible gaze. The city seemed baked hard and dry, brown, yellow and white, in the heat. I looked up; swooping in and out of the dazzle, I saw a falcon's dark wings spread wide, making delicate adjustments as it drifted on the levels and currents of the hot desert air. He was Horus, with the right eye of the sun and the left eye of the moon. What did he see, staring down at our strange little world of statues and monsters, crowds and parades, temples and hovels, wealth and pigsties? What would he think of this ceremonial group of tiny figures, protected by feeble sunshades, making its slow, formal way along the Avenue of Sphinxes, lined with perfectly clipped trees, towards the southern temple? Did he notice me, dressed like a performer in the white robes of a priest? Did he see us all, in our green world of fields and trees, dependent on the glittering serpent of the Great River, and surrounded by the infinity of the eternal Red Land? What did he see beyond the horizon? I watched as he lingered above us for a long moment, then shrugged and tilted away in the direction of the river, before disappearing over the rooftops.

I had slept badly, again. I had dreamed of the boy. In the dream he wore the face of Neferet, the young girl, and she was smiling at me mysteriously. Then slowly, carefully, I began to peel off her face, but she continued to smile. And when I finally pulled her face off over the top of her head, I saw beneath only a mask of darkness, and smelt the sweet stench of decay. I had woken suddenly, my head pounding. Perhaps the rough wine from the night before had been even rougher than I thought. In the morning I had had no sympathy from Tanefert. And when I had returned from the barber with my head shaved, she had just shaken her head.

'How do I look?' I had asked, smoothing my hand over my polished scalp.

'You look like a big baby,' she had said, unhelpfully.

'Not like a priest of the temple, then?'

To her credit, she had laughed out loud.

'I don't think so . . . And don't come home until it has all grown back.'

Along the Avenue of Sphinxes, well-managed crowds stood mutely and in conformity in the searing stillness of the air, crying out praises as the King and Queen passed by in their chariot. Tutankhamun was wearing the Blue Crown, and was carefully surrounded by a tight phalanx of palace guards, headdress feathers nodding bright in the light, bows and arrows polished and glittering. Theban army soldiers stood all along the Avenue. Simut was doing his job, using all the resources under his command. Ay followed in his chariot. Simut and I rode together. He watched everything with intense attention for any detail out of place, any sign of a problem. Then came a long, shuffling train of many other palace officials and priests, Khay among them, all in identical white robes, each with their sweating servants holding sunshades over their masters. I noticed a street dog running along beside this strangely sombre cavalcade, roving in and out of the shadows of the trees and the marching soldiers. He barked and barked, baring his teeth as if he had seen the shadow of an enemy, or an intruder. Suddenly one of the Theban soldiers shot it dead with an arrow. The crowd turned in fear; but no one panicked, and the cavalcade continued.

By the time the procession arrived at the temple entrance, sweat was running down my spine. A linen awning had been set up before the huge double doors, decorated with gold and silver, which led to the new Colonnade Hall. The King's grandfather had begun its construction in my own youth, with an ambitious plan to replace the warren of small, ancient shrines with what was to be a vast, dark modern structure, with towering stone columns big enough to hold crowds of people on their broad tops. It was to be the wonder of the world, and today I would be exceptionally privileged to see it with my own eyes.

The area before the temple was crowded with thousands of priests in robes – so many they made the immense open space look like a great white lake when they prostrated themselves. The temple musicians struck up a new rhythm and melody. Simut's gaze was everywhere, considering all the contingencies, checking the position of his archers on the perimeter walls, the precise formation of his guards that flanked the King and Queen in protection, and examining everyone and everything with his dark eyes. This time there could be no mistakes, no surprises of blood, and no mass panic.

Finally, to a fanfare from the temple trumpets, raised and shining in the light, we processed through the great doors, under the huge carved stones of the outer walls, and into the great colonnade. My first impression was of a realm of shadows. Perfectly carved columns, of a much greater circumference than any palm tree – of the circumference of ten trees – soared up into the cool, dark, mysterious air; fourteen of them, in two great rows, each perhaps thirty cubits high, holding up the massive roof span, like a colossal arcade of stone under a night sky of granite. Thin shafts of light slanted down from the high, narrow clerestory windows, in slices and slivers of intense brightness; insubstantial motes drifted and danced for a brief instant of glory. Wherever the intense light touched the stone, it illuminated the detail of the painted carvings that covered every surface.

The long train of dignitaries and officials shuffled in behind us, all gathering, pushing and complaining to find a place to stand under the vast columns. The grand architecture of the hall made them seem diminished and unimportant. They sounded like a herd of goats, breathing, coughing, shuffling and whispering their little comments of amazement at their first view of this new wonder. Yet these were the men who controlled the power and the glory of the kingdom. The men of the royal domain, the men of the bureaucracies, and the men of the temples; all those who had lost their power and wealth under Akhenaten, the King's father, and now had it back, claiming to have restored *maat* to the Two Lands. Of course, what had truly been restored was their implacable authority and licence to control and develop the infinite resources and business opportunities of the lands for the benefit of their own treasuries. And the King himself, however passively, was the icon of this restoration. In another temple precinct, at the Karnak Temple, early in his reign, he had ordered – or rather, Ay had ordered in his name – a stone stela to be set up on which was carved a statement for all time, and its words were well-known: '*The land was turned upside down and the Gods had turned their backs on the entire land. But after many days my majesty rose upon the throne of his father and ruled over the territory of Horus, both the Black Land and the Red Land being under his control.*' And so it now seemed, for what was left unfinished by the grandfather was completed in the presence of the grandson; and that strange interregnum of Akhenaten had become a piece of great forgetting, his buildings unattended, his images ignored, his name unspoken, his memory unworshipped, as if he had never been. Only the memory of his religious enlightenment, and his attempt to take all power from the traditional priests, remained, repressed but powerful for many.

The royal group were invited to examine the wall carvings that ran all along the length of the new, enclosing walls. Priests held up torches, or gathered together in groups so that their white robes reflected and enhanced the slanting light, to reveal the detail of the brightly painted raised relief work where it lay obscured in the darkness. The flickering flames seemed to make the colourful images move. I worked hard to keep my position close to the King and Queen, but also because I was curious to see these wonders. Firstly, by the entrance, a strong ray of sunlight, by coincidence or contrivance, illuminated the carved features of the King himself. I watched as he stood before his carved stone image greeting the God of the temple. Tutankhamun, flesh and blood, with his childish fears and delicate face, assessed his stone reflection, which bore the wide shoulders and decisive, authoritative gestures of a King. I must confess here they looked unalike, but for the carefully rendered similarities of the profile and the ears.

Everyone moved on, shuffling along the long west wall. Here were carvings describing the water procession of the Gods to Karnak during the Opet Festival. Here were the agile acrobats and the barges with their rigging observed in minute detail, and the blind musicians with their instruments. It seemed each face was a portrait of an individual I might have recognized in a crowd. I wondered if my own face, and those of my family, might also be among them.

Then, with much jostling and tension, the royal group, attended by the officials and servants, moved across to the opposite wall, which continued the story of the festival. Tutankhamun and the Queen moved slowly along, reading the images carefully, as they listened to the High Priest and his acolytes who leaned respectfully towards them, whispering praises and information, no doubt alluding to the astonishing cost and the remarkable statistics of this great work of the temple's glorification to the King's and the Gods' images. The event was following its ordained course.

They returned towards the entrance, and were invited to examine the last register of the wall carvings near the corner, describing the most important scene – in which the King entered the presence of the God within the shrine – when something happened.

Tutankhamun was reading through the inscriptions of this most holy moment, under the direction of the High Priest – when suddenly he stepped backwards in alarm. The High Priest, profoundly shocked and ashamed, held his own hands up before his eyes, as if he had witnessed an appalling desecration. Instantly the palace guard moved into a defensive posture around the royal party, bristling with drawn curved daggers. Behind me, people craned their necks to see what was going on. I pushed my way forward, through the guards. Ay was already scrutinizing the carving the High Priest was pointing to with his staff. He allowed me to stand close to him, in order to examine it. In a cartouche, the King's royal names had been completely erased.

Ay took charge. He spoke quietly to Tutankhamun, who was trembling, while Ankhesenamun tried to help him drink water. He ordered the desecrated carving to be concealed from view, and strictly instructed all those who had seen it never to speak of it on pain of death. The names would be re-carved immediately. Ankhesenamun was whispering into Tutankhamun's ear, and finally he nodded. Then, pretending all was well, the royal party continued with the tour. As she passed by, Ankhesenamun glanced at me. But we could not speak.

We all moved quickly back through the Colonnade Hall, between the great columns, and onwards into the Sun Court, where more crowds of priests had gathered and prostrated themselves in the sunlight of midday, dazzling after the soaring darkness, before the King and Queen. The procession stayed within the high shade of the great papyrus columns that ran along three sides. We walked around the Court in a strange hush – for everyone now knew something troubling had happened, and yet the ceremony continued as if nothing had changed. From there we entered the oldest part of the temple. I found myself in an ancient darkness. Everywhere the carved image of the old King Amenhotep dominated, making offerings to Amun-Ra, God of the temple and the city. The royal party continued through a pillared offering chamber. Along the walls, carved into the eternity of the stone, Amenhotep drove the sacred cattle, and made the ritual offerings of flowers and incense in the place where the gold barque of the God would rest during the festival. Beyond this point I had heard there were many small chapels leading from the Divine Sanctuary, and even smaller antechambers along the side walls, where, folded in deep shadows, stood images of the Gods fashioned in gold. But neither I nor almost any other man could continue beyond this point. Only the King and the highest-ranking priests could enter the Sanctuary of Amun himself at the dark heart of the temple, where his statue, which gave him earthly presence among men, was worshipped, fed and robed.

This was the moment, and Tutankhamun had to go forward alone into the mystery of the Sanctuary. Ankhesenamun could accompany him into the antechamber, but no further. He looked nervous, but seemed to take courage. Ankhesenamun and the King moved forward and disappeared together, and all was silence.

Rich drifts of incense and sweat rose up from the heat of all those human bodies crowded into the small chamber, and in the Sun Court behind us. Prayers were intoned by ranks of priests. Sistra were shaken, tinnily. The temple chantresses intoned the hymns. Time seemed to stretch on and on . . . I saw Ay raise his head slightly, as if wondering whether all was well.

And then suddenly the King and Queen reappeared together. He had exchanged the Blue Crown for the Double Crown of Upper and Lower Egypt. The vulture and the cobra flared in divine protection from his brow. She was wearing the high double-plumed crown that her mother Nefertiti had worn – and in doing so she proclaimed herself as the Queen as Goddess. Far from looking tentative or frightened, Tutankhahmun now stared arrogantly ahead over the amazed crowd of priests and dignitaries gathered in the vestibule, and beyond that in the Sun Court. He waited, and then in his quiet, intense voice he spoke.

'The Gods have revealed themselves to Tutankhamun, Living

171

Image of Amun, in the Temple of Amun. I possess the royal names: the Horus name, Strong Bull, Most Fitting of Created Forms, King of Upper and Lower Egypt, Possessor of the Forms of Ra, Ruler of Truth. In these, my royal names, I wear the Double Crown and I hold the crook of government and the flail of Osiris. I declare from this day I am King in name and deed.'

Names are powers. They bring forth into reality that which they declare. This was a declaration of a new policy of independence. A new coronation. A stir of amazement and awe followed this astonishing, unexpected pronouncement. I would have given gold to behold Ay's face as he listened to these words. But his bony head remained bowed.

The King continued: 'Let this be proclaimed throughout the Two Lands. I declare I will celebrate this day with a new festival in the sacred name of Amun-Ra. Let this be recorded for ever in the writing of the Gods, and let these words go forth in writing throughout all the nomes of the Two Lands so that every subject of the Great House may know this great truth.'

The official scribes hurried forward with their palettes and sat cross-legged, their kilts stretched out over their knees like little tables, and wrote everything down swiftly on their open scrolls.

As I now realized they must have rehearsed many times, Ankhesenamun then rose and joined Tutankhamun, and they remained standing together while the crowd slowly absorbed the revelation and the implications of his words, and then got down on their knees to prostrate themselves. I wondered how Ay would respond to this audacious move in the great game of power. He turned to the multitude of faces, which were alert with anticipation that he would not accept such a demotion without a fight. But he was more intelligent than that. After a long, careful pause, as if it was he who held the destiny of the Two Lands in his hands, he spoke.

'The Gods are all-knowing,' he said. 'We who have laboured all our lives to support and strengthen the Great House, and to restore lost

172

order to the Two Lands, celebrate this proclamation. The King is King. May the Gods make him a great King.'

The scribes wrote this down, too, and on a signal from Ay they passed their scrolls swiftly, hand to hand, down the chamber. They were then taken off by assistants, to be copied and distributed everywhere throughout the land and the dominions, in scrolls and on carved stone stele. And then he led the crowd, prostrating himself before the royal couple like an elderly monster before his children, slowly and stiffly, and with the dangerous irony only he seemed to be able to insinuate into everything he did. Ankhesenamun and Tutankhamun had gambled everything on this moment, and on the success of their declaration. The next days would decide whether they had won, or lost.

22

The King and Queen processed out of the temple complex, back through the Sun Court, where the priests abased themselves on the carefully swept ground, through the colonnade and into their waiting chariot, which drove them swiftly away in a brief blaze of gold.

Before I followed them, to depart with Simut in his chariot, I looked back at the crowded area before the Colonnade Hall, and saw Ay standing at the centre of everything, watching us all go, still as a stone. It seemed as if waves of fervent speculation and excitement were breaking and spreading throughout the multitude all around him. The news would very quickly be communicated everywhere in the city, to the bureaucracies and the offices, the granaries and the treasuries; and the official proclamation would follow in Thebes, and then by messengers directed to all the major cities and towns – to Memphis, Abydos, Heliopolis and Bubastis, or south to Elephantine and the garrison towns of Nubia.

We followed the royal chariot back to the river, where a great crowd had gathered, shouting prayers and acclamations, and then swiftly boarded the royal ship for the river crossing. The King and Queen remained in their private enclosure. The curtain was drawn. As we set off across the water, and as the cries from the dockside faded, I could hear them talking quietly to each other; the words were not audible, but I caught the tone of her voice, calming and encouraging his more querulous one.

When the ship docked at the palace, the royal couple disembarked and were quickly surrounded by a protective phalanx of palace guards. They hurried inside as if sunlight itself was dangerous.

Khay accompanied Simut and me along, talking quickly. For once he looked excited.

'Ay will be incensed!' he whispered eagerly. 'He didn't see this coming.'

'But *you* did,' I said.

'Well, I flatter myself to say I have been the beneficiary of the Queen's confidences. She would not have made this move in the great game without first establishing her network of support among those close to her.'

And she would need it, I thought. Ay gripped the Two Lands by the throat; he still ruled the priesthood, the bureaucracies and the treasury. Horemheb controlled the army.

'But that was very nearly another catastrophe. How could it have happened? It must be investigated immediately. Fortunately, it did not prevent the King making his proclamation,' Khay said.

Simut bristled.

'The Chief Architect is being brought here for questioning, even now.'

'And you, Rahotep, are no closer to discovering the culprit, who seems to have the freedom of not only the royal quarters but now also the Colonnade Hall within the bounds of the sacred temple itself!' said Khay, as if now was the time for accusations to be shared equally among us.

'We are fighting a shadow,' I said.

'Which means precisely nothing,' he scoffed, irritatingly.

'What matters is understanding how this man thinks. Everything he does is a clue to his mind. So we must read each situation carefully, and try to decipher and understand its meanings. The problem is: all

175

our efforts at controlling the situation are undermined by the disruption he is carefully creating amongst us. To him it is a kind of elegant game. He challenges us to understand him, to make sense of him, and then to catch him. So far we have been successful in none of these things. We have hardly even begun to take him seriously. Or perhaps we have taken him too seriously, for if we ignored all of these acts, what power would he really have?'

'You sound like a warrior admiring his enemy,' replied Khay sarcastically.

'I can respect his intelligence and skill without admiring or respecting the uses to which he puts them.'

Ankhesenamun and Tutankhamun were waiting for us in a reception chamber, seated upon two thrones of state. The atmosphere was heady with euphoria, but there was also a tangible edge of anxiety, for everything had not gone quite perfectly.

Khay, Simut and I offered our formal congratulations.

Tutankhamun gazed at us all intently.

'Bow your heads before me,' he suddenly shouted, standing up. 'How is it possible that I should be so humiliated *again*? How is it that there is still no safety for me, even in my own *temple*?'

We all waited, our heads bowed.

'Husband,' said Ankhesenamun, quickly. 'Let us consider our options. Let us take good advice from these trusted men.'

He sat back down on his small throne.

'Look up.'

We did.

'None of you has been able to protect me from all these perils. But I have had an idea. I think it is a very fine idea. It may, in fact, solve all our problems at once.'

We waited with what must have been a mixture of emotions on our faces.

'In what time-honoured fashion does a new King proclaim his

power and courage but in a lion hunt? We have proclaimed ourselves King. Therefore what better means of proving our fitness to the people than for me to go into the Red Land and hunt, and return with the trophy of a lion?' he continued.

It was Khay who spoke first.

'A masterstroke, of course,' he began, very carefully. 'It would create a most positive image for the public. But lord, have you considered how it exposes you to great danger?'

'And what is new about that? Here in my own quarters, which are supposedly secure, supposedly safe, there is still greater danger,' he said petulantly.

Ankhesenamun placed her hand gently on the King's.

'May I speak?' she asked.

He nodded.

'It seems to me the success of kingship is in great part dependent upon the carefully managed display of the powers and virtues of that kingship, in the person of the King. Parades of victory, rituals of triumph, and so on are the means by which we represent to the people the glory of kingship. Therefore, if the King were to be well-protected, a symbolic hunt, conducted within one of the great hunting enclosures, could be most useful at this time,' she said.

'That is a marvellous compromise,' said Khay immediately. 'Such an event can quickly be organized within the safety of the hunting park. A lion, some wild deer too, perhaps . . .' he continued, hopefully.

But the King's face clouded.

'No. Ritual is not enough. Prowess must be manifested. What dignity is there in killing a lion that has already been captured, and cannot escape? I must be seen to kill a lion. And it must take place in the wilderness that is its territory. I must be seen to assert my royal authority over the land of chaos. There must be nothing symbolic about it,' he replied.

This silenced all of us.

Now it was Simut's turn to speak. He was less diplomatic.

177

'In the hunting enclosure we can control the environment. We can ensure your safety. But in the desert lies great danger.'

'He is right,' said Ankhesenamun. 'What matters, surely, is the spectacle?'

But Tutankhamun shook his head.

'Everyone will know all I have done is kill a trapped beast. That is not the right gesture with which to begin my kingship. I am a good hunter. I will prove myself. We *will* go to the desert.'

Khay tried again.

'Has your majesty considered that, in order to reach the hunting grounds to the north-west or the north-east we will have to pass Memphis? Perhaps that is not very ... *desirable*. After all, it is Horemheb's city, and the base of the army itself,' he murmured, uncertain how he should be saying this.

Tutankhamun stood up again, leaning carefully on his gold cane.

'A royal visit to Memphis is *most* desirable at this time. We intend to take Horemheb closer to our hearts. He is an old ally, and in case any of you have forgotten, he was my tutor in Memphis. He has been too long engaged in the Hittite wars. We shall travel with all due ostentation. It is necessary for me to appear there, now more than ever, *because* it is Horemheb's city. I must make my presence and my new authority clear. And when that is accomplished, I will return in triumph to Thebes, and parade my victory through the Ways of the city, and everyone will know, and acknowledge, that Tutankhamun is King not only in name but also in deed.'

The consequences and ramifications of all this multiplied in our minds. Ankhesenamun spoke again:

'The King is right. He must be seen to be King, and to do the things kings must do. This is most necessary, and must be done. But we must request one important thing. This is my personal request . . .'

She looked directly at me.

'Will you, Rahotep, accompany the King? You and Simut will be jointly responsible for his safety.'

How had I ended up, after all, holding the shortest of straws? How had I got myself so far into this situation that there was no choice but to go forward? I thought back to Ankhesenamun's first plea, her appeal based on need and fear. I decided not to think yet about the recriminations, the consequences of all of this, at home.

I bowed my head. Simut glanced at me, and then nodded in agreement.

'We will need a well-trained and completely trustworthy team. But let us take a small one, without extravagance or unnecessary ostentation: a cook, trackers, servants, and a select handful of guards. They must all have been vetted for security by the offices of the palace, as well as by the treasury. By which I mean Ay himself,' I said.

'That is a sensible suggestion,' said Ankhesenamun, 'for then we implicate the Regent in the arrangements, rather than excluding him; for in his exclusion he is more dangerous.'

Khay realized he had no choice but to agree.

'I will make all the necessary security arrangements for the visit to Memphis with Simut,' he said.

'Excellent,' said Tutankhamun. He clapped his hands together. And I realized that for the first time he actually looked happy.

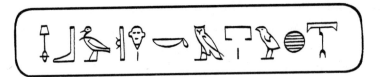

23

The house seemed deserted when I arrived home. I realized how rare it was for me to find myself inside in the daytime. I felt like a stranger, as men do sometimes in their own households. I called out a greeting, but only Thoth responded to the sound of my voice, and came to me, his tail raised.

I found Tanefert watering the plants on the roof. I stood quietly at the top of the stairs, under the portico, for a little while, just watching her as she moved among the pots, self-possessed, self-absorbed. She has a few strands of silver in her midnight hair, which she refuses, rightly, to dye or to pluck out. We have been together for so many years; their number is greater than those of my life before I met her. I realize how lucky I have been. My life before seems a faint dream of another world; and the life since then a new story, with our girls, now almost young women, and the late surprise of my son.

She put down the watering can and stretched her back; her many bracelets glittered as they sifted and tinkled down her soft skin. I thought for a moment they were like the years we have been together, because I had given her one every year, on our marriage anniversary.

Then she realized I was standing there. She smiled questioningly at the strangeness of my appearing here at this hour. I moved over to her. We stood together, side by side, my arm around her shoulder, looking out at the view of the city, in silence. It was late afternoon, the sun had moved across the Great River, and now hung above the western bank. From here we could see all the roofs of our quarter crammed with washing hung out in the heat, and the vegetables drying on racks, and bits of discarded or reused furniture, and birdcages.

'Your plants are flourishing,' I offered, tentatively, to break the silence.

'All they need is water and sun, and a little bit of attention . . .'

She gave me one of her meaningful looks, but said nothing more. She had read my face instantly, as she always does. She was not going to let me off lightly. She waited, playing with a brown, curling leaf.

I wondered how best to broach the subject.

'I have to go away for a few days.'

She continued to gaze out at the horizon, enjoying the fresh, light breeze from the north. She shook her fine black hair loose, and it hung about her face for a moment before she smoothed it back again into a glossy knot.

I gently turned her towards me, and held her. But she was tense within my embrace.

'Don't try to make it all right. I'm afraid.'

I held her closer, and she relaxed a little.

'Nothing in the world means more to me than you and the children. Khety has orders to watch over you all, and to help you if you need anything.'

She nodded.

'How long will you be gone?'

'Perhaps ten days . . . no more than fifteen at most.'

'That's what you said last time. And you promised not to do it again.'

'I'm sorry. Believe me, I have no choice.'

She gave me one of her darkest looks.

'There is always a choice.'

'No, you are wrong. I don't feel I have any choices. I feel trapped by circumstances always beyond my control. And every step I take, in any direction, only takes me deeper and deeper into the trap.'

'And I fear the knock upon the door. I fear opening it to find some grim Medjay messenger standing there, with a formal expression on his face, preparing himself to give the bad news,' she replied.

'It won't happen. I can take care of myself.'

'You can't ever know that for certain. This world is too dangerous. And I know you never feel so alive as when you are at the heart of danger.'

I could say nothing.

'Where are you going?'

'Hunting.'

She laughed, despite herself.

'I'm serious. I'm accompanying the King to the hunting grounds, north of Memphis.'

Her face darkened again.

'Why?'

I took her down the stairs, and we sat in the shady quiet of our small courtyard. Thoth watched us from his corner. The sounds of the world – the street-sellers, children shouting, their mothers shouting back – came to us distantly. I told her everything.

'Ankhesenamun . . .'

'Yes?'

'Do you trust her?'

I hesitated, and she saw it.

'Be careful,' she said. And she was about to say more when the street door banged open, and I heard Thuyu and Nedjmet coming up the passageway, arguing about something of intense importance. Nedjmet threw herself heavily upon the dozing Thoth, who has learned to tolerate her clumsy embraces. Thuyu embraced us both, and balanced herself against my knees, while she ate a piece of fruit. I admired her sleek grace, and her shining hair.

Tanefert went to fetch them water. My middle daughter quickly told me what was on her mind.

'I'm not sure I will get married.'

'Why not?'

'Because I can write and think, and I can look after myself.'

'But that doesn't mean you won't meet someone who you can love . . .'

'But why would you choose to love just one person when there are so many people?'

I stroked her hair.

'Because love is a decision, my darling.'

She mulled this over.

'Everyone says they can't help themselves.'

'That's falling in love. True love itself is different.'

She wrinkled her face up doubtfully.

'Why is it different?'

At this point, Tanefert returned with the jug of water, and she poured out four cups, waiting for my answer.

'Falling in love is romantic and wonderful, and it's a very special time. That's when it feels like nothing else matters. But living in love, year after year, in true partnership, that's the real gift.'

Thuyu looked at both of us, raised her eyes to the heavens, and said: 'That just sounds so *old*.' And she laughed and drank her water.

Then the maid brought Amenmose out into the cooling air of the early evening, awake after his afternoon sleep. He held his arms out, dozily and grumpily, to be picked up; I swung him up on my shoulders so he could rattle the cages of the birds with his little stick. Soon he had them in an uproar of indignant song. I took him down then, and fed him some honey cake and water. Sekhmet returned, too, and joined us, taking her baby brother on her knee, and amusing him.

My father came home from his afternoon game of *senet*, which he plays with his old cronies. We greeted each other, and then he went to sit in his usual place on the bench, his lined face watching us from the shady corner. The girls sat with him, chatting away. Tanefert began to think about dinner, and issued her instructions to the maid, who bowed and disappeared into the storeroom. I set out a plate of figs, and poured my father and myself a small cup of wine each, from the Dakhla oasis.

'A libation to the Gods,' he said, raised his glass, and smiled with his wise gold eyes, observing Tanefert's quiet sadness.

I looked around at my family, gathered together in the courtyard of my house, on this ordinary evening, and I raised my own cup in libation to the Gods who have granted me the gift of such happiness. Surely my wife was right. Why would I risk all of this present, here and now, for the sake of the unknown? And yet it called to me, and I could not say no.

Part Two

To me belongs yesterday, I know tomorrow

The Book of the Dead
Spell 17

24

The sun had disappeared over the Malkata Palace's flat rooftops, and the last of the daylight was abandoning the valleys. The long, low plateau of the western desert glowed red and gold behind us. The great lake was eerily flat, its blackness silvered like polished obsidian, reflecting the dark sky, except when it was disturbed into languorous ripples by the occasional flop of an unseen catfish. The waning moon hung over everything like the curved hull of a white boat, in the deepening indigo of the sky where the first stars were beginning to appear. Servants lit lamps and torches all along the dock so that the place blazed with pools of shadowy, orange light.

All the necessities of a royal progress were slowly, laboriously loaded on to the great royal ship of state, the *Beloved of Amun*. Her long, elegant curves rose to the high, decorated prow and stern's carved finials, beautifully proportioned; detailed scenes decorating the kiosks showed the King trampling his enemies in battle; the great sails were furled, and the long oars were still suspended, tilted up against the cabins; surmounting the high mast-heads, royal falcons stretched their golden wings to the silver light of the moon. The whole construction seemed perfectly balanced upon the still waters of the lake. Docked next to her was another, almost as fine, the *Star of Thebes*.

Together they made a glorious pair, the most superior modes of transport yet devised by any civilization, perfected for every luxury and constructed with the deep knowledge of craftsmanship to take every advantage of the given elements of wind and water: the river currents that sweep perpetually down to the delta, or, returning, the reliable northern winds that blow us home.

I was worried. What I had hoped would prove a swift and relatively small-scale event, had become a problematic exercise in politics and appearances. I should have realized nothing would be simple. There had been confidential meetings, with arguments and correspondence back and forth, between the offices of the King, the security division, and almost every other department of government, about everything from the distraction of the King from the business and appearance of rule, to lengthy disputations between different ministries regarding the passenger list, the supplies, the necessary furniture and the official timetable. Everything had been an issue. But Ay had taken charge of the chaos. I had not seen him since the proclamation in the temple, but he seemed to support the idea of the hunt. It had also been decided that Ankhesenamun would remain in Thebes to represent the King's affairs in the business of government. Ay would also remain. Nothing he had done so far suggested he was other than supportive of the King's proclamation.

I was worried, too about the boy; Nakht told me his progress was very slow, and that I should expect no better. 'Accept the worst, be appeased by anything better, and treat success as an impostor,' he had advised me sententiously, when I had stopped at his city house to check on the boy's condition. The boy looked almost mummified in the splints and linen bandages with which my old friend was attempting to heal his terrible injuries. I had noticed the stitch marks around his face were, gratifyingly, scabbed and beginning to heal. Of course, he could not see, but when I spoke to him, I saw recognition in his face.

'Do you remember me?' I asked quietly.

He nodded.

'I have to go away, but I am leaving you in the care of this gentleman. His name is Nakht. He will care for you until I return. Don't be afraid. He is a good man. And when I return, you and I will talk. Do you understand me?'

And eventually he had nodded once more, slowly. There was nothing more I could do, but hope against hope he was still alive when I returned to Thebes.

I was brought back from this memory by the crying, bleating and indignant calling of the ducks, chickens and goats as they were brought forth, stirred and panicked, to be loaded, alive, on to the ships. Teams of slaves carried trunk after trunk of provisions, already butchered, in crates and boxes, under salt. They carried on whole carcasses, white bones opaque in soft, dark slabs of meat. Storehouses of fruits and vegetables, sacks of grain, silver plates, fine linen cloths, goblets and cups . . . It seemed we were leaving for a visit to eternity. An overseer supervised, striding imperiously through the teams of workers, ticking items on a long papyrus where everything that might possibly be needed was carefully listed. I introduced myself, and asked him to explain to me everything that was being loaded. He nodded and gestured me to follow him towards the storerooms.

'These provisions are just for the King and his entourage – those for the troops and the battalion of attendants are being stored on another transport ship which will go ahead of the royal ships, and prepare each night for the King's arrival and his necessities,' he said.

He turned suddenly between two guards, and entered a storeroom piled high.

'And this is the royal equipment.'

He stood with his hands on his hips, surveying everything with a knowledgeable eye. Servants entered silently, and with his permission and instruction they began to move everything out.

There were four chariots, and a vast array of weapons – gold- and wood-inlaid cases of arrows, bows, spears, daggers, throwing sticks, whips. Also the necessities of royal comfort: fans, chairs, travelling stools, beds, boxes, thrones, canopies, alabaster lanterns, alabaster drinking cups, gold goblets, wardrobes of official robes, hunting outfits, ceremonial linens, jewellery, collars, make-up, unguents and oils. Everything was decorated with the richest of materials, or fashioned from the finest woods. But here, piled on the quayside, in the dark, lit only by the torches shivering now in the cool night breeze from the Red Land, it looked more like the paraphernalia of a homeless god. So much *stuff* for such a short journey; no wonder Ankhesenamun felt stifled by the burdens of the business of royalty, and by the claims of so much gold.

I let them get on with their work. I returned to the ship, to see the King's tame young lion being led aboard by its chain, sniffing the unfamiliar night air, and straining against its short leash. It was a splendid animal, its shoulders and head lolling sinuously as it padded silently along the deck to the prepared comfort of its luxurious cage at the stern. It settled there, licking its soft paws, and glancing with grave eyes at the wide world of the night, so close, and yet unattainable beyond the impassable bars. Then it yawned, as if accepting the fate of its comfortable prison, and settled its head to doze.

But then its ears pricked up, and it turned to look at a small commotion along the quay. A brief trumpet blast followed. The King's slight, elegant figure appeared before a retinue of officials and guards. Ankhesenamun followed behind him, her head covered. They exchanged farewells, politely and publicly, and I saw Ay bending to whisper something into the King's ear. Khay stood attentively to one side, as if he hoped he would be needed. Then Simut, in full military costume, invited the King to board the ship. Accompanied by his little golden monkey, Tutankhamun stepped carefully and elegantly up the gangplank, slim and wary in his white robes like an ibis wading in the reed marshes. When he stepped on to the ship's deck, he turned, and made a gesture to those people still on dry land. It was a strange moment, as if he intended to make a speech, or to wave like a child. Everyone stood in silence, anticipating something. Then, as if he could not think of anything else, he simply nodded, and quickly disappeared into the cabin.

Ankhesenamun beckoned me over, while Ay was engaged in discussions with the captain of the ship.

'Take care of him,' she said quietly, as she turned the gold rings on her delicate and perfectly manicured fingers incessantly.

'I am concerned for your own safety here in the palace. With Ay . . .'

She glanced at me.

'I am used to being alone. And Ay appears to have decided to support what he could not oppose,' she murmured.

'Really?'

'Of course, I do not trust him any more than I would trust a cobra. It is almost more disconcerting to have him as an apparent ally than as a clear foe. But he has brought with him the cooperation of the ministries, and the support of the priests. I suppose he believes he can still manage us according to his own grand designs.'

'He is nothing if not pragmatic. He would have understood at once that opposition would have made things more difficult than collaboration. But he still has great powers . . .' I said carefully.

She nodded.

'I will not make the mistake of underestimating him, or of trusting him. But now there is a balance. His public operation of his powers has to be mediated through the King. And besides, he and I have a common enemy.'

'Horemheb?'

'Precisely. The King remains naive about the general. I am sure, wherever he may be, he will be plotting the next stage of his campaign for power. So take care in Memphis, for it is his city, not ours.'

I was about to reply when Ay, with his perfect ability to appear when least desired, interrupted us.

'You have your authorizations and papers?' he said, in his peremptory fashion.

I nodded.

'The King has made his great proclamation, and those closest to him have supported him in his ambition. Now, the royal hunt must be seen to be accomplished. There would be grave disappointment should he fail to return with a lion as his trophy, ' he continued, more confidentially. His tone was dry as sand.

'I know nothing about hunting lions. My responsibility is to keep him safe and well, and to return him here, and to a secure future,' I said.

'You will do exactly as you are ordered. And if you fail, the cost will be personally high.'

'What do you mean?'

'There can be no question of misunderstanding, surely?' he replied, as if surprised by the innocence of the question.

And then, with no more words, he bowed, and proposed to Ankhesenamun that they prepare for the ship's departure.

The sixty or so oarsmen took up their oars through the gunwales and with a series of great efforts, to the beat of the drum, they began to row the great ship away from the dock. Across the slowly widening distance I saw Ankhesenamun watching us leave, with Ay. Then without a wave, like a pale figure returning to the underworld, she disappeared into the dark palace. Ay remained watching until we vanished from sight. I looked down at the black water, which swirled and eddied in secret currents, as if some sorcerer were stirring up strange fortunes and storms of destiny.

25

Simut joined me at the stern of the golden ship, as the city slipped away behind us. Thebes, city of my birth and my life, dark under the night sky, the shadows of the suburbs and the shanties, the high steep walls of the temples and pylons, pure white where they faced the moon; and it seemed to me, for all the lives within it, that the city looked hollow, precariously balanced, made of papyrus and reeds, as if it could all fall down with one breath of ill wind. The imagination can conquer distance, I realized; but the heart cannot. I thought of the children asleep, and Tanefert awake in our bed, the candle still lit on the table beside her, thinking of me on this disappearing golden ship. I had decided to leave Thoth with her, to guard the house at night. The animal had looked disconsolate at my departure, as if he knew I was leaving him for some time.

'Are you leaving a family here?' I asked Simut.

'I don't have a family. I made a choice, early in my career. I had little family when I was young, and those I had were no help to me; so I decided I would not miss it as a grown man. The army has been my family. And it has been my whole life. I have no regrets.'

It was the longest speech he had ever made to me. After a pause, as if he had been considering whether to trust me with an even deeper confidence, he said: 'I think this journey is more dangerous than protecting the King in the palace. At least there we could control the security situation. We could have managed access, stability . . . but out here anything could happen.'

I agreed with him, and yet here we were, overwhelmed by circumstances beyond our control.

'What did you discover from the Chief Architect of the temple, regarding the desecration of the carving?' I asked.

'He said the last weeks of the construction were chaos. Everything was behind schedule, the carvings were slow in being completed, and he assigned craftsmen according to the advice of the chief artist. Because of the panic, there were lapses in the vetting procedures, many of the workers and craftsmen were not registered as they should have been, and now of course no one will accept responsibility for the carving . . . It would not have been too difficult for some rogue element to gain access to the work site . . .'

He looked balefully at the dark foliage along the riverbank, as if unseen assassins lurked behind each palm tree.

'I am no happier than you at the prospect of this mission. Memphis is a nest of snakes . . .'

'I know it well. I received my training there. Fortunately, I have my own alliances in the city,' he said.

'And what is your opinion of Horemheb?' I asked.

He gazed at the dark river.

'In my military opinion he is a great general. But I could not say the same of his humanity—'

Just then a junior officer approached, saluted to Simut, and addressed me: 'The King has asked for you.'

And so I was admitted to the royal apartments. Thick curtains had been drawn to make this reception space even more private. There was no sign of the King or his monkey. Lit by scented oil lamps, it had been richly, elegantly decorated. I looked around at the array of treasures, any one of which could have funded a family for its entire lifetime. I picked up an alabaster goblet fashioned in the form of a white lotus. It bore crisp, black hieroglyphic inscriptions. I read them aloud to myself:

> *Live your ka*
> *And may you spend millions of years*
> *Lover of Thebes*
> *With your face to the cool north breeze*
> *Beholding happiness*

'It is a beautiful poem,' said the King in his light, high voice.

He had entered without my noticing. I replaced the goblet carefully. Then I bowed and offered him my wishes for his peace, health and prosperity.

'"*Live your ka* . . ." an enigmatic, but beautiful phrase. I hear you once wrote verse yourself. What do you think it means?' he asked.

'The *ka* is the mysterious force of life in all things, in each of us . . .'

'It is that which differentiates us from the dead, and from dead things. But what does it mean to live it fully, in truth?'

I pondered.

'I suppose it is an invocation to each person to live according to that truth, and in so doing, if we are to believe the poem, to gain happiness, which is to say eternal happiness. "*Millions of years* . . ."'

He smiled, revealing his perfect little teeth.

'It is indeed a great mystery. I, for instance, feel at this moment I am finally, truly living my *ka*. This journey and this hunt are my destiny. But perhaps you do not believe in the sentiments the poem expresses?' he asked.

'I struggle with the word *happiness*. I am a Medjay officer. I don't get to behold much happiness. But perhaps I am looking in the wrong places,' I replied carefully.

'You see the world as a harsh, dangerous place.'

'I do,' I admitted.

'You have reason on your side,' he replied. 'But I still believe it can be otherwise.'

Then he sat down in the only chair in the room. Like everything else, it was no ordinary chair, but a small throne made from ebony, partly covered with gold foil, and inlaid with geometric patterns of glass and coloured stones. I was surprised to glimpse, just before he sat down, at the top, the disc of the Aten – the symbol of his father's reign and power, now long banned. He adjusted his slippers upon the inlaid footrest and its picture of Egypt's enemies, the bound captives, and gazed at me with his strange intensity.

'You are puzzled by this throne?'

'It is a beautiful object.'

'It was made for me in the time of my father.'

The monkey jumped up on his lap, and watched me with its nervous, moist eyes. He stroked its tiny head, and it chattered to him briefly. He fed it a nut. He fingered a beautiful protection amulet on a gold chain around his neck.

'But the symbolism is no longer permitted,' I commented carefully.

'No. It is forbidden. But not everything about my father's enlightenment was wrong. I feel I can speak of this to you of all people, isn't that strange? I was raised in his religion, and perhaps for that reason in spirit, if not in the letter, it feels true to me; as rightful as one's true heart.'

'But you led its banishment, lord.'

'I had no choice. The tide of time turned against us. I was merely a child. Ay prevailed, and at the time, he was right – for how else could we have restored order to the Two Lands? But in the privacy of my heart and soul, I still worship the one God, the God of Light and Truth. And I know I am not alone.'

The implications of this were astounding. Here was the King, confessing his attachment to the outlawed religion, despite the destruction of its icons and the estrangement of its priests in his own name. I wondered if Ankhesenamun was implicated in this, too.

'Let me confess to you, Rahotep, while I know it is the duty of a king to be seen to conquer and kill the lion, most noble of the beasts, in truth I have no personal wish to do such a thing. Why would I kill such a wonderful creature, with his wild spirit? I would rather observe his power and his grace, and learn from his example. Sometimes, in my dreams, I have the powerful body of a lion, and the wise head of Thoth to think with. But then I awake, and I remember that I am myself. And only a moment later do I remember I am, and must be, King.'

He gazed at his own limbs as if they were strangers.

'A powerful body is meaningless without a powerful mind.'

He smiled, almost sweetly, as if he appreciated my clumsy attempt at flattery. I suddenly had a strange idea that he might like me.

'Tell me about my father,' he said, gesturing to a low stool where I could sit at his royal feet.

He had caught me by surprise again. His mind moved oddly, suddenly and unexpectedly sideways, by association, like a crab.

'What do you wish to know?' I replied.

'My memory of him is diminishing every day. I hold on tightly to certain images but they are like an old piece of embroidered linen: the colour is fading, and the threads are frayed, and soon I fear his memory will be lost to me.'

'I think he was a great man with a new vision of the world. What he did took great personal courage and political will. But I think he had too high an opinion of the capacity of human beings to perfect themselves. And that was the flaw in his great enlightenment,' I said.

'You do not believe in perfection, either?'

I shook my head.

'Not in this life. Man is half-god, but he is also half-beast.'

'Yours is a sceptical view. The Gods have made many attempts to create a perfect humanity, but each time they have been dissatisfied, and have thrown their work away, and abandoned the world to chaos. I believe that is what befell my father. But it was not the end of the story. Do you remember it? The God Ra, with his silver bones and gold skin, and hair and teeth of lapis lazuli, and his eye from whose vision humanity was born, understood the treachery in the hearts of men, and sent down Hathor, in her form of Sekhmet the Vengeful, to slaughter those who plotted against him. But in his heart Ra felt pity for his creatures. And so he changed his mind. And he tricked the Goddess; he created the red beer of the Gods, and she became drunk with its delight, and did not realize it was not humanity's blood that stained the desert; and that is how we survived her revenge, by the compassion of Ra.'

He stroked the monkey as if it was humanity, and he was Ra.

'You are wondering why I have told you this tale,' he said, quietly.

'I wonder if perhaps it is because you are not your father. And perhaps you told me because although he desired perfection, he brought this world to the brink of a terrible catastrophe. And perhaps because in your compassion you wish to save the world from disaster,' I said.

He gazed at me.

'Perhaps that is what I was thinking. But what of Hathor and her taste for blood?'

'I do not know,' I replied, honestly enough.

'I believe there is a pattern of retribution to events. A crime begets a crime begets a crime, and so on until the end of everything. So how can we escape this pattern, this labyrinth of revenge and suffering? Only by an act of exceptional forgiveness . . . But are human beings capable of such compassion? No. I have not yet been forgiven for the crimes of my father. Perhaps I will never be forgiven. And if that is so, then I will have to prove myself better than him. And here we are, travelling in darkness, surrounded by fear, so that I can bring back a wild lion in triumph. Perhaps then I will establish myself as King in my own name; not as my father's son. It is a strange world. And here you are, to protect me from it, like the Eye of Ra.'

He reached into his robe, and took from it a ring, adorned with a small, but very fine, protective Eye. He gave it to me. I slipped it on my finger and bowed in thanks.

'I give you this all-seeing Eye so that your vision may be as powerful as Ra's. Our enemies travel as fast as shadows. They are with us always. You must see them. You must learn to see in the dark.'

26

The strong current drew us onwards, ever northwards, towards Memphis. Simut and his guard kept watch at all hours. I was restless, unable to sleep, and I felt trapped on the water. Whenever the King took the air, which was not often, we made sure we were away from the villages. Even so, every field and every grove of palm trees presented the possibility of danger, for we made an extravagant target. From our point of view, I saw dirt-poor villages huddled beneath the shade of the date palms, where naked children and dogs swarmed the narrow, crooked mud streets, and families lived crowded on top of each other with their animals in one-room dwellings that were little more than stables. In the fields, women in miraculously bright, clean robes tilled the immaculate green and gold rows of barley and wheat, onions and cabbages. It all looked idyllic and peaceful, but nothing is as it seems: these women would toil from dawn until dusk just to pay the grain taxes to work the land, which they probably leased from one elite family, who lived comfortably inside their richly furnished and luxurious property in Thebes.

After three days' sailing we neared the almost-deserted city of Akhetaten. I stood at the prow to observe the range of broken red and grey cliffs behind the city. Just a few years ago this had been the site of Akhenaten's great experiment: a new, bright, white capital of the future; great towers, open sun-temples, offices and suburbs of luxurious villas. But since the death of the King's father, the bureaucracies had gradually returned to Thebes or Memphis. And then plague had arrived like a curse of revenge, killing off hundreds who had remained, many of them with no work and nowhere else to go. It was said this plague had also killed the other daughters of Akhenaten and Nefertiti, for they had disappeared from public life. Now, aside from a basic staff, the city was said to be largely abandoned, flyblown and falling into dereliction. But to my surprise, and interest, Simut informed me of the King's great desire to visit the city.

And so it was, early the next morning, just as the first birds began to sing, and the river mist drifted insubstantial and chilly over the sinuous currents of the dark water, and while the shadows of the night still lay long upon the ground, we stepped – accompanied by a troop of guards – from our moored ship on to the dry land of history.

With the King in his white robes and Blue Crown carrying a gold walking stick topped with a glass knob, and a troop of front and rear guards in their armour carrying polished weapons to scare away any peasant sightseers dazzled by this unexpected visitation from another world, we set off towards the central city via deserted footpaths that had, just years before, been busy thoroughfares. As we entered the precincts of the city, I saw at once the effects of its abandonment: the walls, once freshly painted, were now faded to dusty greys and browns. The once carefully planted, stylish gardens were now wildly overgrown, and the pools of the rich were cracked and empty. A few bureaucrats and servants still walked to work on these deserted ways; but they seemed to move in a desultory fashion, and they stopped still in astonishment to stare at our group, before falling to their knees as the King passed by.

Finally we stood upon the royal road. The sun's rays had now risen over the horizon, and instantly it was hot. Once an immaculately swept ceremonial way for the arrival of Akhenaten and the royal family in their gold chariots, the road was now an empty pathway for ghosts and the dusty wind. We came to the first pylon of the Great Aten Temple. The soaring mud-brick walls were crumbling. The long, bright flags, which had once fluttered in the northern breeze, were tattered and faded to no colour by the bleaching power of the sun. The high wooden gates hung loosely on their rusted hinges. One of the guards forced them open, with a reluctant creaking and cracking of desiccated wood. We passed through into the vast courtyard. Once it would have been crowded with hundreds of offering tables, attended by thousands of worshippers in their bright white robes, their hands raised in the new ritual to the sun, holding up fruit and flowers, and even babies, for the blessing of the evening rays. The many stone statues of Akhenaten and Nefertiti still stared across the vast space, but all there was to see now was dereliction; the failure of their great vision. One or two of the statues had fallen, and lay face down or face up, staring blindly at the sky.

The King moved ahead, making clear he wished to have some moments of privacy. As we hung back, trying to keep watch, Simut whispered: 'The whole city's turning back into dust.'

'I suppose that's all it ever was.'

'Just add water,' he joked, sombrely.

I grinned at this surprising moment of wit. He was right. Just add water, and make mud; dry the bricks in the sun, then add plaster and paint, and timber and copper from the island of Alashiya, and gold from the mines of Nubia, and years of labour, of blood and sweat and death, from everywhere else – and behold: a vision of heaven on earth. But there had been neither sufficient time nor treasure to build the vision in eternal stone, and so now it was returning to the dust of its making.

The King was standing before a great stone statue of his father. The statue's angular features were chiselled by shadows; all the lineaments of power were embodied in those strange features. Once they had been the epitome of kingship. But now the very style, with its strange, ambiguous elongations, had become a thing of the past. The young King's face was enigmatic as he stood, small, human and frail, before the might of his stone father, among the desolate ruins of his father's great vision. And then he did a strange thing: he sank down on his knees, and venerated the statue. We watched, and wondered whether we should join him. But none of his entourage seemed willing to do so. I moved towards him, and held a sunshade over his head. When he looked up, I saw his eyes were full of tears.

We toured the city's palaces, stepping across the strange evidence of former human occupation: single dusty sandals; pieces of faded clothing; broken jugs and hollow wine jars, their contents long evaporated; small domestic things, cups and dishes still unbroken but full of little drifts of sand and dust. We wandered through high, decorated halls once home to glorious affluence and exquisite music, and now to nesting birds, snakes, rats and woodworm. Beneath our feet, exquisite painted floors of water-gardens full of glazed fish and birds were faded and cracked by time's careless attrition.

'I find I am suddenly remembering things I had forgotten. I was a boy here. I grew up in the Northern Riverside Palace. But now I remember being brought to this chamber.' The King spoke quietly, as we stood in the hall of the Great Palace near the river. The long beams of the morning sun slanted in, dusty and strong. A multitude of graceful columns supported the lofty ceiling still vividly decorated with the indigo of the night sky and the glittering gold of the stars.

'My father rarely spoke. I lived in awe of him. We sometimes worshipped together. Occasionally I would be brought to see him by myself. It was always a special occasion. I would be dressed formally, and carried along many corridors full of silence and alarming, gloomy, ugly old men who bowed low to me, but never spoke. And then I would be ushered into his presence. Often he would leave me to stand

203

waiting for some time before he decided to notice me. I dared not move. I was frightened.'

I was not quite sure what to do with this unexpected confession. So I returned the compliment.

'My own father is also a quiet man. He taught me to fish. When I was a child we would drift along the riverbank for many hours at dusk on a reed boat, our lines in the water, neither of us speaking, enjoying the silence.'

'That is a good memory,' he said.

'It was a simple time.'

'"A *simple time* . . ."'

He repeated the words with a strange nostalgia, and I felt sure he had never had a simple time in his life. Perhaps it was what he most desired; as the poor desire great riches, so the rich, in their appalling ignorance, believe they desire the simplicity of poverty.

The King was staring up at the Window of Appearances where his father had once stood, high above his people, passing down gifts of treasure and collars of honour. Above the window was a carving of the disc of the Aten, and the many rays of the sun radiated like slender arms, some ending in a delicate hand offering the Ankh of Life. But the window was empty now, with no one left to give or receive such blessings.

'I remember this hall. I remember a great crowd of men, and a long silence. I remember everyone staring at me. I remember . . .'

He stopped, uncertainly. 'But my father was not here. I remember I was looking for him. Instead there was Ay. And I had to walk through the crowd into that chamber, with him.'

He pointed.

'And what happened then?'

He moved slowly across the faded river scenes of the great floor, towards a door whose ornate carving had provided a glorious feast for the termites. He pushed it open. I followed him into a long chamber. All the furniture and any other contents had been removed.

It had the hollow acoustic of a long-unoccupied place. He shivered.

'After this, nothing was the same again. I saw my father only once more, and when he saw me he began to shout, like a madman. He took up a chair, and he tried to bring it down upon my head. And then he sat upon the ground, and wept and groaned. And that was the last time I ever saw him. You see, he was quite mad. It was a terrible secret, but I knew it. I was taken away to Memphis. I was educated, and I lived with my nurse, and Horemheb became my tutor. He tried to be a good father to me. No one even spoke my father's name again. It was as if he had never existed. My own father had become a non-person. And then one day, I was readied for coronation. I was nine years old. I was married to Ankhesenpaaten. We were given new names. I, who had all my life been called Tutankhaten, was now renamed Tutankhamun. She became Ankhesenamun. Names are powers, Rahotep. We lost who we were, and became something else. We were like little orphans, confused and lost and miserable. And I was married to the daughter of the woman who they say destroyed my mother. But still there was a surprise to come, for I liked her well. And somehow we have managed not to hate each other because of the past. We realize it is not our fault. And, in truth, she is almost the only person in the whole world I can trust.'

His eyes glittered as emotion brimmed inside him. I decided I could not remain silent.

'Who was your mother?'

'Her name, like that of my father, has turned to dust and been blown away.'

'Kiya,' I said.

He nodded slowly.

'I am glad you know of her. At least somewhere her name lives on.'

'I know her name. I do not know her fate.'

'She disappeared. One afternoon she was there, and then by the evening – she had vanished. I remember I ran to her clothing chests, and I hid inside one, and refused to leave, because all that was left was her scent in her clothes. I still keep them, although everyone has tried to persuade me to get rid of them. I won't. Some days I still catch a faint ghost of her scent. It is very comforting.'

'And you never discovered what happened to her?' I asked.

'Who would tell me the truth? And now, the people who hold such secrets are dead. Apart from Ay . . . And he would never tell. So I am left with a mystery. Sometimes I wake in the night, because in my dreams she has called out to me – but I can never hear what she is saying. And when I wake, I lose her all over again.'

A bird sang somewhere, in the shadows.

'The dead live on in our dreams, don't you think, Rahotep? Their eternity is in here. For as long as we live.'

And he gently tapped his own skull, gazing at me with his golden eyes.

27

Two days later the Great River's deep currents brought us near to the southern domains of the city of Memphis. The ancient necropolises, built in the desert margins above the cultivation, and the ageless temple and pyramid of Saqqara, being the first of the great buildings of the Two Lands, were hidden way up on the plateau. Simut described the other monuments which lay further to the north, but which we could also not see from our river view; the shining white pyramids of Khufu and his Queens; the more recently constructed temple to Horus of the Horizon; and the great Sphinx, where Thutmose IV had erected the Carving of his Dream, in which he vowed to clear the encroaching sands from the Sphinx in return for being made King – and which indeed came to pass, although he had no legitimate claim to the throne at that time.

Thebes suddenly seemed a small settlement in comparison with the vast metropolis that slowly unfolded before our eyes; we sailed for some considerable time, observing the many outlying temple districts, the vast cemeteries that bordered the desert to the west, the middle-class suburbs, and the poor quarters, those slums of humanity that spread out in chaotic shanty districts towards the endless green of the fields; and everywhere, rising above the low dwellings, the white walls of temple enclosures.

Surrounded by welcoming boats and barges, and smaller private yachts and skiffs, we sailed into the main port. Many jetties spread out along the dockside; here were trading and naval ships from many countries, unloading great stacks of precious timber and small mountains of minerals, stone and grain. Thousands of people crowded the long paved ways that ran by the Great River. Fishermen stopped to gaze up at the splendour of the royal ship, their gathered nets dripping in their arms, their catches still twisting and thrashing, silver and gold, in the bottom of the small boats. Dusty workers stared from the supply boats as they stood knee-deep in huge quantities of grain, or on slabs of roughly quarried stone. Children held up by their parents waved from crowded ferries. Onlookers, drawn by the noise, appeared from their workshops and storerooms and shops.

Tutankhamun appeared at the curtain of his apartment. He gestured to me to join him. He was nervously adjusting his costume. He was dressed in his white royal robes, and wearing the Double Crown.

'Do I look well?' he asked, almost shyly. 'I must look well. It is many years since I last visited Memphis. And also time has passed since I met Horemheb. He must see how I have changed. I am no longer the boy under his tutelage. I am King.'

'Lord, you are unmistakably the King.'

He nodded, satisfied, and then, like a great actor, he seemed to centre himself before he stepped into the sunlight, his face beneath the crowns assuming the absolute conviction it had lacked only moments before. Something about the intensity of the moment, and its demands, brought out the best in him. He thrived on an audience. This would surely be his biggest yet. The handler passed the King his young lion, on its leash, and then he stepped up and forward into the light of Ra to a roar of acclaim. I watched as he adopted the ritual posture of power and victory. As if on cue, the young lion roared. The crowd, who could not see the way the beast was prodded to his heroic roar by a spear's sharp point applied by his diligent keeper, called out an even greater enthusiastic response, as if it were now not many individuals, but one great beast.

The spectacle that greeted us upon the quayside was a carefully orchestrated and deliberately overwhelming display of the military might of this capital. As far as the eye could see, stretching back in countless perfectly drilled lines, division after division of soldiers, each one named after the patron God of the district from which it drew its conscripts and officers, paraded in the shimmering arena. Between them were thousands of prisoners of war, manacled and roped together by the neck, together with their women and children – Libyans in cloaks with their long side-locks and goatees, Nubians in their kilts, and Syrians with their long pointed beards, all forced into the posture of submission. Hundreds of fine horses – booty from the wars – danced on their elegant hooves. Envoys from each subjugated state fell to their knees, pleading for clemency, for the breath of life for their people.

And there, at the centre of everything, was a single figure, standing in the sun beside an empty throne, as if all of this display belonged to him. Horemheb, General of the Armies of the Two Lands. I knew him from his ramrod posture as he waited, still as a dark statue.

Tutankhamun took his time, like a god, keeping everyone waiting while he continued to enjoy the acclaim of the multitude; meanwhile the old ambassadors were tottering in the heat, the crowds were gasping for the water- and fruit-sellers, the city officials were sweating in their regalia. And then finally, accompanied by Simut and a phalanx of royal guards, he deigned to descend the gangplank. The crowds renewed their cries of acclaim and loyalty, and the dignitaries made ritual gestures of respect and homage. For his part the King made absolutely no sign of recognition or response, as if all of this pageant was somehow insubstantial and unimportant to him.

On a quiet signal from Simut, the guards fanned out around the

King, organized as dancers, their arms and bows presented, as he stepped down on to the hot stones of the city. Simut and I scanned the crowds and the rooftops for any signs of trouble. Horemheb waited for the right moment; then he respectfully offered the throne to the King. But his every arrogant gesture made the King seem the less powerful man. Something about the cold expression on Horemheb's face even seemed to keep the flies away. He turned to the silent arena. An obedient silence fell. He shouted to every one of the thousands of men present.

'I speak to his majesty, Tutankhamun, Lord of the Two Lands. I bring chiefs of every foreign territory to beg life from him. These vile foreigners who do not know the Two Lands, I lay them beneath his feet for ever and eternally. From the furthest reaches of Nubia to the most distant regions of Asia, all are under the command of his great hand.'

Then Horemheb carefully set his knee to the ground, bowed his sleek head with arrogant humility, and waited for the King to acknowledge his formulaic words. The moments dripped by like the water in a clock, as Tutankhamun left him to stoop in public deference for as long as possible. I was impressed. The King was taking command of the occasion. The crowd remained hushed, alert to this consummate confrontation played out in the language of appearance and protocol. Finally, judging the moment precisely, the King laid a gift of five magnificent gold collars around the general's neck. But he managed to make them look like a burden of responsibility, as much as a gift of respect. Then he raised the general, and embraced him.

The King moved forward, to accept the greetings and obeisance of the other officials as necessary. Finally he ascended the throne on the dais, under the canopy that gave some relief from the burning heat of the sun on the stones. At a command from Horemheb, every division and every group of war prisoners was then paraded before him, accompanied by trumpets and drums. It took hours. But the King maintained his rigid posture, and his distant gaze, even though the sweat was running from under the crowns, and dampening his tunic.

We travelled by chariot into the central city. Simut and I went first, ahead of Tutankhamun, who was flanked by his running guards, their weapons flashing in the high sunlight. I noticed the buildings and headquarters here were like those in Thebes, if far greater in number: the town houses were built upwards for lack of space, and down side passages were the humbler dwellings of those who laboured in the services of the army, the central institution of this city; single rooms which were workroom, stable and home in one, opened directly on to the messy streets. The royal roads and the paved surfaces of the sacred ways, which were lined with sphinxes, obelisks and chapels, were kept clear of onlookers, and so we travelled quickly towards the Palace of Memphis. Over the harsh noise of the wheels on the rutted paving stones, Simut pointed out the famous sights: to the north, the vast old mud-brick construction of the old Citadel, the White Walls, which gave their name to the district, and the Great Temple of Ptah to the south, with its own great enclosure wall. A temple canal ran south all the way to the outlying temple district of the Goddess Hathor. Other canals flashed into view as we passed, linking the river and the port to the central city.

'There are at least forty-five different cults in the city, and each has its own temple,' he shouted, proudly. 'And out to the west is the Temple of Anubis.' I imagined the embalmers, the coffin-makers, the makers of masks and amulets, and the writers of the Books of the Dead, all the specialized craftsmen who clustered into such a quarter to conduct the complex business of that powerful God, Guardian of the Necropolis and of the Tombs against evil-doers. But there would be no time for tours of curiosity.

Simut was eager we should arrive ahead of the King; huge crowds had already gathered in the tight spaces of the passageways and streets, to catch a glimpse of his arrival at the great Palace of Memphis, but they were not allowed near the open area in front of the palace gate towers. Nevertheless this was a security nightmare, for it was packed with foreign and local dignitaries and officials and elite men. Simut's advance guard were swiftly ready; silently and efficiently taking up positions and peremptorily ordering people out of the way to create a path of safety and security for the King. They knew exactly what they were doing, and moved as one in patterns they must have practised and performed many times before. Their brusquely immaculate behaviour left no one, even the Memphis palace guards themselves, in doubt of their authority. Royal archers followed, their great bows drawn and aimed up at the rooftops.

Then the temple trumpets sounded from the walls as the King arrived, surrounded by more guards. Their tribute, the clamour of the crowds, the bellowed orders of the commanders, were deafening; but suddenly the royal cavalcade passed from the dusty heat and light and cacophony of the streets into the cool silence of the first reception hall. At once we were all gathered in relative security. Here, yet more high officials awaited the King's arrival. This was the first time I had seen him closely in a more social situation. Whereas in the palace he had sometimes seemed like a lost boy, now he held himself like a King: his posture upright and dignified, his elegant face calm and composed, his expression seeking no approval in anxious smiles, nor expressing his power in haughty arrogance. He had a charisma that came from his unusual looks, his youth, and his other quality that I remembered from when he was a boy: that of an old soul in a young man's body. Even the gold walking stick which he carried everywhere became an enhancement of his personality.

Simut had warned me there had been a great deal of political pressure from General Horemheb's office for the King to be accommodated overnight in the palace on this royal visit. But Ay's office had insisted the King attend the necessary functions, and then return to the ship for a late departure. It was the right decision. Memphis was dangerous. The city was the heart of the administration

212

of the Two Lands, but it was also the location of the army's head-quarters and barracks; unfortunately the loyalty of the army could not be entirely trusted at this delicate time, especially under Horemheb.

The great chamber echoed with the noise of hundreds of elite men – diplomats, foreign officials, wealthy businessmen, high-ranking officers – bragging, barking and yapping self-importantly at each other as they manoeuvred among the crowds, each working hard to stand near, or speak to and impress, their superiors, or to denigrate their equals and lessers. I moved through the noisy crowds, and kept near to the King. I saw how he nodded as each person in turn was introduced by his two officers, and then dealt with each petitioner and dignitary, managing the brief moments of the interview, responding elegantly to praises and offerings, and giving a sense to each man that he was important, and would be remembered.

Then I suddenly noticed Horemheb standing in the shadow cast by one of the columns. He was being addressed, and evidently bored witless, by some fatuous official, but his eyes were focused, with the poised attention of a leopard, on the King. For a moment he looked like a hunter with his prey. But then the King caught his glance, and Horemheb smiled quickly. Then he moved forward towards the King, and as he did so his face, caught in a dramatic shaft of light, suddenly turned white as marble. Accompanied by the young officer who had proclaimed his letter in Thebes, he made his way deliberately through the crowd. I moved closer.

'It is an honour to receive your Majesty again in Memphis,' said the general formally.

Tutankhamun smiled back, with a slightly cautious affection.

'This city holds many good memories for me. You were a good and trusted friend to me here.'

The King looked delicate and slight next to the confident, well-built, older general. Those attending this dialogue, including the young secretary, waited in silence for Horemheb to continue.

'I am glad you thought so. I was then privileged with the titles of deputy and military tutor. I remember well it was me you consulted on many matters of state and policy, and to me you would listen. It was once said, I could *pacify the palace* . . . when no one else could do so.'

He smiled without opening his mouth. The King smiled back, still more cautiously. He had sensed the undercurrent of hostility in Horemheb's tone.

'Alas, time passes. It now all seems so long ago . . .'

'Then you were a boy. Now, I salute the King of the Two Lands. All we are, and all we have, is held in your royal power.' And he bowed curtly.

'We hold your affection in high esteem. We treasure it. We wish to honour all your works and deeds . . .'

The King let the sentence die away.

'Here in Memphis, you will have noticed many changes,' continued Horemheb, on another tack.

'We hear you have many projects. We hear you are building a great new tomb for yourself, in the Saqqara necropolis,' replied the King.

'It is just a small, private tomb. Its construction and decoration amuses my rare private hours. It would be an honour to show it to you. The wall carvings are very fine.'

He smiled, wryly, as if at a little private joke, but his eyes were distant.

'What do these carvings depict? The General Horemheb's many military triumphs?'

'The glorious campaigns in Nubia, led in triumph by your highness, are described there,' replied the general.

'I remember your glorious and triumphant direction of those campaigns in my name.'

'Perhaps his Majesty forgets his own *distinguished* contribution to their glory.'

'I forget nothing,' replied the King, directly.

There was a little silence in which Horemheb considered his response. There was something of the crocodile about him; his eyes above the surface, ever watchful, the rest of him concealed in the darkness below.

'The King must be hungry and thirsty after his journey. He must eat well before he departs on his royal hunting expedition,' he said, almost in the tone in which one would address a child. Then he clapped his hands, and instantly servants appeared with exquisite food on beautiful pottery dishes. They were respectfully offered on trays to the King, but he ignored them, and I realized I had not seen him eat or drink anything here.

Horemheb issued a peremptory order to the young officer. He disappeared, and we waited, neither Horemheb nor the King speaking to break the stalemate of silence. I wondered what Tutankhamun thought now of this man whom he had called his good father.

The officer returned, leading a high-status Syrian captive, his hands tied harshly behind his back, forcing him to bow in the traditional posture of the captured enemy. The man, who was in a poor state, his head crudely shaven and marked with vicious cuts, his limbs spindle-thin, stared at the floor with the rage of humiliation in his proud eyes. The officer took one of the dishes of food, and offered it to Horemheb, who forced open the jaws of the captive, as if he were an animal. The man was afraid, but he knew he had no choice; and he was starving in any case. He chewed cautiously, and then fearfully swallowed. We all waited to see whether he would double up and collapse from the effects of poison, or just from bad cooking. Of course, no such thing occurred, but Horemheb made him test every dish being offered. Finally he was led away, where he was made to stand facing the wall so that the King could see he suffered from no slow-acting poisons. But the effect of this strange performance was astonishing, for Horemheb made it feel as if the King himself could be that force-fed prisoner.

'We are well aware of the perils and outright threats that the King has suffered, even in his own palace. Now you may, if you wish, eat from our banquet in absolute confidence,' said the general, intently.

215

And everyone watched as the King carefully took a tiny portion of duck meat, ate it slowly, smiled and said: 'Our appetite is satisfied.'

This strange little episode was, as it turned out, a minor skirmish preparing the way for the speeches that followed. As Horemheb stepped up on to a dais the whole chamber fell quickly to a hush. Mouthfuls of food were swallowed, greasy fingers washed clean in fingerbowls, and the servants vanished. The general stared out at the gathering. His handsome face, which seemed never to have indulged in the luxury of self-expression, assumed the lineaments of authority: a certain jut of the chin, and a composed, imperturbable and superior regard. He waited for absolute silence. Then he spoke, not fluently, but with force and conviction, punctuated with assertive gestures that were somehow rehearsed and awkward, and an occasional, almost mocking humour which I sensed could turn, in an instant, into viciousness. He formally welcomed the King and his retinue, and pledged all assistance from the city's resources – which he enumerated at great length, just to remind us all of the powers and riches he could call upon – to his security and pleasure during what he called 'this brief visitation' on the way to the royal hunt. He managed to make it sound like a complaint rather than a compliment, and I watched the King's face for his reaction. But he continued to stare ahead.

Then Horemheb continued: 'At this time of heightened insecurity in the Two Lands, the army remains the force of order and justice, defending the great, eternal values and the traditions of our kingdom. We are successfully prosecuting our territorial interests in the lands of Amurru. Wars are a necessity, to sustain our pre-eminence and authority in the world, and to extend our boundaries. Winning those wars is my responsibility. The perfection of order and justice which our state exemplifies must be maintained and supported, and therefore we petition the King and his advisers to release further funds for this great aim, to extend the army's divisions, and to ensure our glorious success, which will certainly richly repay the investment we now formally request.'

He paused. I looked around the great chamber. Everyone was paying full attention now, waiting for the King to respond. The audience gave him absolute silence, so as to hear every quiet word.

'War is the state of mankind,' he began, eventually. 'It is a great and noble cause. We support and maintain the army of the Two Lands. We acclaim its general. His aim is our aim: the triumph of our order through the rightful exercise of power. We have maintained our support throughout these long years of battle, with confident belief in our general, who continues to assure us of a successful conclusion to these wars. But of course there are many demands upon our great treasury. It is the responsibility of the King and his advisers to balance these many, and sometimes conflicting, requests. *Maat* is the divine order of the universe, but in our cities and our lands that divine order is maintained by proper finance, according to the contributions required of everyone. Therefore we ask the general of the Two Lands to explain and justify, before all of us assembled here, why the army now requests further subsidy, given our already lavish support.'

Horemheb stepped forward, as if prepared for this move.

'Our request is not predicated only upon the successful conclusion to our foreign wars. Its purpose is to reinforce the presence and the power of the army at home. For it has become clear there are disruptive forces at work within our own society. Indeed, from all reports, these forces have found their way to the very heart not just of our temples and our offices of government, but even of our royal palace itself. We wonder how such acts of treachery can possibly have been permitted to come to pass.'

There was a gasp among the audience, for the implication of what Horemheb had said went directly to the heart of the King's authority.

But Tutankhamun was not perturbed.

'It is the way of the world that men are vulnerable to disloyalty and to deceit. There are always those who seek power for their own purposes: men of treacherous hearts and seditious minds. But be assured we shall always triumph over these men, for their petty disaffection has no power over our great kingship. The Gods will be avenged upon them all.'

His calm was impressive. He stared unequivocally at Horemheb. The general moved forward again.

'Words are powers. But actions are still more powerful. We pray for the safety of the King, and remind him that a great army waits, at his disposal, to defend the Two Lands against the enemy that lies within, as well as that which lies without our borders.'

Tutankhamun slowly bowed his elegant head.

'And in recognition of your loyalty, we commit further resources to the wars, for the support of the divisions, and in the anticipation of great victory. We request our general's return to those wars, for where should a general be but with his troops as they fight?'

Those present recognized that this moment in his speech required their vociferous support; they cheered, loudly, and so it seemed like a triumph for the King. But the officers of the army stood around the periphery, observing the drama like jackals waiting for a kill, and making the applauding audience look like monkeys.

28

We departed that afternoon. The sky was milky with heat, and the crowds were small and subdued. The currents carried us swiftly beyond the city's great margins. We had survived the potential dangers of the state visit. Here on this great ship, on the Great River, I felt more in control of the environment. Further north, in the immense marshlands of the delta, the river would begin to change, spreading out in numberless branches that would eventually divide and divide again until at last, like a vast, intricate and unnavigable fan, they would run into the ocean to the north. By evening we had moored at a spot chosen for its remoteness from any towns, and even the local villages lay at some distance. We settled down early for the night.

The caravan that set out before dawn the next morning was not a small one. It included a deputation of diplomats, representatives and officials whose function was to be available to the King in case of need, but more importantly to witness and record the King's deeds, for soon the written statements of his fierce kills and prowess would be commemorated in the carved Scarabs of the Hunts, which would be distributed around the Two Lands. And, of course, the team included uniformed royal guards, out-runners to protect the caravan and charioteers; also armourers who transported the royal weapons, the King's spears, arrows, nets and shields; the Master of the Hunt and his assistants; the dog and cheetah handlers; then the attendant beaters, and the trackers, whose knowledge of the habits and lairs of the animals would be crucial to the success of the hunt. In the royal caravan, our number included myself and Simut, and Pentu the physician.

The dawn air was cold and pure; the moon was low in the sky, and the stars were just fading. Mist drifted across the shadowy waters, and the first hidden birds began to sing as if to conjure Ra himself with their music. Despite the earliness of the hour, everyone seemed aroused and inspired by the beauty of the scene, as perfect as a great wall painting, and by the prospect of the adventure of the hunt. Horses stamped their feet as they were untethered, and the breath of men and animals plumed in the chilly dark.

The green and black fields were still and silent as our strange cavalcade passed along the rutted ways; and only the earliest of the farmers, and a few wide-eyed, bare-footed children arriving at their strips of land before sunrise to take advantage of their water rights, caught a glimpse of the spectacle. They gazed and pointed at us as if at a marvellous dream.

When we came to the margin of the cultivation, we paused. Ahead of us lay the Red Land. I was struck as always by the great silence of its apparent emptiness – holier, for me, than any temple. The sun had just risen about the horizon, and I turned to enjoy the welcome, immediate warmth of its first rays upon my face.

The King stood high on his chariot, and raised his hands to Ra, his God. He was bare-chested, wearing a kilt, and a stole over his shoulder. For a moment his face and body seemed to shine. He held his young lion by its short leather tether, striving for the image of a King, despite his small stature and his golden walking stick. A roar and a long ululation rose up from the hunting teams and the soldiers, a celebration of the start of the hunt, and a shout of warning to the evil spirits of the desert. Then, the moment of ritual accomplished, the King drove his chariot forward, and on this signal we crossed over the eternal border between the Black Lands and the Red.

We followed a course due west, and the rising sun threw the slanted shadows of our marching forms directly ahead of us. The trackers and half of the guard went first, plotting the direction. As we slowly ascended to the desert plateau, the air hummed with heat. The creaking of wooden axles, the occasional stumble of a horse on the loose, gravelly ground, and the panting of the carrying servants and the mules came to me clear and close through the dry air.

We think of the desert as an empty place, but it is not. It is marked and mapped by ancient and newer tracks and by routes worn into the scrub ground by men and animals. As we progressed through the heat of the morning, we encountered occasional drovers and shepherds, those lean and angular nomadic tribesmen who are always on the move; unshaven, their head hair cropped very close to the scalp, their kilts tucked up between their legs, carrying their small rolls of supplies and a few pots on their backs and their long walking sticks in their bony hands as they travel perpetually forward with the same long, languid gait. Their animals, thin and resilient, nibble at whatever they can find, moving at the same slow pace towards some water hole hidden out in the shimmering far places of heat and light.

At times as we progressed through the morning, the trackers cried out, strange high calls like animals or birds, to indicate a sighting: a small herd of desert gazelle or antelope, or ostriches, or caracals, which stood very still, observing us from a safe distance, scenting the wind, and then suddenly vanished in a kicked-up whirl of dust.

As the sun approached its zenith, we stopped to make camp. The trackers found a place which benefited from the protection of a long low bluff to the north – for out here the breeze from that direction at night would be cold, rather than cool – and everyone hurried with practised discipline to their allotted tasks. Quickly a settlement of tents appeared as if out of nowhere. Drills were worked expertly, the sparks quickly blown into flames as the tinder caught; animals were slaughtered; and the rich scent of roasting meat soon filled the desert air. I was hungry. The King sat on his travelling throne, in the luxury of a shady white canopy, fanning himself against the great heat of the day and the flies, and watching the settlement being constructed. Alongside his boxes and his gilded travelling furniture, in this world without walls he looked like a god paying a brief visit to the world. All seemed well.

I walked to the head of the nearest rise to assess the terrain. I shaded my eyes against the harsh glare. In every direction there was nothing to see except the white and grey and red barrenness of the desert, dotted with the occasional tenacious desert bush. I looked back down upon the circle of the encampment. The horses, pack-mules, long-horned sheep and short-haired goats, tethered to thick wooden pegs, were munching on the feed that had been brought along for them. Ducks had been released from their cages, and waddled and pecked furiously at the unpromising desert ground. The hunting dogs and cheetahs, barking and panting in the heat, were kept separate, watched over by their keepers. The tents were all nearly erected, and the King's had been placed in the very centre of the encampment, for maximum protection. Its golden ball-topped central pole shone in the sun. The hunting chariots stood in a line propped on their stands. It all seemed like a vision of civilization. But when I looked again at the distance in every direction, I absorbed the empty, inhuman vastness of the desert. We were here for pastime and amusement, but our little colourful tents and vehicles looked merely like a child's toys set out on a boundless wasteland.

Then I saw, far off, a trail of shadow-sticks, figures as tiny as insects, whose path through the wasteland, I realized, would eventually lead to our encampment. Sweating in the glare of the afternoon sun, I hurried back down to the camp, and alerted the guards. Simut came jogging towards me.

'What?'

'Strangers approaching – they might just be herdsmen, but they have no animals.'

The guards set forth, and soon brought the men into our presence, prodding at them with their flashing spears. It looked like the meeting of two worlds; ours, with its clean white robes and polished weapons, and theirs, nomadic and dirt-poor, their meagre clothing bright with bold colours and patterns, heads shaved, grins wide and spare of teeth. They were honey-gatherers, who inhabited the margins of the desert lands. The leader stepped forward, bowed his head respectfully, and made an offering of a jar.

'A gift for the King, for he is the Lord of the Bees.'

He was a delta man, and as such the bee was not only his livelihood but also the symbol of his land. Wild honey is much prized, more so than the variety cultivated from the clay hives of the city gardens. It is said the flavours are as intense as the tears of Ra, because the bees forage among the rare and earliest-opening flowers of the desert; and so these men spend their lives following the transitory blooming of the seasons along the desert margins. I was inclined to think they offered no harm – they were thin as their walking sticks, dark with use and age, and what use could they be against the power of our weapons? I ordered that they be offered food and water, and then I implied they were welcome to continue on their way. They backed away, bowing with respect.

I weighed the honey jar in my hands. The crude vessel was sealed with bees' wax. I considered opening it, but thought better of it.

'What should we do with this?' I asked Simut.

He shrugged.

'Perhaps you should present it to the King,' he decided. 'He has a notoriously sweet tooth . . .'

At the King's tent, I was announced, and entered. The broad light of the desert filtered in, glowing on the patterns of the linens on the walls. The royal paraphernalia had been set out to make a temporary palace: couches, chairs, objects of great value, mats, and so on. It was warm inside. A fan bearer stood discreetly behind the King, his eyes seeing nothing, slowly wafting the heated air. The King was eating. As I bowed and offered the jar, I saw my own shadow on the tent wall like a figure in a temple carving making a holy offering to the God.

'What is it?' he asked cheerfully, rinsing his fingers in a bowl, and holding them out for a servant to dab dry.

'It is wild honey from desert flowers. An offering from some gatherers.'

He took it in his elegant hands, and examined it.

'A gift from the Gods,' he said, smiling.

'I suggest we store it, and when we are back in Thebes, it will remind you of this hunting trip.'

'Yes. A good idea.'

He clapped his hands, and a servant came and removed the jar.

I bowed, moving backwards, but he insisted I remain with him. He offered me a place on a couch opposite him. He seemed much more light-hearted, and I began to think we had been right, after all, to travel out here. Away from the palace of shadows and its perils, his spirits were already much revived.

We drank a little wine, and some more dishes of meat were brought.

'So this evening we will hunt?' he asked.

'The trackers are confident of finding something. There is a watering hole not far off. If we approach downwind, and silently, then there will be many kinds of creature there at sunset. But the trackers also tell me lions are very rare now.'

He nodded, disappointed.

'We have hunted them almost to extinction. In their wisdom they have retreated deeper into their own domains. But perhaps one of them will answer my call.'

We ate in silence for a little while.

'I find I love the desert. Why do we condemn something so

pure and simple as a place of barbarity and fear?' he said, suddenly.

'Men fear the unknown. Perhaps they need to name it, as if by doing so they might exert authority over it. But words are not what they seem,' I replied.

'What do you mean?'

'I mean, they are slippery. Words can change their meaning in a moment.'

'That is not what the priests tell us. They say the holy words are the greatest power in the world. They are the secret language of creation. The God spoke and the world came into existence. Is it not so?'

He gazed at me, as if daring me to contradict him.

'But what if words are made by men and not by Gods?'

He looked disconcerted for a moment, but then he smiled.

'You are a strange man, and an unusual Medjay officer. One could imagine you think the Gods themselves are our own invention.'

I hesitated to reply. He noticed.

'Be careful, Rahotep. Such thoughts are blasphemy.'

I bowed. He gave me a long, but not antagonistic, stare.

'I will rest now.'

And so I was dismissed from the royal presence.

I stepped outside the tent. The sun had moved beyond its zenith, and the camp was silent, as everyone but the guards along the periphery, under their sunshades, had retired from the conquering heat of the afternoon. I did not wish to think about gods and men and words any more. Suddenly I felt weary of them all. I listened to the great silence of the desert, and it seemed the finest sound I had heard in a long time.

29

The Master of the Hunt, accompanied by his chief tracker, beckoned me forward. I moved as quietly as possible across the scrubby ground to the low ridge from where they were scouting the watering hole. I carefully peered over the scuffed edge of the bluff, and looked down on a remarkable sight. In the late light, herds of gazelle, antelope and a few wild cattle were quietly pushing forward, taking their turn to drink, then gazing cautiously into the now golden distances of the savannah, or dropping their elegant heads to crop. The trackers had dug out the watering hole earlier in the day to lure as many animals as possible; some sniffed the dark ground uneasily, scenting the presence of men, yet drawn by the need to drink.

The Master of the Hunt whispered, 'The water has done the trick. There is good hunting here now.'

'But no sign of a lion.'

'They can survive for long periods without water. And they are rare in our time. Once they were plentiful, along with leopards, which I have never seen.'

'So do we hunt what is here, or do we wait longer?'

He considered the possibilities.

'We could kill an antelope, and let it lie to see whether the lion will come and eat.'

'As bait?'

He nodded.

'But even if we are lucky enough to encounter one, it takes great skill, great courage, and many years of practice to hunt and kill a wild lion.'

'Then it is well we have some skilled hunters among our group who can support the King in his moment of triumph.'

He turned a nicely sceptical eye on me in reply.

The silent tracker, whose keen eyes had not left the spectacle of the watering hole and its sudden population, suddenly spoke: 'There will be no lion here this evening. Nor any evening, I think.'

The Master of the Hunt seemed to agree.

'The moon's light will help, but we could wait many long hours for nothing to happen. Better to occupy the King and his hunters with what is available now. Everything is prepared, so let us hunt. It will be good practice. And there is always tomorrow. We will search further into the wilderness.'

So later we approached from the south and the east, to the lee of the cool northerly breeze that had risen. The sunset was turning the firmament gold and orange and blue. Those invited to hunt, both the elite men in their fashionable outfits and the professional hunters, stood posed on their chariots, waiting, whisking away the inevitable flies with their fans, and quietly soothing their impatient horses. Archers examined their bows and arrows. The air was tense with expectation. I moved through the small crowd towards the King. He rode a plain, flexible and practical chariot. It had hardwearing wooden wheels, and its light, open construction suited it to this rough territory. Two fine horses, themselves decorated with feathered head-dresses, gilded blinkers and magnificent shawls, were ready in the traps. The King stood upon a leopard skin that covered the leather thongs of the floor. He wore white linen, arranged over his shoulders, and a long loincloth tied up for safety and flexibility of movement. His gauntlets were ready, so that his sensitive hands could manage the stresses and tensions of the leather reins, if he wished to take them from his charioteer, who stood respectfully to one side. A fan of gold with an ivory handle and glorious ostrich feathers and his gold cane were propped beside him. Next to them, a magnificent bow, and many arrows gathered in a case, were in place, ready for the hunt.

He looked excited and nervous.

'Any sign?'

I shook my head. I could not tell whether he was disappointed or relieved.

'But there are great gatherings of gazelle and antelope, and ostriches, so all is not lost. And this is only the first hunt. We must have patience.'

The horses whinnied and made a small lunge forward, but he pulled on the reins with practised skill.

Then he raised his hand, to command the attention of the hunt, held it still for a long moment, and then dropped it. The hunt had begun.

Those on foot spread out quickly and silently to the east with their bows and arrows poised. The chariots waited a little before moving from the south. I took my position on my own chariot. I admired the light, singing tension of its construction. The horses sniffed at the excitement in the rapidly cooling air. Up above us the full moon had swung above the horizon. Its pale light illuminated us all as if we were drawings on a scroll for a fable entitled *The Hunt by Night*. I looked across at the King's face; under his crown, with the cobra poised on his brow, he still looked so young. But he also looked determined and proud. He sensed me looking at him, and turned to me, smiling. I nodded to him before bowing my head.

Then we moved out, our wheels crunching across the gritty and uneven ground, until the hunting chariots had spread across an area of the open ground as wide as an arena. Once we were in position, the Master of the Hunt gave a practised cry to the archers who had been deployed to the east. Far up ahead in the shadowy distance, I could barely make out the unsuspecting animals at the watering hole – just some silhouettes highlighted against the last of the light. Several raised their heads nervously at the strange cry. And then at a signal from the Master of the Hunt, the beaters suddenly beat their wooden clappers together in a terrific cacophony, and in an instant the herds of animals were charging in alarm – and running, as was intended by the hunt's strategy, towards the chariots. I heard the distant thundering of their hooves coming towards us. Each man urgently took up his reins, and then, led by the King – who took his instruction from the Master of the Hunt – the chariots hurtled forward to a terrific hue and cry. Suddenly we were in battle.

The hunting dogs and the cheetahs raced ahead towards the approaching beasts, the charioteers had their spears hoisted at their shoulders, or, if they had a driver, their bows balanced and pointed . . . but the terrified herds suddenly sensed the peril that lay ahead, and veered, as one, to the west, so our chariots spread out, the hunt now on under the glory of the moon by whose light it was possible to see every-thing in detail. I looked across and saw the King intent on the quarry, urging his horses on. He was a surprisingly fine charioteer. I followed, keeping as close to him as possible, and saw Simut doing the same, so that we were a kind of protective corral. I feared a supposedly accidental arrow or hunting spear striking him in the midst of the hunt, as they whistled over our heads, through the air, to land ahead of us.

The panicked herds threw up a decoy of clouds of dust, drastically unpleasant on the eyes and the throat, so we steered slightly to the north, still galloping at high speed, to try for a clearer view. The slower animals were already failing, especially the ostriches; and I watched as the King took aim and accurately struck a big one down. A hunting dog grabbed the fallen bird by the neck, and began to drag it back, growling and struggling with its great weight. The King grinned at me, thrilled. But up ahead the bigger prizes were still running fast. We urged our horses on faster and faster. The chariots rattled over the rough ground; I glanced down at the axles and prayed mine would hold strong. My teeth were rattling inside my head, and my bones shaking inside my flesh. My ears filled with a constant humming. I wanted to shout with excitement like a child.

The King managed to place a new arrow in his bow, and raised it up to aim. I decided it was time I did something, and followed suit. Up ahead I saw a swiftly bounding antelope, and chose it as my target. I pulled on the reins, and swerved to the right, and forced the horse faster, until suddenly I had him in my sight; in a sudden gap between the flanks of the other animals I let the arrow fly from the bow. Nothing happened for a moment, but then I saw him miss a stride, tangle himself in his legs, and then crash to the ground. The herd raced on and around the fallen animal, and many of the chariots continued their chase.

Now everything was suddenly very quiet. The arrow had pierced the animal's side, and thick dark blood pulsed and flowed down the steaming flank. The eyes were open wide, but unseeing. Flies, those eternal companions of death, were already buzzing in their disgusting excitement around the wound. I felt both pride and pity. A moment ago this corpse of meat and bones was a living thing of magnificent grace and energy. I am used to the bodies of the dead, to mangled, eviscerated, carved-open corpses, and the sweet rotting stench of decaying human flesh. But this animal, killed in the glory of the hunt, seemed another order of passing. In gratitude and respect, I made the prayer of offering to honour the spirit of the animal.

The King approached on his chariot, accompanied by Simut on his. They drew up, and we waited there in the moonlight, the hot breath of our horses like trumpet blasts in the cold desert night air. The King congratulated me. Simut observed the animal and praised its quality. The Master of the Hunt arrived, added his respectful praise, and directed his assistants to take up the animal, along with those others killed in the hunt. We would not lack for meat.

Back at the camp, torches had been lit, flaring in a circle around the great fire at the centre. The butcher was at his work station at the edge of the camp, his hatchet and knives chopping with assurance down through the soft, vulnerable bellies of the strung-up carcasses. He nonchalantly slung hacked-off hooves on one pile, and gathered the guts in great slippery bundles in his arms, before throwing the best parts into a cauldron. Several archers stood guard on the margin of the camp's penumbra to protect him and the meat from the hyenas and the desert foxes.

The King's kill, the ostrich, had been presented to him. He ran his fingers through the magnificent white and brown feathers.

'I have many fans,' he said, casually. 'And therefore I will have these made into one especially for you, Rahotep, as a gift to remember this fine hunt.'

I bowed.

'I would be honoured.'

We drank water, thirstily, and then wine was poured from a tall jar into our gold beakers. We were served the freshly cooked meat of the kill on dishes of exquisitely crafted metal, placed on the rush mats. I took my pick from the array of bronze knives. The King ate carefully, assessing everything that was placed before him on the plates of gold, and then cautiously trying a little. Despite the physical demands of the hunt, he did not eat with a great appetite. Whereas I was starving, and relished every mouthful of the wonderfully flavoured meat, so much more vivid and tender than anything one could buy from the butchers of the city.

'You do not like antelope?' I asked.

'It feels strange to have seen the living animal running for its life, and now to have this piece of dead . . . flesh in my hand.'

I almost laughed at his childish sincerity.

'Everything eats everything else. More or less . . .'

'I know. Dog eats dog. Such is the world of man. And yet I find the thought of it somehow – barbaric.'

'When my children were younger, and we killed a duck or a rabbit at home, they pleaded pitifully for the animal's life, and then, when the feathers, or the fur and skin had been peeled off like a set of robes, and they had shed their tears, they begged to be shown the heart and to keep the lucky paw. And then they ate the stew with no ill-effects whatsoever, and asked for more.'

'Children are not sentimental. Or perhaps they are taught to become so because we cannot bear their honesty. Or their cruelty.'

'Were you taught to be sentimental?'

'I was raised in a palace, not a home. My mother was taken away from me, my father was remote as a statue. My companions were a wet nurse and a monkey. Is it surprising I gave my love to animals? At least I knew they loved me, and I could trust their love.'

And he gently fed some of the meat to his monkey, then delicately washed his fingers in the bowl.

But we were interrupted, at that moment, by a shadow that appeared on the linen walls at the entrance to the tent. I let my hand fall to grasp the hilt of the dagger hidden in my robe. The firelight out-side made the shadow seem larger than life as it approached. The King called out permission to enter. It was his personal assistant. He carried a tray of freshly baked honey cakes, and a dish of the honeycomb. The King's eyes lit up with delight. The assistant bowed and placed the tray before us. The cook must have decided to make a special treat for the King's hunting-night supper.

His delicate fingers flickered swiftly towards the cakes; but suddenly, instinctively, I grasped his wrist.

'How dare you touch me!' he cried out.

'Forgive me, lord. But I cannot be sure . . .'

'Of what?' he shouted petulantly, rising to his feet.

'That this honey is safe. We do not know its origins. I would rather not take the risk . . .'

Then his little monkey, with its crafty, shiny eyes, darted down from his shoulder, plucked a piece of honeycomb from the dish, and scampered off into a corner.

'Now do you see what has happened?' he cried, annoyed.

He approached the monkey, making little loving noises, but it mistrusted him, and darted along the wall of the tent to the far corner, where it began to nibble at its treasure, blinking with anxiety. Again the King followed him, and I approached from the other angle, in a pincer movement. But the creature was too swift for us, and it darted away again between my legs, snapping at my hand with its sharp little teeth, and ran off again to the far side of the tent, where it sat on its haunches, munching and chattering, until the honeycomb was consumed. The King approached it again, and now that it had nothing to lose, it willingly trotted back towards him, perhaps even in hope of further treats. But suddenly, strangely, it seemed to trip over itself, as if it had forgotten how to walk; and then it curled up into a tight ball, twisting and turning into itself, writhing and uttering little cries of agony. The King's shout of distress quickly brought Simut and the guards. There was nothing anyone could do. Mercifully quickly, the monkey was dead. I was only glad it was not the King who had died in the grip of poison.

He carefully picked up the dead creature, and gently held it close to himself. He turned and looked at us all.

'What are you all staring at!' he shouted.

No one dared speak. For a moment, I thought he was going to throw the little corpse at me. But instead he turned away and carried it into the privacy of his bedchamber.

Outside the moon hung low on the black horizon. It was very cold. The King's guards stamped their feet, and moved back and forth as they resumed their sentry duty, trying to keep warm and awake as they stood beside the brazier that burned like a small sun in its black cage. Red sparks drifted briefly up into the night, and vanished. For more privacy, Simut and I walked beyond the edge of the encampment. Away from the firelight, the vast silvered desert lands spread out for ever; they were more beautiful, under the great blackness of the night sky, than under the harsh light and heat of day. I looked up, and it seemed the heavens burned brighter than ever tonight with the millions of stars that glittered eternally in the perfect air. But here on earth, we were in trouble again.

'It seems he is not safe anywhere,' he said at length. 'It seems nothing we do can assure him of security.'

We had questioned the assistant, and the cook, who hastily explained that Tutankhamun had personally requested the honey be made into cakes. Both were terrified of their involvement in what had happened – and the implication that they were themselves complicit.

'The King has a sweet tooth. He always requires something sweet at the end of a meal,' said the cook, his big, sweaty hands twisted together.

'I did not approve, but the King's wishes must be obeyed in all things,' added the assistant superciliously, nervously regarding the cook.

I had the evidence of my own eyes to confirm their story, and no doubt whoever had sent the honey knew too of the King's pleasure in sweetness.

'If we can catch those honey gatherers, we can question them directly. They will quickly confess who instructed them to deliver the honey,' I said. But Simut shook his head.

'I have already asked the Master of the Hunt. He has persuaded me it will be a fruitless task to track them, especially in the dark. They are experts in the desert, and he assures me if they do not wish to be found they will have disappeared without trace by dawn.'

We pondered the possibilities that remained open to us.

'The King is alive still, and that is the most important thing.'

'Certainly. But whose reach is so extensive that even out here' – he gestured at the huge vacancy of the countless stars and the night desert – 'they can attempt to poison him?'

'I believe there are only two people,' I replied.

He looked at me and nodded. We understood each other well.

'And I know which I would pick as the likelier candidate,' he said quietly.

'Horemheb?'

He nodded. 'We are in his territory, and it would not have been difficult for him to track our progress. And it would suit him for the King to die far from his own court, and the chaos that would follow would be the perfect battleground for him to contend with Ay for power.'

'All of that is true, although it might be said he would be the first suspect one would think of, and perhaps he would not be so – obvious.'

Simut grunted.

'Whereas Ay is clever enough to engineer something from this distance, which would also cast a shadow of suspicion over Horemheb,' I continued.

'But in either case, they would both benefit from the King's death.'

'And in either case, they are men of immense influence and power. Ay cannot control the army, and yet he needs it. Horemheb cannot control the offices, and yet he needs them. And both of them wish to control the royal domain. I am beginning to think the King merely stands between them as an obstacle in their own great battle,' I said.

He nodded.

'What do you think we should do?' he asked.

'I think we should remain here. The priority is to kill a lion. That in itself will give the King renewed comfort, and confidence.'

'I agree. To return in any other way would be a sign of failure. He has set the stakes very high. We must not fail.'

We walked back to the brazier, to warm ourselves.

'I will watch through the night, with the guards,' offered Simut.

'And I will see if the King needs anything, and I'll sleep in his tent, if he requires it.'

And so we parted.

30

Tutankhamun was sitting on his travelling throne, staring at nothing, holding the dead monkey like a baby in his lap. I bowed my head and waited for him to speak.

'You saved my life,' he said, eventually, flatly.

I remained silent.

'You will be rewarded,' he continued. 'Look up.'

I did so, and I saw to my relief that something important had changed in him.

'I confess that everything that has happened in these last weeks has brought great fear into my heart. Sometimes I was afraid to be alive. And fear itself became my master. But the King of the Two Lands must not be afraid. It is time to conquer my fear, to give it no authority. Otherwise what will I be, but the prey of shadows?'

'Fear is human, lord,' I said, carefully, 'but it is wise to learn its deceits and its powers, in order to control and defeat them.'

'You are right. And in doing so, I learn the deceits of those who would use fear against me; those who would use the images of death to terrify me. But if I give death no sway, then fear has no sway. Is that not true, Rahotep?'

'It is true, lord. But it is common to all to fear death. It is a reasonable fear.'

'And yet I cannot afford to live in fear of it any more.'

He looked down at the dead monkey, and gently stroked its fur.

'Death is only a dream, from which we awake in a more glorious place.'

I could not agree with him, and therefore I remained silent.

'I know you well enough now, Rahotep, to see when you are not speaking your mind.'

'Death is a subject I resist discussing.'

'And yet your life's work is the business of death.'

'Perhaps, lord. But I have no love for it.'

'I would imagine, having seen so much of it, you must find it somehow disappointing,' he commented, accurately.

'It is at once disappointing and remarkable. I look at corpses, which were a day before living, talking and laughing, committing their petty crimes and enjoying their love-affairs, and now what is left behind but an inert sack of blood and viscera? What has happened? My mind still blanks at the thought of the experience of being dead.'

'We are alike, we both think too much,' he said, and smiled.

'It is worst in the small hours. I realize death is a day closer. I fear the death of those I love. I fear my own death. I think about the good I have not done, and the love I failed to cherish, and the time I have wasted. And when I have done with all that useless remorse, I think about death's emptiness. Not to be here. Not to be anywhere at all . . .'

He said nothing for a moment. I wondered if I had gone too far. But then he clapped his hands and laughed.

'What wonderful company you are, Rahotep! Such optimism, such cheerfulness . . .'

'You are right, lord. I brood. My daughters tell me to cheer up.'

'They are right to do so. But I am concerned. I hear no word of faith in the Gods in what you say.'

I paused before replying, for suddenly the ground of our conversation felt thin as papyrus.

'I struggle with my faith. And I struggle to believe. Perhaps that is my personal way of being afraid. Faith tells us that in spirit we never die. But I find, try as I might, I cannot yet believe that story.'

'Life itself is holy, Rahotep. The rest is mystery.'

'Indeed, lord. And sometimes, as I lie there thinking my futile thoughts, the light steals up on me; dawn comes, and the children awake, and outside the street fills up with people and activity, as it does in every street, all through the city, as in every city in the land. And I remember there is work to be done. And I get up.'

He said nothing for a moment.

'You are right. Duty is everything. And there is great work to be accomplished. Everything that has happened recently has only encouraged me in my absolute determination to fulfil my kingship, in the line of my great ancestors. When we return to Thebes, I will establish a new order. The rule of darkness will be abolished. It is time to bring light and hope to the Two Lands, in the glorious names of the Kings of my dynasty.'

I bowed my head again at these brave words. And I let myself wonder how the world would be if, perhaps, after all, the light could conquer the shadows.

He poured two goblets of wine, passed me one, and offered a stool to sit with him.

'I understand who has reason to wish me dead. Horemheb is ambitious for power. He sees me merely as an impediment to his own dynasty. And Ay will oppose the new order, because it denies him his authority. But Ankhesenamun and I will deal with him accordingly.'

'The Queen is a great asset,' I said.

'She has a mind for strategy, and I for appearance. It is a fortunate combination. And we trust each other. We have depended on each other since we were children, at first from necessity, but that quickly grew into mutual admiration.'

He paused.

'Tell me about your family, Rahotep.'

'I have three glorious girls, and a young son, thanks to the grace of my wife.'

He nodded.

'You are indeed fortunate. Ankhesenamun and I have not yet achieved that, and it is imperative we raise children to succeed us. Twice we have failed, for the infants were stillborn. Girls, they told me. Their deaths had a grave effect upon us. It made my wife feel . . . blighted.'

'But you are both young. There is time.'

'You are right – there is time. Time is on our side.'

Neither of us spoke for a moment. The faint light from the brazier played across the tent walls. Suddenly I felt tired.

'I will sleep outside your tent tonight,' I said.

He shook his head.

'That's unnecessary. I will no longer be afraid of the dark. And tomorrow we will hunt again, and perhaps fortune will bring us what we seek: a lion.'

I stood, and bowed my head. I was about to step back, and out of the tent, when he unexpectedly spoke again.

'Rahotep. When we return to Thebes, I wish you to become my personal bodyguard.'

I was astonished into silence.

'I am honoured, lord. But surely Simut has that position.'

'I wish to appoint someone who will concentrate on my security to the exclusion of all else. I can trust you, Rahotep; I am sure of it. You are a man of honour and dignity. My wife and I need you.'

I must have looked disconcerted, for he continued:

'It will be a generously rewarded position. I am sure your family would benefit. And you would not have to consider your career prospects in the city Medjay again.'

'You do me too great an honour. May we discuss this again when we return to Thebes?'

'Yes. But do not refuse me.'

'Life, prosperity and health, lord.'

He nodded, and I bowed and stepped backwards. But before I left the tent he called to me:

'I enjoy talking to you, Rahotep. As much as I have enjoyed talking to any man.'

Outside, I looked up at the moon, and thought about the oddness of fate; of the disparate things that had brought me to this place, this wilderness, and this moment. And I realized that, despite everything, I was smiling. Not just at the strangeness of my audiences with the most powerful man in the world, who was still something of a child; but at the unpredictability of fortune, or luck, that now offered me what it had seemed I would never achieve. Preferment. And I indulged myself in a rare, delicious sensation: the thought of triumph over that clod of authority, Nebamun. I would enjoy watching his rage when I told him that I no longer needed anything from him.

31

A tracker returned that evening with news. He had found the tracks of a lion. But they lay far off, deeper into the Red Land. We gathered in Simut's tent.

'He is a nomad,' said the tracker.

'What does that mean?' asked Simut.

'He is not attached to any pride. Young males live alone in the desert, before finding a pride to which they can belong again, in order to father young. Whereas the females always hunt together, and always remain in their home prides. So we have to follow him into his own domain.'

We agreed we would dismantle the camp, and move everything to where the tracks had been found. From the new camp, it would be possible to take our time, track the lion, and choose our moment to hunt. We had sufficient supplies of food and water to last at least another week. And if the lion moved even deeper into the desert, then we could travel further, even as far as the remote oases, if necessary, for supplies of food and water.

I watched as our temporary habitation was taken down again. All the golden furniture, the kitchen equipment and the caged animals were loaded on to carts. The goats were tethered together again. The cook's hooks, knives and great cauldrons were loaded on to the mules.

And finally the King's tent was dismantled, the central pole and its golden ball taken down, and the long lengths of cloth folded and packed away. Suddenly it looked as if we had never been here at all, so transient was the impression we had made upon the vastness of the desert. All that was left was the chaos of our footprints and the brazier's circle of black ash that was already drifting apart in the light northern breeze. I pressed the cinders down under my foot, and remembered the black circle on the box lid back in the Palace of Shadows. Of all the signs, it was the one that had haunted me most. I still did not know its meaning.

The sun was already well past its zenith when we set off deeper into the Red Land. The air shimmered across the desolate, barren landscape; we travelled slowly through a wide empty bed of shale and grit, surrounded by low bluffs, that might once have been a great river in the ancient past – for it is known that the bones of strange sea creatures were occasionally revealed by the wind and the changing sands. But now, as if by some catastrophe of time and the Gods, everything in this world had been transmuted to this grey and red rock and dust under the furnace of the sun. The great slow seas of sand, which I had heard of in tales from travellers, had to be much further to the west.

I rode beside Simut.

'Perhaps fortune is at last gracing us,' he said quietly – for every sound travelled crisply in the silent air.

'All we have to do now is track the lion.'

'And then we must do everything to help the King to his triumph,' he replied.

'He is determined to make the kill himself, but it is one thing to kill an ostrich among a herd of terrified animals, and another altogether to face and kill a desert lion,' I said.

'I agree. We will have to surround him with the best hunters in our team. Perhaps if they can bring the lion down, then he would be content to strike the final blow. It would still be his kill.'

'I hope so.'

We rode on without speaking for a while.

'He seems to have recovered well from the death of his monkey.'

'If anything, it has strengthened his resolve.'

'I never liked that pathetic creature. I would have wrung its neck long ago . . .'

We laughed quietly.

'I pity its suffering, but it turned out to have a use, in the end.'

'As a food-taster, and through its greed, like a creature in a moral fable, it came to an unfortunate end,' he replied, with a rare, wry smile.

After slowly crossing the forsaken ocean of gravel and grey dust for hours, we came at last into a different, strange, wild landscape where the artistry of the wind had carved pillars of pale rock into fantastical shapes, lit now in yellows and oranges by the glory of the sunset. The brazier was quickly set, the tents resurrected, and soon the smells of cooking drifted richly in the pure air.

The King appeared at the entrance to his tent.

'Come Rahotep, let us walk together before it is dark.'

And so we strolled among the curious forms of the rocks, enjoying the cooling air.

'This is another world,' he said. 'How many others, of perhaps still greater strangeness, lie even further away into the Red Land?'

'Perhaps the world is much larger than we can know, lord. Perhaps the Red Land is not all there is of the land of the living. There are stories of lands of snow, and lands where all is green, always,' I replied.

'I would like to be the King who discovers and charts strange lands and new peoples. I dream of how the glory of our empire might one day go forth into unknown worlds, and into the dim future. Who knows but that what we make in this world might survive time itself! Why should it not? We are a great people of gold and power. The best of us is beautiful and true. I am glad we came, Rahotep. I was right to command it. Away from the palace, away from those walls and shadows, I feel alive again. I have not felt alive for so long. It is good. And fortune will smile upon me now. I can feel the goodness of the future, just ahead of me, calling to me to make it come to pass . . .'

'That is a great calling, lord.'

'It is. I feel it, in my heart. It is my destiny as King. The Gods are waiting for me to fulfil it.'

As we had talked, the brilliant stars, in all their glory and mystery, had appeared in the great ocean of the night. We both stood beneath them, looking up.

32

We set out in the chariots, properly armed and provisioned, as the sun was setting on the next day. The trackers had reconnoitred the terrain and found more signs. The lion's territory seemed to centre on the low, shady bluffs at a little distance from the camp. No doubt they provided a haven for whatever life could survive in this harsh place. We carried with us a newly slaughtered goat's carcass, to tempt him. We waited, our chariots arranged in a wide fan, watching from a careful distance as a tracker rode across the grey landscape with the dead animal, deposited it, and then retreated.

The tracker took up a position next to me.

'He will be very hungry, for the prey is limited out here, and we have offered him a fine feast. I hope he will take the bait before it is dark.'

'And if he does not?'

'Then we must try again tomorrow. It would be unwise to approach him in the darkness.'

And so we waited silently as the sun continued its descent. Ahead of us the shadows of the bluffs lengthened imperceptibly, until, like a slowly rising tide, they reached the carcass, as if to consume it. The tracker shook his head.

'We are too late,' he whispered. 'We can return tomorrow.'

But just then, he tensed like a cat.

'Look. There he is . . .'

I peered into the darkening landscape, but saw nothing until at last I noticed the slightest movement of shadow against shadow. Everyone had noticed the tracker's reaction, and a sudden jostling of movement passed down the line of men and horses. The tracker held up his hand for absolute silence. We waited intently. Then the shape moved forward, stealthily, slinking, as it approached the carcass. It raised its head to scan the terrain, as if wondering where this ready-made feast could have come from, and then, satisfied, settled down to feast.

'What should we do?' I whispered to the tracker.

He considered carefully.

'It is too dark to hunt him now, for we would easily lose track of him. This terrain is difficult. But now we know he will accept our offerings, we can return tomorrow, and tempt him out earlier with more fresh meat. A young adult such as this one has a large appetite; he will not have fed well for a long time. And tomorrow we will be well prepared, and in better positions from which to surround him.'

Simut nodded in agreement. But suddenly, without warning and without support, the King's chariot jolted forward, and began to gain speed across the rough ground. Everyone was taken entirely by surprise. I saw the lion raise its head, disturbed by the distant noise. Simut and I spurred our own horses, and set off in pursuit of the King. I looked again and saw the lion was now dragging the carcass away towards the cliffs, where we would never find him. I was gaining on the King's chariot, and shouted at him to stop. He turned around, but gestured as if he could not, or would not, hear me. His face was alive with excitement. I shook my head wildly, but he merely grinned like a schoolboy, and turned away. The chariot wheels clattered alarmingly, and the axles knocked and complained as the wooden structure struggled with the demands of the rough terrain. I glanced up and for the briefest of moments I saw the lion standing and staring. But the King had some distance to cover, and the beast did not seem greatly alarmed.

The King raced onwards, and I saw him struggling to control the chariot, and at the same time to fit an arrow into his bow. Now the lion turned, and his loping strides quickly become full-stretched flight at incredible speed towards the safety of the dark bluffs. I lashed my horse onwards, and gained on the King. I thought surely he would realize there was no chance of hunting the lion in these conditions, but suddenly his chariot jumped up in the air as if it had hit a rock, and then slammed down again. As it did so the left wheel shattered and sheared, the spokes and wheel rim splintered and flew off, and the carriage collapsed on to its left side. It was dragged wildly across the rough ground by the panicked horses. I saw the King gripping on to the side of the chariot in terrror; but in the next moment his body flew up like a rag doll, and then hit the ground at speed, rolling over and over, until it came to rest in the darkness.

I reined in my horse, and my chariot skidded to a halt. I ran to his body. He was not moving. I dropped to my knees beside him. Tutankhamun, Living Image of Amun, was making small sounds that tried and failed to become words. He did not seem to recognize me. There was a puddle of blood, black and shiny, spreading on the dust of the desert.

His left leg above the knee was sticking out at a sickening angle. I carefully peeled the linen of his robe, sticky with blood, away from the skin. Shards of shattered bone protruded through the torn flesh and skin. There was grit and dirt in the horrible, deep wound. He gave a terrible moan of acute pain. I poured water from my flask, and the blood washed away, black and thick. I feared he would die there, in the desert, under the moon and the stars, his head in my hands like a chalice of nightmares.

Simut arrived, and took one look at the disastrous wound.

'I will fetch Pentu. Don't move him,' he shouted, as he rode away.

The tracker and I stayed with the King. He had begun to shiver violently with shock. I tore the panther skin from the floor of the chariot, and covered him with it as gently as possible.

He was trying to speak. I lowered my head to catch his words.

'I am sorry,' he kept repeating.

'The wound is superficial,' I said, trying to reassure him. 'The physician is coming. You will be fine.'

He gazed at me from the strange distance of his agony, and I knew he knew I was lying.

Pentu arrived and examined the King. He checked first his head, but aside from the swelling of bruises and long scratches down one side of his face, there were no signs of bleeding at the nose or ears, and so he concluded the skull was not fractured. At least that was something. He then examined the wound and the broken bone by the light of our torches. He glanced up at Simut and me, and shook his head. Not good. We stood apart so that the King could not hear us.

'We are lucky that the artery in the leg has not been severed. But he is losing a great deal of blood. We must reset this fracture immediately,' he said.

'Out here?' I asked.

He nodded.

'It is imperative he is not moved again until this is done. I will need your help. This is a difficult bone to set, for the fracture is severe, and the muscles of the leg and thigh are powerful. And there will be some over-riding of the shattered bone-ends. But we cannot move him until it is done.'

He assessed the angle of the broken bones. The King's limbs seemed like the parts of a mangled doll. Pentu placed a rolled-up linen cloth between his chattering teeth. Then as I held his torso and upper thigh firmly in position, and Simut held the other side of his body, Pentu swiftly pushed down on the femur, and with a practised motion jammed the shattered bone-ends together. The King screamed like an animal. The gristly noise of the setting reminded me of the kitchen, when I break apart the haunch of a gazelle, twisting its leg bones from the thigh socket. This was butcher's work. Then the King vomited, and passed from consciousness.

Pentu set to work by the flickering torchlight, stitching the ugly wound with a curved copper needle he produced from a case made of bird bone. Then he smeared honey and oil on it, and bound it tightly in linen bandages. Finally he made the leg as secure as possible within a splint padded with linen and secured by knots, for the journey back to the camp.

The King was carried into his quarters. His skin was clammy and pale. We gathered around, in a hushed, urgent conference.

'The fracture is of the worst kind, both because the bone has shattered, rather than snapped across, and because the skin has been torn open, making the flesh vulnerable to infection. There has been loss of blood. But at least everything has been reset. Let us pray to Ra the fever will pass, and the wound heals well,' said Pentu gravely.

A low sense of dread had fallen upon us all.

'But he is now asleep, which is good. His spirit will be pleading with the Gods of the Otherworld for more time, and more life. Let us pray they are persuaded.'

'What should we do now?' I asked.

'The most sensible decision medically would be to transport him swiftly to Memphis,' said Pentu. 'At least there I can care for him properly.'

Simut interrupted: 'But in Memphis he would be surrounded by his enemies. Horemheb is likely still in residence. I say we must return him to Thebes in secrecy, as swiftly as possible. And this accident must be kept secret until a public version of events has been agreed with Ay. If the King – life, prosperity and health be upon him – is fated to die, then it must be in Thebes, among his own people, and near to his tomb. And we must control how his death is understood. Of course, if he lives, then he can best be cared for at home.'

We broke camp that night and started our sorrowful journey under the stars, back across the desert towards the distant ship, and the Great River that would carry us all home to the city. I tried not to let myself think what the consequences would be for all of us, and for the future of the Two Lands, if he died.

33

I kept vigil at the bedside of Tutankhamun as he twisted and turned in feverish agony all through the nights of the river journey back to Thebes. His heart seemed to race in his chest, trapped and frail, like a tiny bird. Pentu treated him with purgatives, to prevent the beginning of putrefaction in the bowels spreading morbidly to the heart. And he contended with the leg wound, tying and retying the wooden splints, changing the linen padding regularly, so that the splintered bones might have some chance of binding together.

He had struggled to keep the wound clean, at first binding it with fresh meat, and then poultices of honey, fat and oil. But each time he changed the bandaging, and applied more cedar resin, I could see the lips were hesitating from binding, and now a deep black shadow was creeping through the flesh, under the skin, in every direction. The smell of rotting flesh was vile. Pentu tried everything: a decoction of willow bark, barley flour, the ash of a plant whose name he would not reveal, mixed with onion and vinegar, and a white ointment made from minerals found in the desert mines of the oasis towns. Nothing worked.

On the second morning of the journey, with Pentu's permission, I spoke to the King. The fresh daylight entering his chamber seemed to calm and cheer him after a long, painful night. He had been washed, and dressed in fresh linens. But already he was drenched in sweat, and his eyes were dull.

'Life, prosperity and health,' I said, quietly, aware of the grim irony of the formula.

'No degree of prosperity, no gold nor treasure, can bring back life and health,' he whispered.

'The physician is confident of a full recovery,' I said, trying to maintain my encouraging expression.

He gazed at me like a wounded animal. He knew better.

'Last night I had a strange dream,' he panted. I waited for him to gain enough strength to continue. 'I was Horus, son of Osiris. I was the falcon, hovering high in the sky, approaching the Gods.'

I wiped the sweat that beaded his hot brow.

'I flew among the Gods.' And he searched my eyes, earnestly.

'And what happened then?' I asked.

'Something bad. I fell slowly to earth, down and down . . . Then I opened my eyes. I was looking up at all the stars in the darkness. But I knew I would never reach them. And slowly – they started to go out – one by one, faster and faster.'

He gripped my hand.

'And suddenly I was very afraid. All the stars died. Everything was dark. And then I woke up . . . and now I fear to sleep again . . .'

He shivered. His eyes glistened, sincere and wide.

'It was a dream born of your pain. Do not take it to heart.'

'Perhaps you are right. Perhaps there is no Otherworld. Perhaps there is nothing.'

He looked terrified again.

'I was wrong. The Otherworld is real. Do not doubt it.'

Neither of us spoke for a moment. I knew he did not believe me.

'Please, take me home. I want to go home.'

'The ship is making good time, and the north winds are blowing well in our favour. You will soon be there.'

He nodded, miserably. I held his hot, damp hand for a while longer, until he turned his face away to the wall.

Pentu and I went out on to the deck. The world of green fields and labourers passed by as if nothing important was happening.

'What do you think are his chances?' I asked.

He shook his head.

'It is unusual to survive such a catastrophic fracture. The wound is badly infected, and he is weakening. I am very worried.'

'He seems to be in much pain.'

'I try to administer whatever I have to diminish it.'

'The opium poppy?'

'Certainly I will prescribe that, if the pain becomes still worse. But I hesitate to do so until it is necessary . . .'

'Why?' I asked.

'It is the most powerful drug we possess. But its very potency makes it dangerous. His heart is weak, and I do not wish to weaken it further.'

We both stared out at the landscape for a little while, without talking.

'May I ask you a question?' I said, eventually.

He nodded, cautiously.

'I have heard there are secret books, the Books of Thoth?'

'You have mentioned them before.'

'And I believe they include medical knowledge?'

'And if they did?' he replied.

'I am curious to know whether they tell of secret substances, which might give visions . . .'

Pentu regarded me very carefully.

'If such substances existed they would only be revealed to men whose exceptional wisdom and status conferred on them the right to such knowledge. Why, in any case, do you want to know?'

'Because I am curious.'

'That is not the kind of approach that encourages one to reveal closely guarded secrets,' he replied.

'Nevertheless. Anything you could tell me would be very useful.'

He hesitated.

'It is said there exists a magical fungus. It is only found in the boreal regions. It is supposed to grant visions of the Gods . . . But the truth is, we know nothing certain of this fungus, and no one in the Two Lands has ever seen it, let alone experimented with it to prove or disprove its powers. Why do you ask?'

'I have a hunch,' I replied.

He was not amused.

'Perhaps you need more than a hunch, Rahotep. Perhaps it is time you had a vision of your own.'

Through that last night of the journey, the King's fever worsened; he was in appalling pain. The black shadow of infection continued to consume the flesh of his leg. His thin face took on a clammy, sallow complexion, and his eyes, whenever they flickered open, were the dull colour of ivory. His mouth was parched, his lips were cracked, and his tongue was yellow and white. His heart now seemed to have slowed, and he barely had the power to open his mouth to take water. Pentu finally treated him with the juice of the opium poppy. It calmed him marvellously, and suddenly I understood its power and attraction.

Once, in the small hours, he opened his eyes. I broke with protocol and took his hand in mine. He could barely even speak in a whisper, struggling to enunciate each word through the softness of the opium trance. He looked at the protective Eye of Ra ring he had given me. And then with enormous effort, summoning his last reserves of strength, he spoke.

'If my destiny is to die, and pass to the Otherworld, then I ask this of you: accompany my body as far as you can. See me to my tomb.'

His almond-shaped eyes gazed earnestly at me from his gaunt face.

I recognized the stark lineaments and the strange intensity of approaching death.

'You have my word,' I said.

'The Gods await me. My mother is there. I can see her. She calls to me . . .'

And he looked up into thin air, seeing someone I could not.

His hand was small, and light, and hot. I held it between my own as carefully as I could. I looked at the Eye of Ra ring he had given me. It had failed him, and so had I. I felt the delicate slowness of his fading pulse, and attended carefully to it, until just before dawn when he let out a long, last gentle sigh, of neither disappointment nor satisfaction, and the bird of his spirit went out of Tutankhamun, Living Image of Amun, and flew into the Otherworld for ever; and then his hand slipped gently from mine.

Part Three

Your face has been opened in the House of Darkness

The Book of the Dead
Spell 169

34

The *Beloved of Amun* sailed silently into the Malkata harbour just after sunset on the next day. The darkening sky was suitably ominous. No one spoke. The whole world seemed silenced; only the sombre, steady splash and draw of the oarsmen made any sound at all. The water bore an odd, flat, silky grey sheen, as before a sandstorm. On the long stone quay of the palace only a few figures waited. I noticed only one lamp was lit along the dock. We had sent a messenger ahead with the news, the worst news. We should have been returning with the King in glory. Instead we were bringing him home to his tomb.

I stood beside the King's body. It seemed so small and frail. It was now wrapped in clean white linen. Only his face was displayed, calm and still and vacant. His spirit had left. All that remained was this stiff shell. There is nothing emptier in this world than a dead body.

Simut went ashore, while I waited with the King for the guards to arrive. I heard their feet upon the gangplank, and then in the silence that followed Ay entered the royal cabin. He stooped over the body of Tutankhamun, contemplating the reality of the catastrophe. Then with effort he bent lower to the King's left ear, the ear through which the breath of death enters. And I heard him whisper: 'You were a useless child in life. Your death must be the making of you.'

And then he straightened up stiffly.

The King lay unmoved by this upon his golden deathbed. Ay scrutinized me briefly, his eyes like little stones, his cruel face untouched by feeling. Then, without a word, he gestured to the guards to bring the King's body on its bier, and they carried him out.

Simut and I followed the bier through the endless corridors and chambers of the Malkata Palace, which were absolutely deserted. I suddenly felt we were thieves returning a stolen object to its tomb. I reflected that at least we were not yet in fetters. But that might only be a matter of time. No matter what the truth of this accident, we would be blamed for the King's death. He was our responsibility, and we had failed. Suddenly I wanted badly to go home. I wanted to walk away from this chamber, and these indifferent corridors of power, and cross the black waters of the Great River, and go quietly up my street to my house, and close the door behind me, and curl up beside Tanefert, and sleep, and then, when I had slept for many hours, wake up to the simple sun, and for this all to be nothing but a dream. Reality was now my torment.

We were escorted to the King's chamber, and left to wait outside. Time passed slowly, obscurely. Muffled voices, sometimes raised, carried through the thick wooden doors. Simut and I glanced at each other, but he gave nothing away of what he was thinking or feeling. Then the doors suddenly opened, and we were admitted.

Tutankhamun, Lord of the Two Lands, was laid out upon his couch, his thin hands folded across his thin chest. He had not yet been properly attired for death. He was surrounded by the toys and game boxes of his lost childhood. They seemed now to be his grave goods, the objects he would truly treasure in the Otherworld, rather than the golden paraphernalia of royalty. Ankhesenamun gazed at the dead face of her husband. When she looked up at me, her face was hollow with sorrow and defeat. How could she forgive me? I had failed her as much as I had failed the King. She was alone now, in this palace of shadows.

She had become the last living member of her dynasty. No one is more vulnerable than a widowed queen without an heir.

Ay rapped his walking stick suddenly upon the floor stones.

'We must not indulge our grief. There is no time for mourning. There is too much to be done. It must appear to the world that this event has not occurred. No one may speak of what they have seen. The word *death* will not be spoken. Fresh food and clean linens will continue to be delivered to the antechamber. His nurse will continue to attend him. But his body will be purified and made beautiful here, in secret, and since his own tomb is far from ready, he will be buried in my tomb in the royal necropolis. It is suitable, and it will not take long to adapt. The gold coffins are already being prepared. His burial treasures and his funerary equipment will be assembled and chosen by me. All of this will be done swiftly, and above all secretly. When the burial has been accomplished, in secret, then, and only then, we will announce his death.'

Ankhesenamun, stirred from her grief by this astonishing proposal, broke the silence that followed.

'That is absolutely unacceptable. The obsequies and funeral must be conducted with full honour and dignity. Why must we pretend he is not dead?'

Ay approached her furiously.

'How can you be so naive? Do you not understand that the stability of the Two Lands is at stake? The death of a king is the most vulnerable and potentially disastrous time in the life of a dynasty. There is no heir. And that is because your womb has failed to produce anything other than stillborn, deformed infants,' he sneered.

I glanced at Ankhesenamun.

'So the Gods have willed,' she replied, staring at him in cold anger.

'We must take control of this situation before chaos overwhelms us all. Our enemies will attempt to destroy us now. I am God's Father, Doer of Right, and what I decree will be. We must maintain the order of *maat* by all means necessary. The Medjay divisions

261

are even now being given instructions to prevent public and private association, and to use all means to quell any signs of public unrest on the streets. They will be stationed throughout the city, and along the temple walls.'

It sounded like preparations for a state of emergency. What dissent could be so alarming? Who did he mean as the enemy? Only Horemheb. He was Ay's greatest threat at this moment; Horemheb, General of the Two Lands, could easily mount a campaign for power now. He was young, he commanded the majority of the divisions of the army, and he was intelligently ruthless. Ay was old. I looked at him, with his painful bones and teeth, and his rage for order; his earthly power that had seemed so absolute for so long, suddenly seemed vulnerable, and weak. But it would not do to underestimate him.

Ankhesenamun saw all of this.

'There is another way. All of this would be resolved by a strong and immediate succession. I am the last of my great line, and in the name of my father and grandfather, I claim the crowns,' she countered, proudly.

He glared at her with a contempt that would wither a stone.

'You are nothing but a weak girl. Do not indulge in fantasies. You have tried to oppose me once, and failed. It is necessary that I will crown myself king shortly, for there is no one else fit to govern.'

She was provoked now.

'No king may be proclaimed before the Days of Purification are completed. It would be sacrilege.'

'Do not contest my will. It shall be so. It is necessary, and necessity is the most compelling of all reasons,' he shouted, his cane quivering in his hand.

'And what of me?' she said, intently, calmly composed against his rage.

'If you are lucky, I may marry you myself. But it depends how useful such an arrangement would be. I am by no means convinced of its value.'

She shook her head in derision.

'And how is it for you to be convinced of anything? I am Queen.'

'In name only! You have no power. Your husband is dead. You are quite alone. Think carefully before you speak again.'

'I will not tolerate you addressing me in this way. I will make a public proclamation.'

'And I will forbid that and prevent it by any means necessary.'

They stared at each other.

'Rahotep is assigned as my personal guard. Remember that.'

He merely laughed.

'Rahotep? The man who guarded the King, and brought him home dead? His record speaks for itself.'

'The King's death was not his fault. He is loyal. That is everything,' she replied.

'A dog is loyal. That does not make him valuable. Simut will provide a guard. For now, you may mourn in private. And I will consider your future. As for Rahotep, he was given a clear responsibility, and yet the very worst has happened. I will decide his fate,' he said casually.

I had known these words were coming. I thought of my wife and my children.

'What about the lion?' asked Simut. 'The King cannot be seen to have returned without the trophy.'

'Kill the tame one, and display it,' replied Ay dismissively. 'No one will know the difference.'

And with those words he departed, insisting she accompany him. Simut and I remained standing before the slender body of the King, the young man whose life had been entrusted to us. He was the very image of our defeat. Something was finished here, in this bundle of skin and bone. And something else had begun: the war for power.

'I doubt even Ay can contain this,' said Simut. 'People read signs, and the King's absence from public life will be noted very quickly. Coming immediately after the fanfare about the royal hunt, and the expectation of his glorious return, the speculation will be uncontrollable.'

'And that is why Ay needs to bury Tutankhamun as soon as possible, and announce himself King,' I replied. 'And he needs to keep Horemheb at a distance for as long as possible.'

'But the general is as watchful as a jackal. I am sure he will scent this death and seize his opportunity to confront Ay,' said Simut. 'It is not an optimistic prospect.'

We both stood staring down at the King's delicate, dead face. It represented so much more as well: a possible catastrophe for the whole of the Two Lands if this power struggle were not swiftly resolved.

'What worries me most is that Ankhesenamun is so vulnerable to both of them,' I said.

'That is a cause for deep concern,' he conceded.

'It would be a disaster if Horemheb returned to Thebes just now.'

'And it would be a disaster if he entered this palace,' said Simut. 'But how can that be prevented while his wife resides here? Perhaps she should be sent away.'

This was news to me.

'Mutnodjmet? She lives within the palace?'

He nodded.

'But her name has never been spoken in all this time,' I said.

He turned his head closely to mine.

'No one speaks publicly of her. Privately, they say she is a lunatic. She lives in a suite of chambers, from which she never emerges. They say she has only two dwarfs for company. Whether this is by her own will, or whether that of her husband has been imposed upon her, I do not know.'

'You mean she is imprisoned here?'

'Call it what you will. But she has no liberty. She is the family secret.'

My mind raced ahead, like a dog on the scent of its hidden quarry, suddenly close.

'I must attend to other matters, but let us talk more, elsewhere. What will you do now?' he asked.

'I have no future, apparently,' I said, with a lightness I did not feel.

'But you are not yet in fetters.'

'I suspect if I try to leave this palace, a strange accident will befall me.'

'Then do not leave. You have a role here. Protect the Queen. I can offer you in turn the protection of my guards, and whatever degree of safety the authority of my name confers.'

I nodded, grateful.

'But first there is something I must do. I must speak to Mutnodjmet. Do you know where her chambers lie?'

He shook his head.

'It is kept a secret, even from me. But you know someone who probably could take you there.'

'Khay?'

He nodded.

'Ask him. And remember: what happened was not your fault. It was not my fault, either.'

'Do you think the world will believe that?' I replied.

He shook his head.

'But it is the truth, and that is still something, even in this age of deceit,' he replied, and then he turned away and left me alone in the King's chamber, with the dead boy.

35

Why had no one ever mentioned Mutnodjmet? Not even Ankhesenamun, her own niece. And yet, all the time Nefertiti's sister, the wife of Horemheb, the general of the Two Lands, had been incarcerated here within the Malkata Palace. Perhaps she was simply a poor madwoman, the living shame of her family, and so they kept her locked away from public sight. But she was nevertheless a connection between the royal dynasty and Horemheb. He had married into power, and now, it seemed, he acquiesced in his wife's imprisonment.

I was considering these matters when the door of the chamber slowly, silently opened. I waited to see who would enter. A figure in dark robes moved silently across the stone floor towards the bed.

'Stop there!'

The figure froze.

'Turn around,' I said.

The figure twisted slowly towards me. It was Maia, the wet nurse. Her contempt for me was undisguised. Grief disfigured her face. Then she carefully and precisely spat at me. She had nothing more to lose. I wiped the spittle from my face. She moved towards the dead body. She bent tenderly over her King, kissing his cold brow reverently.

'He was my child. I fed him, and cared for him from the day he was born. He trusted you. *And behold what you have brought back.* I curse you. I curse your family. May you all be blighted as you have blighted me.' Her face was livid with rage now.

Without waiting for, or apparently desiring, a reply, she began to wash the body with natron-salted water. I sat down upon a stool and watched. She worked with infinite care and love, knowing this would be the last time she could ever touch him. She washed his limp arms, and his dangling hands, taking each finger in turn, and wiping them like a helpless child's. She passed her cloth gently over the unmoving, thin chest, wiping along the length of each rib, and over the narrow shoulders, and under the shallow armpits. Then she drew her cloth down the long length of the sound leg, and then gently around the festering wound of the broken one, as if he were still sensible of his pain. Finally she knelt at his feet. I listened to the quiet splash of the cloth in the bowl of scented water, the little cascade as she wrung it out, the steady repeated movement of the cloth between his toes, around his delicate ankles, and along the length of his dead feet, which she kissed as she finished her work.

Tears dripped from her chin as she wept silently. Then she folded his arms, in time-honoured fashion, ready for the gold crook and flail, the royal symbols of Upper and Lower Egypt, and of Osiris, the first King, Lord of the Otherworld, which others would place in his hands in due course. Finally from one of the clothing chests, she took a fine gold collar and a jewelled gold pectoral, with a scarab inlaid at its heart, pushing a fine red carnelian sun disc above it into the light of the new day, and placed it on his chest.

'Now he is ready for the Controller of the Mysteries,' she whispered.

And then she settled herself on a stool at the side of the room, as far away from me as possible, and began murmuring her prayers.

'Maia,' I said.

She ignored me. I tried again.

'Where are the quarters of Mutnodjmet?' I asked.

She opened her eyes.

'Oh, now that it is too late, he asks the right question.'

'Tell me why that is the right question?'

'Why should I tell you anything? It is too late for me. It is too late for you. You should have listened to me before. I will speak no more. I will be silent for ever.'

I was about to insist when the door opened and the Controller of the Mysteries entered the chamber, wearing the jackal-headed mask of Anubis, the God of the Dead, and accompanied by his assistants. Usually the body would have been removed to an embalming enclosure, away from the living quarters, where it would be washed, eviscerated, dried out with salt, anointed and bandaged. But I supposed because Ay had insisted upon secrecy, he had ordered that the body must remain in the chamber. A lector priest began to recite the first instructions and magical utterances, while the lesser officials prepared the chamber with the necessary equipment – tools, hooks, obsidian blades, resins, water, salt, palm wine, spices, and the many bandages that would be used during the long process. They set the sloping wooden embalming board upon four wooden blocks, and then respectfully lifted the King's body and laid it out there. Later in the long ritual, the embalmed body would be dressed in a shroud, and then bandaged; and then, for this King, priceless jewels, rings, bracelets, collars and magical amulets, many containing spells of special protection, would be secreted within the folds and layers of the fine linens, with utterances and spells to accompany each action – for every action had to adhere precisely to the traditions if it were to have value in the afterlife. Finally, the death mask would be fitted, so that this last face of gold could identify the dead man, and allow his *ka* and *ba* spirits to reunite with his body in the tomb.

The Controller of the Mysteries stood at the foot of the embalming table, looking down at the King's body. Everything was ready for the work of purification to begin. Then he turned his gaze on me. I could see the white of his hidden eyes through the elegant holes in the black of his mask. In the close silence, all his assistants turned to stare at me. It was time to leave.

36

I knocked on the door to Khay's office. After a moment his assistant answered. He glanced anxiously at me.

'My master is occupied,' he said urgently, trying to get between me and the door to the inner chamber.

'I am sure he can spare me a few moments of his precious time.'

I walked through the antechamber, and into Khay's office. His bony face was flushed. He was taken aback, and was not sober enough to cover it well.

'The great Seeker of Mysteries makes his grand entrance . . .'

I saw he had a full cup of wine upon his low table, and there was a small amphora on its stand beside it.

'I'm sorry to disturb you at this late hour. I thought you might be at home, with your family. Do you have a home and a family?'

He squinted at me.

'What do you want, Rahotep? I'm busy . . .'

'So I see.'

'At least some of us are committed to a certain level of competence in our work.'

I ignored him.

'I've discovered a very curious thing.'

'Good to hear our Seeker of Mysteries has discovered *something* . . .'

His mouth seemed to be working slightly in advance of his brain.

'Mutnodjmet resides within the walls of this palace.'

His chin was now raised, his eyes suddenly wary.

'What bearing could that have upon your business here?'

'She is Horemheb's wife, and aunt to Ankhesenamun.'

He clapped his hands together, his face a caricature.

'Such meticulous research into the family tree!'

But he was nervous, behind the irony.

'So can you confirm she is being held within the palace?'

'As I said, the subject has no bearing on the matter at hand.'

I moved closer. Tiny broken veins were pulsing delicately in the puffy, crinkled skin around his eyes. He was subsiding fast into middle age. The stress of his elevated position would not help, and he would not be the first to take to wine as a consolation.

'I have a different opinion of the matter, and so please answer the question.'

'I am not here to be interrogated by you.'

His feathers were up now.

'As you know, I have the authority of the King and Queen to pursue my inquiries wherever they may take me, and I cannot comprehend why there should be such an issue about answering a very simple question,' I replied.

He blinked at me, wavering slightly. Eventually he answered:

'She is not being held, as you put it. She lives out her life in her own wing of accommodation within the comforts and security of the royal quarters.'

'That is not what I have heard.'

'Well, people do talk such *rubbish*.'

'If it is all so nice and easy, why has no one told me about this?'

'Ha! You are desperate for some direction in your futile

investigation of the mystery. But it has now become quite pointless, and I would advise you against pursuing this line of inquiry.'

'Why?'

'Because it will prove a dead end.'

'Why are you so sure?'

'She is a poor lunatic who has not left her quarters for many years. What can she possibly have to do with all of this . . . ?'

He turned away. His hands quivered slightly as he raised the wine cup and drank a deep draught.

'Take me to see her. Now.'

He put down his cup too quickly, and some of the wine splashed on his hand. He looked incensed by this, and instead of wiping it away, he licked it off.

'You have no grounds for such an interview.'

'Should I trouble Ay or the Queen with this request?'

He wavered.

'When there is so much else of really vital importance going on, it really is too ridiculous, but I suppose if you insist . . .'

'Let us go, then.'

'It is late. The Princess will have retired. Tomorrow.'

'No. Now. Who knows what hours lunatics keep?'

We set off down the corridors. I hoped to keep a bird's view of our progress, like a plan inscribed on the papyrus of my memory, because I wanted to be able to locate her quarters exactly, and find them again if I needed to. But it was not a simple matter, for corridors dwindled to passageways, and became more crooked and narrow. Beautiful wall paintings of papyrus marshes, and images of rivers full of perfect fish beneath our feet, gave way to mundane plainly painted plaster walls and dried-mud floors. The finely wrought oil lamps that lined the main passageways became more ordinary, such as one might find in any reasonably comfortable home.

Finally we came to a simple doorway. No insignia decorated the lintel. No guards stood before it. It could have been the doorway to a storeroom. The bolts were tied together, and sealed. Khay was perspiring; tiny beads of sweat gathered on his noble forehead. I nodded. He knocked, not very confidently. We listened, but there was no sign of movement.

'She must have retired for the night.'

He relaxed visibly, and turned to leave.

'Knock harder,' I suggested.

He hesitated, so I did it myself, with my fist.

More silence. Perhaps this was a useless chase, after all.

And then I heard footsteps, very quiet, moving across the floor. The faintest glow of light appeared under the door. Someone was definitely there. A tiny star of light appeared in the door, at eye level. Whoever it was observed us through a peephole.

And then the door rattled with a mad fury.

Khay jumped back.

I broke the seal myself, quickly untied the knots of the cord that bound the bolts, and threw open the doors.

37

The chamber was dreary, lit by the oil lamp she carried, and niches in the wall where cheap candles burned with an oily, smoky light, casting a dismal light on everything. Mutnodjmet, sister of Nefertiti, wife of Horemheb, was very thin; her sunless skin clung to her elegant bones, which were painfully obvious through the folds of her plain robe. Her skull was shaved. She wore no wig. Her shoulders were rounded. Her face, which carried the same high cheekbones as her sister's but had none of its poise, was somehow inert, and her eyes would have been sorrowful were they not also apathetic. She was a hollow thing. She gave off a desperate, sad, unanswerable neediness. But I also knew I could not trust her in any way, for despite her lassitude, need was coiled inside her, like a cobra, poised.

A dwarf stood on either side of her. They wore good-quality, matching clothes and jewellery, and matching daggers, indicating they were of prestigious rank. This was not unusual, for many men of such stature and appearance had made their way into responsible positions within the royal courts of the past. Unusually, however, they were identical. They did not look happy to be disturbed.

Mutnodjmet continued to stare at me uncomprehendingly, her

head lowered, her mouth slack. She seemed unable to make sense of who I might be, or what we might be doing there.

'Why have you brought me nothing?' she mewed, in a tone that was much deeper than disappointment.

'What should I bring you?' I asked.

She considered me with her dull eyes, suddenly yelled a remarkable set of abuses at me, then shuffled off into another chamber. The dwarfs continued to gaze at us, with unfriendly expressions on their faces. I assumed they knew how to use their daggers. Perhaps their small stature would give them an advantage; after all, I thought ruefully, plenty of damage can be inflicted below the waistline.

'What are your names?'

They exchanged a brief look, as if to say: 'Who is this idiot?'

Khay intervened.

'We are here only briefly to visit the Princess.'

'She receives no visitors,' said one of the dwarfs in an unexpectedly resonant voice.

'None?' I asked.

'Why do you want to see her?' said the other one, in an identical voice.

It was like talking to two faces with one mind. There was something comical about it all.

I smiled.

They were not amused, and their little hands went to their daggers' handles. Khay began to prevaricate, but he was interrupted.

'Oh just let them in,' she shrieked, from the other chamber. 'I want company. Anything, to make a change from you two.'

We moved down the hallway, off which I noticed several more or less empty rooms for storage, and a cooking area equipped with shelves and storage pots and jars, and came to a larger salon. We sat on stools, while she reclined on a bed. The room was basic, and somehow under-furnished, as if she had inherited a few second-rate leftovers from the family mansion. She watched us with her jaded eyes, circled with excessive and inaccurately applied lines of kohl. She looked Khay over like a fish that had gone off.

'I bring you Rahotep, Seeker of Mysteries. He insisted on meeting you.'

She looked down her nose at him, and giggled.

'What a cold dish *he* is. I wouldn't feed him to a cat . . . but *you*.'

She looked me directly in the eye.

I ignored her blatant cue. She cackled suddenly, her head thrown back like a melodramatic actor.

I continued to hold her gaze.

'Oh. I see; the strong and silent type. *Perfect*.'

She tried to gaze back like a courtesan, but she faltered, giggled, and suddenly collapsed into hysterics.

Someone had supplied her recently enough. She was still in the happy phase. Soon that would fade, and she would be in the clutches of her grim need again. I felt excitement rising in my chest, like a wonderful panic, for here was the missing connection. But would she be capable of doing the things I thought she had done? Could she have placed the stone carving, the box containing the mask of animal remains, and the doll? She resided within the royal quarters, but her freedom of movement seemed no greater than that of an animal within a cage. Her rooms were sealed from the outside. Someone was controlling her; but who? Not her husband, at least not directly, because he was far away. It had to be someone who had regular access to the palace, and in particular to these chambers. Also, it had to be someone who could supply her. The answer was so tantalizing. Was whoever had killed the young people, also *managing* the Princess? One question at a time, and I might be able to prove the connection, slowly, carefully, precisely.

'Who supplies you?' I said.

'With what?' she said, her eyes glittering.

'With the opium poppy.'

Khay was on his feet instantly.

'This is an appalling breach of protocol, and a disgusting accusation.'

'Sit down and shut up!'

He was deeply affronted.

'You have your own addictions,' I added, purely for my own vindictive pleasure. 'Addiction to wine is no different to what she's doing. You can't live without it, and neither can she. What's the difference?'

He huffed but found he had no reply to that.

'That's true,' she said, quietly. 'It's all there is. I tried to refuse it. But in the end, life without it is disappointing. It's just so boring. So – *nothing*.'

'And yet here you are, living for it. And you look like you're dead already.'

She nodded, sadly.

'But when you have it inside you, everything feels like *bliss*.'

She seemed as far from a state of bliss as a woman in the jaws of a crocodile.

'Who brings it to you?' I asked.

She smiled enigmatically and approached me.

'You'd like to know that, wouldn't you? I can see right through you. You're as desperate as I am. You need your answers, just like I need my drug. You know how it *feels* . . .'

She slid her cold hand down inside my robe. It did nothing for me, so I withdrew it, and returned it to its owner.

She rubbed her wrist, tenderly.

'I'm not going to tell you anything now,' she said, like a petulant child.

'I'll go, then,' I said, and stood up.

'No, don't,' she called out. 'Don't be cruel. Don't abandon a poor girl.'

She mewed like a cat again.

I turned back.

'I'll stay with you for a little while. But only if you talk to me.'

She twisted her hips from side to side, like a seductive child. It was pathetic in a middle-aged woman. Then she patted the bench, and so I sat again.

'Ask me anything.'

'Just tell me who supplies the drug.'

'No one.'

She cackled again, suddenly.

'This is tiresome,' I said.

'It's a little, private joke between him and I. He tells me he is no one. But he does not know I laugh because I see he has an empty face.'

'What do you mean?'

'You know what I mean. Somehow his soul is missing. He is a hollow man.'

'And how old is he? And how tall?'

'He is middle-aged. He is your height.'

I looked at her. I sensed a new thread of connection running in my brain.

'What is his name?'

'He has no name. I call him "the Physician".'

The Physician.

'Tell me about his voice.'

'It is not loud, but it is not too quiet. Not young, but not old. Not gentle, but not violent, either. It is a calm voice. There is a strange kindness in it, sometimes. A kind of gentleness.'

'What about his hair?'

'Grey. All grey,' she sang.

'And his eyes?'

'Oh, his eyes. They are grey, too, or sometimes blue, or sometimes both. They are the only beautiful thing about him,' she said.

'What is beautiful about them?'

'They see things others cannot see.'

I pondered that.

'Tell me about the messages.'

'No, I can't,' she said. 'He would be angry with me. He will not visit me again if I betray the messages.'

I glanced at Khay, who was listening with amazement.

'And when does he come?'

'I never know. I have to wait. It is terrible, when I haven't seen him for days and days.'

'You fall ill?'

She nodded, pathetically, her chin drooping.

'And then he arrives, and leaves me his gifts, and all is well again.'

'When he leaves you these messages, they instruct you to do things for him. Am I right?' I asked.

She nodded, reluctantly.

'To take things, and leave them in certain places?'

She paused, nodded again, and leaned towards me, whispering noisily.

'He allows me to walk the corridors and on occasion the gardens when no one is present. Usually it is night. I am locked up here for days and days. I go crazy with boredom. I get desperate to see the light, to see *life*. But he is very strict, and I have to return quickly, or he will not give me what I need; and he always reminds me I have to be very careful never to be seen, because then everyone would be so *furious* and there would be no more gifts . . .'

She looked at me, her eyes wide and innocent now.

'Who would be angry?'

'*They* would.'

'Your family? Your husband?'

She nodded, miserably.

'*They treat me like an animal,*' she hissed.

'Does no one else ever release you, and allow you some liberty?'

She hesitated for a moment, and glanced at me before she shook

279

her head. So someone was taking pity on her. I thought I knew who that might be.

I watched her as she shifted nervously, her fingers endlessly unpicking an invisible tangle of thread.

'So what is happening out in the wide world?' she asked, as if she had suddenly remembered it was still there.

'Nothing has changed,' said Khay. 'Everything remains the same.'

She looked at me.

'I know he lies,' she said, quietly.

'I can't tell you anything,' I said.

'I have a world in here.' She tapped the side of her head lightly, as if it were a toy. 'I have lived in it for a very long time now. My world is beautiful, and the children are happy, and people dance in the streets. Life is a party. No one grows old, and tears are unknown. There are flowers everywhere, and colours, and wonderful things. And love grows like fruit upon the vine.'

'I suppose your husband is not in it, then.'

She looked up instantly, her eyes suddenly focused.

'You have news of my husband? When did you see him?'

'A few weeks ago, in Memphis.'

'Memphis? What is he doing there? He has not seen me for so long. He has been away at the wars for years. That is what the Physician told me . . .'

She looked betrayed.

'How does the Physician know about your husband?' I asked.

'I don't know. He gives me news. He told me my husband was a great man, and I should be proud of him. He said he would soon return, and everything would be different.'

I glanced at Khay at these ominous words.

'But I fear my husband has never loved me as I loved him, and he never will. You see: he has no heart. And perhaps he even wishes me dead, now that I have served one purpose, and failed in the other. Human beings do not matter to him.'

'What purpose have you failed?' I asked.

She looked at me very directly.

'I am barren. I have given him no heir. It is the curse of our line. And to punish me, look what he has done.'

She raised her hands to her pitiful skull. 'He has made me mad. He has locked the demons in my head. One day I will dash my brains out on the walls, and it will all be over.'

I held Mutnodjmet's hands in my own. The sleeve of her gown lifted a little, and revealed healed scars on her wrists. She wanted me to see them.

'I am going to leave you now. If the Physician returns, perhaps you should not mention my visit. I would not want him to withdraw his gifts.'

She nodded, sincerely, and utterly unreliably.

'Please, please, please come and visit me again,' she said. 'I might remember more things to tell you, if you came again.'

'I promise I will try.'

She seemed satisfied with that.

She insisted on accompanying me to the door. The dwarfs re-appeared, attending her like malevolent pets. She kept repeating *'goodbye, goodbye'* over and over as I closed the door. I knew she was waiting on the other side, listening to the cords being tied on her living coffin.

We walked away in silence. Khay seemed quite sobered now.

'I feel I owe you an apology,' he said, at length.

'Accepted,' I replied.

We bowed to each other.

'You must know the name of this Physician,' I said.

His face fell with disappointment.

'I wish I did. I knew, of course, that she was here, and why. I was given the responsibility of the practical aspects of her care. But the order came from Ay, perhaps in collaboration with Horemheb. This

281

"Physician" would simply have been granted a pass to the royal quarters, and it would all have been done in secret. It all happened so long ago, and she was such an embarrassment, I suppose we all just forgot about her, and carried on with matters that seemed much more important. She was the dirty family secret, and we were all glad to get rid of her.'

'But are you sure Ay is in charge of her circumstances?'

'Yes, or at least he was at the start.'

I thought about that.

'Is she right about Horemheb?' I asked.

He nodded.

'Horemheb married her for power. He seduced her very effectively, but all he wanted was an entrée into the royal family. He knew no one would want her for herself, and so she was a kind of bargain.'

'What do you mean?'

'She was damaged goods, so to speak. She was always a bit strange. Even from her childhood she was troubled, hysterical. So she came cheap. The family were keen to see her put to some use, and the alliance to a rising military star seemed valuable at the time. He was obviously going somewhere. Why not keep the army within the family? And obviously he got a remarkable preferment out of it. The other side of the bargain was that as a member of the family, by the grace of the deal, he would agree to behave; to give her at least the public semblance of a married life, and to harness the army to the strategic business and international interests of the family. After all, under the terms of the deal, that would be in Horemheb's own interests, too.'

'And is that why Mutnodjmet still remains incarcerated within Malkata Palace? Why don't they send her to her husband?'

'They must have come to some mutually beneficial arrangement. She lost her mind. She became a liability to both parties. To Horemheb she became a horrible embarrassment; she is the price he paid for his ambition. She loves him, but she revolts him. He wants to be rid of her. To Ay she was also a problem, for she is part of the dynasty, but she could not sustain a public role. Therefore it was in the interests of both parties that she *disappeared* from life, to become a kind of non-person without actually dying. But she is kept alive, for now. And as you see, she is quite mad, poor thing.'

'And Horemheb?'

'The ruthless young crocodile quickly outgrew his pond. He grew bigger and bigger. And soon all the fine meat and the rich jewels they fed him were not enough. He will rid himself of her as soon as it suits him to do so. He has been watching Ay, and Tutankhamun, and Ankhesenamun, and all of us. And now, with the catastrophic death of the King, I'm afraid his moment has come.'

He seemed thoroughly sobered by his words. He looked about himself, at the smooth, cold luxury of the palace, and seemed for a moment to see it for what it truly was: a tomb.

'But one thing is now clear,' I said.

'And what is that?'

'Both Ay and Horemheb are complicit with the Physician. Ay made the arrangements for her care. Horemheb knows how his wife is being incarcerated. But the question then is: who recruited the Physician to do what he did? Did Horemheb command the Physician to make his wife an opium addict? Or was it his own idea? And did the Physician act on his own agenda in terrorizing the King, or on the orders of someone else? Horemheb, perhaps?'

'Or Ay,' said Khay.

'Possibly. For he would not wish the King to take control of his own power, as he did. And yet his own reaction to what happened indicates he had no knowledge of how the objects came to be in the chamber. In any case, it does not feel like the kind of thing he would do.'

Khay sighed.

'Neither possibility is optimistic. In any event, now that the King is dead, you may be sure Horemheb will arrive here soon. He has important business to conduct. His future is all before him. All he needs to do is conquer Ay and the Queen, and the Two Lands will belong to him. And I for one fear that day with all my heart.'

The hour was late. We had arrived back at the double doors of the Queen's apartment. Guards had been stationed there for the night. I asked Khay to leave me there, to speak to the Queen alone. He nodded, then hesitated, and turned as if to ask me something confidential.

'Don't worry,' I said. 'Your secret's safe with me.'

He looked relieved. But he also looked as if he was about to tell me something else.

'What?'

He hesitated.

'This is not a safe place for you any more.'

'You're the second person to say that to me tonight,' I replied.

'Then you know to be very careful. This is a pool of crocodiles. Take care where you step.'

He patted me on the arm, and then walked slowly away down the long, silent passageway, back to his small, diminishing amphora of good wine. I knew my time too was running out. But I had my clue. And, with luck, Nakht would have saved the boy, and he would now be healed enough to talk. If so, perhaps I could connect everything together. Identify the Physician. Stop him from committing any further acts of mutilation and murder. And then I could ask him the question that was burning in my head. Why?

38

I knocked on the door. The Maid of the Right Hand nervously opened it a fraction. I pushed past her and her protestations, and walked through into the chamber to which I had first been brought. *In another life*, I thought, *before I entered this labyrinth of shadows*. Nothing had changed. The doors to the courtyard garden were still open, the hammered bowls were lit, and the furniture remained immaculate. I remembered how I had felt this was her stage scenery. She appeared, alarmed, from the bedchamber. She was relieved to see it was me.

'Why are you here? It is very late. Has something happened?'

'Let's go outside.'

She nodded, uncertainly, drew a light shawl around her shoulders, and stepped through the doors into the garden. The maid quickly lit two lamps, then scurried away at a gesture from her mistress. We walked in silence to the pool, carrying the lamps, and seated ourselves on the same bench, in the dark, with just the lamps to hold back the darkness of the night.

'Why didn't you tell me about Mutnodjmet?'

She tried for a moment to look innocent, but then she sighed.

'I knew if you were any good you would find out eventually.'

'That doesn't answer my question.'

'Why didn't I tell you? Isn't that obvious? She is our terrible family secret. But why are you asking me? She could not possibly have anything to do with everything that has happened.'

'You thought you were the best judge of that.'

She looked wounded.

'Why are you saying this now?'

'Because she is the person who left the carving, the box and the figurine.'

She laughed briefly.

'That's not possible—'

'She's an opium addict. As you know. She has a doctor. He calls himself the Physician. He has managed her need for his purposes. In return for carrying out the little tasks of leaving his presents around the royal quarters, he supplies her with the drug. So he keeps her in need, and she does whatever he requires. But what is more, that same man has also been killing and mutilating young people in the city, using the same drug to subdue them.'

She struggled to take it all in quickly.

'Well then, you have solved the mystery. All you need to do is arrest him. And then you will have performed your task, and you can return to your life.'

'She cannot name him. I am sure Ay or Horemheb can. But that is not why I am here.'

'No?' she said, apprehensively.

'You have been visiting Mutnodjmet, and taking her out of her apartments.'

'Of course I have not.'

'I know you have.'

She stood up, offended, but she did not deny it again. Then she sat down, her manner more deliberately conciliatory.

'I took pity on her. She is a hopeless creature now, although once she was not so pitiful. And she is still my aunt. She and I are all that remain of our great dynasty. She is my only connection to my history. It is not a reassuring thought, is it?'

'You must have been aware of her addiction?'

'Yes, I suppose I was, but she had always been strange, ever since my childhood. So I avoided thinking about it, and no one else ever talked about it. I assumed it was Pentu who treated her.'

'And then, when you realized what was happening with her addiction, you felt you were not in a position to be able to help her.'

'I did not dare intervene between her husband and Ay. There was so much else at stake.'

She looked ashamed.

'I could not risk a public scandal. Perhaps that was cowardly. Yes, I think now it was cowardly.'

'Do you think Mutnodjmet ever revealed that you would visit, and take her out, from time to time?'

'She knew that if she did, I would no longer be able to come.'

'So it was a secret, and you could trust her to keep it?'

'As far as I could trust her with anything.'

She looked uncomfortable.

'Let me be direct. Perhaps you have seen this Physician. Perhaps he did not know about your visits. Perhaps you chanced upon him, once.'

'I have never seen him,' she said, her eyes intent with truthfulness.

I looked away, disappointed again. The man was like a shadow, always in the corner of my eye, always elusive, slipping away into the dark.

'But still you are afraid of something,' I continued.

'I am afraid of many things, and as you know I do not hide my fear well. I am afraid to be alone, and to sleep. Now the nights seem longer and darker than ever. No candlelight seems powerful enough, in this dismal palace, to keep the shadows at bay.'

She suddenly looked utterly lost.

'I want you to take me away,' she said. 'I can't stay here. I'm too frightened.'

'Where am I supposed to take you?'

'You could take me to your home.'

I was astonished by the idea.

'Of course I can't.'

'Why can't you? We could leave together. We could go now.'

'At this time? When the King is to be buried, and all is uncertain, and then you disappear?'

'I can return for the funeral ceremonies. Take me in disguise. It is night. No one will know.'

'You think of no one but yourself. I have risked everything for you from the moment you called for me. And now you think I will risk my own family? The answer is no. You must stay here, in the palace, and oversee the burial of the King. You must assert yourself in power. And I will stay beside you at all times.'

She turned on me, her face suddenly crude with anger.

'I thought you had nobility, I thought you had honour.'

'I care for the safety of my family above everything. Perhaps to you that is a strange idea,' I replied carelessly, and walked away, too angry to remain seated.

'I'm sorry,' she said eventually, lowering her eyes.

'You should be.'

'You cannot talk to me as you have done,' she said.

'I am the only one who tells you the truth.'

'You make me dislike myself.'

'That is not my intention,' I replied.

'I know that.'

'I promise you, I will not let you come to any harm.'

She searched my face, as if for confirmation.

'You are right. I cannot run away from everything I fear. It is better to choose to fight rather than to flee . . .'

We set off back up the dark path towards the lit chamber.

'What do you intend to do now? Ay is anxious to proceed as quickly as possible with the embalming, the burial, and his own coronation,' I said.

'Yes, but even Ay cannot command time. The body must be made ready for burial, the tomb must be readied, the rituals must be meticulously observed; all of this takes the required and necessary number of days . . .'

'Even so, Ay of all men can find ways to economize on everything.'

'Perhaps. But how can he pretend the King is sequestered for so long? Rumour seeps out of silence like water from a cracked vessel . . .'

She suddenly stopped, her eyes alive with urgent thought.

'If I am to survive, I have very few choices. Either I make an alliance with Ay, or with Horemheb. It is a brutal choice, and neither option holds anything but revulsion for me. But I know if I try to assert my own authority independently as Queen and as the last daughter of my family, I cannot yet command the support I would need among the bureaucracies and – despite Simut's support – the army. Not against the aggression and ambition of those two.'

'But surely there is a third way. You play Ay and Horemheb off against each other,' I suggested.

She turned towards me, her face alight.

'Exactly! Both would prefer me dead, but they realize alive I am a valuable asset to either of them. And if I could make each think the other wanted me, then, as men do, they might fight to the end to possess me.'

Suddenly, as she spoke with such conviction and passion, her mother's face appeared in hers.

'Why are you staring at me like that?' she asked.

'You look like someone I once knew,' I replied.

She understood at once who that might be.

'I am sorry for you, Rahotep. You must miss your family and your life. I know you are only here because I called to you to help me. It is my fault. But from now I will protect you with all my power, such as it is,' she said.

'And I will do everything I can for you. Perhaps we can protect each other.'

289

We bowed our heads at each other.

'But I need to ask you to do something for me now,' I said.

She quickly supplied me with what I needed: papyrus, a reed pen, a palette containing two cakes of ink, sealing wax and a small pot of water. I wrote quickly, and the characters flowed from the pen with an urgent fluency of love and loss.

To my dearest Wife and Children
This letter must stand in my place. I have been detained for longer than I wished on my task. Know that I have returned safely from my journey. But it is not possible yet to return to you myself. Nor can I tell you when I shall once more walk through our door. I wish it could be otherwise. May the Gods help you to forgive my absence. I enclose a sealed letter for Khety. Please give it to him as soon as possible.
I shall shine through love for you all.
Rahotep

Then I wrote to Khety, telling him exactly what had happened to me, and what I needed him to do. I rolled both letters up, one inside the other, sealed them and handed them to Ankhesenamun.

'Give these letters to Simut, and have him deliver them to my wife.'

She nodded, and hid them away in her writing chest.

'You trust him?'

I nodded.

'He will be able to deliver these letters undiscovered. It is not possible for you to do so,' I said.

Thinking of my family, I felt the pieces of my heart grinding against each other like shards of glass in my chest. Then suddenly we both heard something outside the double doors, and they were flung open.

39

Ay entered the chamber, followed by Simut, who closed the door behind him.

Ay gazed at me with his stony eyes. I could smell once again the lozenge of cloves and cinnamon that he sucked constantly in an effort to relieve the pain in his rotting jaw. For him to reappear at this hour of the night could only mean bad news. He sat down upon a couch, rearranged his linens meticulously, and nodded to Ankhesenamun to sit opposite him.

'Horemheb's ship of state has been sighted to the north of the city,' he said, quietly. 'He will arrive here soon. When he does so, I am certain he will request an audience with the Queen. I suspect he must know the King is dead, even though there has been, and will be, no announcement. How he knows this is a matter for investigation. But we have priorities. First, we must agree a strategy for managing this unfortunate eventuality.'

Before Ankhesenamun could reply, he continued.

'Clearly, he will have considered, as I have done, the advantages or otherwise of an alliance with you. Like me, he will recognize the value in your ancestry and the contribution your image might make to the continuing stability of the Two Lands. I am sure he will make an offer of marriage. He will couch it in favourable terms, such as: he will father sons, he will promote you as Queen, and he will bring the security of the army of the Two Lands to support your mutual interests.'

'These are interesting and, on the surface, favourable terms,' she replied.

He glared at her, and continued: 'You are still a fool. He will rid himself of Mutnodjet, and marry you to promote his own legitimacy within the dynasty. He will father sons for the same reason. Once you have supplied him, he will dismiss you, or worse. Look what he has done with his own wife. Accept his offer, and he will destroy you in the end.'

'Do you think I do not know this?' she replied. 'Horemheb despises my dynasty and all it has stood for. His ambition is to create his own. The question for me is whether my survival and that of my dynasty through my future children is more assured with him than it would be otherwise. What other choices do I have?'

'It would be naive to the point of idiocy ever to think anything of yours would be assured with him.'

She rose and paced the chamber.

'But my life and the future of my dynasty is not assured with you, either,' she replied.

He did his crocodile imitation of a smile.

'Nothing in this life is certain. All is strategy and survival. And so you should consider the advantages that might lie in an alliance with me.'

She gazed at him imperiously.

'I am no fool. I have considered instead the advantages to you of an alliance with me. Marriage to me would grant you the final legitimacy of my dynasty. I would be the vessel of your ambitions, now that the King is dead. You could assert your authority even more extensively, as King in name and deed,' she said, as she walked around him.

'My own ancestors have been intimately allied to the royal family for several generations. My parents served your parents. But as King, in return for marriage I would offer you the support of the priesthood, the offices and the treasury, as protection against Horemheb and the army. For make no mistake, he is planning a coup.'

'I see. That is also an interesting prospect. But what of the future? You are very old. When I look at you I see a sad, old man. A man sick of the pain in his teeth and his bones. Sick of the effort of it all. Sick of being alive. You are a bundle of old sticks. Your virility is a withered memory. How could you provide me with heirs?'

His eyes glittered with hate, but he refused to take the bait and reply in anger.

'Heirs can be provided in many ways. A suitable father to your children could easily be found, with my help. But we speak too personally. What is most important is the exercise of authority for the sake of *maat*. All I do is for the stability and the priority of the Two Lands.'

She turned on him now.

'Your progeny is shadows. Without me your paternity will amount to nothing but dust. After your death, which will not be long – for all the powers in the kingdom cannot save you from mortality – Horemheb will erase your name from the walls of every temple in the land. He will bring down your statues, and demolish your offering hall. You will be as nothing. It will be as if you never lived. Unless I decide that you are useful to me. For only through me can your name live on.'

He listened without emotion.

'You make the mistake of hatred. Emotion will betray you, in the end, as it always does with women. Remember this: only through me could you survive to accomplish all that you wish. You should know by now death holds no fear for me. I know it for what it is. He understands.'

And he pointed at me.

'He knows there is nothing to come. There is no Otherworld, and there are no Gods. It is all nonsense for children. All that exists is power in the crude hands of men. That is why we are all so desperate for it. Otherwise what is there for men to shore against the inevitability of their own ruin?'

No one spoke for a long moment.

'I will consider everything you have said. And I will meet with Horemheb. And in my own time, I will come to a decision. It will be the right decision for me, and my family, as well as for the stability of the Two Lands,' she said.

He rose from the couch, and shuffled towards the door. But before he departed he turned around, stiffly: 'Think carefully which of the two worlds is the lesser in evil. Horemheb's army, or mine. And then make your choice.'

And he left.

The Queen immediately began to pace the chamber again.

'Horemheb is here already. That is too soon! But why is he waiting?' asked the Queen.

'Because he knows he can create a situation of tension and fear. This is strategy. He wants to make it seem as if he is in control of what happens. Do not give him that power over you,' I replied.

She gazed at me for a moment.

'You are right. We have our own strategies. I must maintain them. I must not be misled by fear.'

I nodded and bowed.

'Where are you going?' she asked, anxiously.

'I must talk further to Ay. There is something I need to ask him. Simut will remain with you until I return.'

I closed the door, and quickly followed the shuffling figure up the dark corridor. As soon as he heard footsteps he turned, suspiciously. I bowed.

'What is it now?' he snapped.

'I would like to know the answer to a question.'

'Do not waste my time with your foolish questions. It is too late. You have failed in your task. Go away.'

And he waved his bony hand dismissively at me.

'Mutnodjmet is incarcerated here in the Malkata Palace. This was originally done years ago, under your orders, I assume in agreement with Horemheb. And I assume she has been more or less forgotten.'

He looked surprised at the mention of her name.

'So what?'

'She is an opium addict. Who supplies her with the drug? The answer is: someone who attends her, in secret. She has obeyed his instructions in return for the gift of the drug for which she has, of course, a desperate need. It was she who left the death mask, and the carving, and the doll, in the royal quarters. Shall I tell you what she calls this mysterious man? She calls him the "Physician".'

Ay was listening seriously now.

'If only you had discovered this weeks ago.'

'If only someone had told me about her weeks ago,' I replied.

He knew I was right.

'I think you must know his name. For it can only have been you who appointed him to her care in the first place,' I continued.

He considered everything for a long moment. He seemed profoundly reluctant to speak.

'Ten years ago I appointed a physician. He had been my Chief of Physicians. But he failed to be useful to me. His gifts deserted him, and his knowledge was of no help in curing me of the maladies that beset me. So I made Pentu Chief Physician, and I gave that man the task of caring for the needs of Mutnodjmet. It was a private arrangement, in return for which he would be paid well, both for his work and his absolute discretion. He was to keep her alive, for the time being. There were severe penalities for any failure of secrecy.'

'And what was his name?'

'His name was Sobek.'

*

My mind raced back through everything that had happened, to the day of the festival, to the day of the blood, and the dead boy with the broken bones in the dark room, and the party on the roof of Nakht's city house. I remembered the quiet man of late middle age, with short grey hair untouched by dye, and the bony, minimal physique of someone who does not eat for pleasure. I recalled his unremarkable, almost simple face – hollow, as Mutnodjmet had said – and his stony, cold grey-blue eyes bright with intelligence, and with something like rage. I heard him say: *'Perhaps it is the human imagination that is the monster. I believe no animal suffers from the torments of the imagination. Only man . . .'*

And I remembered Nakht, my old friend, and now it seemed also the colleague or acquaintance of this master of mutilation and mystery, replying: *'And that is why civilized life, morality, ethics and so on, matter. We are half-enlightened, and half-monstrous. We must build our civility upon reason and mutual benefit.'*

I saw in my mind's eye the grey man raising his cup and replying:

'I salute your reason. I wish it every success.'

Sobek. The Physician.

'You look like you have seen a ghost,' said Ay.

40

Simut's elite guards took up positions along the dark, adjoining streets, and on the neighbouring rooftops. The city was silent, under the night curfew, apart from solitary dogs barking aggressively to each other across the darkness, under the moon and stars.

Khety had returned Thoth to me, and the animal danced and chattered quietly at my side in pleasure at our reunion. But time was short. Khety and I had urgent news to communicate. As we made our way to this place, he had told me quickly, in urgent whispers, that my family were safe and well; and under Nakht's care, the boy was improving. He had not died. Then he had wanted to know how I had identified Sobek. I explained it all.

'Then we've done it,' he said, delighted.

'Unfortunately not,' I replied.

And having made him swear to keep the secret, I told him the story of the King's death. For once he was utterly silenced.

'Say something, Khety. You always have something ludicrously optimistic to say.'

He shook his head.

'I can't think of anything. It's an absolute disaster. A calamity.'

'Thank you.'

'I don't mean it was your fault. You did everything that was asked of you. You followed your orders from the King himself. But what's going to happen to us all now? The city's already restless. No one knows what's happening. It's as though the whole of the Two Lands is on the precipice of an abyss, and at any moment we could all go tumbling in.'

'These are dark times, Khety. But don't be so melodramatic. It doesn't help. Have there been any more murders in the city, like those of the boy and Neferet?'

He shook his head.

'Nothing. As far as I know. Nothing has been reported. It has all gone very quiet. Word got out on to the streets of the other murders. It travelled around the clubs very quickly. People are spooked. Perhaps they are just taking much more care.'

I was puzzled.

'But a killer like this will always find a fresh victim. The desire for the act grows greater with each murder, usually. It becomes an un-assuageable hunger. We know he is an obsessive. So where has his obsession led him now? Why would he stop killing?'

He shrugged.

'Perhaps he has gone to ground.'

He nodded at the house.

'Perhaps he's in there now. Perhaps you've got him.'

'Don't speak too soon. It makes me feel superstitious,' I replied.

Sobek's house stood in a street of discreet residences, in a good quarter of the city. Nothing distinguished it from the others. I nodded to Simut. He made a signal to the guards stationed on the rooftops, who leapt silently from roof to roof like assassins. Then, at another brief gesture of command, the guards who accompanied us attacked the solid wooden door with their axes. Quickly it was smashed down. A few neighbours, alarmed by the sudden commotion, peered out into the lane in their night robes, but they were peremptorily ordered back into their houses. I pushed ahead into a vestibule, followed by the guards who spread out silently, their weapons poised, and took command of each room, one at a time, gesturing in silence to each other. Others entered via the roof to secure the upper rooms. Each room was less interesting than the last. It seemed like the home of a solitary man, for the furniture was functional, the decoration modest in the extreme, and there was none of the normal detritus of everyday life. The place seemed lifeless. Upstairs were wooden chests containing efficient but unsophisticated clothing, and a few pieces of nondescript, daily jewellery. The place was deserted. He had eluded me again. Surely we had missed something? It was as if he had known we would find him. And he had left us no clues. But how could he have known? Bitterly disappointed, I walked through the rooms one by one, looking for anything that could give me way a forward.

But suddenly a shout came from the back of the house, beyond the inner courtyard. Simut and his guards stood around a small door, like that which would lead to a storeroom. The cords were tied in what looked like the same magical knot as that which had tied the box containing the rotting death mask. On the seal, I saw a single sign I recognized too: a dark circle. The Sun destroyed. Suddenly elation gripped me. I tried to remain calm as I slipped my knife through the cord, so as to preserve the knot and the seal; and then I pushed open the door.

I smelt at once the chilly, airless, hollow odour of a tomb opened after a long time – as if the darkness had slowly suffocated the air itself. Khety handed me a lamp, and I entered, cautiously. The thought that this was a trap flitted across my mind. I held the lamp up before me, and tried to see beyond its shivering light.

The room seemed to be of a moderate size. Along one wall was a long bench, holding clay vessels in various sizes, and an astounding array of surgical instruments: obsidian knives, sharp hooks, long probes, cupping vessels and vicious forceps, all precise and highly ordered. Further on were a series of small glass phials with stoppers, each with a label. I opened one. It seemed to be empty. I kept it to examine in the light of day. Further down the shelves were more jars. I opened them at random; they seemed to contain a variety of herbs and spices. But the last one contained something I recognized: the powder of the opium poppy. Further along the shelf were several more jars, all containing the identical substance: a substantial supply. The bench was highly ordered and efficient.

But as I stepped forward, I felt something crack and shatter beneath my sandals. I squatted down with the lamp and saw the floor was littered with bones: the little skulls and wing-fans of birds; the miniature skeletons of mice, shrews and rats; the jaws and legs of dogs or baboons or hyenas or jackals; and also pieces of larger bones, which I feared were human, smashed into shards. It was as if I had trespassed into a mass grave of all life. I held the lamp up to peer further into the dark. I saw something still stranger: from the ceiling on twine hung many bones, and broken pieces of bones, to make the shattered skeletons of strange, impossible creatures, part-bird, part-dog, part-human.

Shuffling forward, trying not to tread on any more of the remains at my feet, and loathing the creepy touch of the hanging bones in my hair and on my back, I made out out a large, low, shadowy object that stood at the end of the room. As I came closer, I saw it was an embalmer's bench. On the bench was a small wooden box. Behind the bench, I saw a big black circle had been painted on the back wall. The Sun destroyed. I held the lamp up closer, and all around the perimeter of the circle were those strange, disturbing signs I had seen around the box: curves, sickles, dots and dashes. Spattered all across the dark circle were dripping lines of dried, dark blood. I looked again at the embalmer's bench; in contrast to the wall's record of butchery, it was as fastidiously clean as the surgical instruments that lined the walls. But they were not for healing. They were for torture. How many victims had he experimented on in here, as they screamed for mercy, for their lives, or for the mercy of death?

The wooden box carried a label. On it was written, in a neat cursive, one word: '*Rahotep*'. It was a gift from Sobek to me. I had no choice but to open it. Inside I saw something I know I will always see whenever I try to sleep. Eyes. Human eyes. Arranged in identical pairs, like jewels on a tray. I thought of Neferet, and the two boys. All had missing eyes. And here was a box full of staring, quizzical, startled eyes, like a tiny audience paying me the closest attention.

41

I closed the box, and returned the eyes to darkness. This gift was a mockery. He had tricked me. He knew I would track him to his house. He knew I still did not understand what he was doing. The eyes were like signs – he was watching me. And if he was watching me, then what else did he know? Suddenly, fear gripped my throat; perhaps he knew about my family – after all, he had seen them at Nakht's party on the roof of his city house. I must protect them. I would send Khety immediately to organize a secure guard. But then another thought came crashing in against the first; how had he realized I had discovered the connection with Mutnodjmet? And then another, still more alarming. We had left Mutnodjmet unguarded.

The moment the boat docked at the Malkata Palace harbour, Simut and I raced through the guarded entrance doors, and down the long corridors. I racked my brains to recall the route to Mutnodjmet's chambers, but the shadowy labyrinth of the palace confused me.

'Take me to Khay's office!'

Simut nodded, and we ran on. I didn't bother to rap on the doors, but burst through. He was fast asleep, snoring on his couch, his head back, robes still on, the cup of wine empty. I shook him violently, and he started awake like a man in an accident, staring wildly at the two of us.

'Take us back to Mutnodjmet's apartments, now!'

He looked puzzled, but I yanked him to his feet and propelled him through the door. 'Take your hands off me!' he cried in his querulous voice. 'I am quite capable of walking unaided.'

He struggled, trying to rearrange his appearance into something like dignity.

The doors to Mutnodjmet's apartment were shut, and the cords tied and sealed. As we approached, I felt something crunching lightly underfoot. Puzzled, I crouched down and saw, in the light of our lamps, something glittering. I wiped some up on my finger and tested it on my lips. Natron salt. It was most likely the spillage from a sack that someone had carried into the apartments. But why would anyone do such a thing?

I broke the seals on the doors and we entered carefully. All was silence and darkness. There was no sign of the twin dwarfs. Holding my lamp before me, I advanced along the corridor that led to the salon. But as I passed the store chambers, I saw something wrong. Two of the big storage jars had had their contents – grain and flour – emptied on the floor in neat piles. Simut glanced at me. I carefully removed the lid of one of the jars. Crouched inside was a small figure in good clothes up to his chest in his own blood; I looked more closely and saw the hilt of his jewelled dagger thrust into his heart. The back of his little head was smashed in. I opened the other one. The same.

We entered the salon. There had been a struggle. Furniture had been thrown over. Goblets lay shattered on the floor. And there on a low gilded bench was a dark, grey mound. I carefully pushed handfuls of the salt away. Mutnodjmet's eye-sockets stared back at me, white and empty; her hollow face, glittering with scattered salt crystals, was desiccated and wrinkled as if time had suddenly sucked her dry. Her lips were shrivelled and white, and her open mouth was dry as a cloth left out in the midday sun.

'What's happened to her?' whispered Simut.

'The natron has absorbed the fluids from her body. By now all her internal organs will have begun to turn to dark brown mush.'

'So was she alive when he did this to her?' The soldier shook his head at such sophisticated barbarity.

'It would have taken time for her to die like this. She must have been maddened with thirst. And *that's* what fascinates him. Watching people suffer and die, in great detail. But I'm not sure he does it only for the pleasure of witnessing their pain. The pain is only part of the process, not the end of it. He's seeking something else. Something more original.'

'But what?' asked Simut.

I stared down at the poor eyeless woman. It was the only important question.

As we walked back up the passageway, I remembered the little glass phial I had found in Sobek's laboratory. I opened it, but it seemed to contain nothing, despite the stopper and the carefully noted date. I noticed at the bottom a faint dusting of glittery white residue. I dabbed my finger and licked it carefully. More salt; but not natron salt. Some other kind of salt. It tasted familiar. But I could not place it.

42

Horemheb's magnificent ship of state, the *Glory of Memphis*, was now anchored out on the still water of the lake. As it loomed over its lucid mirror image, it looked like a menacing weapon. The Eye of Horus was painted repeatedly all along the hull, granting special protection. In amongst the Eyes there were images of the ram's head of Amun, and winged falcons, and the figure of the King trampling his enemies underfoot. On the side lookouts the figure of Montu, God of War, strode defiantly; and the deckhouses were painted with multi-coloured circles. Even the blades of the oars were decorated with the Eye of Horus. The menace was intensified by the corpses of seven Hittite soldiers, hanging head downwards, twisting slowly as they rotted in the morning sunlight.

'I wonder if he has shown himself yet,' I said to Simut, as we stood side by side, considering this intimidating vessel.

'No. He will wish to make the most of his grand entrance into the palace.'

'Do you know him personally?' I asked.

Simut stared at the ship.

'I was a cadet in Memphis when he was already Chief Deputy of the Northern Corps. I remember he came to address a private feast for the promising officers of the Ptah Division. He had already married into the royal family. Everyone knew he would soon become general, and he was treated almost as if he were King himself. His speech was interesting. He said the priests of Amun had a profound flaw: their enterprise was founded on wealth, and in his view, in human beings the desire for wealth was never satisfied, but would always over-reach itself and turn into decadence and corruption. He argued that this would necessarily and inevitably create a cycle of instability in the Two Lands, and therefore make us vulnerable to our enemies. He said the army had a sacred duty to break this cycle, by enforcing the rule of order. But it could only maintain the right to do so by sustaining itself in absolute moral purity.'

'When men speak of moral purity, what they mean is, they have hidden their moral impurities beneath an illusion of virtue,' I said.

Simut glanced at me.

'You speak well for a Medjay officer.'

'I know whereof I speak,' I replied. 'Men are not capable of absolute moral purity. And that is a good thing, in my view, because if they were they would not be human.'

Simut grunted, and continued to stare at the great ship in the harbour.

'He also said something about the royal family which I have never forgotten. He said their priority was the perpetuation of their dynasty as the representatives of the Gods on earth. And naturally when that priority coincided with the interests of the Two Lands, then all was well. But he said when there was disruption or dissent, or when the royal family failed in its divine duties, the Two Lands should identify its own needs and values as paramount. Not those of the royal family. And therefore only the army, which desired neither power nor wealth for itself, but only the assertion of our order throughout the world, would have a sacred obligation to enforce its rule, for the sake of the Two Lands' survival.'

'And what do you think he meant by "disruption or dissent"?' I asked.

'He was implying the dangers inherent in the inheritance of the Crowns by a King too young to rule in any meaningful sense, under the aegis of a Regent whose interests were obscure. But I think he really meant something else.'

He lowered his voice.

'I think he meant the private continuity of the Aten faith in the family. The father's banished God. That dangerous religion had already caused terrible chaos once in living memory, and it could not be allowed to rise again. He implied the army would not tolerate any sign of its return to public life.'

'I think you are right. And that, too, remains Ankhesenamun's flaw. For like her husband, it is difficult for her to disassociate herself not just from the failings of her father, but from the root of the problem: the banished religion.'

Ankhesenamun was with her ladies of the chamber, who were preparing her for the formal reception. The rich scents of perfumes and oils drifted in the quiet air. Little gold pots and blue and yellow glass containers were opened before her. She held a fish in her hands made of blue and yellow glass, and was pouring some intensely scented essence from its pursed lips.

'Horemheb has requested an audience. At noon today,' she said.

'As we expected.'

She glanced at me, and then returned to a careful consideration of her appearance in the polished copper mirror. She wore a beautiful braided wig of short, tightly curled hair, and a pleated robe of finest linen, fringed with gold, which was tied beneath her right breast, enhancing her figure. On her arms she wore bracelets and gold winding cobras. From her neck, on gold thread so fine it was almost invisible, hung several pendants and an elaborate gold pectoral showing Nekhbet the Vulture Goddess, holding the symbols of eternity and with her blue wings spread out protectively. Then her assistants placed a remarkable garment around her shoulders, a shawl made of many small gold discs. She turned about, and glittered dazzlingly in the candlelight. Next, her assistants slipped on her sandals – thongs of delicate gold, straps decorated with small gold flowers. And finally the tall crown was placed on her head, and held there by a gold band decorated with protective cobras. When I had last seen her dressed in the royal robes, she had looked anxious. Today she looked supremely regal.

She turned to face me.

'How do I look?'

'You look like the Queen of the Two Lands.'

She smiled, pleased. She looked down at the pectoral.

'This belonged to my mother. I hope some of her great spirit will protect me now.'

Then, sensing my sombre mood, she looked at me once more.

'Something has happened, hasn't it?' she asked suddenly.

I nodded. She understood, and dismissed her ladies. When we were alone, I told her the news of the death of Mutnodjmet. She sat very still, tears running down her cheeks, marring the kohl and malachite make-up that had been so carefully applied. She shook her head, over and over.

'I failed her. How could this happen in the palace, while I was here, sleeping?'

'Sobek is very clever.'

'But Ay and Horemheb killed her as much as this evil, repulsive man. They trapped her, and maddened her. And she was the last of my family. Now I am alone. Look at me.'

She glanced at her royal outfit.

'I am nothing but a statue for these garments.'

'No, you are far more. You are the hope of the Two Lands. You are our only hope. Without you, the future is dark. Remember that.'

When the Queen entered, a thousand people bowed low and fell silent. The palace reception hall had been luxuriously prepared for

Horemheb's visit. Incense burned in copper bowls. Vast, elaborate bouquets of flowers were set in vases. The Palace Guard lined the way to the throne. I noticed Ay was not present. The Queen ascended the dais, faced her officials, and sat down. And then we all waited in a silence that had to be endured for longer than anyone expected. The general was late. The dripping of the water clock measured the passing of time and the increasing humiliation of his absence. I glanced up at the Queen. She knew this game, and maintained her composure. And then finally we heard his military fanfare, and suddenly he was striding down the chamber, followed by his lieutenants. He stopped before the throne, stared arrogantly at the Queen, and then bowed his head. She remained seated. The dais still gave her the advantage of height over the general.

'Look up,' she said quietly.

He did so. She waited for him to speak.

'Life, prosperity and health. My loyalty is known throughout the Two Lands. I place it, and my life, at your royal feet.'

His words echoed around the chamber. A thousand pairs of courtly ears listened for every nuance.

'We have long trusted your loyalty. It is more than gold to us.'

'It is loyalty that encourages me today,' he replied ominously.

'Then speak your mind, general.'

He glanced at her, turned back to the chamber, and spoke to the entire gathering.

'What I wish to speak of is for the Queen's ears alone, and would benefit from a more private setting.'

She inclined her head.

'Our ministers are as one with us. What matter could there be which would not be for their ears also?'

He smiled.

'Such matters as belong not to the state but to the individual.'

She considered him carefully. Then she rose, and invited him to accompany her to an antechamber. He followed her, and so did I. He turned to me, furious, but she spoke firmly.

'Rahotep is my personal guard. He goes everywhere with me. I can vouch absolutely for his integrity and his silence.'

He had no choice but to accept.

I stood by the door, like a security guard. They sat opposite each other on couches. He looked curiously inappropriate in this more domestic setting, as if walls and cushions were strange to him. Wine was poured, and then the servants vanished. She played the game of silence, and waited for him to make the first move.

'I know the King is dead. I offer you my sincere condolences.'

He observed her reaction closely.

'We accept your condolences. As we accept your loyalty. And we offer you our own condolences on the dreadful and premature death of your wife, my aunt.'

Instead of surprise or sorrow at this news, he merely nodded.

'This news brings me grief. But may her name live for ever,' he said, according to the formula, and with more than a touch of irony. Ankhesenamun turned away in disgust at his vanity and viciousness.

'Was there anything else the general wished to say?'

He smiled slightly.

'I have a simple proposal to make, and given the sensitivities concerned, I believed it was correct to express myself in a private setting. I decided it was more sympathetic. You are, after all, the grieving widow of a great King.'

'His death has deprived us all of a great man,' she replied.

'Nevertheless, our private grief must necessarily take its rightful place among more urgent considerations.'

'Do you think so?'

'There is now much at stake, my lady. Of that I am certain you are fully aware.'

His eyes glinted. I saw how he was enjoying himself, like a stealthy hunter with his bow, stalking his unsuspecting quarry.

310

'I am fully aware of the intricate perils of this changing moment in the life of the Two Lands.'

He smiled, and spread out his hands in an open gesture.

'Then we may speak freely. I am sure we both have the best interests of the Two Lands at heart. And that is why I am here: to make a proposal. Or perhaps I mean a suggestion for your consideration.'

'And that is?'

'An offer of an alliance. A marriage.'

She pretended to be astounded.

'A marriage? My mourning has barely begun, your own wife is barely dead, and already you speak of marriage? How can you be so insensible of the manners and rights of grief?'

'My grief is my business. It is as well to discuss these issues now, so that you have time to make a full consideration. And time to come to the correct decision in due course.'

'You speak as if there is only one possible answer.'

'I speak with the passion I feel, but I wholeheartedly believe it to be so,' he said, and did not smile.

She looked at him.

'I would also ask you to consider a proposal of mine.'

He looked askance.

'And what is that?'

'In difficult moments like this, there is great temptation to make alliances, for political reasons. Many of these are very attractive. But I am the daughter of kings who have fashioned this kingdom into the greatest power the world has ever seen. My grandfather envisioned this palace, and built many of the monuments of this great city. My great ancestor Tutmosis III transformed the army of the Two Lands into the finest force ever known. A force that you now lead in magnificent triumphs. How therefore should I best represent the responsibility of power that I have inherited, in my blood and in my heart? How else but by ruling in his name, believing I can count upon the support of my faithful officers?'

He listened without emotion, and then he rose.

'A name is very well. A dynasty is very well. But the kingdom is not a toy. It is not only pageantry and palaces. It is a rough beast, dirty and powerful, that must be brought by force of will under the sway of authority that is not afraid, when necessary, to exercise its full strength and power, no matter what the cost. And that is man's work.'

'I am a woman but my heart is as strong with anger and authority as any man's. Believe me.'

'Perhaps indeed you are your mother's daughter. Perhaps you have the will and guts to smite your enemies courageously.'

She considered him.

'Do not mistake me. I am a woman, but I have trained myself in the world of men. You may be sure your proposal will receive our most meticulous and judicious consideration.'

'We must discuss your considerations, and the opportunities I propose, in more detail. I will be available to you at any moment. I have no intention of departing this city until the situation is resolved – to our mutual satisfaction. I am here as a private man, but I am here too as the General of the Armies of the Two Lands. I have my own duties, and I will perform them, with all the rigour of my calling.'

And he bowed, turned, and departed.

43

I walked as fast as I could through the noise and chaos of the crowded streets of the city towards Nakht's house. The air dazzled with light. Every cry and shout of the street vendors, or the mule-men, or the scatterings of excited children, seemed to anger me. Everyone trespassed in the way of my progress. In my mind I felt as if I were attacking flies with a knife. It seemed as if everything that had happened since I was last here were a strange, hollow dream from which I still had not awoken. Sobek was somewhere, and yet I was unable to track him down. How could I do so? I needed to return to the place where I had first encountered him, and to the man who had introduced us.

I knocked on the door. Nakht's servant Minmose opened it cautiously. I was gratified to see two Medjay guards standing behind him, their weapons prepared.

'Ah it is you, sir. I was hoping it might be.'

Inside, I quickly showed the guards my authorities, and Minmose informed me his master was on the roof terrace. I ascended the wide wooden steps, until I came out once more on to the elegant open space. My old friend was reclining under the embroidered awning, taking advantage of the light northern breeze, and pondering a papyrus scroll with a luxury of leisure I had forgotten existed in my world of politics and power struggles and mutilations.

He got up, delighted to see me.

'So you are back! The days were passing swiftly, and I thought, surely he is back by now, but there was no news—'

He saw the expression on my face, and his greeting stuttered to a halt.

'What on earth has happened?' he cried, in alarm.

We sat in the shade, in the dappled light, and I told him all that had passed. He could not sit still, but paced around me, his hands behind his back. When I recounted the King's accident and subsequent death, he stopped as if turned to stone.

'With this death, the whole order, the great dynasty, is thrown into peril. We have had centuries of affluence and stability, and now all is suddenly in doubt. This leaves the way open for others to make a challenge for power, Horemheb, of course . . .'

I told him then about the general's arrival at the palace.

He sat down again, shaking his head, looking as uncertain and afraid as I had ever seen him.

'Unless some sort of truce is agreed, there will be civil war in the Two Lands,' he murmured.

'It looks disastrous indeed. But it is possible that Ankhesenamun could use her status and prestige to exactly the end you describe.'

'Yes, both Ay and Horemheb would benefit from a new alliance with her,' he mused.

'But my friend, momentous as the problem remains, that is not the main reason I am here,' I said.

'Oh dear! What could be yet worse?' he asked, anxiously.

'Firstly, how is the boy?'

'He is making a fair recovery.'

'And can he speak yet?' I asked.

314

'I must tell you, my friend, it is still early in his recovery, but he has responded well, and has been able to say a few words. He has asked about his family, and his eyes. He wants to know what happened to his eyes. He also said a good spirit spoke to him in the darkness of his suffering. A man with a kind voice.'

I nodded, trying not to reveal how gratified I felt by this last comment.

'Well, that is a piece of good news.'

'But you have still not told me why you are here. And that is making me quite anxious,' he said.

'I believe I have discovered the name of the man who has been leaving the objects in the Malkata Palace. The man behind the threats to the life and the soul of the King.'

He sat forward, delighted.

'I knew you could do it.'

'I also believe the same man committed his cruelties on the boy, and on the dead girl, and on the other dead boy.'

Now Nakht looked dismayed.

'The same man?'

I nodded.

'And who is this devious monster?' he said.

'Before I tell you that, let me speak to the boy.'

When the boy heard two pairs of sandals he cried out, alarmed.

'Don't be afraid. I have with me a gentleman, who is one of my oldest friends, to visit you,' said Nakht gently.

The boy relaxed. I sat down next to him. He lay on a low bed, in a cool, comfortable room. Much of his body was still bandaged with linens, and another bandage was wound around his head, to hide the disfigured eye-sockets. Where the girl's face had been sewn on to his, the little holes had healed, leaving a pattern of tiny white scars, like stars. I could have wept at the pity of it.

'My name is Rahotep. Do you remember me?'

He tilted his head in my direction, listening to the character of my voice like a bright bird with a distant comprehension of human speech. And slowly, a small, gratifying smile spread across his face.

I glanced at Nakht, who nodded, encouragingly.

'I am glad you are well. I would like to ask you some questions. I need to ask you about what happened. Would that be all right?'

The smile vanished. But eventually he gave the slightest of nods. This gave me an idea.

'What I will do is ask a question, and you can reply either yes, by nodding your head, or no, by shaking it. Can you do that for me?'

Slowly he nodded once.

'The man who hurt you; did he have short, grey hair?'

The boy nodded.

'Was he an older man?'

Again he nodded.

'Did he give you something to drink?'

The boy hesitated, and then nodded.

And then, my heart beating faster, I asked:

'Were his eyes a kind of grey-blue? Like stones in a stream?'

A chill ran through the boy. He nodded, once, then twice, and then on and on, nodding and failing to get his breath as if he were suddenly maddened in fear at the memory of those cold eyes.

Nakht rushed to the boy's side, and tried to calm him, soothing his brow with a cool, wet cloth. Eventually the panic subsided. I wished I had not had to cause him such distress.

'I am sorry, my friend, to ask you to remember such things. But you have helped me very greatly. I will not forget you. I know you cannot see me, but I am here as your friend. That is a promise. No one will hurt you again. Will you accept my word?' I asked.

And I waited until slowly, untrustingly, he gave me the slightest nod.

Outside, Nakht confronted me.

'What was that about?'

'Now I can tell you the name of the man who did all of these things. But prepare yourself. Because you know him,' I replied.

'I?' said Nakht, with astonishment and some degree of anger.

'His name is Sobek.'

My old friend stood still as a statue. His mouth hung open foolishly.

'Sobek?' he repeated, incredulously. 'Sobek . . . ?'

'He was Ay's physician. Ay sacked him and replaced him. He gave him another, lesser job. Caring for the mad Mutnodjmet. But he cared for her in his own way. He made her an opium addict, and in the end she did anything he asked of her. And now she too is dead.'

He sat down slowly on the nearest elegant bench, as if exhausted by too much information.

'So have you apprehended him?' he asked.

'No. I have no idea where he is, or where he will strike next. And I need your help.'

But Nakht continued to look horrified.

'What is it?' I snapped.

'Well, he is a friend. It is a great shock.'

'Certainly. And you introduced him to me here. That does not make you guilty or complicit in any way. But it does mean you can help me catch him.'

He looked away.

'My friend, why do I get the feeling there is something you are not telling me, once more? Is this another of your secrets?'

He said nothing.

'I need you to answer all my questions clearly and fully. If you refuse, I will have to take the necessary measures. This is too important, and time is too short, for games.'

He was astonished by my tone. We stared at each other. He saw I meant what I said.

'We are both members of a society.'

'What sort of society?

317

With the utmost reluctance he continued: 'We are dedicated to the pursuit of knowledge for its own sake. I mean the research, investigation and study of secret knowledge. In our times, such esoteric knowledge has been driven underground. It has become unacceptable. Perhaps it was always something that could only be appreciated by an initiated elite who valued knowledge above all else. We preserve and continue the ancient traditions, the ancient wisdom.'

'How?'

'We are initiates, we preserve the secret rites, the secret books . . .' he stuttered.

'Now we are getting somewhere. And what are these books about?'

'Everything. Medicine. Stars. Numbers. But they all have one thing in common.'

He hesitated.

'And what is that?' I asked.

'Osiris. He is our God.'

Osiris. The King who, in the ancient story, once ruled the Two Lands, but was betrayed and murdered, and then resurrected from the Otherworld by his wife Isis, whose love and loyalty made this possible. Osiris, who we depict as a man with black or green skin, to indicate his fertility and his gift of resurrection and eternal life, dressed in the white bandages of death, holding the crook and flail, and the white crown. Osiris, who we also call 'the perpetually good being'. Osiris, who offers the hope of eternal life, provided his followers make the right preparations for death. Osiris, who it is said waits for all of us after death in the Hall of Judgement, the supreme judge, ready to hear our confession.

I sat back and considered Nakht for a moment. I felt as if this man, who I counted as a close friend, had suddenly become almost a stranger to me. He stared at me as if he was feeling the same.

'I am sorry for the way I spoke to you. Our friendship is very important to me, and I would not see it imperilled. But I had no choice. I had to make you tell me this. You are my only possible link to this man.'

He nodded slowly, and gradually a touch of warmth returned to the feeling between us.

'You said I could help you. What did you mean?' he asked eventually.

'I will explain. Tell me something first. Does this secret society have a symbol?'

Once more he hesitated.

'Our symbol is a black circle. It is the symbol of what we call the night sun.'

At last I had found the answer to that enigma. I quoted back his own words to him: '*The Sun at rest in Osiris, Osiris at rest in the Sun.*'

He looked askance.

'My friend. I must ask you this. When I described the carving with the sun disc destroyed, and when I asked you about the eclipse, and we went to the astronomical archives, you must have recognized the connection. Is that not the truth?'

He nodded, miserably.

I let him dangle on the sharp hook of his own guilt for a little while.

'What does it mean?' I said, eventually.

'In the simplest form, it means that in the darkest hour of the night, the soul of Ra is reunited with the body and soul of Osiris. This allows Osiris, and indeed all the dead of the Two Lands, to be reborn. It is the holiest, most profound moment in all creation. But it has never been witnessed by any mortal. It is the greatest of all the Mysteries.'

He was silent for a moment, unwilling to meet my eye.

'I asked you about this before. And you did not tell me this most crucial detail. I might have identified Sobek much more quickly. I might have saved lives.'

He was frustrated again.

'We are a secret society! The relevant word is "secret"! And at the time I did not see any truly compelling reason to betray the sacred oaths I took.'

'And, as it turned out, you were wrong,' I replied.

To his credit, he nodded and looked appalled.

'The consequences of our slightest deeds seem never to be in our power. I try to control my life, but I see now, life controls me. And at moments like this, I feel I have the blood of innocent people on my conscience.'

'No, you don't. But if you are feeling in need of moral redemption, then help me now. Please.'

He nodded.

'I suppose, logically, Sobek is working for either Ay or Horemheb, most likely the latter, for he benefits greatly from the King's death.'

'And if that is so, then catching him before he can wreak any more chaos is imperative. Horemheb's ship of state is moored by the Malkata Palace. He has proposed to Ankhesenamun. She is considering his offer.'

'May the Gods preserve us from that destiny. Tell me your plan,' he said quietly.

'I believe Sobek is obsessed with visions. I also believe he is fascinated by hallucinogenic mysteries and substances. He seems to be also fascinated by what happens in the moment between life and death. I think that is why he drugs his victims and watches closely as they die. He is searching for something in that moment. This might bear comparison with the interests of your secret society – the moment of darkness and renewal?'

Nakht nodded.

'Now, Pentu, the King's physician, mentioned to me that there is said to be another, very rare, fungus reputed to give the power of immortal vision; he said all that was known of it is that it grows only in the far boreal regions of the world. Do you know anything about this?'

Nakht nodded.

'Certainly. It is mentioned in the secret books. I can give you a much more detailed account. It is said to be a red-capped fungus, which only thrives in remote forests of silver trees with golden leaves. Its existence is highly speculative. No one has ever *held* such a thing in his hand. Anyway, it is said to be a means by which its priests die to the world, experience a vision of the Gods themselves, and then return to life. They also say that, used incorrectly, it is a powerful poison, and results in madness. I always considered it a kind of esoteric fable of spiritual enlightenment rather than something that existed in the real world.'

'What matters now is that it *might* exist, and that if one had such a fungus, it would be an object of obsessive fascination to such a man as Sobek. A vision is sometimes far more powerful than reality itself . . .' I said.

Nakht shook his head doubtfully.

'Your plan depends upon something that does not exist.'

'Sobek has used the power of the imagination against us himself. And so there's a kind of poetic justice in using it against him, isn't there?'

'What a strange world this is,' he replied, 'Medjay detectives describing their work in terms of poetry and justice.'

I ignored his quip.

'In any case, the person who will pretend to have obtained the mysterious, magical fungus is you,' I replied quickly.

He looked aghast.

'Me?'

'Who else? I cannot very well present myself at your secret society, can I?'

He shrugged, realizing he was trapped.

'We'll need to concoct a good story about how you obtained it,' I continued. 'Where do you get your seeds from, the rare ones in the gardens?'

'They are sent to me by merchants from all over the kingdom. Let me think. Ah! There's one in the town of Carchemish on the Mittani border. He supplies me with very rare and interesting seeds and bulbs which come from the north.'

'Excellent. A connection like that will bear investigation. You could say he obtained the hallucinogen from a dealer with contacts along a new trade route,' I suggested.

'That is just about plausible; to the east of the great inland sea beyond the northern borders of the Hatti kingdom there is a fabled and impassable mountain range where snow reigns permanently, and no traveller can survive. But it is also said that there is a secret route through those mountains, leading to another realm beyond, of endless forests and desolate plains, frozen in ice, white as the purest limestone, where primitive peoples, pale and straw-haired and blue-eyed, wearing the furs of beasts and the feathers of golden birds, live in palaces of ice.'

'It sounds horrible,' I said.

I had put Nakht in a dangerous situation. But he knew I had no other choice. If, as I believed, our man was obsessed with dreams and visions, and since I knew he was a member of the secret society, then this was the best lure.

'So all you need to do now is send a discreet message in your no-doubt secret language, proposing to your secret-holding fellows that you will bring the hallucinogen to a meeting tomorrow night, so that they can inspect and experiment with this mysterious marvel of visions. Perhaps you could even offer the temptation of a live experiment.'

'On whom, may I ask?' he said nervously.

'I am sure Khety will be willing to represent the victim, given what is at stake.'

'Well, a message is not necessary. Tomorrow night we celebrate the last night of the Mysteries of Osiris. I suppose you do not know that the last month of the inundation is the time of his festival? As the flood waters recede, so we celebrate the rites of resurrection. Following the days and nights of lamentation, we celebrate the triumph of the God. Tomorrow night, in fact.'

44

I was desperate to return to my home, to check that all was well, and that the guard I had ordered Khety to organize was in place. I could afford to take no chances with my family. But as I turned a corner in the riddle of the lanes of the oldest part of the city, I saw a shape whirring through the air, and felt a blow, spreading with something like painful warmth across the side of my head, and then all was darkness.

I came to my senses on the filthy floor of the lane. Thoth was nuzzling my face with his wet muzzle. The shadows of four men stood over me. They were wearing the kilt of the army. One of them tried to kick Thoth, but he turned on him, his teeth bared.

'Call your animal off,' said one of them.

I quelled the bile in my throat, and slowly got to my feet.

'Thoth!'

He came instantly, obediently, to stand beside me, at attention, gazing at the soldiers. I allowed them to shackle me, and then, with them forming a guard of dishonour, I was hurried away, down to the docks. They hustled me on to a boat, and, with Thoth anxious at my side, we set off across the Great River. We landed on the opposite bank, further north. I was pushed on to a waiting chariot, Thoth bounding up to sit at my feet, and we were driven off at speed along the stone ways that led directly towards the desert hills and mortuary temples; and then we turned north-east, towards the hidden valley. Then I was summarily taken from the chariot, and marched up the baking slopes of the rocky grey and orange hills. Our breath sounded loud in the tinder-dry silence. I wondered suddenly whether I was being escorted to some desert grave, but this seemed an absurd way to go about disposing of me. They could simply have caved in my skull and thrown me to the crocodiles, if my death was their intention. No, I was being taken to meet someone.

When we reached the top of the hill, with the great green plain surrounding the city of Thebes stretching far away to the east, hazy in the late afternoon heat, behind me, I was not surprised to see in the shimmering haze a figure waiting for me under a sunshade, with a horse standing nearby. I knew his profile. Horemheb seemed as unaffected as a lizard by the heat. He looked at me, sweating and out of breath, with contempt. He made me stand in the sun, while he remained in his circle of deep shade. I waited for him to address me.

'I am puzzled. Why does the Queen trust you?' he said, suddenly.

'If you wanted to have a conversation, why did you bring me up here?' I asked.

'Answer the question.'

'I am the Queen's personal guard. You would have to ask her why she trusts me.'

He came closer.

'Understand me well. If I do not receive satisfactory answers to my questions, I will not hesitate to cut your baboon's head off. I see you are fond of the creature. I was not happy to have you listening to my conversation with the Queen, and that inclines me further towards the necessity of violence,' he said.

I considered my few options.

'I am a detective in the city Medjay. I was called by the Queen to investigate a mystery.'

'What was the nature of this mystery?'

I hesitated. He nodded to one of his men, who drew out a knife.

'Suspicious objects were found within the royal quarters,' I offered.

'It will save time if you answer as fully as possible.'

'These objects were threats to the life of the King.'

'Now we are getting somewhere. And what was the result of your investigation?'

'No culprit has been decisively identified.'

He gazed at me doubtfully.

'You can't be much good, then.'

He beckoned me to follow him to look the other way, down into the hidden valley that lay beyond and far below us, deep into the hills to the west. On the scarred dust-grey of the valley floor I saw tiny figures moving about: workmen.

'Do you know what that is?' he asked.

I nodded.

'That is the King's tomb being readied,' he said. 'Or rather, it is Ay's tomb being adapted to receive the King.'

It seemed wiser to say nothing.

'You may be wondering what it is I want from you.'

'I assumed there must be something,' I replied. 'Although what a mere Medjay detective could offer you is unclear.'

'You have influence with the Queen. I wish you to do two things. One is, to encourage the Queen to a favourable reply to my offer of marriage. The other is, to report to me on Ay's conversations with her. Is that clear? And of course, there will be great advantages for you in the future. You are an ambitious man, and that should be respected, and your ambitions satisfied.'

'Presumably, if I do not do as you ask, you will execute my baboon.'

'No, Rahotep. If you do not do as I wish, and if you are not successful in persuading the Queen of the advantages of marriage to me, I will execute your family. I know more about you than you can imagine. Your three girls. Your young son. Your beautiful wife, and your ageing father. Just think what I could do to them, if I chose.

And of course, I would have you live to endure and witness every moment of their suffering. And then I would condemn you to the gold mines of Nubia, where you could lament their deaths at your leisure.'

I tried to keep breathing, and not to give myself away. I was tempted to reveal everything then about the identity of Sobek, and his connection to Horemheb's wife. I was tempted to ask him about the balls of blood that had been thrown at the King and Queen during the festival. But at this moment, when he seemed to control everything, I held on to my information. It was all I had. I would save it.

I was about to accept his proposal, when somehow, impossibly – for evening was still some hours away – the brilliance of the daylight noticeably faded. It was as if the air and the light were slowing down in time. Everyone noticed it. For a moment Horemheb and his guards looked confused. Thoth began to run in circles, muttering anxiously, his ears laid flat against his skull. Now unnatural cries and animal howls rose from every corner of the valley, and from the more distant settlements. We all stood staring up towards the sun, shading our eyes to try to understand what was happening. A great catastrophe seemed to be taking place in the realm of the sky. Suddenly vast shadows massed and moved across the slopes, hollows and hidden depressions of the mountainside, and, it seemed, from out of the red rock itself, as if the underworld's ghosts and spirits were rising up to conquer the light of the living.

Distantly, I heard a high-pitched music calling urgently through the air; it must be the ceremonial trumpets blasting their emergency from the temple walls. The great pylon gates would be closing firmly now against the people. Inside, priests in white robes would be scurrying to offer sacrifices to sustain Ra from the unprecedented threat of darkness that was suddenly sweeping over everything.

It felt like the end of the world. I thought of the children, and Tanefert. I hoped they would be at home together, where at least they could shelter behind the solid wooden door. I hoped they would not be afraid. The vast shadows drew even more strength and gathered together into a strange twilight; and then everything suddenly went very quiet. Even the northerly wind, which always sprang up in the late afternoon, faded and then completely died. It was as if the world was abandoned; down below in the far fields, I could only see a few mules standing uncertainly, untended, and the last few workers running for their lives across their carefully tilled rows. I heard the tiny screams of an abandoned child, but I could not see him, and anyway he too was swiftly lost in the encroaching gloom.

By now the sun had faded so much it was possible to watch, between the woven mesh of my fingers, the extraordinary, unaccountable spectacle that was taking place in the heavens. A black curved sword's edge had imposed itself upon the great disc of the sun. Then, bands of shadow like those at the bottom of a sunlit pool rippled vastly and at speed across the land below, then over us, then onwards across the Red Land; I held my hands out to catch at them, but somehow they made no impression on my skin. As the light dimmed further it turned to something strangely grey, as when all colour is leeched away from an over-washed garment.

Everything accelerated; the great black bird of night swept completely over the face of the day, and instantly the imperishable constellations of the heavens shone brilliantly, as day passed into night in a moment of time that could not be measured by the dripping of a water clock. Ra, Lord of Eternity, disappeared as surely as if he had departed below the horizon of the sky at sunset. Now all that remained was a thin corona of light around the great black conquering disc of darkness; it looked as if the God of the Sun had been forced to offer his glory in surrender. All around me was night; and yet impossibly I saw the very edges of the distant horizon in every direction displaying the oranges and yellows of sunset. It was suddenly cold, as in winter, and utterly still.

And then I saw with my own eyes a sight I shall remember until the moment of my death: the great Eye of Creation, staring down at me; the ebony of the pupil, the brilliant white corona of the iris, and momentarily a thin band of crimson, like blood, flickering around the edges of the darkness. I could not breathe, and the world ceased and was silent; and it seemed to me the most beautiful mystery I had ever seen.

But as suddenly as the darkness had conquered the light, the balance of power shifted again, and a shimmering arc of the thinnest brilliance, like the honed blade of a gold knife catching the sunlight, emerged from the opposite side to dazzle the darkness with its triumph. At first the world turned opalescent grey again, and the strange battalions of shadow rippled quickly over and away from us again, but this time in the opposite direction; and quickly the familiar blue of the sky was restored. The stars faded fast; and the world began to fill again with colour and life and time.

Horemheb was fascinated. I had never seen him so enraptured. He turned to me with a look of triumph on his handsome, harsh face.

'Did you see? The Aten was consumed by the darkness. It is a sign from the Gods that they will not sustain the corrupt power of this pathetic dynasty. There will be a new order! This is a new Sun, shining on a new age!' he shouted decisively, and he beat his fist against his chest triumphantly. His officers gave him a disciplined cheer.

And with that he rode off down the barren hillside, accompanied by his running officers, leaving Thoth and me to make our own way back to the palace. And as we returned along the dusty path, the image of the Eye of heaven haunted my imagination. It was the symbol of the dark circle made real. My instinct had been right. It was not just the mysterious symbol of a society; it was also a prophecy of something real to come. I suddenly recalled what Nakht had said about the dark circle: 'It means that in the darkest hour of the night, the soul of Ra is reunited with the body and soul of Osiris. This allows Osiris, and indeed all the dead of the Two Lands, to be reborn. It is the holiest, most profound moment in all creation.'

But the more I thought about that, the more ambivalent it seemed. Did this heavenly event foretell a miracle of the return to life, or an impending catastrophe?

45

The palace officials were running up and down the corridors in great confusion like ants in a colony that has been disturbed by children poking sticks. I entered the Queen's chamber, and found her in intent conference with Ay, Khay and Simut.

Ay glanced at me briefly. His face was hollow with tiredness. For once he looked discomposed.

Simut was giving an account of the aftermath of the eclipse.

'There has been significant disorder in the city. Crowds that gathered in front of the temple gates are refusing to disperse. There has been looting, buildings have been set on fire . . . and I must report the Medjay have only worsened the situation by their attempts to control the crowds. There have been running battles in some quarters with certain dissident elements . . .'

Khay interrupted.

'The people are calling for the King. They refuse to leave until the King appears and speaks to them.'

Ay sat very still, his brain whirring, seeking a solution. His refusal to announce the death of the King had now trapped him. He was caught out by his own lie.

'That is only one of our problems. Horemheb will seize this

opportunity to bring his divisions into the city to control the unrest,' said Simut.

'And where are those divisions?' snapped Ay.

'As far as we can tell, they are in Memphis. But our intelligence is not clear,' he admitted. 'Even the fastest messenger cannot relay orders between here and Memphis in less than three days, and then they will need to mobilize, and sail south. Unless Horemheb has foreseen everything, and prepared divisions to march on Thebes more quickly.'

There was a moment of silence, while each person considered what ought to be done with the precious time that remained to us.

'I will speak to the people,' said Ankhesenamun, suddenly.

'And what could you possibly say?' Ay replied. His sinister eyes flickered, curious now.

'I will tell them the truth. I will say the events in the heavens are a sign of a renewed order on earth. I will explain that the King was united with the God during the darkness, and is now reborn in the Otherworld. I remain here, as his successor, with his sanction. If I do that, then Horemheb's bid for power will be annulled.'

They gazed at each other, adversaries joined by mutual necessity.

'You are a clever child. It is a good story. But many will be suspicious of it.'

'The darkness was a great and rare event. It is a spectacle without parallel, and people need to understand it. My words will have to persuade the people.'

Ay quickly thought through the ramifications and possibilities of her proposal.

'I will support you, but words are powers and must be chosen carefully. When you speak of yourself, I would prefer "representative" to "successor".'

She considered this.

'We return to our original disagreement once again. There is little time, and I see no other solution. Why should I not name myself as successor? For that is what I am.'

'You carry the blood of your family. But remember this: you cannot enact your power without authority over the offices of the government. And I alone exert that authority.'

'In my name,' she replied quickly.

'Indeed. And that is why we must fashion a strategy to our mutual advantage.'

She considered the situation. She had to make a swift choice.

'Very well.'

'And the content of the speech will be agreed between us?' he said. She glanced at Khay, who nodded.

'Of course.'

'Then prepare yourself well, for this appearance is the most important one of your life.'

As soon as Ay had left, she jumped up.

'Where have you been?' she said fretfully, and with a touch of anger. 'I was concerned for your safety.'

'I went to visit my friend Nakht in the city. And on the way back I was offered an invitation I could not refuse to an audience with Horemheb.'

She looked astonished.

'And you went?'

'I had little choice. They took me captive.'

'And what did he say to you?'

We sat down together, and I recounted everything I had discovered about Sobek, and that I had now proved, through the witness of the boy, that he was also responsible for the killings in the city. Finally I described to her everything Horemheb had said to me. She looked astounded for a moment.

'We must protect your family from his attentions.'

'Yes, but we must also think. So far, he has only made threats against them, and he will not carry them out until you have informed him of your decision. So we must keep him in uncertainty for as long as possible. At the same time, I have a plan to catch Sobek. And we can then interrogate him and discover if and how Horemheb or Ay are connected to his actions. And that information will give you great power.'

She nodded, her eyes on fire with the exhilaration of the moment. Suddenly she could see a way forward for herself and her dynasty.

'This darkness has shocked me. I feel the Gods' eyes upon me. I feel they can see inside me. Everything is at stake, not just the future of my dynasty, but also the fate of the Two Lands. But strangely, I find I feel, for the first time in many months – entirely alive.'

Smoke drifted across the great open space before the Temple. The crowd stretched back along the Avenue of Sphinxes. Some were chanting, others shouting, most praying. I watched from the vantage of the pylon gateway roof. We had travelled swiftly and secretively by ship and then chariot to the temple itself, under the protection of Simut's guard. Now, at his signal, the trumpeters raised their long, silver instruments towards the horizon and blasted out a fanfare. Suddenly the attitude of the crowd shifted, from chaotic discontent to attention. The spectacle they had demanded was about to begin.

The Queen appeared from the gateway, arrayed in the gold robes of state and the crowns, and the silence gave way again to screaming and shouting when it became clear she was alone. But in the long, low angles of the late light, she glowed. She continued forward, ascended the dais, ignoring the cries and laments, and then stood to confront the great beast of the multitude. She waited to be heard. It would be a battle of wills. Finally silence fell. I saw thousands of faces, rapt, anxious, devoted to her glorious presence.

'This has been a day of wondrous omens,' she called out. 'The Gods have revealed themselves to us. So let us worship them.'

She raised her arms, serenely; and then, slowly, many in the crowd followed suit. Those that did not were at least silenced.

'Ra, the King of the Gods, has triumphed over the forces of darkness and chaos. Life is renewed. The glory and power of the Two Lands is renewed. But in that moment, he has taken something he greatly desired. What he has taken is of great value to us. Greater than gold, and greater than life. I stand before you now, as the daughter of Kings, and the daughter of the Goddess Maat who brings justice and order, to give you the news of our great sacrifice, and the God's great gain. For in the moment of darkness, witnessed by all living things, the King Tutankhamun was united with Ra, as the King must be, and, as it is written in the great books, he is now one with the King of the Gods. And the world is remade. The world is reborn again.'

Her words echoed around the open space. A vast wail of lamentation rose up and spread out through the crowds and the city. I saw people turning to each other, many persuaded, a few shrugging, uncertain. They knew this story of the sacrifice of the King for the renewal of life, for it is one of the oldest of the stories that explain to us how things are in the world. And she had used it wisely. Her words might well convince the multitudes. The elite would certainly require a more sophisticated explanation, but it would be difficult for them to question the story.

She pressed on.

'I stand before you now. I am the best-loved daughter of Ra. I am *maat*. I am order over chaos. I am the Eye of Ra at the prow of the Ship of the Gods. Under me, our enemies will perish in the darkness, and our world will flourish in the light of the Gods.'

This was followed by another persuasive fanfare from the trumpets; and now, most of the multitude roared their approval. The Queen's spirit and her beauty seemed to have won them over. But I saw there were others who turned away, unsatisfied, shaking their heads. The battle to win the Two Lands after the death of Tutankhamun remained to be won. If I could prove a connection between Horemheb and Sobek then Horemheb's position would crumble. If I did not, then I could not see, at this moment, what could prevent him from appropriating, in the name of the army, the kingship.

46

That evening, Thoth and I returned to Nakht's town house. Minmose offered to shave my head, for if I was to pass through the temple gateway, I needed once again to transform myself into the appearance of a priest. As I was sitting under his blade, with a cloth around my neck, Khety arrived. Luckily for him, he would not need to perform these ritual ablutions, for he was to attend as Nakht's experimental victim – a non-elite character.

'Is the guard in place at my home?' I asked first.

He nodded. 'Tanefert was not happy about the imposition. But I explained the necessity as well as I could, without frightening her.'

I sighed with relief.

'And did you impress upon her to make sure the children do not go out, in any event?'

'I did. Don't worry. They are safe. They will be guarded night and day.' Then he allowed himself a quiet chuckle. 'You make an unconvincing priest,' he said.

'Be careful, Khety. You will soon find yourself in a much more compromised position.'

He nodded.

'That's what I enjoy about my work. Every night is different. One night patrolling the streets; the next, taking dangerous hallucinogens . . .'

'Nakht has concocted something that will look plausibly like the fungus, but will have no effect at all.'

'So I have to pretend?' he asked.

'Yes,' said Nakht, as he entered in his robes. 'I have made up a simulacra of the dried fungus using ground beans.'

'I hate beans,' replied Khety. 'My wife cooks them, but they have a horrible effect on me . . .'

'You will not need to consume more than a mouthful, and so the noxious effects should be absolutely minimal,' Nakht replied. And then added: 'Which is surely a relief for all of us.'

'But what sort of thing should I talk about when I've taken the powder?' asked Khety.

'Nothing to start with. And then, slowly, imagine that the light of heaven is revealed to you. Let your mind accept the illumination of the Gods.'

'And what does that look like?' asked Khety.

Nakht glanced at me, dubiously.

'Think of light. Describe the beauty of the light, and how you see the Gods moving in light, as if light were thought and thought were light.'

'I'll try,' said Khety, hesitantly.

Nakht had ordered chariots to carry us from his house, up the long Avenue of Sphinxes, to the Great Temple of Karnak. The streets were dark. I noticed boarded-up shop fronts, and some blackened interiors – the damage done during the riots. But the city seemed quiet again. We arrived at the gates, and Nakht spoke to the temple guards, who assessed Khety and me by the light of their lamps. Nakht's fame here was great, and I prayed that they would ask few questions. He chatted cheerfully to them for a moment, and then, with a last questioning look, we were swiftly waved through. We passed under the gateway and once more into the vast shadowy arena within the temple walls. Beyond the great raised hammered bowls of oil that had been lit throughout the Enclosure, like a constellation of small suns, everything disappeared into an obscure penumbra.

Nakht lit his oil lamp, and we set off across the open ground in the direction of the House of Life. But instead of entering there, he led us further to the right of the building. We followed down several dark passageways between separate buildings – workshops and offices, all deserted for the night. The passageways narrowed and the buildings gave way to storage rooms and magazines, until we reached the high back wall of the Great Enclosure itself. Just there stood a tiny, ancient structure. As we approached I saw the figure of Osiris, God of the Dead, was carved everywhere on its walls, in his white crown flanked by two plumed feathers, surrounded by column after column of dense inscriptions.

'This chapel is dedicated to Osiris,' whispered Khety.

'Precisely. The God of the Otherworld, of night, and darkness, and death before life . . . but of course he is in truth the God of the light beyond the light, as we say. Of illumination and secret knowledge,' Nakht replied. Khety nodded, as if he understood, then raised his eyebrows at me.

We passed through the outer chamber, and into the small, dark inner chamber of the temple. Quickly Nakht lit oil lamps in niches around the walls. Rich drifts of incense floated on the shadowy air. He installed me behind one of the pillars, near the entrance, from where I could observe everything that came to pass, and anyone who approached. Then we settled down to wait. And eventually, one by one, twelve other men in white robes arrived. I recognized some of them from the party at Nakht's house. There was the blue-eyed poet, and the architect. Each man wore a gold pendant on a gold chain around his neck. On each one was an obsidian circle: the dark disc. They greeted Nakht with great excitement, and then examined Khety like a servant for sale. Finally, only Sobek had failed to appear. I felt my plan crumbling away between my fingers. He had not, after all, taken the bait.

Nakht played for time:

'One of our number is missing,' he said eventually, loudly enough so that I could hear. 'We should wait for Sobek.'

'I disagree, time is passing, and so we should begin the ceremony without him. Why should the God wait for Sobek?' called out one of the men, followed by a chorus of agreement. Nakht had no choice but to begin. From my vantage behind the pillar, I watched as Khety's eyes were bound with a black cloth, so that he could not witness anything. Then a small chest was carried in, and from within that a gold coffer was brought forth. This was opened to reveal a human-shaped pottery dish, and within that was something that looked like a wheat loaf or cake, baked in the rough shape of a human being.

Nakht intoned a hymn over the cake: '*Homage to thee, Osiris, the lord of eternity, the King of the Gods, thou who hast many names, whose forms of coming forth are holy, whose attributes are hidden . . .*' and so it went on. Finally, the incantation finished, the cake was raised up and then divided into fourteen parts, and each man ritually ate one of the pieces. I suppose these were the fourteen parts into which Seth, the jealous brother, cut up Osiris's body after he had murdered him. Now, ritually, the God was reborn in each man. One piece of the cake was left over for Sobek.

The mystery accomplished – and I must confess I was disappointed that it seemed merely to be a symbolic meal – the twelve men gathered around Nakht for the evening's experiment. He drew forth from his robe a leather pouch, and then spoke at length, partly playing for time, reiterating what he knew of the powers and nature of this food of the Gods, and his hope that it could offer visions of the Gods. Still there was no sign of Sobek.

Finally, realizing that there was no more time left, Nakht opened the pouch, and, on a cosmetic spoon, produced a sample of the powder. The initiates observed it minutely, fascinated by its legendary potency. By now the blindfolded Khety must have been quite concerned, for the moment was approaching for the experiment. But Nakht suddenly said: 'Let us not waste this marvel on a servant. I myself will eat the food of the Gods.'

The men all nodded enthusiastically. I could imagine Khety's relief. Nakht must have decided Khety's acting skills were not going to be adequate, and perhaps, too, he thought he could take up more time with his own performance, just in case Sobek finally appeared.

'You will be able to describe to us your visions in intellectual detail, which the servant could not,' said the blue-eyed poet, condescendingly.

'And we shall be here to record anything you may speak of when you are possessed of the vision.'

'You may become a living oracle,' said another, excitedly.

With a great performance of ritual, Nakht mixed a spoonful of the powder into a cup of fresh water, and then drank it in slow, careful sips. The chamber was utterly silent, each man gazing with rapt anticipation at Nakht's serious face. At first nothing happened. He smiled and shrugged slightly, as if in disappointment. But then, a look of seriousness stole over his face, and became one of intense concentration. Had I not known he was performing, I would almost have been persuaded of the authenticity of the vision myself. Slowly he raised his hands, palms up, and his eyes followed. He seemed now to be caught in a trance, his eyes wide open and unblinking, staring at an airy mirage of something that was not there.

And then what had been an act became real. Between the small, steady lights of the oil lamps, and the greater penumbra of the chamber, a shadow entered. The figure that cast the shadow was all darkness; small, like an animal almost, its shape and features hidden in the wrapped folds of the black cloak that covered it from head to toe. I felt fear like a cloak of ice descend upon me. I drew my knife from its sheath, and grasped the figure from behind and held the blade to its throat.

'Take three steps forward.'

The figure shuffled ahead like an animal in the market place into the light of the lamps. The faces of the initiates stared incredulously at these unexpected and unacceptable intrusions.

'Turn around,' I ordered.

It did so.

'Remove your hood.'

It did so, slowly slipping the cloth from its head.

The girl was not much older than my own daughter Sekhmet. I had never seen her before. She looked like a girl one would pass on the street, and not notice. She sat on the low bench, a cup of water clenched between her fists, shivering and panting. Nakht carefully placed a linen shawl around her shoulders, and went away, to leave us some privacy, and to try to calm the hubbub of protestation that now rose from his fellow society members.

I lifted her chin, and gently tried to persuade her to look at me.

'What has happened? Who are you?'

Tears squeezed out from her eyes.

'Rahotep!' she managed to say before the intense chattering of her teeth overwhelmed her again.

'I am Rahotep. Why are you here? Who sent you?'

'I do not know his name. He said to say: "*I am the demon who dispatches messengers to lure the living into the realm of the dead*".'

She stared at us. Khety and I glanced at each other.

'How did he find you?'

'He stole me from the street. He says he will kill my family if I do not deliver a message to Rahotep.'

Her eyes filled with tears, and her face contorted again.

'And what is the message?'

She could barely enunciate the words.

'You must come to the catacombs. Alone . . .'

'Why?'

'You have something he wants. And he has something you want,' she replied.

'What does he have that I want?' I asked, slowly.

Now she could not look me in the eye. Great convulsions shook her.

'Your son,' she whispered.

47

I ran through the shadows of the night. Thoth kept pace with me. Perhaps Khety was following behind. I did not look back. As if from far away I could hear the distant pounding of my sandals upon the dusty ground, and the low hum of the blood in my skull, and the thumping of my heart in the cage of my chest.

A guard had been in place. Khety had ordered Tanefert not to let the children out, under any circumstances, nor to open the door to anyone. The house was to look as if it were closed up. So how had Sobek managed to take him? I imagined Tanefert's grief and the children's terror. *And I was not there to save them.* What if it was a bluff? What if it was not? I ran faster.

He would meet me at the catacombs. I must come alone. If I came with anyone, the boy would die. I was to bring the hallucinogen. If I failed, the boy would die. If I spoke to anyone of this, the boy would die. *I was to come alone.*

I came to the harbour, tore a reed skiff from its moorings, and began to paddle, demented, across the Great River. I thought nothing this time of crocodiles. The moon was a white stone. The water was black marble. I sailed upon the surface of shadows like a tiny statue of myself on a model boat, accompanied by Thoth, passing over the waters of death to meet Osiris, God of Shadows.

From the western shore I ran on, and the air cooled as I passed the border of the western edge of the cultivation. I was an animal now, all senses alert, and all vengeance. I had a new skin, the colour of rage. My teeth felt sharp as jewels in my jaws. But time was passing too fast, and the distances were too great, and I feared I would be too late.

I only stopped running at the low entrance to the catacombs. I looked down at Thoth, who had kept pace with me. He gazed up, panting hard. His eyes were clear and bright. I slipped the bridle on his muzzle to stop him from barking. He understood. I had not come alone, but he would be silent. Then I took my last breath of open night air, and we passed under the ancient carved lintel, and descended the steps into the darkness beyond darkness.

We came out into a long low-raftered hall. I listened to the monumental silence. It seemed possible in such a holy hush to hear the dead gasping as they crumbled to dust, or sighing to persuade us to join them in the delights of the Otherworld. Someone had left a lamp lit in a wall sconce for me. It burned without movement or sound, undisturbed by currents of air or time. I picked it up and walked forward; tunnels disappeared unfathomably in every direction, and off each one of them deep, low-ceilinged chambers were stacked high with clay pots of all shapes and sizes. There must have been millions and millions of them, containing the embalmed remains of ibises, falcons and baboons . . . Thoth, surrounded by the remains of his own kind, scented the cemetery air, his ears alert, to catch the smallest revealing sounds – a sandal treading on dust, the whisper of linen across living skin – such things as would be inaudible to me but might betray the presence of Sobek and my son to his acute attention.

Then we both heard it: a child's cry, lost and stricken, calling pitifully from deep within the catacombs. *My son's voice* . . . but where was it coming from? Thoth tugged suddenly on his leash, and we scrambled along the passage to our left, our shadows tracing us along the walls in the sphere of light cast by the lamp. The passage sloped downwards. More passageways led off in different directions into branching infinities of darkness. *Where was he? How would I save him?*

Then we heard another high, echoing cry, this time from another direction. Thoth turned and tugged on the leash, urging me to follow. I let him lead me down a side passage. At the end, it divided into two. We listened, vigilant, every nerve sharpened, every muscle tense. Another cry came, this time to the right. We hastened along the passage, past still more low chambers crammed with pots, most of them smashed now, with small bones and bits of skull sticking out at odd angles, as if they had been here for a very long time.

Every time the cry came echoing up to us, it led us deeper and deeper into the catacombs. It occurred to me then how impossible it would be, even if I could save my son, to find our way out again. And the thought followed: *this was a game.* He was trapping me. I stopped. When the next cry came I shouted out: '*I will go no further. Come to me. Show yourself.*'

My voice echoed down the passages, resounding and repeating throughout the labyrinth, before fading to nothing. Thoth and I waited in the vast obscurity, in our small circle of weak, propitiatory light. At first, there was nothing. But then the faintest glow glimmered in the darkness. Impossible to gauge how close or how far away it was, this tiny point of light. But we watched it bud and flower, as it lit up the sides of the passageway, I saw within it: *a shadow, walking.*

48

He wore the black mask of Anubis, the jackal, Guardian of the Necropolis. His painted teeth were white in the dark. I saw a ceremonial gold collar around his neck.

'You have brought your baboon,' he said, in his low, grey voice.

'He insisted on meeting you.'

'He is Thoth, Recorder of the Dead. Perhaps he deserves a place at this gathering,' he replied.

'Take off that mask, Sobek, and look me in the eye,' I said.

The great catacombs, with their labyrinth of darkness and silence, seemed like the vast, echoey ear of the Gods. Were they were listening to every word? Slowly he removed the mask. We faced each other. I stared with hatred into his stone-grey eyes.

'You have my son, and I want him back. Where is he?' I said.

'He is here, hidden. I will return him to you. But first, you must give me something.'

'I have it but I will not give it to you until my son is safe, with me.'

'Show it to me.'

I held up the leather bag so he could see it in the lamplight. He gazed at it hungrily.

'We have an impasse. I will not tell you where the boy is, until I have the bag. And you will ensure I do not gain possession of the bag unless you have the child. So let us be intelligent, and think about this in another way,' he said.

'And what is that?'

'The price of your child's life is nothing more than a little conversation with me. I have long thought of you as an honoured colleague. We are very like each other, after all.'

'We have nothing to discuss. I am nothing like you. All I want is my son. Alive. Now. If you have hurt him, if you have hurt any particle of him—'

'Then to get him you must be patient, or I will tell you nothing,' he replied coldly. 'I have waited for this moment. Think, Seeker of Mysteries. You, too, have questions. Perhaps I have answers.'

I hesitated. Like all murderers of his kind, he was lonely. He desired to be understood.

'What do you want to talk about?'

'Let us talk about death. For this is what fascinates us both. Death is the greatest of gifts, for it alone offers transcendence and perfection from this hopeless and banal place of blood and dust,' he said.

'Death is not a gift. It is a loss,' I replied.

'No, Rahotep. You feel most alive when closest to death. I know you do, despite the sweet little world of your family. All those dear children, and your loving wife . . . But mortals are mere bags of blood and bone and vile tissue. The heart, the famous heart of which our poets and lovers speak, is nothing but meat. All shall rot.'

'It is called the human condition. We make the best of it. What you do is also very banal. You kill helpless, drugged boys and girls, and small animals. You skin them, you break their bones, and you pluck out their eyes. So what? That is nothing special. In fact, it is pathetic. You are no more than a schoolboy torturing insects and cats. I have seen much worse. I don't care why you killed them in the way you did. It doesn't matter. It was some kind of freak show of death done for your own benefit. You speak of transcendence, and yet here you are, deep in the catacombs, a lonely, frustrated little man, despised, a failure; and desperate for what is contained in this little leather bag.'

He was breathing faster now. I needed to goad him.

'Did you know that one of the boys did not die? He is alive. He described you. He can identify you,' I continued.

He shook his head.

'A witness with no eyes? No, Rahotep, it is you who are desperate. It is you who are the failure. The King is dead, your career is finished, your son is in my power.'

I struggled not to slam him up against the wall of the catacomb and smash his face with the lamp. But I must not, for how then would I find Amenmose? And I still needed answers.

'As for those absurd objects you left for the King; your strange little gifts. Did you really think they would frighten him?'

He scowled.

'I know they caused him terror. They showed him, and that girl, everything they feared; all I had to do was to hold up a mirror to their terror of death. Fear is the greatest power. Fear of the dark, of decay, destruction and doom . . . and above all, fear of death; the fear that drives all men. The fear that underlies everything that we have made, and everything we do. Fear is a glorious power, and I used it well!' Sobek's voice was tighter now.

I moved closer to him.

'You are a pathetic, sad, twisted old man. You were sacked by Ay, and in revenge you found a way to make yourself feel important again.'

'Ay was a fool. He did not see what he had before him. He dismissed me. He betrayed my care! But now he regrets it. Everything that has come to pass, all the chaos and the fear, has been caused to happen by me! Even you, the famous Rahotep, Seeker of Mysteries, could not stop me. Do you still not see? I called to you. I laid a path for you, from the beginning, to this moment. And you have followed like a dog, fascinated by the stink of corruption and death.'

I had known this, and denied it to myself. He saw it.

'Yes. Now you understand. Now fear touches you. The fear of failure.'

I kept moving to ward off that fear.

'But why did you hate Tutankhamun? Why did you begin to attack him?'

'He was the seed of a declining and deteriorating dynasty. He was not fit. He was not virile. His mind was weak and his body imperfect. His fertility was blighted, and offered only a progeny of twisted, useless things. He had no prowess. I could not permit him to become King. That had to be stopped. Once, in the time of wisdom, before this time of fools, there was a sacred custom of killing the king when his failures jeopardized the health and power of the land. I have restored that noble ritual. I have followed the old rites. His bones were broken, his face was cast away, his eyes were cast out, his death mask was composed of rotting things, so that the Gods will never recognize him in the Otherworld. I have renewed the kingship. Horemheb will be King. He has power and virility. He will be Horus, King of Life. And as for the boy King, he will vanish into the obscurity of oblivion. His name will never be spoken again.'

At last, he had mentioned the general. I pushed on.

'Why Horemheb?'

'This is a land of lamentation. Our borders are harassed; our treasuries and granaries are empty; whores and thieves and fantasists govern our temples and palaces. Only Horemheb has the authority to restore the Two Lands to glory. I am he who has power over the living. I am he who sees the Gods. I am the dark sun. I am Anubis. I am the shadow!' he shouted.

'And so everything you did was on Horemheb's orders? The objects, the carving in the Colonnade Hall, the murder of Mutnodjmet? And in return he promised you glory and power?'

'I do not take orders! Horemheb recognized my gifts and he commissioned my acts. But he is a soldier. He has no comprehension of the greater truths. He does not yet know the extent of my work, for it goes far beyond the power and politics of this world. What use is this world if the Otherworld too is not within our grasp?'

I walked around him with my lamp. I knew there was more.

'Thank you for the gift of the box of eyes. I suppose they came from the victims I found.'

He nodded, satisfied.

'They were gathered for you. A tribute. And a sign.'

'Eyes are everything, are they not? Without them, the world disappears to us. We are in darkness. But as in an eclipse, the darkness is itself a revelation. "The Sun at rest in Osiris, Osiris at rest in the Sun!"'

He nodded.

'Yes, Rahotep; at last you begin to see, to see the truth . . .'

'In your workshop I found some glass phials. What did they contain?' I asked.

'You have not solved that either?' And he suddenly barked with contempt. Thoth growled and stirred at my side.

'I tasted salt . . .' I said.

'You did not think far enough. I collected the last tears of the dead, from their eyes as they saw their approaching deaths. The secret books tell us that tears are an elixir that contains the very distillation of what the dying witness in their last moment, as they pass from life to death.'

'But when you drank the tears – nothing. Just salt and water, after all. So much for the mysteries of the secret books.'

He sighed.

'There were compensating pleasures in the act.'

'I suppose you drugged your victims to make it easier to commit your barbarities? I suppose they did not struggle. I suppose you were able to show them the agonies of their poor flesh in great detail,' I said.

'As always you fail to see the deeper meaning. I left them as signs of warning for the King. But I wanted something else, something more profound.'

'You wanted to watch.'

He nodded.

'Death is the most glorious moment in life. To behold that moment of passing, as the mortal creature yields up its spirit, from the greatest of darkness into the light of the Otherworld, is to behold the finest elation this life can offer.'

'But your experiments failed, didn't they? All the broken bones, and the gold masks, and the dead faces turned out to be just ridiculous props. There was no transcendence. The drug gave illusions, not visions. The dead simply died, and all you saw in their eyes was pain and sorrow. And that is why you need this.'

I dangled the leather bag before his fascinated eyes. He reached out for it, but Thoth suddenly leapt at him, and I held it away.

'Before I give it to you, and you return my son to me, tell me one thing. How did you obtain the opium poppy?'

I was gratified by the flash of surprise in his stony eyes.

'It is easily obtainable,' he replied, carefully.

'Of course it is, medicinally, in small quantities, for a physician such as yourself. But there is more to it than that; there is a secret trade. I think you know a great deal about that.'

'I know nothing about it,' he muttered.

'Nonsense. The demand for the luxury of its pleasures is so strong now that no number of desperate girls and boys, used as traffickers, could satisfy it. But that remains a useful way to distract the city Medjay from the bigger plan. Let me tell you about that plan. The opium poppy is grown in the Hittite lands, and then its juice is smuggled into Thebes by ship, through the port. The drug is stored and sold through the clubs. All the officials, at every stage – from the border guards, through the port officials, to the bureaucrats who approve the clubs – are bribed. Everyone needs to survive, especially in these tough times. But what fascinates me is this: how do the cargoes manage to pass from the land of our enemies, the Hittites, in a time of war, through the border security of the army? There is only one answer. And that is: the army itself is complicit in the trade.'

'What an extraordinary fantasy! Why would the army connive in such a thing?' he scoffed.

'The treasure from such a secret trade enables Horemheb to achieve economic independence from the royal treasury. This is the modern world. The days of primitive looting and plundering and pillaging are long gone. And an independently financed, well-equipped and highly trained army is a very dangerous monster.'

For a long moment he was silenced.

'Even if this outlandish fantasy were true, it has nothing to do with me.'

'Of course it does. You know all of this. You are the physician. Your knowledge of hallucinogens makes you very valuable. Horemheb employed you not just to administer to his mad wife, but as overseer of the business here in Thebes. You oversee the arrival of the cargoes at the port, and you make sure it is transferred reliably to the clubs. But I don't think Horemheb knew the full extent of your nasty private activities. Did he?'

He gazed at me with his empty eyes.

'Very good, Seeker of Mysteries. My works of art were personal tributes to Horemheb. They were a contribution to his campaign for power; my offering of chaos and fear. But how does this knowledge profit you? Rather, it now condemns you. I cannot let you go. You are trapped in this underworld of darkness. You will never find your way back to the light. So now I will tell you the truth. And I will watch you suffer. The vision of your misery will more than compensate me for the loss of the other vision. I am no fool. Who is to say whether what you carry is real, or fake?'

And then he uttered a cry, imitating my lost boy, exactly. The obsidian knife of fear slipped between my ribs and pierced my heart. Was Amenmose, my son, dead? I sensed I was too late. He had won.

'What have you done with my son?' My voice was cracked.

I took a step towards him. He took a step backwards, raising the light of the lamp to dazzle me and disguise his face.

'Do you know what Osiris cried to the Great God when he arrived in the Otherworld? *"Oh what is this desolate place? It is without water, it is without air, its depth is unfathomable, its darkness is black as night. Must I wander hopelessly here where one cannot live in peace of heart or satisfy the longings of love?"* Yes, my friend. I have made your son a little sacrifice to Osiris, the God of the Dead. I have hidden him far, far away, in the depths of these catacombs. He is still alive, but you will never find him, not even with all the time in the world. You will both starve here, lost in your very own Otherworld. Now, Rahotep, your face has been truly opened in the House of Darkness.'

I lunged at him, Thoth rose on his hind legs, snarling and baring his teeth, but Sobek suddenly threw his flaming oil lamp at me, and disappeared into the darkness.

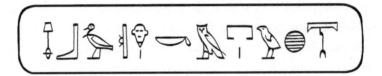

49

I released Thoth's muzzle, and he bounded into the darkness. Red light flared from the burning oil that had splashed from Sobek's lamp, and spread across the wall behind me. I heard barking, and then, gratifyingly, screaming. But I needed Sobek alive, to give evidence, and above all to return my son to me. I shouted an urgent order to the baboon as I ran along the dark gallery towards the figure huddled on the ground. I held my lamp up. Thoth had bitten deeply into Sobek's throat; there was a great gash down one side of his mauled face, tearing his eye from the socket, and the ragged flesh of his cheek hung loosely from the face, exposing bone and vessels. Black blood was pulsing from the neck wound. I knelt down and dragged his ruined face close to mine.

'Where is my son?'

Blood gurgled in his mouth as he tried to laugh.

I pressed my thumbs down on his eyes.

'What do you see now?' I whispered into his ear. 'Nothing. There is nothing. You are nothing. There is no Otherworld. This darkness you see is your eternity.'

I pressed harder and harder, forcing his eyes back into their sockets, and his legs kicked in the dust like a swimmer drowning on dry land, and he squealed like a rodent, and I felt blood under my fingers, I kept pushing until his vicious heart pumped the last of his black blood from his body, and he was dead.

I kicked his useless corpse, over and over, stamping on the remains of his face until I lost all strength. Then I collapsed on the ground, sobbing in defeat. For his death had achieved nothing. I had done wrong. The oil lamp was dimming fast. I no longer cared.

And then – I heard something. Far, far off: the sound of a child, waking from a nightmare to find himself alone in the darkness, weeping and screaming . . .

'I'm coming!'

Amenmose's screams came back louder.

Thoth bounded ahead of me, into the greater depths of the darkness, but sure of himself as he moved left and right, making the choices for me. And all the time we cried out to each other, father and son, screaming for life.

Thoth found him at the end of one of the deepest galleries. His small head stood out above the rim of a pot large enough for a fully-grown baboon. His face was sticky with tears and dirt, and his cries were inconsolable. I scrabbled around for a stone with which to smash open the pot without hurting him. And I kissed the howling boy, and tried to calm him a little, calling "*Amenmose, my son*" over and over. The first blow did not crack the pot. He howled louder still. Then, with another surer blow, the pot split open. I dragged the shards apart, the dirt cascaded out, and at last I held my son's shaking, cold, filthy body in my arms.

The lamp was guttering now. We had to try to find our way out before we lost the light. I shouted a command to Thoth. He barked as if he understood me, and bounded ahead. I held the boy under my arm, and ran after him, unable to protect the flame at the same time.

But too soon, it flickered and died.

Utter darkness. The boy whimpered, and began to cry again. I shushed him, tried to comfort him.

'Thoth!'

The baboon bounded to my side, and by feel and habit I fastened the leash on to his collar. He moved on into the blackness, and all I could do was follow, trying to protect the boy from harm as we bumped into walls, and tripped on the uneven floor. Hope, that most delicate of emotions, flickered in me as weak as the lamplight had been. I kissed my son's eyes in despair. He was quiet now, as if my presence in the dark comforted him, and any fate would now be acceptable.

And then, I saw a brief flash in the obscurity. Perhaps I had imagined it, a figment of my desperate brain. But Thoth barked again, and then the light duplicated itself, and I heard calls coming to me, as if from the lost world of life and sunlight. I shouted back. The lights turned and gathered, coming towards me, like sacred deliverance from the shadows. As they approached I looked down at my son's little face. His eyes opened wide as he watched the lights in the darkness, like something from a fable bringing him to the happy ending of a scary story.

In the shaking light of the first lamp I recognized a familiar face, at once fearful and relieved. Khety.

50

When I had carried Amenmose up the lane and into the house, Tanefert had fallen to her knees, her mouth open in a silent howl of agony and relief. She held him in the vigil of her arms, and would not let go. When eventually, speaking to her gently, I had been able to prise him from her and lay him on his couch, she then turned to me and beat me with her fists, slapping my face with her hands as if she would tear me apart; and in truth I was glad to let her.

Then she washed the boy in cool water, with a cloth, with infinite tenderness, talking to him quietly. He was tired and fractious. Then she watched over him sleeping, as if she would never leave him again. Her own face was still wet with her tears. She avoided my gaze. I could not speak. I tried brushing my hand gently against her cheek, and she ignored it. I was about to withdraw it, but suddenly she grasped it, kissed it, and held on to it. I encircled her with my arms, and held her as tightly as she had held our son.

'Never forgive me, as I will never forgive myself,' I said, eventually.

She looked at me with her now-calm, dark eyes.

'You promised me you would never allow your work to hurt our family,' she said simply.

She was right. I put my head in my hands. She stroked my head, as if I were a child.

'How did he take him?'

'I had to find food for us all to eat. The children were sick of the same old dinners. They were bored, and frustrated. And I couldn't stay inside the house all the time. It wasn't possible. So I decided to go out to the market. I left the servant girl in charge of them. The guard was on the door. She says they were all playing in the yard, and she was doing the washing. And suddenly all she could hear was screaming. She ran out – and Amenmose had disappeared. The gate was open. The guard was lying on the ground, blood pouring from his head. Sekhmet had tried to stop him taking Amenmose. He punched her. That monster punched my daughter. It was my fault.'

She curled into herself, sobbing. Futile tears startled my eyes. Now it was my turn to comfort her in my arms.

'That monster is dead. I killed him.'

Tanefert raised her tearful face, taken aback, and she saw it was the truth.

'Please don't ask me any more today. I will talk about it when I can. But he is dead. He cannot harm us any more,' I promised.

'He has harmed us too much already,' she replied, with an honesty that broke my heart.

The girls' heads appeared around the curtain. Tanefert looked up, and tried to smile.

'Is he all right?' said Thuyu, chewing her side-lock.

'He's asleep, so be quiet,' I said.

Nedjmet stared at him.

But Sekhmet, when she saw him, broke down. I saw the black bruising around her eye, and the scratch marks on her arms, and the long grazes on her legs. She gulped and swallowed, and the plump tears came extravagantly.

'How could you let that happen to him?' she cried in her broken voice, hardly able to breathe.

I felt shame come upon me, like a mantle of mud. I kissed her gently on the forehead, wiped her tears, said to all of them, 'I am so sorry', and then I walked away.

I sat on the low bench in the courtyard. From outside the walls of the house the sounds of the street came to me distantly, from another world. I thought about everything that had happened since the night Khety knocked upon the wall by the window. My own heart was knocking now, in my ribs. I had done my family a terrible wrong by leaving. It had not seemed so at the time. And perhaps I had had no choice. But Tanefert is right: there is always a choice. I had chosen the mystery, and I had paid the price. And I did not know how I could heal this.

It was Sekhmet who came out to find me. She was sniffing, and patting away at her face with her robe. But she sat down next to me, curled her legs elegantly beneath her, and leaned into my side. I put my arm around her.

'I'm sorry, that was a horrible thing to say,' she said quietly.

'It was the truth. I trust you to tell me the truth.'

She nodded wisely, as if her head were just a little bit too heavy with thinking these days.

'Why did that man take Amenmose away?'

'Because he wanted very badly to hurt me. And he wanted to show me he could take one of the most important things in the world away from me.'

'Why would anyone do such a thing?'

'I don't think I know. Perhaps I will never know.'

'What happened to him?'

'He's dead.'

She nodded, and thought about that, but she didn't say anything more, and so we sat together, listening to the noisy chaos of life in the street, watching as the sun rose higher, dispelling the shadows, and listening to the sounds of the girls starting to prepare the meal in the kitchen, arguing and laughing again together.

51

Once I knew my family was safe, I visited the palace one more time, and made my final report. I felt sick to the heart at the thought of re-entering that domain of shadows. But Ankhesenamun desperately needed to know what I had discovered about Horemheb – about how he was financing the new army, and about his commissioning of Sobek. These things would be crucial weapons in her negotiations. She could use that information against the general, intimating that she knew everything, and could reveal her knowledge, and so expose him and replace him. She would have the power to negotiate a truce between herself, Ay and Horemheb. She, Khay and Simut had gazed at me in astonishment as I explained everything. And once they had questioned me to their own satisfaction, I had excused myself. I had said I needed time alone with my family, to recover from everything that had happened. I bowed, stepped backwards, and then, without permission, turned away. I sincerely hoped I would never again be required to set foot in those hushed chambers.

Over the next days, a steady, sweltering heat settled on the land. The sun blazed remorselessly down, driving even the shadows into hiding; and the city stirred with prognostications and mirages and rumours.

Horemheb's ships, carrying several of his Memphis divisions, had arrived, to a clamour of alarm, and they remained anchored near the harbour on the east bank; at any moment a raid or an occupation was feared, but day after day nothing happened. The constant heat and the inconstancy of the future made daily life difficult and insubstantial, and yet still people carried on with their ordinary business of work, and eating, and sleeping. But by night the curfew was imposed more strictly than ever, and as I sat upon my roof with Thoth, unable to sleep, looking up at the stars, drinking too much wine, listening to the guard dogs and the stray dogs barking furiously at each other, and thinking about everything and nothing, I felt like the last man alive under the moon.

Sometimes I stared across the chaotic shambles of rooftops in the direction of the Malkata Palace, far away across the city. I imagined all the tensions and power struggles that must still be taking place there, while Tutankhamun's body underwent the final Days of Purification, in preparation for his burial. I thought of Horemheb on his ship of state still floating in the harbour, Khay drinking wine in his office, and Ay alone in his perfect chambers, clutching his fist to the endless pain in his jaw. And I thought of Ankhesenamun pacing her lamplit apartments, thinking of ways to win the board game of politics, and ensure the future of her unborn children. And I saw myself, mulling and drinking in the dark, and talking more to Thoth than to anyone else, perhaps because he had been with me through everything. He alone understood. And he could never speak.

And then one evening, soon after sunset, I heard someone knocking. When I opened the gate I saw a chariot there, and an accompanying troop of palace guards like a vision in my chaotic street. Faces up and down the lane gawped in awe at the apparition. I somehow expected Khay's bony, gloomy features to greet me. But the face that peered cautiously at me was Ankhesenamun's. She was carefully wrapped in the disguise of a linen robe.

'I see I have astounded you. May I enter?' she said, uncomfortably.

I had imagined I would refuse to have anything more to do with any of these people and their palace intrigues. But I found I could not close the door in her face. I nodded, and she stepped gingerly down from the carriage in her gold sandals of excellent quality – far too good for this street – and under the disguise of a sunshade quickly entered the modest accommodation of my home.

Tanefert was in the kitchen. As we passed through towards the reception room, where we almost never sit, she saw who it was, and suddenly seemed to be caught in a trance. Then she remembered herself, and bowed low.

'Life, prosperity and health to your majesty,' she said quietly.

'I hope you will forgive this unexpected visit; it is rude of me to arrive uninvited,' said the Queen.

Tanefert nodded through her amazement. The two women took each other in carefully.

'Please, go to the reception room. I will bring refreshments,' said Tanefert.

We settled on the benches, in an awkward silence. Ankhesenamun looked about her at the ordinary room.

'I never thanked you for everything you did for me. I know you paid a very high price for your loyalty. It was much too high, in the end. Perhaps you will accept this as some compensation, however inadequate.'

She handed me a leather bag. I slipped it open and drew out a gold Collar of Honour. It was a beautiful and valuable object, of superb quality and craftsmanship, and I would be able to support the family for years on its value. I nodded and slipped it back inside the bag, feeling none of the things I should, perhaps, have felt on receiving such a treasure.

'Thank you.'

Silence followed. I could hear Tanefert in the kitchen, preparing the tray.

'The gift is an excuse. The truth is I have wanted to see you every day, and I have refrained from calling for you. I could not bring myself to do so,' she offered. 'I realize how greatly I have come to depend upon you.'

'And yet here you are,' I replied, perhaps too harshly.

'Yes. Here I am. I have often imagined you in your home, with your family. I should like to meet them. Would that be possible?'

The girls were in any case alert to all visitors and the opportunity to meet them, and had gathered in the kitchen where I could hear them urgently questioning their mother about the identity of the unexpected stranger. I brought them in. To their credit, they approached, wide-eyed, and fell to their knees, bowing in perfect style.

Ankhesenamun thanked them, and asked them to stand up and introduce themselves. Then my father entered. He sank awkwardly to his painful knees like an old elephant, in wonder at this extraordinary guest. Tanefert returned with Amenmose in her arms.

He was sleepy, rubbing his eyes.

'May I hold him?' asked Ankhesenamun.

My wife passed her the child, and the Queen of the Two Lands held him cautiously, gently gazing down at his face, which stared up at hers, doubtfully. She laughed at his timorous expression.

'He is not sure of me,' she said.

But then the boy honoured her by responding to her laugh with his best grin, and her own face lit up, reflecting the delight of the moment.

'It is a great gift to have children,' she said, quietly, and held him for a long moment before returning him reluctantly to his mother.

I persuaded the girls to leave us, and they did so, enjoying the business of bowing over and over as they moved backwards, bumping into each other in their enthusiasm, out of the room. Then we were alone again.

'I imagine you are not here simply to pay me, and to meet my children.'

361

'No. I have a kind of invitation for you. But it is also an appeal.'

'And what is that?'

She took a long breath, and sighed.

'The Days of Purification are complete. It is time to bury the King. But I have a problem.'

'Horemheb?'

She nodded.

'It is absolutely necessary that I decide what course to pursue. I have sustained him carefully, and I think he almost believes I will accept his proposal. Ay also believes I will see the wisdom of his proposition.'

'So it will be a dangerous moment when you reveal your decision,' I said.

'Yes. And once the King is buried, I must act. So I have decided for now I need them both, if I am to claim the crowns and continue my dynasty. Where Ay is concerned, he has offered to support me as Queen, provided he continues to control the offices and the strategy of the Two Lands. I would have to accept his accession as King—'

She saw my startled expression, but continued: 'But in return I maintain my position and my independence, and I develop my own contacts, relationships and support among the offices of the government. I will confer useful legitimacy upon his authority. Ay is old, and he has no children; it will only be a matter of a few years of his kingship, before he settles all his authority and influence on me, and then he can conveniently die. This is agreed between us. It is the best I can do.'

'And Horemheb?'

'That is more difficult. Despite my revulsion for him, I have had to consider every choice, every option. He has powerful forces on his side; he commands in total more than thirty thousand soldiers. His generation are all new men, and the new army has been a path towards power and success for those who would otherwise have had none. Imagine what they could do! However, his accession to power would bring him into direct conflict with Ay and the offices, and I believe this would make the Two Lands as unstable as if we were at war with ourselves. Both of them know this, and both recognize it gives neither a clear advantage. Civil war would benefit no one at this time. And it is also the case that most of Horemheb's divisions are still far away, engaged in the Hittite wars; even if a truce were negotiated there, it would take months for them to return, and that would be seen as a major defeat for the general. But he remains very dangerous.

'Thanks to you, I have the intelligence I need now about the trade in the opium poppy, and I could use this to damage his reputation for moral purity. But it will be very difficult to prove, and above all I believe almost impossible to identify him, comprehensively, as the master of this trade. I have also decided such a controversy would be too damaging at the very time when everything must be done to create a new unity. So, I still need to contain him, like a lion in an enclosure, and in a way that ensures the army remains more or less willingly a collaborator within the scope of our authority. And to do this, in the real world of men and ambition, I must tempt him with something he wants. So I shall offer the prospect of marriage, but on the condition he waits until Ay is dead. And perhaps, with fortune on my side, a better possibility will reveal itself before then, because in truth I could never share my bed with that man. He has the heart of a rat.'

We sat in silence for a moment.

'You said you had a request,' I reminded her.

'I said it was an "appeal", and an invitation, in fact,' she replied.

'What is it?'

She paused, nervously.

'Will you accompany me to the King's burial? It is to take place tomorrow night.'

52

And so it was I joined the funeral party of Tutankhamun, once Living Image of Amun, and Lord of the Two Lands, accompanying him, as he himself had asked me to do in his final hours, to his eternity. The body lay within his chamber in the palace, wrapped in its white linen shroud, within the innermost of the coffins. He looked neat and tidy, like a large, well-made doll tied up with gold thread and decorated with amulets.

Ankhesenamun formally placed a collar of fresh flowers, blue and white and green, around his neck. A gold vulture and below it a scarab pectoral had been placed around his neck, and a gold falcon on his breast. His arms were crossed, and a pair of gold hands held the crook and flail of kingship. I remembered I had been the last person to hold the King's real hand, as his life slipped away. Surmounting the shroud was an object of impossible glory and wonder: a death mask created with the most profound metalworkers' skill from pure gold into the proud face of the God Osiris. But the craftsman had also accurately recreated the eyes of Tutankhamun, sly and watchful and brilliant, under the dark lapis lazuli curves of his eyebrows. Fashioned from quartz and obsidian, they stared into eternity with confidence. The vulture and the cobra flared protectively above his face. I felt it was a face such as he would have wished to possess to meet the Gods.

We processed through the palace. I was permitted to walk behind Ankhesenamun, next to Simut, who nodded, pleased to see me. Ay walked beside the Queen. He was sucking on another clove and cinnamon lozenge whose scent occasionally wafted in my direction. He had toothache again. It was hard to feel pity. When we emerged through the western gateway of the palace, the open air of midnight was cool, and the stars were shimmering lucidly in the depths of the eternal ocean of the night. The mummy in its open coffin was placed upon a gilded catafalque protected by friezes of carved cobras, and decorated with garlands; the other coffins, one inside the other, followed behind on another bier dragged by oxen, for their weight was enormous. Twelve high officials, including Khay and Pentu, were dressed in white, and wore white mourning bands upon their brows. At a signal they called out in one voice, and then heaved on the ropes to drag the first, light catafalque on its runners along the stones of the Processional Way.

We proceeded along the main Way, going west and then north. In the distance, the long low structures of the Temple of Hatshepsut were etched against the moon-silvered cliffs. It was a laborious, slow journey. Everywhere along the strategic points of the route, Simut had placed troops of guards, equipped with powerful bows. The land was silent, under the moon's inspection. The shadows of the night fell in strange divisions. We eventually reached the Valley of the Kings' embrace, and then proceeded west, turning left and then left again into the most secret eastern necropolis valley, and passing slowly between the vast, eroded ramparts of rock towards the entrance to the tomb.

When we finally arrived, I saw hoards and stacks of objects had already been unloaded and set under white linen sheets, as if a great household were moving palaces; these must be the funeral treasures that would furnish the tomb after the rites had been completed and the coffins had been set and sealed within the sarcophagus.

Lamps lit the sixteen carved stone steps that led down into the tomb, and while everyone prepared for the rites to take place, I descended. I was shocked by what the light of the lamps revealed: the entrance to the tomb was not yet finished, indeed the passageway seemed barely to have been tidied in time for this ceremony. Left on the steps were jars of bandages and natron, and the workers' water skins, hastily placed to one side. I passed through the rock-cut doorway into the Hall of Waiting.

Here again, the work was unfinished. On the sloping floor and the still-rough stone of the walls were the masons' red marks and guide-lines. Flakes and chips of limestone had not been swept up from the floor. Gold glittered here and there on the walls where the movers of the royal furniture had scraped their burdens in their haste. The air smelled of burning things – candle wax, oils, incense, rushes – even the rough-hewn stone of the walls and the low roofs seemed to be permeated with the acrid history of the many chisels that had worked through the bedrock, chip by chip, blow by blow.

I turned right and entered the burial chamber itself. The walls were decorated, but only in a simple, unostentatious way. There had evidently not been enough time for anything grander and more sophisticated. The many massive sections of the golden shrine, comprising four huge boxes, one inside the other, were set against the walls, waiting to be assembled within the confined dimensions of the dark space, once the coffins had been manoeuvred into place within the sarcophagus. Each section of glorious gilded wood was marked on the ungilded inner side with instructions – which end matched which, and so on. Already occupying almost all the space in the chamber was an immense yellow stone sarcophagus. Each corner was intricately carved with the detailed, overlapping protective wings of the deities.

I turned right again and looked into the treasury. It was already furnished with many objects; the great shrine would make it impossible to carry anything beyond the burial chamber. The first thing I saw was a life-like carving of Anubis, sleek and black, his long ears pointing up as if listening attentively, under a blanket that someone had, oddly, wrapped over his back as if to keep him warm in the endless dark of his watch. Behind him was a huge gold canopic shrine. Along one wall many black shrines and chests had been placed and sealed. On the opposite wall were more shrine boxes. Alongside Anubis was a row of ivory and wood caskets.

When no one was looking I opened one, carefully; inside was a beautiful ostrich feather fan. Its inscription read: "Made with ostrich feathers obtained by his majesty when hunting in the deserts east of Heliopolis". I thought of the fan he had promised me. On top of these boxes, several miniature boats were balanced, beautifully detailed and painted in bright colours, complete with miniature sails and rigging. I noticed a small wooden box at my feet. Tempted, I lifted the lid, and saw two tiny coffins contained within it: Ankhesenamun's stillborn daughters, I guessed.

As I stood pondering these small remains left among the jumble of golden objects, Khay joined me.

'If only those children had come to full term, and been born well, then we would be living in a very different world,' he said.

I nodded.

'There are many family heirlooms here. Objects with the family names on, and others bearing the image of the Aten,' I said.

'Indeed. Look at these, for instance: palettes, boxes and bangles that belonged to his half-sisters. And waiting up there, hidden under the linens, is wine from the city of Akhetaten, and thrones of state bearing the Aten symbol. They are private things, but forbidden now, and consigned to eternity here in this tomb. Which is just as well.'

'I imagine it would be to Horemheb's advantage to get hold of these treasures. He could use them to blackmail Ankhesenamun, accusing her of secret loyalty to the failed religion. So Ay is using this opportunity to bury the symbols of a failed past, along with the last King of that time.'

'Exactly. Hence this unseemly haste and secrecy.'

'And look at what it amounts to, after all: wood, gold, jewels and bones.'

We returned up the steps to the night world. I saw the stars were already beginning to fade. Dawn would soon be revealed. The moment had come to complete the last rituals. Ay was now dressed in the leopard skin of a priest, and wore on his old head the Blue Crown of kingship, adorned with gold discs. It was he who would perform the rite of the Opening of the Mouth, and in doing so establish his succession. The coffin containing the mummy was lifted into an upright position, and Ay hurriedly raised the forked *pesesh kef* to the King's dead mouth, and then to the other organs of sensation – the nose, ears and eyes – to restore their powers, and allow the King's spirit to rejoin his body so that he could Come Forth by Day in the next life. It was all done according to the Instructions, but as swiftly as possible, as if Ay feared he would be interrupted. I noticed Simut's guards were stationed along the tops of the Valley, and near the entrance.

The coffins were carried, with a great struggle, down into the tomb. Our small group of mourners followed in our orders. Once in the Hall of Waiting, the air was hot and thick. No one spoke, but the breathing of those present sounded loud, nervous and laboured in the strange acoustic of the chamber. Over the heads of the other men I could glimpse only fragments of activity, as the rites were continued in the burial chamber: I saw the side view of the coffin being lifted up with enormous effort; the flash of an amulet; and I smelt the scent of warm resin as it was poured into the innermost coffin. Prayers and incantations drifted inscrutably in the dark air. Finally the stone lid of the sarcophagus was lifted into place; I heard the complaint of ropes and pulleys, and the grunting of men as they struggled within the tight restrictions of the space. But then there was a sudden, loud crack, and a gasp of shock from the witnesses; one of the workmen had dropped his corner, and the stone lid had cracked into two pieces as it hit the sarcophagus. But their overseer, realizing nothing could be done, clapped his hands. The broken pieces were set back together, quickly sealed with gypsum, and the crack painted yellow to disguise the flaw.

Then the construction of the four shrines around the sarcophagus continued. It took a long time. The men worked with almost comic difficulty, trying to make sense of the parts in the lamplight, struggling with each other to discover the space and the logic by which to manoeuvre each piece, in the right order, into place, in silence. Finally it was completed, and the men, shining with sweat and breathing like exhausted mules, retired. By now there was just two cubits' space between the great gold shrine and the decorated walls; priests finished laying out ritual objects according to a pattern that made sense only to them: wooden oars, lamps and boxes, wine jars and a bouquet of olive and persea. The doors of the shrine were sealed. Inside lay shrine within gilded shrine; and at the heart of this large cold nest of carved and inlaid gold and wood and yellow stone, small and vulnerable within all this panoply of gold, this accumulation of treasure, lay the thin, eviscerated, mummified body of the dead King. I remembered him suddenly, and the look of delight on his face as he waited for the hunt, under the desert stars, alive.

We stepped backwards in respect, our heads bowed. Ay and Ankhesenamun came last; and then we slowly retreated, backwards, out of the Hall of Waiting, leaving the King in his stone chamber with all his gold, his grave goods, his couches and masks and little boats, with his game boards, and stools on which he had sat as a child, and the bowls from which he had drunk – all the things of this world he would need again in the next, where time had no power, and darkness was changed into eternal, unchanging light. So they say.

We ate the funeral meal and watched as the last of the grave goods were carried down to furnish the Hall of Waiting and the smaller crypt to the left: chariot wheels and the sawn-off or disassembled parts of gold chariots; beautiful painted and marquetry-inlaid boxes; and three elegant couches, one of which was decorated with lions. Their gold faces and blue muzzles and the looks of pity in their wise, serious golden eyes glimmered at me in the darkness, and then threw powerful shadows against the wall in the dim lamplight as they passed. White food-offering containers were stacked under one of the couches. Here was the lotus cup of alabaster, pale and luminous in the lamplight, which I had seen in Tutankhamun's chamber on the ship. There were chairs and thrones decorated with the signs of the Aten, and two life-sized guardian statues studiously ignoring the disorder; silver trumpets wrapped in reeds, gold walking sticks and gold-tipped arrows had been stacked by the walls. Many wine jars, whose dockets indicated they were already old, from the time of Akhenaten, and many more alabaster vessels of oils and perfumes were carried through into the small crypt, together with hundreds of baskets of fruit and meat which were then stacked on stools and boxes and a long, gilded bed. There was gold everywhere; enough to make me sick of its famous lustre.

Finally it was time to seal Tutankhamun in his tomb of eternity. I had a strange feeling that we, the living, crowded into the passageway, were on the wrong side of the stone door that was hurriedly constructed between ourselves and the now deserted Hall of Waiting. The gathered faces – nobles, priests and the young Queen – looked like conspirators at a crime in the candles' nervous, gusty light. I felt something like disgust as well as pity as the masons in their dirty work-clothes manoeuvred the last stones into place with a grinding sound, then crudely slapped and smoothed dark wet grey plaster with their trowels over them for the necropolis guards to apply their oval insignias of Anubis; many hands reached forward to record their signs for eternity, in a manner perfunctory, anxious and at odds with the meaning of the other symbols. *Great of love of the entire Land . . . creating images of the Gods that they may give to him the breath of life . . .*

Then, like a herd of animals, we shuffled backwards up the passageway holding our frail lamps. Ankhesenamun laid a last bouquet on the steps – mandrake, blue water lily, nightshade, olive, willow; hopeful, frail, transitory flowers from the world's spring. Her face was wet with tears. I came last, and as I looked back I saw, like a dark, rising flood, the shadows of our departing forms joining the great darkness of eternity that now followed us up the sixteen steps, until it was sealed in by more stones, for ever.

53

The half-moon had sunk to the edge of the black and blue outline of the Valley. We stood together, uncertain under the late stars, in the land of the living. But we were not alone. In the darkness an imposing figure stood waiting, with armed men behind him, their arms polished by the moonlight. Horemheb. I looked for Simut's guards; I saw dark shapes, slain bodies, slumped in the darkness.

The general walked forward to confront Ay and Ankhesenamun.

'You did not see fit to invite me to the last rites of the King?' he demanded.

Ay faced him.

'I am King. I have performed the rites, and taken the succession. I will announce my accession and my forthcoming coronation in the morning.'

'And what of you, Queen? Did you think so little of my offer that you failed to discuss it with me before making whatever decision has led to this sorry situation?'

'I considered everything. I am the widow of Tutankhamun, Restorer of the Gods, and the granddaughter of Amenhotep the Glorious. And you are not noble.'

'How dare you question my nobility!' he growled in his low, menacing voice.

She paused. The moment had come. Horemheb was impatient to hear what she would say.

'Information has come to us, privately and secretly, which has astounded and disappointed us. It concerns the reputation and integrity of the army.'

She let the dangerous words hang in the dark air.

'The reputation and integrity of the army is untarnished,' replied Horemheb, menacingly.

'Perhaps then, the general is not aware of everything that is happening within his own division. There are elements within the army which are trading with the Hittites, our ancient enemies, for personal profit,' she said.

He approached closer, his breath pluming in the cold night air.

'You actually dare to accuse my divisions of treachery? You?' He gazed at her in derision. But she confronted him.

'I am reporting that which was told to me. Perhaps it is not true. But then again, perhaps it is. The opium poppy, I hear. Transported across the lines of battle. Trading with the enemy? It would be most unfortunate if such a suggestion were to reach the offices, the temples, and the general ear,' she said.

Horemheb swiftly drew out his curved sword, its polished outer blade glinting in the moonlight. For a moment, I feared he would slice off her head. He held his weapon aloft in his gloved fist, and his soldiers instantly aimed their elegant, powerful arrows at our hearts, in preparation for an order to slaughter us all in silence. Simut stepped forward to protect the Queen, his own dagger now raised at Horemheb. The two men stared at each other, tense as dogs before a vicious fight. But Ankhesenamun held her ground and intervened.

'I do not think our assassination would help your cause. You do not have sufficient power to take control of all the offices and temples of the Two Lands. Too many of your troops are fighting the war. Think carefully. Listen to my proposition. All I desire is order for the Two Lands, and therefore an equitable sharing of the powers necessary to maintain that order between the three of us. Ay will govern as King, for he controls the offices of the kingdom. You will remain as general. The secret trade must stop. If it does, then there is be much to be gained for you. There is the future.'

Slowly Horemheb lowered his sword, and gestured for his men to lower their bows.

'And what is that future? Will you marry this shambles of age and infirmity?' he asked, gesturing with contempt at Ay.

'My King is dead, but only I can bring forth a successor, a son who will be King in turn. That is my destiny, and I will fulfil it. As for the father of my son, I will choose him carefully, the fittest and the best among the best of men. I will choose him myself, and no man will have authority over me. Whoever proves himself to be this noble man, I shall take as my husband. And he shall become King, beside me. In due course, we will rule the Two Lands together. Perhaps you, sir, will prove yourself to be this worthy man.'

Ay, who had remained silent throughout this exchange, now intervened.

'Those are the terms. You should know that there are a thousand palace guards stationed above us, and at the entrance to the Valley. They are prepared to do whatever is necessary to secure our safety. What is your answer?'

Horemheb looked up, and there on the escarpments on either side were new lines of dark figures holding bows.

'Did you think I would not anticipate everything you could have thought of?' continued Ay.

Horemheb considered them both. Then he approached them very closely.

'Wonderful: an old man with toothache and a feeble girl with dreams of glory grasping at the reigns of power, and a useless Medjay officer who knows now his family will never be safe. Listen—'

And he opened his arms to the vast silence of the night and the desert that dwarfed us.

'Do you know what that is? It is the sound of time. You hear nothing but silence, and yet it is roaring like a lion. There is no god but time, and I am his general. I will wait. My hour is nigh, and when it arrives, in triumph and glory, you will both be nothing but dust, and your names will be nothing but dust, for I will erase them, every single one, from their stones, and I will usurp your monuments, and in your place there will be a new dynasty, carrying my name, valiant son succeeding each strong father, generation after generation, into the future, for ever.'

And then he smiled, as if victory were assured, turned away and marched off into the dark, followed by his troops.

Ay gazed after him balefully.

'That man is full of wind. Come, there is much work to be done.'

He suddenly winced and grasped his jaw. It seemed that all the power in the world could not alleviate the pain of ruined teeth.

Before she departed, to her uncertain future, Ankhesenamun turned quietly to me.

'I came to you, asking for help. You have risked everything to help me in these days. I heard his threat against your family. So be sure I will do all within my power to ensure their safety. You know I wish you to become my private guard. That offer remains open. It would make me happy to see you.'

I nodded. She looked sadly at the sealed entrance to the tomb of her late young husband. Then she turned away, followed by Khay and the other nobles, and they all took to the chariots that would carry them back on the long paved way to the palace of shadows, and the merciless work of fashioning and bringing to pass the secure future of the Two Lands. I remembered what Horemheb had said about power; that it was a rough beast. I hoped she could learn to ride it well.

*

Simut and I stood watching them go. Darkness was falling quickly from the dawn air.

'Horemheb is right, I'm afraid. Ay will not live long, and the Queen cannot govern without an heir. Not while Horemheb is waiting.'

'True. But she is becoming a powerful woman. She has her mother in her. And that gives me hope,' I replied, with a feeling of optimism that caught me by surprise.

'Come, let us walk to the top of the hills and watch the sun rise on this new day,' he suggested.

So we scrambled up the tracks, like scars on the rough, dark, ancient hide of the mountainside, and soon before us lay the vast panorama of the shadowy world: the rich, ancient fields, the endlessly flowing waters of the Great River, and the sleeping city with its glorious temples and towers, its rich, silent palaces, its prisons and hovels, and its quiet homes and poor districts, in the dark distance. I breathed in the cold, fresh air. It was bracing and fortifying. The last stars were fading, and there was a hint of red on the horizon beyond the city. The King was dead. I thought of his eyes, and his gold face, down in the dark, perhaps – who knows? – now seeing the Otherworld appear before him as the light of eternity dawned and his spirits rejoined him.

As for me, what my eyes beheld of the world was enough. Smoke from the first fires began to twist into the still, pure air. Far off I heard the first birds begin to sing. I rested my hand on Thoth's head. He gazed at me with his wise, old eyes. My children and my wife would still be asleep. I wanted very much to be there to greet them when they woke. I needed to find a way to believe we could be safe, despite the perils and threats of the future to come. I looked up at the indigo sky, and the horizon that was brightening with every moment. It would soon be light.

THE END

Author's Note

Since 1922, when Howard Carter made his momentous discovery in the Valley of the Kings, Tutankhamun has become the most famous, compelling and in some ways mysterious of all Ancient Egyptians. As a child, in 1972, I was taken to see the great Tutankhamun exhibition at the British Museum. His grave goods – among them the golden shrine, gilded statuettes showing him poised with a spear or holding the flail of power, the alabaster 'wishing cup', a gold sceptre, glorious jewellery, a long bronze trumpet, a boomerang and an intricately decorated hunting bow – seemed like the treasures of a lost world. Above all, his death mask of beaten, solid gold – surely one of the most beautiful works of art from the ancient world – seemed to sum up the powerful mystery of the so-called 'boy king', who possessed such power and lived among such wonders, and yet who died mysteriously young – probably less than twenty years old – and was then hurriedly buried and entirely forgotten, for about 3,300 years.

The discovery of the tomb promoted a huge revival in the popular fascination with Egypt; but perhaps it emphasized the occult mysteries of the pyramids and tombs, and the B-movie curses of the mummies, at the expense of a more balanced view of that remarkable culture. For Tutankhamun, for instance, the pyramids were already about as ancient as Stonehenge is for us today.

Ancient historians and archaeologists have given us a great deal of detailed information about Ancient Egypt, and about the New Kingdom in particular. By the 18th Dynasty, Egypt commanded the most powerful, rich and sophisticated empire the ancient world had ever known. It was a highly complex, highly organized society, constructing astounding monuments, fashioning gorgeous art, objects and jewellery, sustaining its pre-eminence in international power politics, and supporting lives of luxury and affluence for its elite – all on the back of a large labouring workforce. Beyond its own borders, it ruled and administered a vast territory from the third cataract in what is now Sudan, through much of the Levant. Its routes of trade in rare goods and labour stretched much further. It had an advanced army, led by General Horemheb, an extremely powerful priesthood that administered and profited from vast tracts of land and property, a sophisticated civil service, and something recognizably like a national police force in the Medjay.

The Medjay were originally nomadic Nubian people. During the Middle Kingdom, the Ancient Egyptians appreciated their fighting skills, employing them as trackers and foot soldiers, and using their scouting talent to collect intelligence on strangers, at the borders especially. Fortunately for us, Ancient Egypt was a bureaucratic culture, and a report from that time still survives: 'The patrol which set out to patrol the desert edge . . . has returned and reported to me as follows: "We have found a track of 32 men and 3 donkeys"' (Kemp, 2006). By the 18th Dynasty the term Medjay could be applied more widely to describe a kind of early urban policing force. Corruption and crime are richly attested to during the New Kingdom, as throughout time and culture, and so I have extrapolated from the available evidence a police force functioning similarly to a modern one, with a coded hierarchy, a strong assertion of independence from other forms of authority, and of course independent-minded detectives, or 'Seekers of Mystery', of which Rahotep is the finest.

All the earthly powers, accomplishments and triumphs of New Kingdom Egypt were made possible by the life-giving waters of the Nile, the Great River, which defined for the Ancient Egyptians the 'Two Lands': the Black, which was the richly fertile soil of the river lands, and the Red, which was the apparently endless desert that surrounded them, and which represented the things they feared – barrenness, chaos and death. The perpetual cycle of the daily rebirth of the sun in the east, the setting of the sun in the west, and the sun's mysterious night journey through the perilous territory of the afterlife inspired their beautiful, complex religion.

We know Tutankhamun inherited the throne when he was only about eight years old. We know Ay, essentially the Chancellor, governed in his name. And we know Tutankhamun was born and raised in a turbulent time. He inherited the difficulties of his reign from his father, Akhenaten. The introduction, or imposition, of Akhenaten and Nefertiti's revolutionary Aten religion, and the foundation of a new temple-capital at Akhetaten (modern-day Amarna), had created a profound crisis of politics and religion, which I explored in *Nefertiti: The Book of the Dead*. After the end of Akhenaten's reign, the old orthodox religion was restored, as powerful factions battled for power and new influence. One clear indication of how this forceful period of reform affected Tutankhamun, and the political necessity of disassociating himself from his father's reign, was that he changed his name from Tutankhaten ('Living Image of the Aten') and reinstated the name of Amun, 'the hidden one', the all-powerful god whose temple complex at Karnak remains one of the great monuments of the ancient world.

The Ancient Egyptians feared chaos greatly. They recognized its forces as a constant threat to natural and supernatural order, and to the values of beauty, justice and truth. The goddess Maat, who was depicted as a seated woman wearing an ostrich feather, represented order at both the cosmic level of seasons and stars, and at the social level of the relations between the gods, in the person of the king, and men. A graphic description of the sense of chaos prevailing at the time of Tutankhamun's coronation is recorded on the Restoration Stela (a stone slab bearing inscriptions) which was set up in the temple complex of Karnak in the early years of his reign. Of course, its purpose was partly propaganda; but its description of the state of the world before Tutankhamun's ascension is incredibly vivid. (A passage from the text forms the epigraph to this book.) The new king's duty would be, as for all kings before him, to restore Maat to the Two Lands of Egypt; as the stela asserts, 'He has vanquished chaos from the whole land . . . and the whole land has been made as it was in the time of Creation.'

Evidence for a biography of Tutankhamun is extremely sketchy, and most accounts are interpretations based on shards of often highly ambiguous evidence. Many compelling mysteries remain unsolved. How and why did Tutankhamun die so young? Recent CT scans of his mummy have disproved the old theory that a blow to the back of his skull killed him. The new scientific evidence implies a broken leg, and septicaemia. If so, how did this happen? Was there an accident? Or did some more sinister crime befall him? We can still only guess why the funeral arrangements seem to have been so strangely hurried – the tomb paintings crude and unfinished, the funeral furniture haphazard, the parts of the golden shrine damaged as they were put together, and the two mummified foetuses buried with him unidentified. Why was the wine out of date, and why were there so many walking sticks in the tomb? What was the role of his wife Ankhesenamun, who was also his half-sister, and daughter of the great queen Nefertiti and Akhenaten? What was Ay's claim to power, and under what circumstances did he become the next king? And where was the powerful figure of Horemheb during this strange, dark time?

The great poet Robert Graves wrote that his historical novels were attempts to solve cryptic historical puzzles. There can be few greater remaining historical mysteries than the life and death of

Tutankhamun, and this novel has been my endeavour, through imagination, careful attempts to be as historically accurate as possible, and a wish to depict these long-dead people as being fully alive in their own present tense, to offer a solution to the mystery of the young man who briefly held the crook and flail of earthly power in his hands, and who was then entirely lost to history until that day in 1922 when the seals of his tomb were broken open.

Howard Carter famously answered, when asked if he could see anything: 'Yes . . . wonderful things!' Everyone who has since looked on Tutankhamun's golden death mask remembers the eyes: fashioned from quartz and obsidian, and decorated with lapis lazuli, they seem to gaze through and beyond all the mere mortals shuffling past in wonder. They seem to stare into the light of eternity.

Select Bibliography

Andrews, Carol, *Egyptian Mummies*, British Museum Press, 1998

Darnell, John Coleman, and Manassa, Colleen, *Tutankhamun's Armies*, Wiley and Sons, 2007

Kemp, Barry J., *Ancient Egypt, Anatomy of a Civilization*, Routledge, 2006

Kemp, Barry J., *The Egyptian Book of the Dead*, Granta Books, 2007

Manley, Bill, *The Penguin Historical Atlas of Ancient Egypt*, Penguin 1996

Meskell, Lynn, *Private Life in New Kingdom Egypt*, Princeton University Press, 2002

Nunn, John F., *Ancient Egyptian Medicine*, British Museum Press, 1997

Pinch, Geraldine, *Egyptian Myth, A Very Short Introduction*, Oxford University Press, 2004

Pinch, Geraldine, *Magic in Ancient Egypt*, British Museum Press, 1994

Reeves, Nick, *The Complete Tutankhamun*, Thames and Hudson, 1990

Sauneron, Serge, *The Priests of Ancient Egypt*, translated by David Lorton, Cornell University Press, 2000

Shaw, Ian, and Nicholson, Paul, *The British Museum Dictionary of Ancient Egypt*, British Museum Press, 1995

Strudwick, Nigel, and Strudwick, Helen, *Thebes in Egypt*, Cornell University Press, 1999

Wilkinson, Richard, *The Complete Temples of Ancient Egypt*, Thames and Hudson, 2000

Wilson, Penelope, *Hieroglyphs, A Very Short Introduction*, Oxford University Press, 2003

Acknowledgements

Many people helped me during the writing of this book:

Bill Scott-Kerr, Sarah Turner, Deborah Adams, Lucy Pinney and Matt Johnson at Transworld are a writer's dream team. Heartfelt thanks to them for their patience, support, great notes, and enthusiasm.

Without my exceptional agent, Peter Straus, this book would not exist. I would also like to thank Stephen Edwards and Laurence Laluyaux at Rogers, Coleridge and White. Many thanks also to Julia Kreitman at The Agency.

Carol Andrews, BA, PADipEg, my wise Egyptological expert, generously shared her remarkable knowledge, scrutinized every draft, and corrected my mistakes with great fortitude. I should say, in time-honoured fashion, that any errors inadvertently remaining are my responsibility.

Broo Doherty, David Lancaster, John Mole, Paul Rainbow, Robert Connolly, Iain Cox and Walter Donohue kindly read drafts of the novel, and their acute and accurate responses guided me forward. Jackie Kay gave me constant support and encouragement. The Dromgoole family, Dom, Sasha and the glorious girls, Siofra, Grainne and Cara, give me inspiration. My profound thanks to Edward

Gonzales Gomez; as a song from the New Kingdom says, 'from my innermost heart'.

To all I would raise Tutankhamun's glorious alabaster goblet, known as the 'wishing cup', with its beautiful inscription:

> *Live your ka*
> *And may you spend millions of years*
> *Lover of Thebes*
> *With your face to the cool north breeze*
> *Beholding happiness.*